Dear Reader,

I am so excited Avon Books is re-releasing *The Seduction of Sara*! From sexy villain in *The Abduction of Julia* to sexy redeemable hero in *The Seduction of Sara*, Nick Montrose must undergo a drastic and dramatic transformation. He does so at the not-always-gentle hands of our heroine Sara, a widow with ideas of her own despite her brothers' many attempts to "guide" her through life.

In this book, Nick suffers from what he calls "headaches" which are, in fact, panic attacks reminiscent of some forms of Post-Traumatic Stress Disorder, an illness that went undiagnosed and untreated at that time. The symptoms of his illness leave Nick fearful that he's slipping into madness. A man of great pride, he attempts to hide his affliction, which only worsens his condition. With Sara's insistence and help, he finds that by sharing his pain he becomes stronger. That's a lesson that's difficult for many of us.

One of my friends suffers from this illness and I must thank him profusely for sharing such a difficult and intensely personal experience.

I hope you enjoy *The Seduction of Sara*. For excerpts of upcoming books, my publishing schedule, and/or an occasional free contest prize (and pictures of me stalking my favorite hot Australian actor), please check my website: *www.karenhawkins.com*.

All best!

Karen Hawkins

Karen Hawkins

D0051743

Karen Hawkins

The Seduction of Sara

AVON

An Imprint of HarperCollins*Publishers*

This is a work of fiction. Names, characters, places, and incidents are products of the author's imagination or are used fictitiously and are not to be construed as real. Any resemblance to actual events, locales, organizations, or persons, living or dead, is entirely coincidental.

AVON BOOKS
An Imprint of HarperCollins*Publishers*
10 East 53rd Street
New York, New York 10022-5299

First Avon Books paperback printing: November 2001

Avon Trademark Reg. U.S. Pat. Off. and in Other Countries, Marca Registrada, Hecho en U.S.A.
HarperCollins® is a registered trademark of HarperCollins Publishers.

Printed in the U.S.A.

20 19 18 17 16 15 14 13 12 11

Prologue

Paris
January 14, 1815

Normally Madame du Mauier's salon was thick with male talk and laughter, but tonight all attention was turned to the card table in one corner of the room, where Nicholas Montrose, the Earl of Bridgeton, regarded his opponent with ill-disguised contempt. Baron Parkington was a slovenly snob who spent his entire life sneering at those he thought beneath him. Nick generally ignored such petty specimens of humanity, but for some reason, he felt a compulsion to flatten this particular toadstool. And damned if he wouldn't enjoy every second.

Parkington's beefy fingers thudded a sudden tattoo on the table. "Well, Bridgeton? Match the five hundred or withdraw."

The baron's shrill voice grated along his nerves. Nick gazed at the man until he reddened. It was ludicrous to continue playing; the baron had lost almost every hand. Nick should have been happy with that.

But it wasn't enough. He wanted to humiliate the baron the same way that the baron wanted to humiliate him. To drag his name into the mud and leave it there, quivering flotsam in the stream of life.

"I will meet your five hundred, Parkington." Nick reached into his coat and withdrew a sheaf of papers from his inner pocket, then dropped them onto the table. "And raise you forty thousand pounds."

The baron blanched as a collective gasp arose from their audience. Like ravenous wolves, they smelled blood and wanted to be in on the kill.

A bead of sweat rolled down Parkington's cheek to join the others on his wilted collar. "Forty thousand? You must be joking."

"I never joke about cards." The devil's luck was with him tonight, and Nick couldn't lose. Besides, defeating a man like Parkington has its own pleasures. For as much as Nick despised the baron, he also envied him. Once the game finished, the baron would return to his lodgings, pack his belongings, and go home to England.

It had been three years since Nick had set foot on the shores of his own country—three long, lonely years. The thought held him, tightening his throat and weighting his chest.

God, but he was getting maudlin. Nick gestured for a servant to refill his glass with Madame's excellent brandy. He might wish to return home, but not because he missed the soggy English countryside. No, he wished to return home because he had been slighted. Nick had been forced to leave England under a cloud of suspicion, and the memory rankled still.

A distinguished, white-haired gentleman who stood near Nick's elbow murmured quietly, "Tempting fate, are you not, *mon ami*?"

Nick flicked a glance at the Comte du Lac. He was dressed in a puce coat with sumptuous silver lacing, and his patrician face expressed nothing but polite sincerity. He looked the quintessential nobleman, but Nick knew Henri had neither title nor breeding. He was an imposter who made his way through the *ton* offering comfort to wealthy widows and lonely wives.

While a moral man would have exposed such perfidy, Nick found Henri too amusing to waste his company. Besides, Nick understood what it was to be a pretender. Unknown to society, his fortune hadn't come from ancient family coffers, but had been hard-won, wrested from the fingers of Lady Luck herself.

Viscount Gaillard, a small, dark man who had taken on the duty of dealer, lifted a brow at the baron. "Well, Parkington? The earl has wagered forty thousand pounds. Can you meet it?"

Parkington's gaze remained glued on the draft that lay atop of the pile of money. He wanted it. Nick could see it in the way the man's damp, pudgy hands tightened about the cards, the way his pink tongue traced the dry line of his too-fat lips.

"By God, yes!" Parkington motioned for a pen and paper. It was swiftly brought and he wrote two lines across it, then signed with a flourish. "There."

Gaillard frowned at the paper. "What is that?"

"Hibberton Hall," the lackwit sneered. "My family seat in Bath."

An estate in England. Something shifted deep within Nick's heart, and, for an instant, he could only stare at the piece of paper that had been tossed into the center of the table. A dull ache tightened his throat, and he was assailed with images of damp, fog-shrouded mornings and gentle rolling green hills.

Damn it. He'd made his way alone since the age of thirteen, and his experiences had taught him the uselessness of emotion. If he returned to England, his decision would be based in reality, in necessity, not some elusive sentiment. But the time was drawing nigh when change was indeed a necessity. He must find a home of his own, somewhere secluded. Somewhere he could spend the last few lucid moments of his life.

And those would be far sooner than anyone would have guessed. Nick looked at the baron's scrawled writing, aware of a dull pounding at the base of his skull. "I accept," he said quietly. From the corner of his eye, he caught sight of the comte shaking his head. Someone would stumble from the table a loser, a broken man with nothing left to his name, and it could well be he.

A servant refilled his glass, and Nick took a deep drink, the ache behind his eyes increasing. It was a sign of the impending darkness. He suffered from headaches; yet they were more than headaches. They were hours and days of interminable pain, of swirling blackness and paralyzing fear, all combined into one. He met his opponent's avid gaze with a bland one of his own, even while he cursed the fates that so ill-timedly drilled inside his head. "We play."

Gaillard dealt a card faceup in front of Parkington. The eight of clubs lay on the green felt, and a discontented murmur burst from the crowd.

Parkington's face beamed through the sheen of sweat. "Only a queen or higher can change your luck now." A sneer curled his overly red lips. "I shall enjoy spending your money, but not as much as I shall enjoy telling everyone in London how I won such a sum from the infamous Earl of Bridgeton."

Nick glanced at the dealer. "My card, Gaillard."

"*Oui*, my lord." The Frenchman wiped his hands on his coat, aware that every eye was upon him. He took a steadying breath, then flipped a card onto the table. The queen of hearts smiled sweetly up at Nick.

The entire room burst into a roar of excited babble. Parkington stared, his mouth slack. "It cannot be—"

Nick stood and nodded to the Comte du Lac, who obediently came forward to collect the winnings. Henri glanced at Parkington and smiled gently. "It happens, monsieur. Luck is a fickle creature. She loves many, but is faithful to none."

The baron shook his head as if to clear it of a nightmare. "I was winning until—" His breath hissed between his teeth. "Bridgeton, you bastard."

The comte paused in collecting the scattered banknotes. Gaillard's black eyes widened as everyone within hearing froze in place.

Nick continued to pull on his gloves. "My beloved parents were in fact legally wed, so I am not a bastard in the strictest sense of the word. However, if you were to question my parentage . . . I fear not even my mother was certain on that issue."

Parkington lumbered to his feet, his face now as red as it had been white. "The game was damned irregular. I demand an accounting."

The silence grew louder, bolstered by a silent hum of excitement. Nick flicked an infinitesimal bit of dirt from his sleeve. Damn them all. They wanted blood, and he was about to provide it for them. But he had very little time; the throb in his head had increased, and a horrible heaviness weighted his limbs.

Henri cut a sharp glance at the baron. "Perhaps the baron has made a mistake. After all, he is English. Certainly he knows better than to imply the earl has cheated."

The baron sneered. "I said it once, and I will say it again: the Earl of Bridgeton is a cheat." His lips twisted in contempt. "But what can one expect from the son of a French whore?"

The growing ache in Nick's head turned into a writhing pain, pushing against his skull, spreading inky spots to the corners of his eyes. He placed his hand on the edge of the table to steady himself. "Henri, will you serve as my second?"

Henri groaned. "Not again."

Parkington's beady eyes darted nervously from one to the other. "Again?"

Henri nodded morosely. "For him, it is a hobby. We go, he fights, he kills, we leave. Then we have breakfast."

"There will be no breakfast this time," Nick said quietly. He picked up the note and tucked it in his coat pocket. "We fight tonight. Name your second, Parkington."

The baron glanced nervously about the room and encountered a wall of seething French nobility. His desperate gaze finally alighted on a familiar face. "Billingsworth."

Nick could see that Mr. Billingsworth, a wealthy banker held in some esteem in Paris, had no wish to be embroiled in this drama. But the baron didn't give him the opportunity to refuse. He immediately began to remove his coat. "Shall we go outside?"

Nick raised his brows. "Why? This room is large enough."

"*Quelle domage*," Gaillard exclaimed. "You cannot fight a duel in here."

"Yes, we can." Nick removed his gloves, flicking a contemptuous glance at the baron. "What will it be? Swords or pistols? I have both in my carriage."

The baron loosened his cravat with a quick jerky movement, then yanked his arms out of his waistcoat. "Pistols."

Nick turned to a servant. "Ask my footman for my dueling pistols."

The servant scurried off as Henri shook his white head. "The things you do, *mon ami*. There is no stopping you in this folly, I suppose." He sighed. "If you are to fight in the salon, then we must have more room. Gaillard, help me move these tables."

In a matter of moments, the room was cleared of furniture, the pistols brought and examined by both seconds, and everything prepared for the duel.

Nick smiled briefly at Henri. "It appears it is my lot in life to relieve the world of as many fools as possible."

"At this rate, there will be no one left in Paris."

"Then perhaps the time has come for us to go to England."

The comte pursed his mouth. "They say the women in London are without compare."

Nick nodded. Though the Parisian women carried their own allure, he missed the freshness of a true English beauty.

Within a remarkably short time, Gaillard had counted off the paces in the silent room. Leaving Henri, Nick took his mark opposite the baron. Anyone seeing the earl might think him unprepared, for he held his gun loosely to his side, his stance negligent.

But the comte apparently thought otherwise, for he called out, "Don't kill him, Bridgeton. Not here."

Gaillard signaled for quiet. "Fire on three, gentlemen. Are you ready?" At their nods, he began the count. "One."

Nick met the baron's furious gaze and smiled gently through the swell of pain behind his eyes. The baron's mouth thinned, perspiration gleaming on his upper lip.

"Two," Gaillard said.

There was a second of deathly stillness, then Gaillard opened his mouth to give the signal. But before he had time to speak, Parkington yanked up his hand and a brack of red fire exploded from his pistol.

A vase over Nick's shoulder shattered into a thousand pieces, falling to the marble hearth in tinkling discord.

The comte started forward. "Foul! Gaillard did not count three!"

"*Oui!*" Gaillard said, his face frozen with disgust. "The baron fired early."

Behind Nick's eyes, hot, red anger flickered to a flame. "Finish the count."

Gaillard hesitated, then agreed, his visage stern.

Parkington dropped his gun, his eyes wide. "It was an accident! I didn't mean—"

"Three," Gaillard said.

Nick lifted his gun and sighted down the barrel.

The baron backed away, his hands before him. "Please! I was only—"

A sharp crack echoed through the room. The baron gave a startled cry as the bullet ripped away the flesh of his left ear and sent him whirling backwards. He stumbled against the wall, then slid to the floor. There he sat, his eyes wide with fright, moisture dribbling from the corner of his mouth, a slow well of blood soaking into his collar. A frantic babble erupted from the crowd.

The comte wiped his brow. "*Mon Dieu*, I thought you would kill him."

Nick tossed his gun to a slack-mouthed servant. "And mar Madame du Mauier's Persian rug? Not even I could commit such a crime." He gripped the back of a chair in an effort to halt the swell of black spots that danced along the edges of his sight, his stomach roiling in protest at the abrupt movement.

The comte looked at him with a dark frown. "You look pale. The headache, *non*?"

Nick nodded once, praying he hadn't waited too long to leave. "Make my apologies to Madame du Mauier. I will, of course, pay for any damages she thinks necessary." He swayed as he turned, and Henri caught his arm.

"Perhaps I should see you home. You look—"

"*No*." Nick shook off Henri's hand. "I don't need a nursemaid."

Henri hesitated, then stepped away. "Send word if you need me."

Nick didn't answer, focused on staying upright. He walked from the room, only vaguely aware of the congratulations offered at all sides. He didn't worry what they thought of his lack of response; they would think him disdainful and rude, and merely respect him all the more.

With relief, he saw his coach was pulled up to the entrance. He climbed in and sank against the squabs as a footman silently closed the door and waved the coachman on his way. Jaw clenched, Nick tried to still the grip of nausea. All he had to do was make it home, he told himself, fisting his hands tightly, willing himself to remain conscious as the coach jolted down the road.

Through the unrelenting agony, a thought sprang forth, clear and cool like the quiet trickle of a fountain under a relentless summer sun: *I own a house in England, my own estate.* As soon as he was able, he would plan his triumphant return and show those who'd dare scoff at him that he was not a man to be dismissed.

No. He was the Earl of Bridgeton, and to hell with the world.

Chapter 1

London
January 28, 1815

The only thing that stood between Saraphina Lawrence and Hades was a respectable marriage bed. Given her choice, she would have leapt over the bed and raced straight into the flames wearing nothing but the famed Lawrence sapphires, her arms spread wide to embrace the wild heat. It was a pity her brothers wouldn't get out of the way.

"Damn all interfering men," she muttered, staring morosely out the window of the slow, plodding carriage.

Her aunt's eyes widened in the uncertain light

that shimmered across the silver strands at her temple. "I beg your pardon?"

That was Aunt Delphi's answer to everything—pretend you didn't hear and look annoyingly innocent. So far it had won her a duke who'd had the good grace to die within twelve months of the wedding, and a handsome jointure that gave her a startling amount of independence. Not that Aunt Delphi ever used it.

"I said, '*Damn all interfering men*,' " Sara repeated more loudly. "I have been grossly misused, and you know it. I was dragged out of my house—"

"To attend the social event of the season."

"—and forced to ride in this decrepit coach—"

"As if Marcus would have anything other than the best coach made."

"—just because my brothers are determined to make me into something I'm not." Sara scowled down at the brightly jeweled slippers that peeped from beneath her skirts. They pinched hideously, and had she not been determined to irritate her brothers' tedious sense of decorum, she wouldn't have worn the gaudy things. She slipped her feet free and wiggled her toes in the cool evening air, ignoring Delphi's look of disapproval.

Though she hated his arrogance, perhaps it was just as well that Marcus had summoned her. It was time they settled this issue once and for all. She was beyond listening to solemn advice; every minute that she walked on the border of ruin and challenged the stolid face of society exhilarated her. For the first time since Julius's death, she felt alive. Alive and free.

Aunt Delphi shook her head. "You have run mad. Since Julius died, you—"

"He died, but I did not. And I refuse to act as if I did."

Everyone had watched and waited for her to show some remorse, some hint of sadness, but she felt nothing. Not after her handsome husband died much the way he'd lived—with his breeches about his ankles and his private member where it didn't belong. It was no wonder Lady Georges had retired to the country after his death; it must have been a shock to watch her near-naked lover fall out of her carriage when her screams of ecstasy frightened the skittish horses into bolting.

Even worse was the fact that the entire *ton* knew the sordid truth. It had been the whispered joke of the season. The mere thought of it pinched Sara's pride worse than her shoes ever could. But strangely, the pain of Julius's public betrayal had freed her in a way that his death hadn't. She would never again waste her life trying to be something she was not, no matter what Marcus said. "My brother should pay more attention to his own affairs and stop torment-ing me."

"He cares about you, Sara. All of your brothers do."

"And I care about them. But I don't go around telling them what to do. Marcus has sway over my funds until I am twenty-five years old, and then I am free. If he wants any peace in the next four years, he'll let me be."

Shaking her head, Aunt Delphi regarded her

niece with compassion. While Sara's behavior might befuddle her brothers, Delphi understood it perfectly. Before Sara had married, there had always been a touch of wildness to her. She'd ridden harder, laughed louder, and been more spontaneous than any gently bred woman should be. But she'd always been surrounded by her brothers, all five of them startlingly handsome and larger than life, just as passionate in nature as their sister. To them, Sara was just Sara—exuberant and in love with life.

Then Sara had met Julius and all her passion had focused on one man: she had loved him dearly. Julius had been in love, as well, for his marriage had shocked his friends even more than it had Sara's. She was not the sweet, demure miss everyone expected him to wed.

But the relationship was doomed from the beginning. Julius, for all his wild ways, was brought up in a very traditional manner; he had one place in his life for his wife and another for his mistresses. Meanwhile, Sara came from a large, extended family and her ideas were quite different. She believed that love included complete fidelity and it never crossed her mind that her husband might believe otherwise. Had Sara been older, perhaps she would have demanded Julius give up his paramours. But she'd been seventeen, with no mother to confide in and too proud to ask for advice.

Delphi smoothed her silk skirts, a heavy lump in her throat. If she had not been so occupied with silly society pursuits, she might have been able to help her niece during what must have been an increasingly confusing and painful time. But Delphi, like everyone else, had missed the desperation of Sara's subsequent actions. Directed by Julius's critical mother and condescending sisters, she traded her sparkle for a distressingly cool elegance. To Delphi, it seemed that Sara's natural exuberance died a slow and agonizing death while all hint of happiness faded from her eyes.

And the more Sara changed, the unhappier Julius became as the very things that had captivated him about his young wife disappeared. By the time Julius died he and Sara were little more than strangers, while the manner of his tragic death had finally awakened her family to the true state of affairs.

Delphi slanted a glance at her niece and noted the unhappiness that darkened Sara's blue eyes. It was too late to do anything about Julius's behavior, but there was still a chance she could help her niece. And thanks to Marcus, that was exactly what Delphi intended to do. "Sara, promise me you will listen to your brother. He only wants what's best for you."

"He wants what is *easiest* for him," Sara said. "There is a wide gap between the two."

The carriage turned a corner and came to a halt. Her heart heavy, Delphi lifted the curtain and peered outside. Treymount House was the largest residence in Mayfair, boasting a magnificent ballroom and two grand salons. The carriage pulled into the long line in front of the brightly lit house. Horses neighed and link boys darted between the carriages, while a welter of footmen jostled for position.

Even though it was still months away from the season, everyone flocked to London for the annual Treymount ball, a tradition set by the late marquis in what Delphi thought was a vulgar display of wealth. But it worked. It didn't matter how poor the roads were, how frigid the wind, or how inconvenient it was to return to London in the middle of winter; the Treymount ball was a huge success each and every year.

Sara looked out at the crowded street. "It looks like someone kicked over an anthill."

It certainly did. People clamored for an invitation to Treymount, and frankly, Delphi didn't blame them. It wasn't just the residence, imposing as it was, or the sumptuous entertainment, but more the way the entire St. John family exuded power and arrogance, unconsciously reminding one that here was the embodiment of true nobility.

The carriage finally arrived at the front door, and soon she and Sara were walking toward the entryway, breathing in the spicy scent of the flowers strewn down each side of the red carpet to mask the unpleasant scents of the winter-grim city. Muted laughter and music swelled to meet them as they entered the great hall.

Marcus was not at the head of the receiving line, but was waiting in the library for Sara's arrival. Which was a good thing, Delphi decided as she handed her cloak to a waiting servant, shivering slightly in the chill. It was about time Marcus took a more direct hand in managing his sister's affair. She turned just as Sara undid the clasp of her own blue-velvet cloak and swept it from her shoulders.

Oh dear, no. Sara's sapphire blue gown was low cut and diaphanous enough to cause even the most risqué of the *ton* to raise their brows. And draped over Sara's lush figure, it was beyond scandalous. It was a complete disgrace.

From beneath the edge of the silk peeked sparkling slippers, while a cacophony of sapphires covered her throat, head, and arms. It seemed a bad omen that Sara had worn every piece of the Lawrence sapphires, from the wide gold necklet to the sparkling tiara that held her shining black curls from her face. To Delphi, the deep blue gems echoed the desperate brilliance of Sara's eyes.

Sara smoothed her skirts, the unconscious gesture pushing her breasts into a precarious position at the edge of her neckline. Swallowing hard, Delphi nervously fingered her own decorous bracelet. Already people had begun to recognize Sara. And while some of Delphi's friends could be counted on to halt any talk that resulted from such an outrageous costume, others would seek Sara out, determined to discover an interesting tidbit that could be exaggerated into a scandal. The bracelet broke with a snap. "Blast!"

Sara looked at the broken bracelet, her gaze softening slightly. "Don't worry about me, Aunt Delphi. I will be fine."

"Not unless you listen to your brother."

The softened expression vanished, and the new, coolly elegant Sara lifted one barely clad shoulder. "Marcus can go to hell."

"At least meet with him, Sara. Please. He's waiting for you in the library."

Sara met Delphi's gaze for a long moment, then she sighed. "Oh, very well; I suppose I had best get this over with. The sooner he realizes he can't order me about like a servant, the better." Her back ramrod straight, Sara turned and walked out of the foyer, her silk skirts brushing the floor behind her, draping across the graceful length of her legs.

For a dismal moment, Delphi wondered if she should accompany her niece. But the days had long passed since she could hug away Sara's hurts. Delphi closed her eyes. *Please, God, grant Marcus the patience of a saint. He's going to need it.*

Sara marched to the library, threw open the door, and halted. She'd expected to see Marcus behind his desk, his face carved in disapproval. Instead she found herself facing three of her five older brothers, their expressions ranging from outright disapproval to genuine concern.

"Damn," Sara muttered. "If Brand and Devon were here, it would be the whole bloody army."

"What a lovely way to greet your family." Chase stood by the fire, his broad shoulders resting against the mantel. Hair the color of a raven's wing and eyes the purest blue, he was the youngest of her five brothers, and the most intemperate. Right now, his face was rigid with anger, his arms crossed over his chest in stiff disapproval. "I suppose I shouldn't be surprised at anything you say or do. Not after seeing you at Hell's Door."

Marcus looked up from where he sat at his desk, his dark eyes glinting. "Hell's Door? Not Farley's newest gaming hell?"

"That's the one," Chase said. "Our dearest sister was there not a fortnight ago."

"Where I saw you," she replied calmly. "If it's not a fit place for me, then it's not a fit place for you."

Chase flushed. "I'm not female. Nor am I so green that I don't know an ivory turner at a glance."

"No, you just lose your shirt at the faro table and then stumble out the door on your merry way."

Chase pushed himself from the mantel, his jaw set. "Now, see here—"

"Easy, children," Anthony said in a lazy murmur from the settee by the fire.

Sara caught a glimmer of understanding in his brown eyes. Her half brother was the only one who had, at one time, understood her. With tawny gold hair and brown eyes, he was the very image of their mother. Anthony's father had died of a fever within a year of his marriage, leaving behind Anthony, who was barely three months old, and a lovely widow, who promptly fell in love with the tempestuous Marquis of Treymount, Sara's father.

The marquis had been a passionate man who firmly believed in family. Deeply in love with his wife, he fully welcomed Anthony as the oldest of his soon-growing brood and made it a point to never distinguish between any of his children. They accepted one another without question and only Anthony's name bore evidence that he was not a St. John.

She nodded to him now. "Anthony."

"Sara. You look well."

"She looks like a hardened flirt," Chase said, glowering. "Look at that gown."

"Indeed," Marcus said, his deep voice a threatening rumble. "It's time someone put a stop to your antics, Sara."

She lifted her chin, controlling the anger that flashed through her at his high-handed tone. She had to remind herself that he was not used to being challenged.

Marcus was often called "the Golden Treymount" for his almost mystical ability to turn his investments into cold, hard coin. Men eagerly watched where he invested and followed his lead by the score.

Sara slid a glance at the all-powerful Marquis of Treymount, the patriarch of the family since the death of their parents. He was a man who reveled in his ability to command. His icy gaze was fastened on her with brooding intent, the hard line of his jaw seemingly carved in granite.

Annoyance made her hand curl into a fist. She was not afraid of Marcus. In a way, he was just like her—born with the desire to force fate onto his path, instead of the other way around. Perhaps that was why they couldn't speak without arguing. She walked to a small chair near Anthony and stood beside it, unwilling to sit. "Where are Brand and Devon?"

Anthony answered. "Brandon is missing, as is his wont of late."

"It must be a woman," Chase said with a smirk. "He always has a flirt in progress somewhere."

"And Devon?" Sara asked.

Marcus stood and came around to the front of the desk, picking up a leather box as he went. "I sent him to Bristol to see about our shipping interests, or he would be here as well."

They were all puppets to do Marcus's bidding, Sara decided bitterly. "What do you want, Marcus? I have things to do this evening, and none of them include this little gathering, pleasant though it is."

Marcus's cool gaze flickered across her form. "I should send you home to change into something more suitable to your station."

"But you won't," she replied in a voice that was amazingly calm considering the angry pounding of her heart. "I wouldn't return."

"Oh, you would come back," he said softly, "if I had to drag you here myself."

She managed a shrug that cost her more than she liked to admit. "Why are the others here? Were you afraid to face me alone?"

"I asked them to come because each one has, at some time within the past month, requested that I put a stop to your wild ways."

Sara shot a glance at Anthony. He met her gaze steadily enough, regret shadowing his face. A hollow pain flickered across her heart. *The traitor*. She returned her gaze to Marcus. "It is none of your concern what I do."

"Everything you do affects us. You are our sister."

"He's right," Chase said. "And lately, I cannot even sit at a game of dice without hearing my sister's name bandied about like one of the Prince's paramours."

Oddly, her wildest brother had a streak of prudery that extended only to her. Sara suspected it would expand to include his wife if he ever settled down to marry. She favored him with a brief glance. "I don't know how you can complain about my gown when you are wearing that atrocious waistcoat."

Anthony looked at his brother's chartreuse-and-pink waistcoat, an amused gleam in his eyes. "She has you there, Chase."

"We are not talking about fashion," Marcus said, setting the leather box beside him on the desk. "Chase doesn't step outside the bounds of propriety. Sara, once and for all, I'm asking you to give up this wild life." His voice softened with a hint of understanding. "If not for yourself, then for those of us who care for you."

For an instant she wavered, a wash of loneliness making her yearn for the closeness she'd once had with her brothers—a closeness that had disappeared when she'd gotten married. She understood her brothers' concerns, misguided as they were. Yet as much as she hated facing their disapproval, she could not become the complaisant, demure female they so obviously expected.

She'd tried that route once, and it had earned her nothing but pain. "I cannot change the way I live just to make other people happy. Not even you."

Marcus's face hardened. "Very well. You leave me no choice." He opened the leather box and withdrew a stack of papers. "Do you recognize these?"

She could see her signature sprawled across each sheet; they were her markers. In her months with the demimonde, she'd been far more reckless than was her wont. "How much are they?"

"Thirty-four hundred pounds."

Sara's mouth went dry. Surely not . . . Pride made her shrug. "I will see my solicitor first thing in the morning."

"I've already seen him. The only way you can come up with such a sum is to sell all your holdings—a move I, as your guardian, would never approve."

Anger sharpened her tongue. "Then what am I to do?"

He tossed the papers back into the box and shut it. "Send me your allowance for the next twelve months. All of it."

"I would have nothing to live on!"

"Which is why you will once again become dependent on me for support."

"*No.*"

"You have no choice," he retorted. "Furthermore, I have made arrangements for you to live in Bath for the next year."

"But everyone will be in London by April!"

"Not you. Too many people know of your exploits here in town."

Sara closed her eyes and tried to still the angry thundering of her heart.

"Sara," Anthony said softly, his voice lulling a way through her anger. "You are still young. You have your whole life ahead of you. This is just a small inconvenience."

"Perhaps you'll even meet someone you could care for," Chase added.

It was all suddenly clear—they wanted to bury her in the wilds of the country, leave her to "settle down," perhaps even marry again. She leveled a glare at Marcus. "I suppose you have already selected a groom. Who is it? Cavendish? Southland? Perhaps one of the royal dukes?"

"That—" Marcus's gaze flickered to Anthony and then back "—is something we have not yet agreed upon."

Had Julius not been so foolish as to appoint her stern brother the executor of his will, Sara was certain she would have been free to do what she pleased, when she pleased. But for now, all she had was a silk gown, her tattered pride, and the Lawrence sapphires clasped about her throat. She always wore them when facing adversity, as a reminder of the things she'd already dealt with and survived. Normally they gave her a feeling of invincibility, but tonight they felt cold and heavy on her bare skin. A reminder of her failures and fears.

Anthony shifted in his chair. "Sara, we don't wish to cause you pain. We realize that Julius was the wrong husband for you. You need someone more solid. More stable."

Sara's anger threatened to choke her. "Who are you to know what I want and need? Marriage is *not* the answer."

Chase spread his hands wide. "Think about it, Sara. You wouldn't be so . . . alone. Marriage can be a wonderful thing."

"Oh? I don't see any of *you* galloping to the altar."

Her brothers looked at one another, unease settling among them like a haze of acrid smoke. But she knew their unease would not make them rethink their decision—they were determined to ship her off to Bath as soon as possible.

She couldn't stay in London without funds; she wouldn't have the money to maintain her household, her stables, or anything else. But her brothers were crazed if they thought she would quietly retire to Bath, chastised into becoming some sort of demure schoolroom miss—especially while they were shopping about for her next damned husband.

Sara looked down at her fingers where three sapphire rings glittered, anger settling into a hard knot of resolve. It was time she took matters into her own hands. She would go to Bath, but *she* would be the one to select her next husband. And this time there would be no affection, no risk of pain. Nothing but a polite agreement to marry. And then, like all society couples, they would go their own ways, free from her brothers' smothering interference. It was an idyllic picture.

Of course, she'd lose her widow's jointure the second she married. That meant that her future husband would have to be well-heeled, as well as having an undemanding nature. Perhaps an older man. A widower, if there was one to be found. Someone who would settle for friendship, good conversation, and nothing more. It was a difficult proposition, but not impossible. And fortunately for her, if ever there was a place to find an older, settled widower, Bath was it.

Sara looked at Marcus. "Is there anything else you wished to speak to me about?"

He frowned, a flash of uncertainty in his dark blue gaze. "You will be leaving within the month."

"Fine." Sara went to the door and opened it. "I have no recourse other than to capitulate. But don't expect me to like it."

Marcus's jaw softened slightly. "Sara, trust us. We are only thinking of your future."

"So am I," she replied, her fingers tight about the doorknob. "But I'm seeking more than safety. I want happiness, Marcus. And I won't settle for anything less." Without waiting for his reply, she left, slamming the door behind her.

Damn them all. The angry clip of her jeweled heels was loud in the empty hallway. In the distance came the noise of the ball, the swell of music irritating her ragged spirits.

She knew exactly the type of man her brothers would choose for her—someone as arrogant and overbearing as they were. Someone who would try to control her every move. But they had forgotten one thing: she was a St. John through and through. In all the blood-wrought battles throughout all the ages, no St. John had ever cried defeat. And Sara wasn't about to become the first.

Chapter 2

Bath, England
February 21, 1815

Delphi had never been able to refuse a plea from one of her nephews, or from any of her numerous family members, for that matter. So when Marcus had unexpectedly asked her to chaperone Sara in Bath, Delphi had meekly agreed, even though she was no match for her niece's natural liveliness. Especially not since she admired that very trait.

When Delphi arrived at the Lawrence town house for the trip to Bath four weeks after the Treymount ball, she found Sara in an unexpected mood—smiling and excited. She even laughed heartily at all of Delphi's weak attempts to jest, which made Delphi experience a growing spasm of uncertainty. Whatever was Sara up to?

Her unease grew when an old school friend of Sara's, Miss Anna Thraxton, called within an hour of their arrival in Bath. Granted, Miss Thraxton's family was well-known and connected to almost everyone worth knowing. It could not be denied, however, that they had fallen on hard times. This was due mainly to the eccentricity of Anna's esteemed grandfather, a retired judge who spent a considerable amount of time writing pamphlets calling for the disposition of wealth from the upper classes to the lower classes in a fashion he called "redistribution."

Since Sir Thraxton was connected to so many of the best names in society, no one was willing to question his acceptability. Still, it was widely felt that the gentleman's political tendencies bordered on treason, and only the most foolish allowed the conversation to drift from such safe topics as the weather or horse racing.

Miss Anna Thraxton, however, was a very pleasant companion. Tall and auburn-haired, with gray eyes, a serene smile, and an unfortunately autocratic nose, it was a shame that financial circumstances rendered her ineligible as a potential wife for one of Delphi's handsome nephews. A woman of such Junoesque proportions would surely complement the family line.

Be that as it may, within a very few moments of sitting with Anna and Sara, Delphi became aware that there was a private conversation going on beneath the innocuous small talk. Sara's eyes positively glowed with excitement, and Anna more than once made a mysterious reference that sent Sara into a paroxysm of choked laughter.

Delphi's heart sank. There was no denying it; Sara was up to something. And whatever it was, Delphi was certain she had no ability to stop it. Yet as nervous as the thought made her, Delphi had to admit to some secret excitement at being in Bath.

She was tired of the *sameness* of her life. Perhaps it was the approach of her forty-third birthday that was so oversetting. That was the age at which her own mother had died, and Delphi didn't want to be like her mother, who had given her whole life to her children and husband and then just faded away.

No, Delphi wanted something . . . else. A surge of excitement was quickly followed by guilt. Who was she to decry her circumstances? She possessed more than her fair share of good fortune. She had a warm and loving family, more money than she could possibly spend, several properties—it was a shame that she was so ungrateful. Unaccountably depressed, she left Sara and Anna alone to gossip about their school friends.

Sara was pleased to discover that Anna was just as she remembered—quick-witted and pragmatic, with a flair for scheming that was unrivaled.

"The nerve of your brothers," Anna exclaimed upon being told the circumstances leading to Sara's arrival in Bath. "And now they expect you to sit idly by while they find a husband for you? That is positively medieval!"

"Yes. Julius is dead and Marcus will not rest until he has buried me, as well. Which is why I have made a decision." Sara picked up a tasseled pillow from the settee and plumped it mercilessly. "I plan to find my own husband. Someone who is malleable, who understands a civilized union and will not dictate to me. I want my freedom."

"Hmm." Anna looked at her thoughtfully, then said, "We will also need to find a man with a fortune. It can be done; 'malleable' and 'wealthy' are not always disparate traits."

Sara nodded. "I lose my jointure the day I marry."

"You'd want a handsome man, too," Anna mused. "One young enough to understand your need for enjoyment."

"If possible—although I may have to compromise on such things." She refused to think of how much she might have to compromise. Still, armed with their set of criteria, she and Anna began to make a list of prospects.

Two weeks later, after a flurry of visits, Sara began to realize how difficult her search really was. She stood with Anna at the Jeffries ball watching the meager company fill the grand parlor. In London, a gathering this miniscule would only have declared itself a "soiree." But here in Bath, with over forty couples present and two dozen single persons, the Jeffries "ball" was already being touted a glittering success.

"What about that one?" Anna whispered.

Sara turned to where Anna pointed. A young man stood by the wide white doors that led into the ballroom. Thin, with a wisp of yellow hair drooping over his shiny forehead, he reminded Sara of a wilted sprig of thyme. She hunched a shoulder. "He looks delicate. I don't want a sickly husband."

Anna looked around. "This side of the room appears to be lacking eligible males."

"Maybe we would fare better on the other side." Sara took Anna's arm, and they sauntered across the Jeffries ballroom, eyeing every man they passed. It was a depressing exercise in futility. Bath was populated with an astounding number of stodgy, respectable men—men who would want their wives to sit at home and sew samplers and bear a horrendous number of children. Sara could read it in their eyes.

It was yet another dastardly aspect of Marcus's plan: since the season had started, all the eligible men would be safely ensconced in London, waiting for the new batch of heiresses.

Anna blew out a disgusted sigh. "I don't see a one that will do. They are all either too timid or too conventional. I thought about Captain Rothschilde, but he's fifty years old if he's a day, and I don't think he'd be at all lenient with a young wife."

"The man I need could be a hundred years old for all the difference it makes." Time was marching on, and she just knew that Marcus was already holding interviews with potential candidates for her hand.

She narrowed her gaze on a young man who

hovered nearby, as if gathering his nerve to ask one of them to dance. He froze when he caught her gaze. The more she stared, the redder he became until, finally, he turned and almost ran from the room, his head tucked as if afraid she would follow.

Sara made a sound of disgust. "Are there no real men here tonight?"

"It doesn't appear so," Anna said with genuine regret. "I've been wracking my brain and I can think of only two men who might suit your purpose, though neither are perfect."

"Who?"

"Mr. Stapweed or the Earl of Bridgeton. Unfortunately, Stapweed has an annoying tendency to spit when he speaks."

Ugh. "What about Bridgeton?"

"The earl is, as Grandfather would say, morally corrupt." Anna made a face. "Grandpapa has taken to reading Methodist literature."

"Tell me more about this earl. Who is he?"

"He recently moved into Hibberton Hall, Parkington's old place. Lady Chultney told Grandpapa that the earl is the most depraved man on Earth."

"Lady Chultney also thought Lord Collinsworth killed his wife, when she was only visiting relatives in the north."

"That is quite true, the poor dear. However, Grandpapa told me the same thing about the earl. He is familiar with the family, you know. And Lord Peebleton refused to recognize the earl when they met in the park last week—gave him the cold shoulder as soon as he saw him."

Well, that was interesting, indeed. Lord Peeble-ton was not known to be a stickler. "Whatever has the earl done?"

"No one will say . . ." Anna glanced around as if afraid someone would overhear. Then she opened her fan and whispered behind it, "But Lady Chult-ney believes he once abducted a woman for *unsavory* purposes."

"Sounds like a Banbury story to me."

"I think he must be excessively romantic to go to such lengths to secure a woman's affections." Anna smiled, a wistful look in her eyes. "Just imagine! A man who would defy the law in your name and whisk you away to his palace—"

"The earl has a palace?"

"Well, no. He has been renovating Hibberton Hall for the past month, which is why he hasn't been in town much. But I've heard it said that he is as handsome as an angel—a *fallen* angel." Anna lowered her voice. "At one time, just being seen talking to him could ruin a woman forever."

"And now?"

"He inherited a title," Anna said matter-of-factly. "Not to mention that he just returned to England with a tremendous fortune."

"Which immediately cancels all crimes he has committed, short of murder."

"Exactly. And Grandpapa thinks the earl wants to reestablish himself in society. It would do him a lot of credit to marry into your family, as the St. Johns are above reproach." Anna suddenly chuckled. "I never thought of it this way before, but this is just like a novel from the lending library—only there is no hero."

"I don't need a hero. I was blessed with a large amount of common sense, which is of infinitely more use than a man."

"Hear, hear," Anna said approvingly. "If you want true affection, get a pet. They are much cleaner and far more amusing."

"And infinitely more loyal. A pity Marcus wouldn't be content with my purchasing a greyhound for company."

"Yes, I—" Anna suddenly clutched her friend's hand. "Good God, Sara, he's here."

"Who? Marcus?" That would be just like him—to send her to Hades, then come to keep an eye on her himself.

"No, no," Anna said, grabbing Sara's arm and yanking her around a potted palm so they could stare undetected at the entryway. "The Earl of Bridgeton just walked in. Look!"

Sara followed her friend's wide, fixed gaze.

Striding into the room as if he owned the world, was the most beautiful man she had ever seen. Tall and broad-shouldered, the newcomer walked with a negligent grace, his movements as fluid as melted silver. His flawlessly cut coat clung to his athletic shoulders, his breeches molded over muscular thighs. His patrician nose and sensual mouth had been carved by a master hand. Every inch of him bespoke power and decadence, from hair the color of gold to skin brushed with the slightest touch of bronze.

He was beyond beautiful—he was as magnificent as sin.

"Good God," Anna breathed. "I've never seen such a perfect man."

"Perhaps we should pinch him just to be certain he's real."

Anna chuckled. "I'd volunteer, but your Aunt Delphi already looks at me as if she thinks I might begin sprouting horns."

"Aunt Delphi? She loves you."

"No, she doesn't. She's worried I'm a bad influence on you, and if she had any idea what we were doing right now, she'd blame the whole thing on me without a second's pause."

"Do you think so?" Sara said absently, her mind still on the earl. Perhaps she'd been going about this all wrong. Maybe what she really needed was a rakehell. Surely a man given to sin would never stop his wife from attending gaming hells, or dressing as she pleased, or doing whatever took her fancy, providing she was discreet.

The idea held immense appeal.

She watched the earl walk to the receiving line and bow to Lord Jeffries, who frowned, his face turning a bright red. There was no mistaking the surprise on the man's face. "I wonder if Bridgeton even had an invitation," she murmured.

"Surely he wouldn't come without one!" Anna exclaimed.

Just as Sara wondered if Lord Jeffries would eject the earl from his ballroom, the portly older man bowed. Sara supposed she shouldn't be surprised.

What else could he do? Make a scene at his own ball?

She had to admire the earl's boldness. Even from this distance, she could tell he was a man who'd transgressed more than his fair share. Someone called out the earl's name and he turned, his sensual mouth curved in a lopsided smile that made Sara's throat go completely dry.

"Look," Anna said, "Lady Bedford is dragging your Aunt Delphi into the cardroom. She'll be occupied for half an hour at least."

"Excellent," Sara said, glancing around. She was not the only one affected by the earl's presence. Olivia Charles already had her smelling salts clenched in her hand, while Melinda Loundry was positively gawking. There wasn't a woman in the room who wasn't staring, openly or otherwise.

In fact, even Anna was once again staring. She went so far as to lick her lips, as if regarding a particularly succulent pastry. "Our coloring would blend well."

"Yes, you would make a lovely set of statues. Once I convince him to marry me, perhaps your grandpapa will commission a portrait of the two of you."

Anna grinned. "You can't blame me for dreaming. I never knew he was so beautiful."

"On the outside, perhaps. But on the inside, he has a hard lump of coal for a heart—all rakes do." Just like Julius—and this time Sara would be very careful to remain emotionally detached. "I rather like the fact that he has no heart. I don't plan on using mine, either. Come on. I want a word with him."

Anna's gaze narrowed on Sara. "What are you going to do?"

"I'm going to see if he'll accompany me to the terrace, so that I can interview him. I'm not going to make another mistake."

"Sara, if anyone catches the two of you alone, you will be compromised."

"Who said anything about being alone? *You* will be with us."

"But—"

"I have to talk to him and make sure that he suits our purpose. Wait for me by the terrace door, Anna. I'll be right back."

Ignoring Anna's sigh of exasperation, Sara slipped from behind the palm and made her way toward the decadent Earl of Bridgeton and all his golden glory. For the first time since she'd arrived in Bath, a wing of hope brushed Sara's bruised spirit. Trying to still the thud of her heart, she planted herself in the earl's path and waited.

Nick stifled a yawn. What mad impulse had possessed him to attend such an insipid affair as Lord Jeffries' ball? He hadn't been here for five minutes and already tedium was pulling at his lids, as if he had risen from a deep sleep and could not awaken. He supposed he should just consign himself to an evening of unrelieved boredom. After all, like it or not, this was where he had to begin if he was to rebuild his place in society.

When he'd been younger, he had been judged on his association with his mother, measured by her erratic, immoral behavior, and branded a dangerous youth even when he'd been too young to understand the whispered comments. But such treatment had toughened him, and he had eventually grown into his initially undeserved reputation, accepting it with a boldness that added to his notoriety.

At Nick's side, the Comte du Lac gave a satisfied sigh as he watched a small cluster of women swish by in a cloud of satin, lace, and scent. "I begin to see why you so desired to return to England. The women, they are—" he kissed his fingers to the air, smiling dreamily. "Each and every one of them."

Nick glanced at a stiff-lipped matron who was staring at him from across the room as if she'd like to flay him with her fan. She was as round as she was tall, with thin, wispy hair piled high and adorned with a variety of flowers and ribbons in an effort to make the scanty tresses look more substantial. She glared at him as if for a ha'pence, she'd have ordered the footmen to escort him to the closest door and slam it in his face. Eyelids twitching, she leaned over to her thin, angular companion and began talking rapidly.

He knew what the matron was saying. She was cataloging his every fault—telling tales about his mother, exaggerating his youthful escapades, repeating every story she'd ever heard.

He shrugged the thoughts aside, unbothered by memories. Despite his errors, he would not apologize for his past. It was his, and he was content that it should be so. Nick had never aspired to perfection, or even such a lamentable state as goodness. He was, and would always be, his mother's son. The thought both pained and reassured him.

Nick waited until the matron again fixed him with her venomous gaze, then he lifted his brows and smiled—slowly, surely, letting his lashes lower just enough to cause her to stutter to a halt. Her eyes widened; her mouth gradually dropped open to hang in limp wonderment.

Satisfied, Nick turned away and murmured to the comte, "You exaggerate, as usual. Some of these women make me ill."

"Well, there might be one or two exceptions," Henri amended affably. "Perhaps you should find a mistress, *mon ami*. It will give you new energy. A new focus. And I, as your friend, will assist in the selection." The comte rubbed his hands together and looked about the room with an appraising eye. "What shall it be? Tall or petite? Blond or brunette? Perhaps a tasty little redhead, *non*?"

"I don't really care about hair color or height."

"Then what? Perhaps you care if she is . . ." The comte made a rounded gesture at his chest.

"Just do not burden me with a woman who expects me to declare my love every time she sighs. Or one who attempts to weigh me down with the boring details of her daily activities. I have enough tedium in my own life without enduring someone else's."

"Already we have narrowed the field. You want a woman of character who neither talks nor complains nor expects declarations." Henri frowned. "*Voyons!* You don't look for a woman, but a saint."

"I've always been selective."

"You can afford to be. You have the face, the funds, the title. But that is the problem for you, no? Too many willing women."

"I've never found it to be a difficulty."

"But of course. It is a little like eating too rich of food. At the time, it is almost impossible to turn away. But later . . . then begin the regrets. You need a challenge, *mon ami*. Someone who will inflame your interest to new levels. Someone who will obsess your every waking moment. Someone who—"

"What I need is a drink. And of a quality I am unlikely to discover here."

"Come, you must admit you would like to meet such a woman."

For a brief instant, Nick wondered about the allure of true love. He'd never felt an all-consuming need to be with someone, to know what they were doing every minute of the day, to believe they were essential to his happiness. The thought was almost laughable. The ugly truths of his life had burnt away whatever tender sensibilities it took to fall in love. "Love is for fools, Henri. I am not a fool."

The comte frowned, his bushy brows lowered over the bridge of his nose. "Do not tempt fate, Nicholas."

"I tempt no one. However, you are right about one thing—I would like a mistress: someone who, after several months of mutual pleasure, I can leave without having to look back."

So far, things were working out well. He'd managed to brazen his way into this gathering, and sometime tonight, he'd be sure to garner an invitation or two to other events. All he had to do was display a few social graces and his wealth, and his feet would be solidly on the path of social acceptance. Once Nick conquered Bath, he would move on to London, where his real detractors resided. By that time he would already be established, with a score of connections to hold him in good stead. All told, his reentrance into society was proving to be exceptionally easy.

"I believe I will retire to the cardroom," Henri said thoughtfully, his gaze on a trim woman in puce who had just disappeared through the doors.

"I won't be staying long," Nick said.

"If I'm fortunate, neither will I," murmured the comte. Flashing a grin, he left, a jaunty bounce to his step.

Nick tried to shake off a sense of heaviness. His three years on the Continent had spoiled him. Three years of wild living, drinking to excess, and gambling 'til dawn. But that time was over—now he had Hibberton Hall, and soon he would take his rightful place in society.

He looked around the room, feeling an overwhelming desire to escape the heat and stifling respectability of the silk-swathed ballroom. He hated to be around so many people. The sights and sounds inevitably irritated his head and made it ache worse than usual.

You've been alone far too long, he told himself

firmly. How else was he to find a suitable mistress for his last few months of sanity, if not at this parade of feminine charms? A whirl of bronze silk caught his eye, and he watched a plump beauty dance by on the arm of a young lord. Just beyond them stood a pale lady in pink, smiling up at a foppish gentleman whose shirt points forced his chin to a ridiculous angle.

They were all here for the same reason—searching for a dalliance. Of course his case was different, for his mistress would have to be something out of the ordinary, someone with character and intelligence. He'd had his chance at wealth and beauty and had found them both lacking.

At the thought, he lifted a hand to his brow, the familiar ache tightening like a band around his head. The monsters were restless tonight, but not dangerous. They teased and tormented, but he remained amazingly sober, his thoughts lucid, his eyesight clear. It was a relief, and he could only pray that the headaches stayed at bay. Perhaps all he'd needed was the fresh air of England.

The music changed to a slow waltz, and Nick watched as a sea of colored gowns swirled across the gleaming floor. Tall and short, plump and thin, dark and fair, the room was packed to the walls with eligible women.

A pair of dark eyes caught his gaze. Hmmm ... Lucilla Kettering, the infamous Lady Knowles, stood in the corner by a potted fern, conversing with a dashing blade who looked a good five years her junior. Nick knew the young widow from his travels on the Continent. He'd met her in Paris and had enjoyed her perfumed skin and wild abandon between the sheets. Tall and shapely, she was the picture of cool composure and feminine strength—precisely the type of woman he was looking for. That she possessed a lascivious nature that exactly matched his own would only make their partnership the sweeter.

Nick bowed to her, his gaze lingering on her rounded bosom. Her mouth curved in pleasure, one hand lifting to where the pulse beat at her throat as if she remembered his mouth seeking that very spot. Her eyes flared in excitement as Nick made his way toward her through the crowd.

He had not taken more than a few steps when someone bumped into him.

"I beg your pardon," said a velvety feminine voice.

Nick glanced down and came to an abrupt halt. He was staring into the face of a schoolroom miss who was surely no more than seventeen years of age. But seventeen or not, he was rooted to the spot. He forgot about Lucilla, forgot the heat of the room, forgot his boredom. Forgot everything but the most damnable dimple in the woman's right cheek.

She stared back, but not with the admiration he usually stirred. There was a hint of calm evaluation behind the polite smile that curved her rosebud mouth. Inexplicably amused, Nick could not help admiring the startlingly white skin and full, red mouth. Like a cloud of black silk, her hair sprang from a wide forehead and curled charmingly in a profusion of ringlets on either side of a heart-shaped face.

Young, delicate, and blessed with an ethereal air, she escaped being a true beauty by the shortness of her lower lip and the suggestion of willfulness in her stubborn little chin.

For three years, Nick had traveled the Continent and tasted what each country had to offer—the dark beauties of Italy, the pale sophistication of the Parisian ladies. What he'd missed the most was embodied in the vision before him—the seductive scent of lavender, creamy skin hidden beneath tantalizing layers of clothing, and the direct, wide-eyed gaze of a true innocent.

There were no innocents among the demimonde of Paris or the dirty streets of Rome. Which was why every diminutive inch of this little charmer spoke to his soul, lifted his spirits, and lessened the ache in his head.

Somehow, he found himself capturing her slim hand, his gaze irrefutably drawn by her tender lower lip, which begged to be tasted.

Nick lifted her hand and placed a warm kiss to her delicately gloved fingers. "I beg your pardon for not watching where I was stepping. Allow me to introduce myself; I am Nicholas Montrose, the Earl of Bridgeton."

She dipped a curtsey, her hand tightening over his. "How do you do? I was hoping to have a word with you, my lord."

The calm, self-assured voice was at odds with her youthful appearance. Nick was intrigued; which was she—a blasé creature of society or a country innocent attempting to hide her inexperience behind a mask of composure? His gaze lingered on her eyes. They were the pale blue of a morning sky, fringed with ridiculously long lashes that tangled at the corners. "Have we met before, Miss . . ."

"We've never met, but I've heard of you from many people."

He moved his thumb over the back of her hand in a brief, tantalizing movement. "Perhaps I can dispel some of the rumors."

"I doubt it." She freed her hand as her tongue slipped nervously across her lower lip, and her gaze darted toward the cardroom before settling back on him. "I don't mean to pry, but I've heard it said that you are a known rake."

Amusement banished the last vestige of his boredom. "At times." He would have agreed to anything after witnessing the tantalizing trail of moisture left by her pink tongue.

She nodded once, then said in a well-rehearsed manner, "It is quite stuffy in here. It would be pleasant to take a turn about the terrace."

His attention jerked from her mouth to her eyes. "I beg your pardon?"

"I said, 'It is quite stuffy in here, and it would be pleasant to take a turn about the terrace.'" Her brows lowered. "Perchance you don't hear well?"

"No, indeed. I just didn't expect such a . . . munificent offer so early in the evening." He raked a gaze across her petite form, taking in the generous swell of her breasts and the graceful slope of her white shoulders. Munificent, hell. A dull ache lifted in his groin and swelled.

The heat intensified when she gave an impatient sigh, the movement pressing her bosom against the thin fabric of her gown. Small, embroidered roses rested at the cleft of her breasts, and they rose and fell with her every breath. Nick's cravat tightened a notch.

It was a dilemma. The old Nick would have taken her up on her offer and swept her onto the terrace, pleasuring her until she cried out with ecstasy. The new Nick realized that such an action would cause the pudgy matrons of Bath to slam shut many of the doors just now opening for him.

With true regret, he looked down at his fascinating companion and shook his head. "It wouldn't be wise for us to leave the safety of this room."

She could not have appeared more astounded if he'd announced he was the pope. "But I have asked a friend to serve as chaperone."

Nick followed her gaze to where a tall, auburn-haired woman stood by the terrace door. It was tempting. Tempting, but . . . "Another time, perhaps."

After a moment of stunned silence, she cleared her throat and then spoke in a slow, careful voice, as if she suspected him of limited understanding. "You won't even join me for one moment?"

Nick wondered if she was one of those silly females who viewed his appearance and title as a challenge—a trophy to be won and then displayed. Yet she did not appear enamored of his appearance or title. Indeed, she looked . . . annoyed. Almost as if she thought him guilty of wasting her time.

Of the many reactions Nick had engendered in women—fascination, attraction, admiration, excitement, fear—none had ever looked so obviously unimpressed. In fact, the little vixen had begun to look past him, her gaze assessing a man just to his right.

Nick's interest fanned to a roaring flame. The dreary confines of the ballroom brightened, warmed, and gleamed. "I don't even know your name."

She hesitated the briefest instant. "Lady Carrington. My husband died not long ago."

Ah. This is becoming more interesting by the moment. "I'm sorry."

"I'm not."

She said the words simply, without rancor or emotion, but so surely that he knew her heart was free. This was no grieving widow, but a woman in search of passion.

Nick was a sensual man, and he would take great pleasure in sharing his bed with the fascinating Lady Carrington. But if they were to embark on a delightful flirtation, they would have to carefully mask their interest in one another whenever they were in public. For Nick, who had never had a truly clandestine relationship, the thought was unexpectedly provocative.

He looked down at the little charmer. He imagined her naked and in his bed, her skin flushed by passion, her hair unbound and flowing over her shoulders. He imagined her breasts, full and lush, dewy from his kisses, the crests pink and thrusting. He pictured himself lowering himself between her damp thighs as he rode her until she cried out with passion. He saw himself bending over her, tasting her core, ecstasy nestled among her tight curls. . . .

Her gaze widened and she took an unsteady step backward. "I-I have changed my mind about the terrace, my lord. You won't do at all." She spun away, but her slippered foot tangled in her skirts and she tilted unsteadily.

Nick caught her just before she fell. He let his hands linger possessively on her arms, his temper sparked. *What does she mean, I won't "do"? The little chit needs to be taught the cost of playing with fire.* Especially the kind of fire that raged through him at this very moment, heating his blood, burning away his thin grasp on civility.

She jerked free and fled for the safety of her tall friend.

Swallowing the bitter taste of unfulfilled desire, Nick tried to still the blood that pounded through his body. Across the room, Lucilla attempted to gain his attention, her brows drawn in irritation, a petulant thrust to her lips. But Nick had no use for Lucilla at the moment. He remained rooted where he stood, watching the much-too-tempting Lady Carrington whispering to her friend, who stared at him with a mixture of horror and fascination.

He tried to ignore the relentless ache in his groin. How had he allowed something as simple as thickly lashed eyes and a dimpled cheek to get past his defenses?

Then Nick became aware of the avid gazes of two matrons who looked as if they'd like nothing better than to see him strung from the closest lamppost. Tonight of all nights, he did not need to make a spectacle of himself. One misstep, and he would find himself once again on the outside, looking in. He forced himself to remain in the ballroom, and allowed himself to be introduced to faceless woman after faceless woman. Word of his fortune soon spread and Bath society cracked open its door for the former prodigal son.

But all evening, Nick was much too aware of Lady Carrington as she flitted about the room, smiling at anyone who caught her eye. Grimly irritated, he watched her progression. The *ton* loved scandal almost as much as it loved money and gorged itself on whatever tidbits were available. If she didn't have a care, Lady Carrington would become the next main course—and if she became a social pariah, he would have to give her up. Society loved to declare guilt by association. Still . . . his gaze wandered toward her as she stood talking animatedly to her companion. She was a conundrum, a flash of fire, unexpected and unknown.

Perhaps Henri had been right—he needed a challenge. But not one that could destroy his chance to reenter society. The evening suddenly seemed flat. Taking one last look at Lady Carrington, Nick turned on his heel and left.

Chapter 3

Hibberton Hall had gone too long without a master. The roof leaked in a dozen places, fallen bricks blocked five of the twelve chimneys, and black mold splotched the once elegantly decorated walls in almost every room. All told, the rundown manor was a rotten board away from collapsing.

An ordinary man would have balked at the idea of attempting to return the manor to its former beauty. Fortunately for all concerned, the Earl of Bridgeton was not an ordinary man. Hibberton Hall belonged to Nick and he would see it restored, regardless of the cost, personal or otherwise.

The way Parkington had allowed the Hall to fall into such disrepair was revolting, Nick thought as he stood in the center of the library. This room was in better condition than most of the others, though far from perfect. The floor needed staining, the heavy oak paneling had warped from the constant dampness that pervaded the house, and the fine plasterwork was threaded with tiny cracks. Nick stifled an impatient sigh and crossed to look out the window. "Pratt, we will need some men skilled in plaster work."

"Yes, my lord," his longtime solicitor said from where he sat at the desk, making a list of needed repairs. His fine, tiny writing already covered three entire sheets.

Nick lifted the latch and swung the window open, the hinges protesting loudly. Cold winter air invaded the room, dispelling the moldy odor and clearing his head. Despite almost a century of neglect, Hibberton Hall remained an impressive site. The main part of the house, built during Tudor times, contained a large banquet hall that had been converted to a ballroom almost a hundred years ago by one enterprising owner.

The rest of the Hall represented a succession of owners who built with little consideration to the style of the existing house. Strangely, the resulting architectural hodgepodge was both pleasing and intriguing.

"My lord?" Mr. Pratt's soft voice interrupted his thoughts. "I've prepared a list of materials needed for the repair of the east wing."

Nick nodded, not bothering to examine the paper. His solicitor was more than thorough. "Give it to Ledbetter. Make a note that we will need more men, too. I want as much of the repairs completed as possible before spring."

"Yes, my lord. I will have him scour the country-side for skilled laborers."

"We'll need a steady supply of lumber, as well. Perhaps we should ship some in from France."

"I'll make inquiries." The solicitor adjusted his spectacles, his gray eyes almost obscured by the thick lenses. "My lord, how . . . how are you today?"

Jaw tense, Nick recognized the reference to his headaches. Ah, the joys of old family retainers—yet another aspect of settled life that he had not missed. He caught Pratt's concerned gaze and managed to say, "My headaches are less frequent here than in France."

"Excellent, my lord. Perhaps they will fade away altogether."

"Perhaps," he said, more to end the conversation than because he agreed. He stirred restlessly and pushed aside the edge of the new window hangings, his fingers lingering on the velvet curtains. The lush, sensual feel sparked a sudden vision of Lady Carrington as she had appeared three nights before. Small and delicate, with thick black hair and creamy white skin, she would make a stunning mistress. Every diminutive inch of her was quality—exactly the type of woman to fit a setting like Hibberton Hall. Exactly the kind of woman who would fit Nick's new station in life. All he had to do was win her to his bed.

A brief knock heralded the entrance of the butler. Wiggs tottered into the room, a tray laden with silver and delicate china resting in his gnarled hands. "Your tea, my lord." The butler's voice cracked in the middle of the word "lord" making it sound like "lard."

"Thank you." Nick noted how the butler kept his gaze averted. Since his arrival, the resident servants had treated him as though they expected him to sprout horns and a tail, and it was beginning to get as annoying as hell. "Wiggs."

The butler looked up from adjusting the china on the tray, his gaze uncertain. "Yes, my lord?"

"How long have you served Hibberton Hall?"

"Almost fifty years, my lord."

Mr. Pratt lifted his head from his list making. "All of the servants have been here for quite some time, which is amazing considering that they haven't received a decent wage in years."

Wiggs nodded, pride shining in his face. "We love the Hall, sir. It is a pleasure to serve it."

Pratt dipped his pen into the inkwell and carefully adjusted a column. "Well, you need never again fear missing your wages."

"Indeed not," Nick said, who could not understand such misplaced loyalty. A house was just a house, and Hibberton Hall, for all its potential beauty, was nothing more than that. "Wiggs, I cannot help but notice that the staff seems uneasy."

The butler's Adam's apple bobbed up and down in an alarming fashion. "Do they, my lord? I-I hadn't noticed."

"Indeed they do. And it bothers me. So let me say this once, and you can carry it to the others. If you, or anyone else employed at Hibberton Hall, find you cannot bear to see me in your master's place, then I shall have Pratt find you employment elsewhere."

The butler paled. "My lord, with all due respect, the staff was glad to see the baron sent about his business."

Nick frowned. "Then why the devil do all of you jump like rabbits every time I call for you?"

Mr. Pratt cleared his throat. "Ah, perhaps I can explain—"

"Mr. Pratt," Nick said softly, not taking his gaze from the butler, "while I appreciate your desire to assist Wiggs, he appears quite capable of answering for himself."

Wiggs straightened. "My lord, I apologize for any peculiarities you may have witnessed in the household staff, but you must realize that we've never had a gentleman in residence. In all my years as butler, Lord Parkington was here only once. I believe he stayed all of three minutes." Visibly trembling, the butler clasped his gloved hands before him. "The staff and I are doing our best to accommodate you, and we only hope you won't turn us out."

"Turn you out? I have no intention of doing any such thing."

The butler let out his breath in a long wheeze of relief. "Thank you, my lord! You have no idea—"

"Provided," Nick continued inexorably, "that you prove your worth. I cannot abide laziness."

"My lord, you will have no cause to dismiss anyone."

"I certainly hope not. Still, I must ask why is it that after almost a month in residence, only my bedchamber and the comte's are fit for habitation?"

"I have *frequently* spoken to Mrs. Kibble on that subject, but I'm afraid I was unable to convince her that the quiet countryside around Bath could hold the interest of such a, ahem, man of the world."

Nick noted the pause but decided not to pursue it. "So the redoubtable Mrs. Kibble believes I might leave at any minute and not return?"

The butler looked pained. "The current odds are twenty to one that you won't see six more weeks."

Nick certainly understood the appeal of a wager. "Wiggs, I wish to make a small wager myself."

"My lord?"

"I wager ten guineas that the bedchambers in the east wing will not be cleaned and aired by the end of the week."

"But sir . . . that's almost two entire floors!"

"Then I will be keeping my ten guineas," Nick said gently.

After a startled moment, a reluctant smile creased the lines on the butler's elderly face. "I will notify the staff at once, my lord. We will complete the task; see if we don't." Beaming, he left the room, a surprising spring to his ancient step.

As soon as the door closed, Mr. Pratt stood, his chair sliding silently over the thick rug. "Some of this is my fault, my lord. Before you returned, I fear that I mentioned to Wiggs that you might not need the services of all the servants here. I wasn't certain what household staff you might be bringing from France."

"I had no household servants in France, Mr. Pratt. In fact, I had no household."

"I was unaware of that fact, my lord. Since you sent me a considerable sum each year for investing, I assumed you were living well." A hint of concern deepened the solicitor's voice. "You . . . you did live well, didn't you, my lord?"

He shrugged. "I had the money from the sale of Bridgeton House." And he sincerely hoped its drafty fireplaces were the bane of his damned cousin's life. Alec deserved no less.

Those three, long, lonely years on the continent, Nick had lived the life of a wanderer, even when well-heeled. Somehow he'd always known he would return to England, regardless of the promise he'd made Alec.

Mr. Pratt cleared his throat. "I hope you don't think I'm being forward, my lord, but when I heard you were returning to England, I feared the intervening years might have . . ."

"What?"

"I don't know. Humbled you in some way."

Nick raised his brows. "And now?"

"You have not been humbled, my lord. I'm not sure why you felt it necessary to leave England, and your cousin, Viscount Hunterston, has never mentioned the events that led to your travels. But there were rumors . . ." The solicitor reddened, then gave an apologetic shrug.

"I was banished from England," Nick said shortly. "Forced into a nomad's life due to my errors in dealing with my cousin."

"Of course, my lord," Pratt murmured, gathering his ledger. "Very understandable." He paused, then said quietly, "Lady Hunterston is an exceptional woman."

"She is also my cousin's wife; a fact I managed to forget." Nick smiled coldly. "Don't look so crestfallen, Pratt. It was inevitable. Alec and I cannot be in the same room more than ten minutes without coming to blows."

"I daresay some of that is due to the way your grandfather used to play the two of you against each other."

"My grandfather believed Alec worthy. He was not so generous with me."

"That was his error, my lord. It has been my pleasure to serve the Montrose family for nigh on thirty years, and regardless of what has happened between you and Lord Hunterston, I'm glad you have returned."

"Are you? Alec inherited the fortune, not I."

"Lord Hunterston does not hold the title. You do." Behind his thick spectacles, the solicitor's eyes warmed. "I can never forget that. In fact, I didn't even notify Lord Hunterston that you had returned. I thought it would be best if you saw him once you were more settled."

Nick flashed a humorless smile. "And could show him my new magnificence?"

Pratt met Nick's gaze steadily. "And show him

how you've changed. You have, sir. And we both know why."

Because the headaches had finally come to him, just as they had come to his mother. It was only a matter of time before his true weakness was exposed, until he sank into the same blackness that had claimed her, the search for relief that had led her down more and more depraved paths.

The bleak hole that festered in Nick's soul ached anew. He managed a shrug and turned away. "You mistake the matter, Pratt. I am the same as always, only wealthier. And you may tell my bloody cousin that, with my compliments."

A long silence filled the room, then Pratt sighed and Nick could hear the solicitor gathering his papers. "I see His Lordship but little. Viscountess Hunterston keeps him well occupied." The solicitor hesitated, then added, "Lady Hunterston has recently retired to the country."

"At this time of the year? Is she ill, or—?" Nick broke off, comprehension dawning. "Ah, she is having another of Hunterston's brats. What does that make? Ten? Twenty?" Sourness rose in his belly, hot and heavy. It wasn't disappointment, for he'd come to realize that what he'd felt for Julia had been nothing more than hope—hope that she could, somehow and some way, save him from himself. It had been a vain and foolish dream, all tangled up with his desire for what he couldn't have.

Mr. Pratt adjusted his glasses. "I believe it is only their second child, my lord, although they have adopted several others."

"How perfectly dreadful." Nick clasped his hands behind his back and stared out at the lawn. "At your meeting with Ledbetter, tell him to set a date for completion. I want the repairs to the Hall finished as quickly as possible."

Pratt bowed, then crossed to the door. "Yes, my lord. Is there anything else you require?"

"No. Just . . . Pratt?"

The solicitor turned around, his pale eyes curious. "Yes, my lord?"

"Thank you for protecting my interests while I was away."

A pleased smile touched the solicitor's face as he bowed again. "It is a pleasure to be of service." The door closed quietly and Nick was left alone at the window.

On the brown lawn, the winter wind chased a small swirl of leaves down the gentle slope to the pond. As barren and wasted as it appeared, it was his, and he took satisfaction in the notion.

A soft knock sounded at the door, and the comte entered. He was dressed for riding, his deep blue coat making his white hair seem brighter, a jaunty lift to his step.

"Where have you been?" Nick asked. Since the Jeffries ball three days ago, Henri had been in hot pursuit of a widow. Though Nick had not asked, he was certain the woman was blessed with both a fortune and a title, for the comte did nothing that did not progress him further into society.

Henri crossed to the crackling fire. "I have been riding with the lovely Delphi. Ah, Nicholas, you should see her! She is—" The comte kissed his fingers to the sky and dropped into a chair, his legs stretched before him, a smile on his face.

Nick turned to sit at the desk. "So you have been telling me for three days. I'm amazed I didn't notice this paragon when we attended the Jeffries ball."

"Ah, that is because she has no brilliance of expression. No forward, playful manner. No blinding beauty. None of the things you prize in a woman." The comte held his hands toward the flames. "She is quality. Very pretty, and quite charming. A shy butterfly who wants to fly like a bird. And I am willing to teach her all she needs to know."

"Henri, please. I haven't had breakfast yet, and I've a million things to see to this morning, none of which will get done if I must listen to your drivel on an empty stomach."

Henri stiffened. "A million things to do! But you cannot! I told Lady Langtry that you—"

Nick shot a swift look at the comte. "Lady who?"

"Langtry."

"Your Delphi is the Duchess of Langtry?"

"*Oui*. But that should be no surprise. Every day I have told you that I—"

Nick broke in impatiently, "Henri, have you met the duchess's niece?"

"Lady Carrington? But of course. She rides with us every day."

"Damn it, Henri!"

Henri blinked. "What, have I done something wrong, *mon ami*?"

"No, but I have an interest in Lady Carrington."

Comprehension lit Henri's eyes. "Ah, the lovely Sara is your quarry. That is a pity."

"Why?"

"She has only been a widow for a year and her husband was not faithful. I fear she did not accept it well."

So the intriguing Sara was a romantic. That was useful information, indeed. In Nick's experience, women who yearned for the romantic often interpreted the simplest gestures as declarations, which made them all the easier to seduce.

"Mon Dieu!" Henri said with a disgusted look. "I know that expression. Do not even think it. From what Delphi has let slip, Lord and Lady Carrington had a love match at one time, but it turned sour."

"She has been disappointed, then."

"Oui, and Delphi has hinted that Sara had fallen into some impropriety because of it." Henri frowned. "Nicholas, she is the type of woman one falls madly in love with, not the type for a dalliance. You know I am not one to interfere, but I have a feeling you should let her be."

"You have a feeling?" Nick's lip curled. "The next thing I know, you will be reading tea leaves."

"If I could read tea leaves, I would be a very wealthy man. Unfortunately I have only my instinct, and it tells me Lady Carrington is not the woman for you."

"What does it tell you about the lovely Delphi?"

Henri gave a reluctant smile. "Lady Langtry is different."

"How fortunate for your conscience." Nick stood. "Pray continue your association with the aunt. It could prove very beneficial to us both."

After the barest hesitation, Henri clutched at his heart. "Oh, the pain! To have to endure another half hour in the presence of such a beautiful lady. It cannot be borne."

"Go to hell, Henri."

"*Voyons*, but you are irritable this morning."

"I have been attempting to get the servants more focused on their duties. Like the Hall, they have not had proper supervision in some time, and they are incapable of doing a decent day's work."

"Ah, that is because of Napoleon. You might think him safely ensconced on Elba, but he is alive and well in the sitting room at Hibberton Hall." At Nick's questioning gaze, Henri chuckled. "There is a damp spot on the wallpaper. Your estimable housekeeper, the devout Mrs. Kibble, decided it looked exactly like the silhouette of Napoleon from the *Morning Post*."

"Did she, indeed."

"*Oui*. Half of the staff believes her, while the other half are steadfast that the stain looks more like Wellington. It has caused such dissension that the footman and the groom came to blows over the matter last night."

Nick shook his head. Of all the houses in England, he had to win one that possessed a staff worthy of a Shakespearean farce. "I gave Wiggs a powerful incentive to refocus everyone's efforts on the east wing. Perhaps some honest work will distract them from their search for Napoleon's likeness."

"Perhaps. Me, I'd start anew."

"I don't have the time to retrain an entire staff." Nick looked down at one of Pratt's endless lists. "I fear that Lord Parkington cheated me in giving me this house. I should have shot him in the privates."

Henri waved an airy hand. "But with a little paint, a little hammering . . . the Hall will be as good as new, no? A man should leave his mark on this world. Hibberton Hall will be yours."

"So I hope," Nick said. Though the cost would be high, most of the main work had already begun. Soon he would have a home as befitted his name, a home his mother would have been proud of.

Henri watched as the shadows slowly passed from Nick's face, the stiff façade shifting and then disappearing altogether. Most people thought the Earl of Bridgeton a hard, unsympathetic man. And most of the time, he was exactly that. Life had not allowed the earl the luxury of having a heart.

But every once in a while, Henri caught a glimpse of something in Nick's face—something very human. Something worth befriending. "Tell me something, *mon ami*. Now that you have returned to England and you have this beautiful house, what are your plans?"

The earl's cold blue gaze lifted from the sheet of paper and fastened on Henri. "I will ensure repairs to the Hall are well under way, and then . . ."

"And then?" Henri asked, although he already knew the answer.

"Then I will conquer a black-haired innocent with a propensity for teasing." Nick turned to the window and stared with unseeing eyes at the front lawn with such intensity in his expression that Henri shivered.

Mon Dieu, things were not going at all as he had planned—he'd meant for the earl to find a pleasant companion, one who would beguile and tease him from his moods. But it was obvious Bridgeton had something else in mind—a taste of the forbidden.

For one mad moment, Henri wondered if he should uncharacteristically drop a word in Delphi's ear. But a moment's reflection made him abandon such a foolish course of action. The young woman had been married, after all. And any attempt to sway Nick would only antagonize him further.

His only hope was that his information was wrong and the lady was not so innocent. For her sake, Henri hoped she was very well experienced indeed.

Sara stared absently at a small fire screen improbably adorned with hummingbirds and riotously colored parrots. The screen shielded the costly rug in the green salon from popping embers and generally got in the way whenever Sara was about. "Men are fools. Every last one of them."

Anna looked up from where she was regarding a creation in *Costume Parisien*. "That's the third time you've said that in as many minutes. Am I supposed to agree with you or argue?"

"Neither. It is an irrefutable fact of life." Sara

sighed and used the tip of her slipper to outline one of the hummingbirds. The last few weeks had been trying—more than trying, in fact. When she'd first embarked on her quest to find an acceptable husband, it had never occurred to her that there would be so few in Bath. Worse, as she and Anna culled the thin list of prospects, she'd begun to worry what would happen when she *did* find a suitable candidate. Would she be able to bring him to point before her brothers decided to visit?

Surely it wouldn't be too difficult. After all, she wasn't hideous, nor was she of unacceptable birth. It all came down to one thing: her lack of fortune.

"I've flirted and smiled and batted my eyes until I've feared for the life of my lashes, to no avail. I'm at my wits' end."

Anna obligingly set the magazine aside. "Perhaps part of the problem is your devoted brothers. I daresay just the thought of facing one or more of them could scare off even the most honorable man."

Sara ran the tip of her finger along the embroidered lines of the fire screen. Even miles away, her brothers still plagued her. "It's so discouraging. I haven't met a single man who would do."

The image of the Earl of Bridgeton rose clear and strong. Of course, he was far from being an ideal husband; she'd seen that in the hotly possessive way he'd looked at her. Just the memory of that one glance made her shiver still. Smoldering and dangerous, Bridgeton was the kind of man who either possessed a woman, body and soul, or didn't bother with her at all.

Somehow, she hadn't been able to bring herself to admit to Anna exactly what had happened between her and the earl. But the image of his face had stayed in Sara's dreams and a shivery sigh flashed up her spine. For an instant, she'd had the distinct impression of his lips touching hers, his hands on her bared skin . . . A trace of raw desire smoothed the shiver into a whisper of heated anticipation.

Heaven help the woman he decided to make his—he would demand her attention. All of it. Worse, Sara feared she'd *want* him to be demanding. Had she kissed the earl, she never would have wanted it to end. She'd have melted like a chip of ice in a hot cup, turning into a useless puddle before his astounded eyes.

Anna suddenly sucked in her breath. "Sara! What about Viscount Hewlette? He just arrived in town last week and is not so bad looking. He's here visiting an elderly aunt and is very agreeable. Even my grandfather has mentioned that he seems to be looking over all the available women, and Grandpapa is not the most observant of men."

Sara bit her lip. The viscount was a definite possibility. He was attractive enough, and polite. The only negative thing she could think of was that he had a propensity to talk about himself at every turn. But on the positive side, he already had a goodly set of children from his first marriage. It was rumored that his wife died giving birth to their fifth child and that his mother had taken over their care at that time. A man who already had family would not be wanting more. She brightened. "Anna, you might have something there. Hewlette might be the perfect choice."

"I hope so; I'm at a loss to think of anyone else. What is it about this place that attracts bores and elderly lechers? I'm inclined to agree with Grandpapa, who says Bath is stodgy and monotonous."

Sara regarded her friend curiously. "Then why do you live here?"

"Because he insists London is full of scalawags and cretins, Brighton is inhabited by nothing but scoundrels and nincompoops, and York is crawling with vermin and weak-willed naysayers. Grandpapa would rather be crushed by respectability than sullied by despicability."

"How difficult of him."

Anna chuckled. "Yes, isn't it? But being difficult is the one thing he does well." She pursed her lips thoughtfully. "I really can think of no other candidates. If Hewlette will not do, then we are lost."

Sara frowned. "Surely not. There must be some other men about."

"If you wish to marry someone who will pander to your brothers I can think of at least a dozen men who would welcome a connection with the St. Johns. Other than that . . ." Anna shrugged. "If Hewlette does not come to fruition, we will have to make a second attempt at Bridgeton. He is the only other man who meets your qualifications."

Sara picked up one of Aunt Delphi's embroidered pillows and absently tossed it into the air. "That's not an option," she said, keeping her voice carefully neutral.

"You may not have a choice." Anna put her elbow on her knee and rested her chin in her hand. "At least Bridgeton is handsome, and he doesn't smell of garlic like Mr. Dotley."

No, he smelled of maleness and danger and shivery desire. And Sara would never again allow herself to be in the position of wanting someone more than he wanted her. "Doesn't Viscount Hewlette frequently ride in the park?"

"Every morning at nine."

Well. A man who was both reliable *and* the father to a large brood of children should be delighted to have a wife who was more interested in the gaieties of life.

The door to the sitting room opened, and Aunt Delphi appeared, waving a folded missive as she floated into the room. "There you are, Sara! You have a letter and—" She stopped when she saw Anna. "Miss Thraxton, how delightful to see you. Sara has received a letter from her brother."

Sara took the letter and stared at the seal. "It's from Anthony." She opened the letter quickly and scanned the contents.

"What does it say?" Aunt Delphi asked, her head cocked to one side as she tried to read the missive from where she stood. "Is everyone well? Does he tell you the latest gossip from London? Was the Cowpers' dinner party a shocking squeeze? I just know Maria Lockton wore that shocking pink stole to the opera. I asked him to relate all the details of the Oldenhams' rout, too, but he hasn't sent me a single missive."

Sara was trying to decipher his quick scrawl. Anthony had never been much of a correspondent, once sending her a letter mentioning a "trifling injury" that turned out to be a serious fall from a horse that had left him with a broken leg. "He says Marcus has been detained by business." She raised her gaze to her aunt's. "I don't understand. Was Marcus coming here?"

Aunt Delphi blinked rapidly and then glanced down at her shoes. "Ah. Yes. I do believe he was."

"Why?" Sara asked bluntly.

"To visit you, of course. He is your brother, you know."

"He was coming to bully me, wasn't he?"

Aunt Delphi looked uncomfortable. "Well, he did mention that he wanted to see how you were getting on in your new situation."

"Naturally," Sara said dryly. "I wouldn't be a bit surprised if he intended on parading me before every available vicar or lily-livered curate as a potential bride."

"Oh, dear." Aunt Delphi edged toward the door. "If we aren't having any visitors quite yet, then I had better tell Cook to go ahead and serve that leg of lamb I've been saving." Delphi fluttered from the room trailing silk and the scent of lavender, the picture of domestic bliss.

Anna looked at the closed door with a mutinous expression. "Is she always like that?"

"Like what?" Sara asked absently, staring at the letter in her hands.

"Floating about as if she was a blasted fairy."

"Yes, but only when she's not showing an annoying tendency to worry over you and treat you as if you were a child of twelve."

Anna shuddered. "I'm glad I live with my grandfather. He may curse like a coal scuttler, but he doesn't flit about in that disconcerting way. I don't know how you stand it."

"She has a good heart. I just repeat that to myself every five minutes." Sara looked at the letter in her hand. Damn! She should have foreseen this. She jumped to her feet and began pacing rapidly.

Anna watched her for a moment, then said, "What else does the letter say?"

Sara stopped long enough to hand her friend the missive. "It says that if Marcus is unable to get away, another of my brothers will be joining me, but they have not yet decided who."

Anna whistled silently. "Determined to keep an eye on you, aren't they?"

"They are far too involved in my business." Sara crossed her arms over her chest and resumed pacing. "I don't want any of my brothers hovering over my shoulder, making my life a misery. We have a week to find a husband, Anna. Maybe less."

"Then we will have to use every day to our advantage." Anna handed the letter back to her friend. "Tomorrow morning we will ride in the park at precisely nine and meet Viscount Hewlette and see what is to be done."

Sara dropped back onto the settee, her heart heavy. She didn't have time for delicacy. No, she would be very explicit—she'd put all of her cards on the table and hope that the viscount understood the need for urgency. Once she was wed, she was certain Marcus would make a handsome settlement. It would irk him, but his pride would allow no less.

All she needed was to win the viscount's acceptance to a whirlwind courtship. If that didn't work, more drastic measures would be needed. Shivering slightly, Sara didn't even want to think what those might be. Yet even as she had the thought, she had an image of Bridgeton's face. Resolutely, she banished it. Viscount Hewlette had to be her answer. She wouldn't accept any other.

Chapter 4

If there was one thing Nicholas Montrose knew, it was the game of seduction. It would not do to appear too eager to reengage the delicious Lady Carrington in flirtation so soon after the Jeffries ball. He decided to wait at least another week before arranging a "chance" meeting with his intended quarry.

So for several days after his conversation with the comte, Nick stayed occupied with the repairs of Hibberton Hall, taking a personal interest in the hiring of the various craftsmen. To those who did not know him, he appeared completely absorbed by the tasks at hand. Yet every once in a while, he would look up and imagine himself fixed in the finished manor house, his reputation reestablished, his staff well trained, a vague shadowy figure by his side. As the days progressed, the figure took on a more substantive form. One with a cloud of raven black hair and eyes of the palest blue.

He wanted Sara Lawrence. He wanted her in his house and in his bed. The comte was incorrect in thinking Nick needed a deeper, more permanent relationship. He wanted only passion. A tantalizing companion who could make him forget the shadow that hung over him, and nothing more.

Sara was perfect—well-bred, fascinating, and a widow, which meant she had a certain amount of knowledge, however limited it might be. In his experience, Englishwomen were less likely to have been educated in the erotic art of dalliance as the women were in Paris. With the exception of a few dashing souls like Lucilla Kettering, who spent more time abroad than at home, most Englishwomen were unaware of the more erotic physical pleasures.

The thought pleased Nick no small amount. He was more than willing to teach the lovely Lady Carrington the secrets of the boudoir. After all, he'd spent a considerable amount of time perfecting those very pleasures, and it would be wildly exciting to explore them with someone less versed than he.

To learn about his quarry, he sent one of the stableboys to watch the house she occupied. The stableboy faithfully reported Lady Carrington's activities each morning. Nick was pleased to hear that her aunt rarely left her alone and that few of her visitors were men who offered him any competition. Few, but not all.

He scowled at the thought of someone else touching her white skin, kissing her soft lips. The image of Sara Lawrence locked in another man's embrace made him grind his teeth.

It was madness, for Nick had never been a possessive man. He'd taken pleasure as he'd found it, and given it freely. In his experience women were far too ready to commit to him without being asked. Far too anxious to own him.

As the days progressed, Nick found himself thinking of Sara more and more, imagining her velvet-soft voice murmuring his name, her black hair spread across his pillow, her lavender scent mingling with the cool, crisp sheets of his bed. Just as he always did, once he set his sights on an object, he focused on it to the exclusion of all others, and his determination grew each day.

Even his renovations at Hibberton Hall were subtly affected by his preoccupation. He actually ordered a striking red wallpaper for the library because he'd had a wayward thought that it would contrast well with the rich black of her hair.

So, despite his decision to wait, only four days passed before Nick found himself riding into Bath. Henri had reported that Lady Carrington rode in the east park each morning with a small group of her friends and admirers. Nick rode the paths until he finally saw her, her diminutive form atop a feisty bay gelding.

Nick pulled up his horse and watched. If the fascinating Sara had looked appealing wearing a dull gown of watered silk, she was devastating in a form-fitting sapphire blue riding habit, its severe lines accenting her curves. A high collar framed her face; her cheeks were warm with color, her blue eyes sparkling. A long white feather decorated her tall hat and brushed her shoulder temptingly.

She was magnificent.

Laughing, she turned to reply to something her companion said, the movement highlighting her delightful profile for a moment against the shrubbery. Nick's body responded with a rapidity that caused him to curse the tight cut of his breeches.

He smiled grimly at the reaction. For the first time since he could remember, all things were turning in his favor. The repairs of the Hall were moving quickly; Pratt had so wisely invested his funds that he would easily be able to afford the highest quality of life; and best of all, his headaches had diminished greatly. The fresh country air left him sharper, more alive than he'd ever felt.

And soon he would have a mistress. Nick turned his horse toward Lady Carrington's party. To her left rode the tall, auburn-haired woman she'd been with at the Jeffries ball. Miss Thraxton, if he remembered correctly, and she seemed to be an unusual female in her own right. On Sara's right rode three gentlemen; one was a groom and one was a footman. Her aunt was obviously taking no chances that her willful charge would slip away. His gaze flickered to the third man, and Nick's smile faded.

Tall, dark, and impeccably dressed, Viscount Hewlette appeared the perfect escort for any lady of fashion. His face and manner were always charming, his smile respectful, his manner ingratiating.

Still, Nick thought he could discern just the tiniest hint of boredom in Lady Carrington's countenance. Without further preamble, Nick pulled his horse into their path and waited.

Sara saw the earl an instant before anyone else. After listening to Viscount Hewlette expound for the last half hour on the magnificence of a new hunter he'd bought, the earl appeared like a burst of sunlight in a world of murky, mundane trivialities. Viscount Hewlette was proving to be an enthusiastic suitor, a fact Sara was beginning to regret. Since she and Anna had arranged a "chance" meeting with the viscount three days ago, he had hardly left her side. Sara was more than weary of his constant expostulating on his triumphs in the hunting field and elsewhere.

She stole a glance at the earl from beneath her lashes, and her heart stumbled a little as she pulled her horse to a halt. Taller than the viscount, broad-shouldered and impressively fit, he emanated power and wealth. And he rode a magnificent black gelding that made her poor mount look like a slug.

Some inner part of her leapt awake at the sight of his smile as he approached, and she found herself smiling in return. It had immediate effect—the earl perused her from head to foot, his gaze lingering on her mouth. A heavy warmth trickled a path across her breasts and settled in her stomach.

"Lord Bridgeton. How pleasant to see you again," she said demurely.

He lifted his hat and bowed, a glint in his eyes. "Lady Carrington. It has been several days since the Jeffries ball, has it not?"

"Almost a week, in fact," she said, then bit her tongue at her impetuousness. His knowing glance told her that he remembered the ball all too well. Still, the fact that he had remembered her name was vastly encouraging. Sara sent an appraising glance at him, noting how the sunlight glinted off his hair and deepened it to the tawny gold of a lion's mane, and limned the hard line of his jaw.

Though she'd thought her memory had exaggerated his perfections, she now found it had been lamentably remiss. Somehow she'd forgotten the exact curve of his sensuous mouth, and the way his thick lashes cast shadows over his eyes, making the blue appear almost black.

"Sara?" Anna said from her side.

Belatedly, Sara remembered her companions. "Lord Bridgeton, may I introduce you to Miss Thraxton? And this," she gestured vaguely to her side, "is Viscount Hewlette." For some reason, Sara was suddenly embarrassed to be seen with the viscount and his stuffy theories on farming.

Bridgeton ignored Hewlette. Instead, his gaze flickered toward Anna, and he bowed. "Miss Thraxton. I am delighted to make your acquaintance."

Sara noted that even the pragmatic Anna was affected by the earl's handsomeness. Her face was bright pink as she returned the bow with a jerky nod. "My lord, how do you do? Perhaps you would like to join us for a ride about the park?"

Sara cast a glance at Aunt Delphi's elderly groom. Hopkins gazed at Nick with a frowning stare, as if trying to place him. Sara bit her lip and wished there were some way she could get rid of the groom and his minion.

Hewlette nudged his horse forward. "Bridgeton, I had heard you were back in England."

"Did you?" the earl asked, looking less than interested. "How nice." The subtlest hint of a threat threaded through the words and Sara shivered. There was something almost hypnotic about his voice, something dangerous and dark, yet seductive.

"It appears the gentlemen know each other," Anna said brightly.

Hewlette managed a tight, superior smile. "Actually, no. Lord Bridgeton and I do not travel in the same circles."

Sara ground her teeth. The imbecile. Of course they didn't travel in the same circles. She could hardly imagine a man like Bridgeton enjoying a discussion on the values of fertilizer application.

Bridgeton merely appeared amused. Indeed, he flicked a faintly contemptuous glance at Hewlette before saying, "Then I daresay you aren't familiar with Lord Wilkins. When I was in Rome, I was the guest of the consulate."

Hewlette reddened. "Naturally I know Lord Wilkins. I didn't stay with him, of course—"

"Of course," murmured Bridgeton. He smiled at Sara. "Lady Carrington, may I say how lovely you appear this morning."

Sara managed to say with tolerable composure, "Thank you, my lord. May I compliment you on your horse? He is lovely." She patted her own mount's neck. "Unlike poor Petunia. She cannot walk for ten minutes without needing a good nap."

Bridgeton leaned over and rubbed a gloved hand along her horse's side. Sara watched as his hand moved breathtakingly near her knee before he straightened.

"She's not worthy of you." He met Sara's gaze so directly that she blushed. "And it appears she is forming a splint. If you find yourself without a mount, I would be pleased to lend you one from my stable—"

"That won't be necessary." Hewlette almost glared. "I have several mounts in my stables that would be more than adequate for a gentlewoman of Lady Carrington's standing."

"I'm sure you do," Bridgeton said. "But I wasn't offering her an 'adequate' mount. Lady Carrington can handle a much livelier horse—one that won't bore her to death."

Sara knew he wasn't speaking about horses. She also knew that it was pure folly to assume that his interest in her was anything other than prurient in nature. Still, some part of her responded to the thought of riding a horse like his, of flying through the park, leaping over the hedgerows and letting chance take her where it would.

Bridgeton's smile deepened and warmed. "Yes," he murmured, as if hearing her thoughts, "a handsome black gelding with a lilting gait. One to match the color of your hair."

The picture made her smile and a spark shimmered between them. It was as if he knew her and her impulses, her desire to taste freedom and to live life minute by minute.

Anna cleared her throat loudly. "Dear me! Look

at the time. Sara, aren't we supposed to meet your aunt at ten?"

Lord Hewlette inched his mount forward until his horse was between Sara's and the earl's. "Lady Carrington, I would be glad to escort you home. I would like to have a word with your aunt." He spoke in a loud, proprietary manner, sending a warning glance at the earl.

Bridgeton still ignored the man. He touched the brim of his hat to Sara and Anna. "Lady Carrington, Miss Thraxton, perchance you will be at the Kirkwood rout tomorrow evening?"

Sara nodded. "I believe so."

"Excellent," said the earl, his voice deepening to a deadly purr. "I look forward to seeing you there." He cast a glance at the viscount. "By the way, Hewlette, Lord Edgerwood mentioned you might be of a mind to sell a certain set of bays."

Hewlette's eyes brightened. "Indeed I am. Are you looking for a pair?"

"I ordered a phaeton. In fact, I'm off to look at Oglethorpe's knockoffs in an hour."

The viscount stiffened, his broad face darkening with concern. "I fear you may be disappointed; Oglethorpe's grays aren't nearly so well matched. Don't make up your mind until you've seen my pair. Perhaps tomorrow—"

"I must purchase a matched pair this morning," the earl said softly.

Hewlette's mouth dropped open. "This morning?"

"The phaeton will be delivered to Hibberton Hall by noon. I wish to have the horses by then."

Bridgeton glanced past Hewlette to Sara. "But you have plans this morning, so I will just call on Oglethorpe and hope—"

"No, no! I can visit Lady Langtry another time." He turned to Sara and offered an apologetic grimace. "You will make my apologies to your aunt, won't you?"

Sara managed a stiff smile. "Of course."

Hewlette took Sara's gloved hand and pressed his lips to her fingers, sending her a look fraught with meaning. "In the meantime, I hope to see you at the rout. May I have the honor of the first dance?"

Over Hewlette's shoulder, the earl watched, his gaze thick with mockery. Sara suddenly had the feeling that he was laughing at her. She jerked her chin in the air. "Only one dance, Lord Hewlette? I was hoping for two."

The viscount's gaze flared with warmth, and he tightened his hold on her hand. "The *first* two, my lady." With an air of reluctance, he turned his horse to the earl. "Well, sir? Shall we go?"

Bridgeton didn't grace Sara with another glance. Instead, he pulled his horse beside Hewlette's and, together, they rode down the path.

"Well!" Anna said. "I have now seen a master at work."

"Who? Hewlette? I would hardly call him a master."

"Not Hewlette. Bridgeton, of course. He came, sized up the competition, tossed out one tiny lure, and cleared the field without firing a shot. He is a very dangerous man."

Sara thought so, too. Her heart beat far too quickly whenever he was about. "I'm sure he is just being polite."

"Hmm. I think he's irked you rejected him at the Jeffries ball, and he's decided to have you."

"I didn't reject him, he rejected me. I asked him to go out on the terrace, and he flatly refused. And then he looked at me as if—" Sara swallowed. *As if he wanted to bed me, right there on the floor of the Jeffries ballroom.* And Sara hadn't been shocked; she'd been excited beyond belief.

"As if?" Anna asked, looking far too interested.

"As if nothing," Sara muttered. She turned her horse toward the path. "Come on. Aunt Delphi will be waiting."

Anna wisely held her tongue and turned her mount beside Sara's. Out of the corner of her eye, Sara watched the earl's broad back as he cantered across the park, turning the heads of more than one woman as he went. Hewlette struggled to keep up with him; it was almost laughable the way the stout viscount bumped along on his mount behind the earl's lithe figure.

Sara sniffed. It was true that Hewlette appeared at a distinct disadvantage beside Bridgeton, but what man would not? In a way, Bridgeton was exactly like Julius—he depended far too much on his charm and wit. Well, she would not be fooled by such shallow intrigue. Pasting a smile on her face, she entertained Anna with every naughty bit of gossip she could think of, all the while praying that this odd attraction for the earl would disappear as quickly as it had occurred.

Chapter 5

The heavy clock in the hallway outside the Kirkwoods' grand salon chimed, the sound mingling with the swirl of music and the noisy discord of a hundred voices.

"Midnight," Sara muttered. And still the Earl of Bridgeton had yet to walk through the door. Not that she'd been looking for him; *her* attention was solely for Viscount Hewlette, who was also mysteriously missing.

"I cannot believe Hewlette has not yet appeared," Anna said, echoing Sara's thoughts. "He is usually quite prompt."

"He said he was coming," Sara said absently. "Of course, I—damn!" Her gaze fixed on the receiving line, her heart sinking.

Anna tried to peer around the feathered head-dress of a stout matron in green satin. "What is it? Has he come?"

"No. It's my brother."

The stout matron moved, exposing Anthony at the head of the receiving line, his massive frame dressed in a black coat, his cravat impeccably arranged about his neck, his breeches stretched over his strong thighs.

"Sweet saints," Anna said in a faded voice, "*that's* your brother? Which one is he—Adonis?"

"Anthony is my half brother," Sara answered shortly, stepping behind a clock. She should have known he would come, since Marcus could not. She grabbed Anna's arm and yanked that bemused maiden to her side. "We don't have any more time. Now that Anthony is here, I won't have the free-dom to sneeze, much less convince someone to marry me."

"And the viscount isn't the kind of man you can goad into action."

"If he's not ready to make a proposal, then I shall just have to propose to him," Sara said resolutely. She had no choice now. A slight stir at the door made her peer around the edge of the clock. "There's Viscount Hewlette! I can't speak with him in the ballroom, not with Anthony lurking about. Maybe I can get him to take a turn with me on the terrace."

"In this cold?"

"I wouldn't care if it was snowing; I must speak with him tonight!"

Anna sighed. "I don't like this at all."

"We have no choice. Look, Anthony is going into the ballroom now. I'll ask Hewlette to walk outside with me. So long as you are with me, no one should pay much attention."

"Very well," Anna said, her voice heavy with doubt. She turned her clear, gray eyes on Sara. "What will you do if he refuses to marry you?"

Sara swallowed. She'd already thought of that, for no matter how marked Hewlette's attentions were, he was reticent on the topic of marriage. Her stomach tensed, and she hoped with all her heart that the viscount listened to her proposal. "We'll think about that later."

Hopefully it would not be an issue. Hewlette stood talking to their host, no doubt discussing his rousing triumphs on the hunting field last season. Strangely, she found her gaze drifting past him to the foyer. Bridgeton had specifically asked her if she would be present, and she thought he'd have arrived by—Heavens, what was wrong with her?

Here she was, on the verge of attempting to secure the viscount's suit, and all she could do was think of the earl, damn his black soul. She didn't want to admit how much time she'd spent imagining all the witty things she should have said when he'd accosted them in the park.

Well, it didn't matter. She didn't have time for games now. Sara waited until Anthony had stopped well inside the ballroom to talk to an acquaintance before she whisked herself across the doorway toward Viscount Hewlette.

He drew himself up as soon as he saw her, his expression brightening. "Lady Carrington! I apologize for coming so late, but I was detained and—"

"Oh, it is of no consequence." She laid her hand on his arm and leaned toward him, looking at him through her lashes. "But now that you are here, I wonder if I might secure your assistance."

"You have but to ask," he said with ponderous gallantry.

Sara suppressed a grimace with difficulty. "I am afraid that I have become separated from my friend, Miss Thraxton. I wondered if you would help me look for her."

"Have you tried the refreshment room?"

"Oh, I'm certain she's not there. I rather think she went out on the terrace."

An arrested expression touched his face. "The terrace?"

Sara laid her hand on his. "I believe I saw her walk out just a few moments ago."

"My dear Sara," Hewlette said, his voice deepening, his gaze narrowing on her face. "I had no idea that you were . . . By all means, let us take a turn on the terrace."

It was like holding bacon in front of a hound. She took a step toward the wide doors that led outside, but halted when she realized that Anna really *had* disappeared from sight. Perhaps she had already gone outside.

Hewlette's hand on the small of her back propelled her gently toward the terrace. He pushed the curtains from the doorway. "After you, my dear."

Just as she crossed the threshold, she cast one last glance behind her. But it wasn't toward her brother or in search of Anna, but rather toward the entryway. It was several minutes after midnight and still the Earl of Bridgeton had not come. Banishing a strange sense of disappointment, Sara placed her hand on the viscount's arm and stepped onto the terrace.

At exactly ten minutes past twelve, Nick walked into the Kirkwood ballroom.

The comte followed a desultory pace or two behind, resplendent in a mauve waistcoat adorned with silver trim. He handed his multicaped cloak to a footman and took a deep, exhilarating breath. "Do you smell that, *mon ami*? It is the scent of the chase, the heady fragrance of *l'amour*."

Nick made no comment. Since last night, he'd been plagued with one of his headaches. Though it wasn't nearly as bad as previous ones, it was severe enough that he'd considered not attending this evening. After all, his absence would only make the lovely Lady Carrington wonder about him even more. The only problem was, he'd thought of little else but her since his ride in the park.

The comte sighed his satisfaction and rocked back on his heels. "All of Bath has come out tonight."

"Indeed," Nick agreed, searching the room for signs of his quarry. "A plaguey nuisance it is, too."

"That is your headache speaking." The comte's bright gaze narrowed. "Ah, there is my delicate Delphi. No, do not look her way! Tonight, I pretend I do not see her, and she must watch me flirt with every woman present."

"Uncertainty keeps them panting."

"*Exactemente!*" The comte waggled his brows, then turned to a lady in blue silk and asked her to dance, his French accent more pronounced than ever.

Nick barely noticed Henri's disappearance; he was too busy searching for Sara. It took him only a few moments to realize that she was nowhere in sight. Clenching his teeth against the sparkle of pain behind his eyes, he set out to find her. Almost immediately he realized the grim truth—she wasn't here. Disappointment gnawed at his temper and as he left the ballroom he wanted to ram his fist into someone's face.

He didn't even bother to tell Henri that he was leaving, but that was nothing new. He'd send a coach later, though he doubted the comte would leave anytime soon. Henri enjoyed functions like these, while Nick detested them.

He stood in the front hall, away from the racket of the ballroom, and pressed a hand to his right eye where the throbbing had increased to a near-frantic tempo. The evening had been a complete waste, and he had the sneaking suspicion that he'd been made a fool of. Damn the heat, damn the crowded room, and damn Lady Carrington.

He spun on his heel and had just reached the front door when a light hand touched his sleeve. He turned immediately, disappointment weighing his brow when he met Lady Knowles's gaze.

"Nick," Lucilla purred, slipping her fingers inside his sleeve, her mouth soft with invitation. "I was afraid you were not coming."

"As you can see, your fears were unfounded." He looked impatiently toward the door. "But I fear I cannot stay."

"No?" She brushed her breasts along his sleeve, tightening her hold on his arm. "Perhaps I should leave with you. We could . . . relive old times."

Nick looked down at Lucilla. He'd forgotten how persistent she was, how possessive. He placed his hand over hers and freed his arm. "I think you have made a mistake, Lucilla."

The pleasant expression on her face froze. "What do you mean?"

"Only that I am not interested in pursuing this relationship."

She looked at him for a long, cold moment, her face hardening. "You have settled on someone else."

"No. I have merely realized we would not suit. Meanwhile—"

"Nick!" Henri said, entering the corridor and crossing to his side. "Have you seen Lady Carrington? Her aunt is looking for her everywhere."

Lucilla flicked a frigid gaze at Nick. "Sara Lawrence? Surely not."

He smoothed his cuff where Lucilla's clinging grasp had creased the fabric. "Pardon me, Lucilla. I must assist Henri in his search."

Lucilla's hands had curled into claws, and a feral gleam entered her gaze, a certain smudge of self-satisfaction. "My dearest Nick, I don't believe I have ever seen you like this before."

He merely raised his brows, his temper sharpening. "And what way is that?"

Lucilla's smile widened, as unpleasant as it was vicious. "I don't believe I've ever seen you as a cuckolded lover."

The comte muttered a curse as a red haze settled over Nick's eyes. He grabbed Lucilla's arm and yanked her against him. "Explain yourself."

Lucilla's nostrils flared, triumph glittering in her eyes. "Sara Lawrence is on the terrace with Viscount Hewlette. I saw them leave a few minutes ago."

Nick spun on his heel and swiftly made his way through the ballroom. He ignored the smiles sent his way, the outstretched hands and curious gazes.

Whether she knew it or not, Sara Lawrence was his, and she had no right to be alone in the garden with another man.

Chapter 6

Sara allowed the viscount to lead her a short distance down one of the dimly lit paths before coming to a halt. Where was Anna? Sara cleared her throat nervously. "Viscount Hewlette, I have a question I must ask you."

He placed his hand over hers. "Ask anything, dearest Sara."

She freed her hand, noting the dampness of his palm. "I know this is rather forward of me, but I . . . I . . ." *Oh, fudge. This is harder than I imagined.* She shivered in the cold.

Hewlette immediately pulled her against him. "Let me keep you warm."

Sara tried to step away, but he held her tight. She frowned up at him. "Release me at once."

He didn't move, just looked at her with a superior expression that made her want to slap him. "We are alone now, Sara. And we both know what you want."

"Yes—marriage."

He stepped away so quickly that he almost stumbled over the uneven walkway. "You are not serious."

"Yes, I am."

"That's a pity. As tempting an armful as you are, you have no fortune. I made inquiries; your jointure ends the day you wed."

"Then why have you been calling on me?"

He smiled in a placating manner. "Because, my little pigeon, I was hoping we could . . ." He trailed a broad finger down her arm.

Sara jerked away. "I am not a pigeon." She suddenly realized that she wouldn't marry this pompous bag of wind for all the freedom in the world. "I would like to return to the ballroom. Now."

His brow lowered. "Surely we can come to some sort of an agreement—"

"Please step aside. I have nothing more to say to you."

Hewlette's jaw hardened, his gaze narrowing. "You little tease," he hissed.

"I am *not* a tease."

"Then why have you been dangling yourself before me for the last week like an overripe plum waiting to be plucked?" he demanded.

Sara sighed her exasperation. "I was not dangling anywhere, and I am getting very cold. Please move aside."

For an instant she thought he would comply, but

his gaze focused on her. "I think we should stay in the garden a bit longer."

"My brother will be looking for me."

He leaned so close, his cologne threatened to gag her. "Your brothers are in London."

Sara cast a desperate glance at the shrubbery, hoping Anna was nearby for protection. The silence seemed to scream a warning, and her mind quavered on the brink of panic. *What if Anna isn't here?* Sara took a quick step backward.

Hewlette's hands shot out and he grasped her by the shoulders. "Oh no, you don't, my dearest Sara. I've been waiting for this since Julius died."

She stilled. "Julius?"

"We were friends, though I daresay you never knew it. He was a generous man, and allowed me use of his best hunter and his phaeton. He even let me sample his mistress—a tasty actress with a penchant for riding whips."

"I have no wish to discuss my husband with you," Sara snapped. Damn it, would Julius continue to sully her life even now?

Hewlette's large hand slid up her arm. "You always fascinated me, you know. So pristine and pure. You were the one thing he would not share."

"Lord Hewlette, that is more than enough. Release me *now*. I will not—"

His hot mouth covered hers. Sara couldn't breathe, and she fought wildly, but Hewlette's embrace pinioned her arms to her sides.

Hewlette's tongue pushed roughly against her

clenched lips. *Where is Anna?* There was only one thing to do. Sara twisted to one side and thrust her knee upward. She caught him in the side of the thigh, completely missing her target. Still, the solid contact made Hewlette yelp, and his grip slackened for a moment.

That was all Sara needed. She fisted her hand in the manner learned from countless tussles with five bigger, less-than-gentle brothers, and slammed it into his nose. Fate favored her, for the viscount was just reaching out to grab her, his motion propelling him directly into her fist and increasing the force of the contact. To her surprise, he fell like a stone and lay on the pathway, making little mewling sounds like a kitten.

"A pleasant night for a stroll, isn't it?" drawled a low voice, so deep and husky, it sent a shiver down Sara's back.

Oh God, not him. Not now. But it was. The Earl of Bridgeton stepped from the path and into the shadows of the hedgerow to stand over Hewlette's prone body. "Tsk, tsk, Hewlette. You really should stay away from the port."

"What are you doing here?" Sara demanded, her heart racing.

"Strolling. I do so love gardens." Nick sauntered forward, golden and imposing even in the lantern-light. His faintly amused gaze flickered from Sara's face to where Hewlette struggled to gain his feet. "Lord Hewlette. Strange as it may seem, you are just the man I was looking for."

Using a stone bench for support, Hewlette managed to stand upright. "Go to hell, Bridgeton."

"But I've information to impart. Your mother is searching for you. You had best go to her."

Swaying dangerously, Hewlette cautiously felt his nose before glaring at Bridgeton. "My mother is in London."

"All the better," the earl said in a silky voice.

The young lord reddened. "Damn you, Bridgeton! This is a private affair."

Nick regarded the viscount's face with a considering frown. "Whatever happened to your nose? It is turning the color of a plum."

"Nothing. I fell, that's all." Hewlette cast a sullen glare at the earl.

"Lady Carrington's aunt is looking for her. It is time she returned to the ballroom."

"I suppose her aunt sent *you* to rescue her?" the viscount said, his mouth twisted with rage. "I can't imagine such a thing."

The earl shrugged, his broad shoulders never making even a crease in the fine coat. "I'm in an odd mood this evening . . . almost quixotic. Like a knight in a fairy tale."

"Perhaps something you ate has disagreed with you," Sara said, feeling ill-used. "I'm sure it will pass."

The earl's gaze rested on her for a moment, an amused curve to his lips. "I'm sure it will. But until then, I am at its mercy."

Despite Sara's annoyance, she had to admit that the earl at least appeared heroic, his tall, lithe form making Hewlette appear short and stocky. And the viscount's florid waistcoat and exaggerated cravat were garish in the face of the earl's quiet elegance.

Oblivious to the fact that he was far outclassed, Hewlette sneered. "Tell the truth, Bridgeton. You have your eyes on her yourself."

The earl turned a considering look at Sara. "No, I have never been in the nursery line."

Sara gasped. "Nursery? I'll have you know I am twenty-one years of age and perfectly able to—" At the flare of amusement in Bridgeton's gaze, she swallowed the rest of her protest, seething.

Bridgeton chuckled. "I stand corrected. The lady is indeed old enough to have an *affaire de coeur*. That is very useful information, indeed."

What was it about this man that made her flare up like dry kindling? Whatever it was, it unnerved her and sent her stomach spiraling into a thousand knots.

Hewlette gave an ugly laugh. "I have to agree with you, Bridgeton; she's an exciting bundle." His gaze narrowed speculatively. "I don't suppose you'd be interested in settling this as gentlemen? A turn of the cards, perhaps?"

Sara balled her hand back into a fist. "My lord Hewlette," she said in her frostiest voice, "I am *not* a 'bundle,' and I am not about to allow you to wager me in a game of cards."

"Don't play the innocent with me," Hewlette snarled, gingerly touching his nose again. "You were the one who invited me to the garden, weren't you?"

"Only because I wished to ask you to—" She stopped, remembering Bridgeton's presence. "I only wished to ask you a simple question. Nothing more."

Nick raised his brows. What was the delectable Sara up to now? Well, it was time the troublesome Hewlette made his way home. "Viscount Hewlette, I hate to be rude, but Lady Carrington has other plans this evening."

Hewlette's mouth twisted into a bitter scowl. "I understand perfectly."

"I doubt it," Nick said, "but it doesn't matter. You will not, I think, be mentioning this evening's encounter to anyone."

The viscount drew himself upright, his nose already faintly purple. "If you were not so damned proficient at dueling, Bridgeton, I would call you out for your impertinence."

"But I am damned proficient at it," Nick said softly. "And you would do well to remember that fact as you take your leave of the lady."

There was nothing more to be done, and Hewlette knew it. Stiff with anger, he bowed to Sara. "Lady Carrington, I look forward to speaking with you at a more convenient time." He tossed a glare to Nick, turned on his heel, and marched stiffly across the terrace and into the ballroom.

Smiling faintly, Nick turned to the damsel he had just rescued.

She met his gaze with a look of blazing contempt. "You, sir, are not needed here."

"Wasn't I? I rather flatter myself that I was right where I needed to be. Hewlette is not a man of honor."

"And you are?"

He couldn't help himself. A slight smile curved his mouth. "No. Although you must admit that my presence was convenient."

"I did not stand in need of any assistance." She glanced toward the bushes beside them, where a sudden rustle announced the arrival of a visitor.

Nick followed her gaze and discovered a blue feather sticking up from behind a tangle of leaves. A swell of irritation gripped him. Instead of rescuing a demure innocent from Hewlette's evil clutches, it appeared he had instead rescued Hewlette from a marriage trap the size of France.

For some reason, the fact that Sara looked so angelic, so innocent, annoyed him further. He grabbed her by the waist and hauled her against him.

She lifted a shocked face to his, her soft lips parted, her eyes shimmering in the uncertain light. "Unhand me!"

"Tell your titian-haired shadow to come out now."

"But I—"

His grip tightened until she gasped for breath. Her slight form was melded to his length, her breasts pressed against his lapels, her feet scarcely touching the ground. "I—I cannot speak . . . if you hold me . . . so tightly."

He loosened his grip just enough for her to catch her breath. "Call her."

"No."

Scowling, Nick released her, then turned to the shrubbery.

Ignoring the damage to his coat and gloves, he

plunged his hands through the branches. A terrified squeak met his actions, and he smiled grimly when his fingers closed around a feminine arm. Without ceremony, he dragged her through the bushes and stood her before him.

"Let me go," Miss Thraxton protested, struggling mightily.

"And have you run into the ballroom, screeching at the top of your voice that your friend is being ravished in the garden?"

"Leave her be," Sara said from his side.

"Do you see the bench by the terrace door?" Nick asked the troublesome Miss Thraxton.

She nodded mutely, her eyes appearing ready to pop out of her face.

"Lady Carrington and I need a few moments of private conversation, but I have no wish to see her good name discredited. Therefore, instead of behaving like an idiot and helping your friend to ruin, you will play the part of chaperone."

Her mouth opened and closed, but she was bereft of speech.

Nick controlled his impatience. *This* was why he eschewed innocents and imbeciles. He took the redhead's elbow and led her down the path and up the terrace stairs to the stone bench, walking so swiftly she nearly had to run to keep up. He dropped her onto the bench's cold surface, her skirts billowing about her. "I am glad to see that we are in agreement. Now stay here. At no time are you to leave this bench, or I will see to it that you are very, very sorry."

Her gaze fixed on his face, she nodded in mute agreement. Nick suppressed an exasperated sigh as he turned to where Lady Carrington awaited him.

She stood in the pathway, arms crossed over her modest white gown to ward off the cold air, her round chin firmly in the air, the very picture of youthful indignation. "That was uncalled for."

"*That* was necessary to preserve your good name." Nick leaned against a tree and crossed his own arms, watching her grimly. "You are a fool if you thought to trap a man like Hewlette into marriage."

Sara thought she was more of a fool to be in the garden with a man who looked like a gilded devil. "If you are about to give me a lecture on the horrors of marriage, pray spare your breath. I know more about them than I wish to."

A flicker of amusement softened Nick's scowl. "All marriages are miserable, sweet. It is the nature of the beast." His gaze traveled over her, resting on her breasts and hips as if he could see through the material of her gown. "If you don't wish to marry, then what do you want?"

She wanted him. The thought came to her so suddenly that she caught her breath. She wanted to touch his face and smooth away the hint of aloofness that marred his handsomeness. She wanted to curl into his arms and feel the strength of him. But that was not to be. She wasn't interested in an affair; she wanted marriage.

But perhaps . . . She eyed Bridgeton carefully. He *was* a man of the world. She would simply explain her circumstances and ask for his assistance. "Despite my dislike of marriage, I must have a husband."

"And you chose Hewlette?"

There was a hint of sneer in his satin-smooth voice and her anger flared. "He seemed an excellent choice until this evening."

"And now?"

"Now I must find someone else. My brothers have decided it is time I wed, and since they control my fortune—" She shrugged. "I want my freedom, but the man my brothers would choose for me will be as staid and controlling as they are. Therefore, I want a husband who will not interfere with my pleasures any more than I intend on interfering with his."

"You want someone who will marry you, and then leave you be?"

"Yes." She paused, marshaling her arguments to persuade him. "Would you be interested in—"

"No."

He hadn't even hesitated. Sara refused to look away, locking her gaze with his. "You are rebuilding Hibberton Hall. Surely you—"

"I just want to live in peace."

"I would leave you in peace. I don't even wish to live under the same roof."

His mouth quirked into a smile. "Then what would be the point of marrying at all?"

"You would have access to my name. The St. Johns are accepted everywhere."

Nick pushed himself from the tree, the shadows flickering across his face. "Under normal circumstances, I might well be tempted."

Sara took an eager step forward, but he held up a hand. "Unfortunately, I have no wish to marry. Not now, not ever."

"But I *must* marry."

He regarded her for a silent moment. "Perhaps you can convince your brothers that you are willing to go along with their scheme."

"What would that accomplish?"

"They would leave you alone if they thought you had capitulated. It might give you more time."

"Time? For what?"

His wicked smile was her answer. Sara's disappointment was so keen it was like the cut of a knife. "I've misjudged you," she said bitterly. "I thought you were . . . oh, I suppose it doesn't matter."

"Doesn't it?" he asked, taking the remaining two steps that brought him to her. "I am not the kind of man you would ever wish to marry, Sara. But if you decide you are interested in a more casual arrangement . . ." He lifted her face with a warm hand, cupping her cheek in an intimate gesture.

Her breath hung in her throat as the moonlight gilded the sensual line of his mouth. She couldn't move away, caught in the slow heat of the moment. Caught in the feel of his bare hand on her skin. Caught in the swift pounding of her own heart. Without thought to anything, Sara lifted her face to his.

His lips came to softly cover hers, his breath mingling with hers in a slow, sweet dance. Sara's resistance melted before the heady onslaught, her body tingling with swirling emotion as he deepened the kiss, opening his mouth over hers, parting her lips with his tongue. She opened her mouth, eager to get closer, to absorb his warmth, to taste his passion.

Thoughts swirled to a halt as Sara lost herself in the kiss. Her body tightened, and for the first time in her life, she yearned for a man other than Julius.

Nick broke the kiss and lifted his mouth until it was a scant breath from hers. "We really are at opposing ends of the spectrum, aren't we?" he murmured, his thumb brushing across her cheek. "I wish for a mistress, not a wife. You wish to be a wife, not a mistress."

He wanted her. Desired her just as she desired him. Some secret part of Sara leapt at his words and she craved his touch even as she admitted that he was right. They were at cross-purposes. He was not the man she was searching for. With the greatest reluctance, she forced her stiff legs to move her away from him, away from the tantalizing scent of male temptation, away from the raw heat that simmered in his gaze.

His hands dropped to his side. "I want you, Sara. And you want me. I can tell."

Despite her determination otherwise, she swayed toward him. She knew from the way he moved, from the fascinating line of his mouth, from the lithe way he walked, that he would be an exhilarating lover—passionate and erotic beyond her dreams. But a few moments of physical pleasure would not gain her what she desired—a complaisant husband who would keep her troublesome brothers at bay. "Thank you for your offer, my lord, but I must decline."

To her surprise, he smiled—a masculine, knowing smile, as if he knew her better than she knew herself. "We shall see, my lady."

Anger stiffened her wavering resolve. Damn the man for thinking he knew her at all. "It was just a kiss, Bridgeton. Surely it wasn't your first." Sara had the felicity of seeing his smile fade as she turned on her heel and walked away.

There! She had put the arrogant earl in his place. But the taste of triumph eluded her. He had read her all too easily, and it irked her. No matter how tempting he might be, the Earl of Bridgeton was to be avoided at all costs. Her head held high, she marched back to the terrace, achingly aware that it was the last thing she wanted to do.

Chapter 7

S ara swept to the terrace with as much dignity as her shaking knees would allow. Bridgeton was a cold-hearted rakehell, about as caring as a coiled snake. She'd thrown herself on his mercy, explained her desperate circumstances, and instead of assisting her as he could so easily have done, he'd used the opportunity to suggest a mere affair.

She clenched her teeth. The trill of excitement that had warmed her at his forbidden proposition proved that Bridgeton had his own charm, a subtle, heady draw, and she had to be very wary in her dealings with him. She had watched her husband flitter through a succession of mistresses and had no intention of becoming one herself.

Sara's foot reached the terrace step, and Anna

jumped from her seat as if released by an invisible hand. She rushed forward, her gaze flickering over Sara's shoulder into the darkness of the garden. "He's gone."

Sara slumped in relief, and managed to make the last few steps to the bench before she sank gratefully on the hard, cool surface.

Anna joined her. "I vow, I've never been so shocked in all my life as when he grabbed me through the branches! What did he say to you? I tried so hard to hear, but the music from the ballroom was too loud."

If the truth were told, some of what had occurred this evening was Anna's fault. Sara turned to her friend. "Where were you?"

Anna blinked. "Here. On this bench. After the earl—"

"No," Sara said grimly. "Earlier. When I came outside with Viscount Hewlette."

"Your brother caught me just before I reached the terrace doors."

"What did Anthony say?"

"He was determined to find you. I told him you were in an antechamber pinning a torn flounce and that you would be back shortly, but he didn't believe me." Anna's eyes sparkled dangerously. "He suggested I was lying."

"You were."

"Yes, but he didn't know that. It's rude to accuse someone when you've no proof. I was tempted to slap him."

Sara, perceiving how tightly Anna's hands were

curled into fists, rather thought Anthony would have gotten more than a slap. "How did you get away?"

"Your aunt returned from the cardroom. When he turned to greet her, I slipped out the terrace doors. Tell me, Sara; are all of your brothers so overbearing?"

"Yes."

Anna muttered something under her breath. "I'm sorry I was late in arriving. I truly thought you would be safe with Hewlette. He seems so dull."

"It took him less than ten seconds to pounce on me. It was like trying to fight off a cat with forty paws."

"Hewlette has been nothing but a disappointment." Anna leaned forward. "But Bridgeton? How did he come to be involved?"

"He was wandering down the path and stumbled upon us just as I disengaged Lord Hewlette."

"I can't imagine a man like Bridgeton walking the gardens alone." Anna tilted her head to one side. "My grandfather heard that Lady Knowles knew the earl when she was on the Continent. Perhaps he was going to meet her."

That would be just like the man, to proposition her on his way to another assignation. Worse, Sara couldn't think of a woman she disliked more than Lady Knowles. Lucilla Kettering had been hunting married men with the voraciousness of a hungry lioness since the first day she'd set foot out of the schoolroom. She'd met and married old Lord Knowles in a whirlwind courtship that left His

Lordship in such a fevered state that he'd keeled over a scant month after the nuptials. Naturally he'd left his considerable fortune to his unblushing bride, who had done her best to run through it in record time.

Sara had many reasons not to like Lucilla Kettering, the least of them being the fact that Julius had once been her paramour. But then, there were few ladies of loose virtue whom Julius had missed.

Forcing a smile, she stood, shivering slightly in the cold. "We should return to the ballroom."

"I'm surprised your brother isn't already out here," Anna said as she joined her.

"So am I." Sara opened the door to the ballroom and stepped inside. A swelter of heat and noise immediately engulfed them.

Anna's attention riveted on the other side of the room. "I spoke too soon—here's Lord Adonis now. If you don't mind, I think I'll go see if my grandfather is ready to leave. I've no wish to face your brother a second time this evening."

Sara didn't feel like facing Anthony for even a first time. "Anna, thank you for your assistance. I'll call on you tomorrow."

"Fine, provided you don't bring *him*," Anna responded, jerking her head toward Anthony, who was a scant two steps away and heard every word. Flashing a smile at Sara, Anna slipped into the crowd.

Anthony stopped long enough to glower at the departing woman. "That woman is a menace."

"She's a good friend."

Obviously unimpressed, Anthony turned his glare to Sara. "Where in the hell have you been?"

"Fixing my gown. Would you like to see where I pinned it?"

His jaw tightened. "Don't press me, Sara. Aunt Delphi has a headache and wishes to go home."

Sara caught sight of her aunt just beyond Anthony. The older woman appeared flustered. Her thin mouth was clamped tightly closed, her hands nervously worrying the edge of her shawl, her gaze flittering about the room in a distracted manner. Sara walked past her brother and placed her hand over her aunt's. "Oh, dear! I'm so sorry you are indisposed. Shall we go?"

A look of gratitude crossed Delphi's face. "Yes, please."

They took their leave of their hosts and were soon safely ensconced in their carriage. If Sara had hoped for a reprieve, she was mistaken. Anthony barely waited for the footman to close the door before he sent her a piercing glance. "It was far too cold to take a turn on the terrace."

Sara thought briefly of denying her whereabouts, but decided against it. Anthony was no one's fool. "It was cold, but not unbearably so," she said. Especially not with the Earl of Bridgeton's mouth covering hers. What a pity she would not be experiencing any more embraces from the man. "Where is Marcus?"

"Attending to business. He invested in a shipping venture and the fleet just returned."

Marcus had a score of minions who scurried every time he sneezed, and it was highly unlikely that he would dash down to the docks to count his new funds personally. No, Sara knew her brothers well, and they were notorious for using a deck of cards to settle every argument. "Lost the draw, did you?" she asked without sympathy.

An answering glimmer lit Anthony's brown eyes. "Yes, but Marcus cheated. I caught him dealing from the bottom of the deck."

"If you caught him, then why isn't *he* here now?"

Anthony gave a reluctant grin. Sara was too intelligent by far. "Because I was cheating, too, and he knew it." However, they had both been attempting to lose. Sara was their only sister and as such, she held a special place in their hearts. Especially for Anthony. Of all his half siblings, he understood Sara better than the others.

She didn't appear at all appreciative of his sacrifice. She fixed a glum glare on him, and said, "I am not made of porcelain, Anthony. Nor do I need to be wrapped in wool and placed in a box for safekeeping. I don't like boxes; I never have."

Anthony regarded his sister through narrowed eyes. Something had occurred this evening, something important. Sara almost shimmered with it. Her skin was flushed, her eyes luminescent even in the dim light cast from the street. The only thing that reassured him was the way her mouth was set in such a thin line. Whatever had happened, she wasn't happy with the outcome.

She sighed now, and leaned her head against the squabs, regarding him through her lashes. "I don't want to argue, Anthony. I'm tired."

"I can tell," he said dryly.

A slight quiver touched her lips. "But I'm still glad to see you."

He lifted his brows in polite disbelief. "Are you?"

"Of course. Now you can go home first thing in the morning and report to Marcus that I am safely tucked away and bored to death. Buried alive, just as he planned."

"That's not what we wanted, Sara. All we ask is that you give yourself a chance to find happiness. And that does not include taking long, unescorted walks in the garden."

Aunt Delphi cleared her throat. "Sara had an escort. Miss Thraxton was with her, so they were perfectly in the bounds of propriety."

To be honest, Sara's redheaded friend worried Anthony more than anything else. Tall, statuesque, with flashing gray eyes framed by thick black lashes, Anna Thraxton was far too attractive to supervise anyone, not least his headstrong sister. And the fact that she'd lied to him about Sara's whereabouts, smiling so sweetly that he'd almost believed her, made him even more irritated. "That hoyden is not a suitable companion. She's barely more than a child herself."

Sara raised her brows. "She's twenty-four and a perfectly acceptable companion."

"Miss Thraxton is untruthful, obstinate, and *wrong*," he stated with certainty.

"Wrong? About what?"

Anthony shifted in his seat. "About everything," he said finally. Before Sara could respond to his weak rejoinder, he turned to Aunt Delphi. "Are you aware of the type of literature Miss Thraxton's grandfather ascribes to?"

"Oh. Uhm, yes," Aunt Delphi said in an uncertain voice, her fingers toying with the fringes of her shawl. "Something to do with taxation. And trade, I think."

"Sir Thraxton is within a hound's breath of being an anarchist. Were he more successful, he'd be swinging from Tyburn, a branded traitor."

"I don't know about anarchy," Aunt Delphi said, "but Thraxton is well known to Wellington, and that counts for a great deal. As for Anna, I've never seen her behave in any but the most circumspect manner."

Anthony opened his mouth to reply, but Sara interceded, sending him an annoyed glance. "Aunt Delphi, how was the ball? Did you win at cards?"

"No." Her fingers were tangled in her shawl, but she made no move to free them, her gaze drifting to the window. "I lost."

Sara frowned. "I've never seen you so upset over a card game. Did anything else happen?"

Delphi attempted to collect herself with an obvious effort. "I had a lovely time. Didn't you, dear?" She immediately began to chatter with an air of forced gaiety.

They finally arrived home, and Anthony stalked off to the library while Delphi and Sara retired to their bedchambers. Splendidly free from the presence of females, he dropped into a wide leather chair. His coat was gone, tossed over a chair by the door, his waistcoat loosened, his cravat hung open about his neck. He stretched his legs before him and reflected on the evening's events.

Something was definitely afoot. Sara had been far too secretive, and her prolonged absence from the ballroom was a particularly ominous sign. Sighing, he rested his head against the high back of the chair and stared at the ornate plaster ceiling.

From the day Sara had been born, she had been his special charge. Though his stepfather had always treated Anthony as if he were his own son, Anthony was always aware that he was different from his half brothers. The knowledge hadn't made him lonely or discontent; it had merely given him the confidence to pursue his own road, wherever it might lead.

Anthony had remained aloof until the day he was called into his mother's room some ten years later to meet his newest sibling—Saraphina Elisia St. John—the first girl born into the St. John family in three generations. Anthony, already embarrassingly aware of how much larger he was than any of his brothers, had felt like a giant when his father handed him the tiny baby.

Eyes wide, he'd stared down at the small, heart-shaped face and the smile that danced in her blue eyes. He'd been so afraid of hurting her that he'd held his breath the entire time she'd lain in his arms. But she hadn't been hurt. Instead, she'd reached up and stuck a small finger in his nose, squealing loudly.

From that day on, Anthony had been Sara's self-appointed champion. He loved her fiercely and protected her against the overexuberance of her other brothers. When Brand helped Sara up into a tree and promptly forgot her during an especially engrossing game of pirate ship, it was Anthony who heard her cries and rescued her. When Chase tested the safety of jumping from the loft into a stack of hay by throwing one of Sara's precious dolls over the railing and then giving her a push when she leaned over to see where it had landed, Anthony was the one who swooped her out of midair, saving her neck and then thrashing Chase soundly to prevent it from happening again.

Now Anthony was protecting his high-spirited sister from herself.

Anthony rubbed a hand over his face, then reached for the port. He should have never allowed Sara to wed Julius Lawrence. He'd been against the match from the beginning, but Sara had been so in love that he'd let his better judgment be swayed by her pleas. Anthony's jaw tensed at the memory of how Sara had changed during that endless year, how the laughter that had once danced in her eyes had slowly faded to nothingness.

Never again, he vowed silently. Never again would a worthless whoreson destroy his sister's happiness. They had all hoped that coming to Bath would give Sara time to reestablish herself, some room to recover her dignity. But it appeared that she was still determined to fling her life away, helped by a tall, auburn-haired beauty who deserved a thrashing in her own right. If anything happened to

Sara, Anthony would know where to lay some of the blame. Miss Anna Thraxton had best beware.

Tossing back the last of his port, he climbed to his feet. In the morning, he would send a missive to Marcus, mentioning his suspicions and hoping against hope that he was wrong.

Upstairs, Sara barely waited for her night rail to settle over her shoulders before she dismissed the maid, grabbed her robe, and padded across the hallway to Aunt Delphi's room.

She was glad to see her aunt was alone and already dressed for bed, sitting at a dressing table where she was absently brushing her hair. Sara didn't wait another minute. She pulled up a low stool, then reached out and clasped Delphi's hand in her own. "What has upset you?"

A quaver passed over Delphi's face, but she quickly suppressed it. "I'm fine, Sara. Really."

"Fudge," Sara said. "If you aren't upset, then why is your robe inside out?"

Delphi blinked down at her arms, where the seams of her cuffs lay revealed. "Oh, dear. I didn't even notice." She sighed, her shoulders sagging. "I'm sorry if I seem out of sorts."

"Nonsense. I'm out of sorts all the time; why should you be any different?"

A smile quivered on Delphi's lips. "I suppose that's true." She looked down at her dressing table and absently fingered the handle of her silver brush.

Sara waited patiently, noting the play of emotions on the older woman's face. Finally, Delphi looked up, a blaze of such anger in her brown eyes that Sara was stunned.

"I was treated most rudely this evening."

"In the cardroom?"

"Yes. By a *man*." She almost spat the words.

"Heavens! What happened? Did he accuse you of cheating?"

Delphi looked down at the brush. "No."

"Did he say something unpleasant to you?"

"No." Delphi's mouth quivered before she burst out, "He didn't say anything at all. That is the problem."

Heavens. This was far more serious than Sara had realized. She racked her brain to think of any man who had paid particular attention to Delphi and could think of several. After all, Delphi possessed a considerable fortune and was still an attractive woman. "Tell me more about this man."

A slow blush climbed Delphi's cheeks. With her blond hair in a braid over one shoulder, the silver barely visible, she looked much younger than her age and as vulnerable as a newborn. "He is no one. I mean, he is French and he is a comte, or at least he said he was."

Ah, the Comte du Lac—Bridgeton's companion. He had accompanied them on several of their morning rides and was quite a charming man— almost too charming. Sara shook her head at her own blindness. She'd been so engrossed in her own affairs that she hadn't noticed Delphi's growing infatuation.

Delphi bit her lip. "Sara, I asked Lady Dupree

about the comte, and you know how she has those connections at the embassy. She's never heard of him and she quite thought he might be an imposter. Since the war, there are a number of people who claim to be titled though they are not."

Sara could hardly contain her outrage. *Of course* Bridgeton's companion was an imposter. And Sara would bet that Bridgeton knew it and thought it amusing to spring the false comte onto unsuspecting Bath society. "You should stay away from him."

"But I cannot help but think that Henri must be in horrible straits to undertake such a deception." Delphi grabbed Sara's hands. "What if he is a fugitive? What if his true title made him a wanted man? You know how things were in France, it is possible he is just afraid to tell people who he really is."

"Yes, and he may be the kind of man who makes his way through life preying on the souls of lonely women, gaining their confidence and then stealing their money. Aunt Delphi, you must have a care."

Delphi's shoulders straightend, and, to Sara's surprise, she turned back to her dressing table, and said stiffly, "You don't know the comte like I do, Sara. He would never do such a thing."

Sara was almost speechless. Shy and retiring, Delphi always agreed rather than argue, no matter what her opinion. Perhaps it was a good thing Anthony had come to Bath after all. "Delphi, tell me more about Henri. Perhaps I am being judgmental."

"Oh, he is a true gentleman, Sara. At least he was until—" Tears filled Delphi's eyes.

"What?" Sara asked, leaning forward, full of indignation for her gentle aunt.

Delphi gulped back a sob. "Oh, Sara, he spent the entire evening talking to Lady Prudhomme and Mrs. Walton, and never once did he even look in my direction!"

Sara impulsively hugged her aunt. "That was certainly rude, but surely it isn't cause for shedding tears."

Delphi pulled away, finding a handkerchief and mopping her eyes. "No, no. It isn't. It's just that I met Henri and I thought—Oh, it doesn't matter what I thought. I was wrong. I see it all now." She gave a nervous laugh. "He will never speak to me again. I daresay it was just my imagination that he even fancied me."

"Perhaps it is for the best," Sara said quietly. This was what she got for focusing solely on herself. Well, no more. Sara would keep an eye on both the comte and Delphi from now on.

After a strained second, Delphi took a deep breath, then shook her head, smiling slightly. "I am just excessively tired, that's all. Dear me, look how late it is. You had best get to bed, dear."

Sara hugged her aunt good night. "If there is anything I can do—"

"I'll let you know." Delphi smiled and gently tucked a stray strand of Sara's hair behind her ear. "I've always admired the way you meet life, Sara. Nothing ever defeats you."

An image of the Earl of Bridgeton still fresh in her mind, his kiss warm on her lips, Sara grimaced. "Oh, I am defeated often enough."

"Disappointed, perhaps, but never defeated. I wish I had your courage."

"Anthony wouldn't call it courage. He thinks it naught but stubbornness."

"Perhaps they are one and the same," Delphi said. "Whatever you call it, I wish I had more of it. You've grown into an amazing woman, Sara. Exactly like your mother."

Her aunt's unexpected approval warmed Sara. She hugged Delphi again fiercely, and silently vowed to do what she could to keep the dashing Comte du Lac from her aunt. It was with a troubled step that she returned to her own room.

Unable to sleep, Sara found herself lying on her bed, arms crossed beneath her head, her thoughts drifting to the Earl of Bridgeton and his tempting threat.

It hadn't really been a threat. More of a promise. Which was thrilling and challenging and wildly terrifying all at the same time. Sara hugged her pillow and stared up at the ceiling, where the candlelight cast intriguing shadows.

No matter how tantalizing the earl and his improper proposal might be, Sara could not give up her scheme. Now that Anthony was here, the urgency had increased tenfold. She forced herself to push away all thoughts of the fascinating Nick and instead think about the other men in Bath. Slowly she went through the men she'd seen this evening.

Just as she was about to give it up as a lost cause, her mind snapped to attention. Sir Francis Bawton.

Sara almost shuddered at the thought. Only twenty-two, His Lordship had an appallingly fixed eye and a sad tendency to wear lace. But he was available, possessed an incredibly thick skin which would protect him from her brother's barbs, and he enjoyed social events to the exclusion of good sense, which guaranteed her a good deal of freedom after the ceremony.

After thirty minutes of consideration, Sara decided that he would suffice though he was far from perfect. There was only one perfect potential husband, and he had already removed himself from her list. Gritting her teeth, Sara rolled to her side and gathered her pillow to her, eventually falling asleep. She dreamed of a handsome prince of a man with a cold, cynical smile and heated blue eyes. A man who beckoned to her from the shadows while promising to teach her the forbidden arts of love.

Snuggling deeper into the covers, Sara smiled in her sleep and dreamed on.

Chapter 8

"**I** can't believe I let you talk me into this," Henri said, hunching his shoulders against the cold morning air.

Nick dropped the curtain over the carriage window and settled back in his seat. "Then do not come."

"Bah. I will never have it said that I am not man enough to brave a sunrise. I only wish the sun did not rise so early."

"It is ten o'clock, Henri. I would hardly call it sunrise."

"That depends upon what time one went to bed, *mon ami*." Henri cast him a stern glance. "And to rise so early to visit a sickroom . . . I cannot believe you wish to do this."

"It isn't a sickroom. It's the Pump Room, and it is where many members of the *ton* gather to exchange news and to talk about the triumphs of the night before. Not to mention take the waters. You might want to try it yourself."

"Why?"

"It is held to greatly improve the disposition of people who suffer from aging."

The comte straightened in his seat. "Aging? Who is aging? I'm only forty years old."

Nick raised his brows.

"Or so," the comte amended, shrugging. After a long moment, he sighed. "*Voyons*, I am in a foul mood, no? I do not know what it is. Ever since the Kirkwood ball, I have been—" He broke off and muttered a curse. "Forgive me. I am not fit company this morning."

Neither was Nick. For the past three days, he had thought of nothing but the taste of Sara Lawrence. The kiss in the garden had inflamed him, invading his dreams and interrupting his sleep. And Sara was even more of a challenge now that her huge, hulking brother had attached himself to her side. Nick smiled to himself. Even that was in his favor, for it deterred Lady Carrington's search for an accommodating husband.

His one concern was that it was highly possible that her reckless search could be successful. She showed a lamentable tendency to ask whatever man she was with to marry her. It was only a matter of time before she ended up wed to a complete lummox.

Nick usually did not care whether or not his mistress was married. But this time . . . this time was different. Now that Nick was attempting to win his way into society, he didn't want to deal with the possible jealousies of a husband. He wanted unfettered access to Sara, not to mention her complete attention. A husband could be . . . distracting.

Therefore, he had to show her the error of her strategy, not to mention the dangers of being found unchaperoned in a garden at a heavily attended ball. She could easily end up ruined herself. Few understood the price of being an outcast—the mortification of being cut, the pain of watching those you assumed were your friends turn away in disgust. Nick resolved to keep his future paramour from the clutches of scandal as much for her own sake as for his.

So, he was now cast in the unenviable position of protector. He knew her brother was doing the same, but the huge oaf had no concept of the lengths his sister was prepared to go to obtain her objectives. And that was what gave Nick the advantage. He knew exactly what Sara had planned, and he understood her desire to escape the confines of society far too well.

The carriage finally arrived at the Pump Room. As Nick and Henri strolled up the steps, Henri glanced at the inscription on the door. "*Water is best*. What fool wrote that?"

"The same fool who convinced all of England that drinking this foul, contaminated poison will cure them of all manner of ills."

The comte snorted. "The world is populated with idiots. You cannot spit without hitting one."

Nick wondered at the comte's ill humor. Surely there was more to it than a sore head caused by a night of overindulgence—though it was rare that the comte drank to excess. Perhaps his pursuit of Lady Langtry was without success. Whatever it was, it was beginning to annoy Nick to no end.

When they entered the room, he forgot about the comte and his problems. Just as he had known she would be, Sara sat in an alcove with her aunt and her titian-haired friend, her brother standing guard nearby like a great golden bear.

Dressed in pale yellow muslin decorated with blue rosettes, her hair arranged in careless black curls over one ear, Sara looked as young and fresh as spring. Nick smiled to himself. Her air of fragility and innocence was deceptive, and no one knew it better than he. Unless, of course, one counted the bruised Viscount Hewlette.

Nick and Henri had not been in the Pump Room more than a moment before they were swarmed with acquaintances. Henri became deeply engaged in conversation with an imposing matron in sprigged India muslin, his low spirits melting away under her bright smiles. Ignoring the press of people, Nick found a chair and moved it so that he had a fine, open view of the fascinating Lady Carrington and her companions.

Sara knew the precise moment the Earl of Bridgeton made his entrance. It was more than the stirring of people who craned their necks to catch a glimpse of him, more than the wave of panting women who stared after him in slack-jawed wonder. No, it was a feeling, an awareness of his presence that was more than physical. Sara told herself it was irritation, but she knew better. It was fear. Pure, unquestionable fear.

Though it took an extreme amount of will, Sara forced herself to keep her gaze steady. Damn the man. She'd never felt so self-conscious in her life.

Anna flipped open her fan, her wide, gray gaze fixed on Anthony. "Tell me, Sara. Is your brother always so severe?"

Sara sent a glance at Anthony, who stood leaning against the wall a few feet away, his arms crossed over his broad chest. To the casual observer he appeared relaxed and at his ease, his sleepy-lidded gaze concealing the bright glint of his eyes. But she knew him too well to be taken in.

She sniffed and turned her shoulder, saying loudly enough for the wretch to hear, "He is not usually so somber, but then, he doesn't usually play the part of nursemaid. It must be wearing after so many days."

He slanted her a smile. "It isn't often I'm with anyone in such need of having a nursemaid." His gaze flickered to Anna. "That includes you, Miss Thraxton."

Anna colored hotly, but before she could answer, a commotion arose as a small party arrived and seated themselves in the empty chairs to the left. At the center of the activity was a very tall and elderly woman dressed in an astonishing fashion. Her bright orange-and-blue turban was adorned with a haphazard spray of jewelry, her thin shoulders covered with a heavily fringed shawl of swirling mustard and purple. Her gown, while the height of fashion, was a shocking shade of pink and clashed violently with her red slippers.

But even in this cacophony of color, Sara's gaze was immediately drawn to the woman's face. Narrow and pale, with a high forehead lined by age and a nose worthy of Caesar, there was something compelling about her.

"Bloody hell," Anthony muttered, straightening when he saw the newcomers. "I thought she'd died."

"Who?"

"Lady Birlington. She is the world's rudest woman."

"Who are the others?" Anna asked.

"The young man with her is her nephew, Edmund Valmont, while that fade-away mouse of a woman is her companion. A distant cousin, I believe." Anthony grimaced. "They're gabsters, every one. Except the cousin. I don't believe I've ever heard her say a word, but that may just be because she has so little opportunity between the other two. The last time I saw Edmund, it took me three hours to be rid of him."

"Lady Birlington just saw you. I think she's trying to get your attention," Anna said.

Anthony turned to Sara. "I'm going to step outside a moment. Do you think you can behave yourself while I'm gone?"

"Please stay away as long as you like," Sara said with some asperity. "I certainly won't miss you."

Anthony grinned and winked, then left.

Sara stole a glance at the new arrivals. The imposing woman was perched on a low settee, her back ramrod straight, her gnarled hands clutched about a gold-encrusted cane.

Lord Valmont, a harassed-looking young man sporting mussed golden curls and an unfortunately round face, deposited an extra shawl, a book, and a small red-velvet case on the table beside the woman. "Here you are, Aunt Maddie. All settled and right as rain. Stay here and I'll fetch you some water."

"I won't drink it."

The lady by her side fluttered uncomfortably. "Oh, please, Lady Birlington," she said in a soft, anxious voice. "You must drink the water. Dr. Tumbolton said it would do you a world of good."

"Dr. Tumbolton is a fool," Lady Birlington replied.

"Dr. Tumbolton is one of the best physicians in London," her nephew protested. "Not much he doesn't know about. In fact, if I were a betting man, I'd say he knows more than just about anyone. Even the Prince."

"That doesn't say much."

Her companion giggled nervously.

Lady Birlington glared. "For God's sake, Althea. Must you titter? I've had to listen to that sound all day, and it's beginning to make me bilious." Satisfied she'd cowed her companion, she jabbed her cane toward Edmund's feet. "Don't just stand there. Get me a glass of wine."

"It is ten o'clock in the morning and there's none to be had," her nephew said. "Furthermore, the doctor wouldn't like it. Wants you to take the waters twice a day for two weeks and abstain from wine and red meat. And you agreed you'd try."

"Humph. That was before I knew the water would taste like horse piss."

"Aunt Maddie!" the young man said, his face as red as his horrendous waistcoat.

The old woman sighed. "Oh, very well! I'll have a little of that blasted water. Only have them put some ice in it. It's bad enough they serve it luke-warm, like some sort of tisane."

Edmund appeared relieved and immediately hurried off to complete his errand, his portly figure disappearing in the crowd.

As soon as he left, the old harridan settled her brilliant shawl about her shoulders. "You see, Althea. Edmund can be handy to have around if you know how to deal with him."

Aunt Delphi returned at that moment, her hand clutched about a small glass. She'd heard that taking the waters reduced wrinkles and sharpened the mind, which was why she came to the Pump Room each morning. Since she only managed to choke down one tiny sip before setting the glass on the nearest table, Sara didn't expect to see any significant results.

As Delphi went to take her seat by Sara, she halted on seeing the new arrivals. "Why, Lady Birlington! How are you?"

"Demme, it's Delphinea." Bright blue eyes surveyed her up and down, then whipped past her to the room beyond. "Don't tell me you convinced that dullard of a husband of yours to bring you to Bath for a kick up."

"Langtry died several years ago," Aunt Delphi said in a repressive tone.

"That's right. Never seem to remember that, but it's not surprising. I knew Langtry, and you were well rid of him—for a dowdier, more prosy bore of a man, I've never met."

Edmund returned with a glass of water. "Here you are, Aunt Maddie."

Maddie pointed with her cane. "Put it on that table. It makes me ill just to look at it." She turned back to Delphi and gestured to the chair beside her. "Come and sit. I'm bored stiff."

"Did you come for the waters?"

"So my doctor thinks, but I'm really here to find a wife for my idiot of a grandnephew."

Edmund made a sound of pure frustration. "Don't want a wife. Got plenty of my own worries as it is."

Lady Birlington snorted. "Like what? You've no household to speak of, you've funds aplenty, and you've no ambition. What worries could you possibly have?"

"Well," he said, looking a little desperate. "Been thinking of buying a horse. Maybe two."

"I vow, Edmund, that's exactly the reason you need a wife. Someone to govern these impulsive decisions of yours. That and for breeding. You owe it to the line to have a few sons. I'd hate to think of the title passing to your cousin Farley." She turned to

Delphi, ignoring the choking sounds coming from her nephew. "Do you know Lord Faulkherst? He's my other grandnephew and the biggest jackanapes this side of Dover. Wouldn't let him in my house without first counting the silver."

Sara had to strangle a laugh, garnering the old lady's attention. "Eh? Who is this?" Lady Birlington said, subjecting Sara to a piercing gaze.

Delphi instantly responded. "Oh! This is my niece—"

"Capital," Lady Birlington said. "Very pretty gel." She turned a gimlet stare on her nephew. "Well, Edmund. Don't *you* think Miss St. John is a very pretty gel?"

"I'm not Miss St. John," Sara corrected. "I'm Lady Carrington. My husband was Viscount Carrington."

Lady Birlington frowned. "Carrington, eh? Tall, slender, something of a talker? Died not long ago. Something of a scandal if I recall; died with his pe—"

"That would be he," Sara agreed hastily.

Aunt Delphi sent her a sharp glance, but Lady Birlington gave a nod. "Not one to keep his business to himself, was he? Well, it is a good thing he died young. Most men don't have the good sense to know when to quit this earth. At least your husband didn't drag on and on like some do."

"How true," Sara said, refusing to flinch under Lady Birlington's gimlet stare. "But it is not a subject I like to dwell on."

Lady Birlington nodded her approval. "You may do. Edmund needs a woman who knows her way about life. No white-and pink-miss for him."

Edmund cast a wild glance toward the door. "Aunt Maddie, *please* don't say another word."

"Nonsense! Lady Carrington is fascinated. You can see it in her eyes." Lady Birlington glanced at Anna, who returned her stare with a calm one of her own. "And who are you, gel?"

"Anna Thraxton, my lady."

Lady Birlington snorted. "Anna? What kind of a name is that? Sounds like something you'd name a milkmaid."

"Fortunately for us both, it isn't your name but mine, and therefore it isn't your concern whatsoever," Anna returned, a decided edge to her voice.

Sara expected Lady Birlington to bridle in anger, but instead a quiver of laughter lit the blue eyes. "Humph. You seem familiar, now that I look at you. Aren't related to Phineas Thraxton, are you?"

"He's my grandfather."

"A good man, Thraxton. Not the best of blood, but good, hardy English stock." She turned to Edmund. "You would do well with either Lady Carrington or Miss Thraxton. You have my permission to call on them both."

"At the same time?" Edmund asked, tugging at his cravat and only succeeding in tightening the knot.

"If you wish." His aunt cast a narrowed glance at Anna's tall form and nodded her turbaned head. "Your best bet might be the tall one. She's got spirit to her, and her hips look wide enough to bear any number of childr—"

"Thank you, Aunt Maddie," Edmund interrupted in a voice of anguish. He stared stoically ahead, his face so red he appeared in imminent danger of bursting into flames.

Lady Birlington then began to gossip loudly about various persons in the room and Aunt Delphi, though slightly stiff at first, soon added her comments and discovered all sorts of scandalous information. Suddenly Lady Birlington stopped talking, her gaze fixed just past Sara.

Without looking, Sara knew who stood by her chair. The air about her hummed, like a thick swirling mist that only she could feel. Only this mist was hot, heated by a desire that had, over the last three days, grown strong enough to see.

"Lady Carrington," said a low, seductive voice. "How are you this morning?"

"By God, it *is* Bridgeton!" Lady Birlington exclaimed.

Edmund whirled to look, openly gawking. "But how . . . you aren't supposed to be . . . Lud, I hope Alec doesn't find out about this. Or has he unbanished you?"

Sara blinked. Someone had dared to banish the Earl of Bridgeton? Why? And who was Alec? Who possessed the power to change the path of a man like Nicholas Montrose?

Lady Birlington frowned. "Hope you aren't planning on staying, Bridgeton. Your cousin wouldn't like it at all."

Nick's gaze narrowed, and Sara was aware of a strange tenseness about him, but he merely shrugged. "Then let him tell me that himself." He turned to Sara. "Lady Carrington, I came to see if you and Miss Thraxton could join me for a carriage ride this afternoon."

Having seen the mount he rode in the park, Sara immediately pictured a dashing phaeton and the spirited horses he'd own, and she yearned to agree. But she had Bridgeton's measure and was not about to become another of his conquests. "I'm afraid I have plans this afternoon," Sara said, keeping her voice as far from enthusiastic as possible.

"Indeed?" he murmured. "What a pity."

Over his shoulder, Sara caught sight of the comte as he bent his white head in answer to something Lady Phillipson had said. Sara glanced at Delphi and discovered her aunt watching the comte with a sad, yearning expression. In that instant, Sara knew she had to speak with Bridgeton. Only he would know the truth about his friend. "But perhaps I might be able to postpone my plans for a day or so."

Anna blinked. "Sara, do you think you should—"

"I will come at two," the earl said. "I believe I know your direction." He bowed, feathering a kiss over her hand, lifting his eyes to hers as he did so. The stark promise that lit his gaze made her shiver. He released her hand and took his leave of the others, gathered the comte, and left the Pump Room. The sight of the horde of women who stood staring after him like a pack of adoring spaniels made Sara feel slightly ill. She hoped she didn't have such a pathetic glaze to her eyes.

"You know, Bridgeton looks nothing like his father," Lady Birlington said, her sharp gaze missing nothing. "Though he was a well-favored man, too. At least he was before his megrims made him so pale."

"Megrims?" Sara asked.

"Lud, yes," Lady Birlington said. "Bad ones, too. They got worse once he married that Frenchwoman. She was far too common for him, as anyone could see. But he was besotted and would listen to no one."

"I'd heard she was prodigiously handsome," Delphi offered in a soft voice.

"Humph," Lady Birlington said. "She was more than handsome; couldn't help but stare whenever you saw her. Bridgeton has much the look of her. Unfortunately, he also inherited her tendencies for ruin."

"Tendencies?" Sara asked, leaning forward.

"He is on the road to hell, my dear. His mother had a weakness for laudanum. It eventually destroyed her, and I daresay it will destroy him, too." The old lady cast a shrewd gaze at Sara. "If I were you, I'd stay away from Nicholas Montrose."

Sara intended to do just that. Once she found out more about the too-charming Comte du Lac, of course.

"I'm sure my niece will have nothing to do with the man if he is so ineligible," Aunt Delphi said, a slight huff to her voice. "However, you can hardly expect her to avoid him because of some old gossip."

Lady Birlington poked her cane at her nephew's feet. "Tell Her Grace that my memory is as sharp today as it was forty years ago."

"Can't do that," Edmund said. "Wasn't born forty years ago. She'd think I was lying." Edmund looked at the door where Bridgeton had just disappeared. "Daresay you'll think me silly, but I think that man is dangerous."

Dangerous. Sara shivered. Oh yes, he was dangerous. He was dangerous because every time she saw him, her resolution wavered. His very presence put her plan at risk, and she was rapidly crumbling. And now that she was forced to seek him out to discover what she could of the comte, she was in even more danger of losing sight of her goal.

But she had too much at stake to waver. As soon as she arrived home, she would send a note to Sir Bawton. She would not waste another moment's thought on Bridgeton.

Chapter 9

Sara sanded the letter she had just written and held it out to Anna, who quickly scanned the contents.

"Well," she said after a noticeable pause, "it is certainly direct."

Sara returned the quill to the holder. "All it says is that I hope I meet him at the Fairfax spectacle. I'm tired of all this dallying about. As soon as it dries, I'll have one of the footmen deliver it."

Anna obediently waved the missive in the air to dry it quicker. "Sara, are you certain you should pursue this? We know very little about Sir Bawton, and we were so wrong about Viscount Hewlette—"

"Which is why I won't be seeing Sir Bawton alone. *You* will be with me the entire time. Besides, we know that Sir Bawton is very persuadable, and his family only recently gained acceptance."

"Grandfather says the family reeks of trade."

"That's quite a compliment from him," Sara said.

"True. Still . . . I don't know about this."

"Neither do I. But at least I am doing *something*."

Anna folded the missive and handed it to Sara. "Won't Anthony try to stop you from seeing Sir Bawton?"

"He might, if he thought I was the one wishing to see him. Therefore, I hinted that you had a *tendre* for the man."

Anna's face pinkened. "Lovely."

In actual fact, Anthony had reacted rather strangely to the news that Anna had developed an unanswered passion for Sir Bawton. Anthony had first stared, his mouth agape. After a stunned moment, he had broken into loud, guffawing laughter, which had irritated Sara even as it had assured her that he would pay no attention to Sir Bawton when next they met.

"I suppose it doesn't matter," Anna said finally. "What did Anthony say about our ride with Bridgeton? He seemed livid when he discovered we were going."

"He thinks Aunt Delphi is accompanying us. I told him that we were all leaving at two, which is true—only Delphi is going to the lending library."

Anna raised her brows. "Delphi? At a lending library?"

"I was rather surprised myself. But she said she

was going to try and improve the tone of her mind. I'm just glad to see her getting out of the house."

A soft knock sounded at the door, and the butler entered. "My lady, the Earl of Bridgeton has arrived. I left him in the sitting room."

A trill of nervous excitement raced through Sara. "Thank you, Jacobs. I will be there immediately."

The butler bowed again and left.

Anna waited until the door had closed before she said, "I still don't feel right about Sir Bawton. Even Grandfather had little information about him, and you know how he loves a good gossip."

"That's because there is nothing to impart. Trust me, Anna. This will work out fine." She went out into the hallway and handed her missive to one of the footmen.

In the sitting room, Nick listened to the low murmur of feminine voices approach the door. He'd been surprised when Sara had agreed to accompany him on his ride, and he fully expected her to greet him with some excuse as to why she could not attend.

The door opened, and she whisked into the room with a brisk, no-nonsense step. She was dressed in a gown of pale pink that made her skin glow. He bowed. "Lady Carrington."

"Lord Bridgeton."

Miss Thraxton entered the room after Sara, and Nick bowed again. "Miss Thraxton. And how are you this afternoon?"

"I'm fine, thank you," Miss Thraxton said.

"Except for your ankle," Sara said.

Nick looked at Miss Thraxton's foot where it peeped out from beneath her skirts.

"Oh, yes," she said, her face reddening. "I fell on the steps, and I'm afraid I won't be able to accompany you on your ride through the park."

"I certainly hope you brought a groom with you," Sara said, sending him a blinding smile.

Nick suddenly had the feeling he'd been lured into a lion's den. The redoubtable Lady Carrington wanted something—he was sure of it. But what? Bowing, he said, "Of course I brought a groom. The proprieties are an important part of life."

She looked as if she'd like to disagree with him, but then thought better of it. Amused, he bid good day to Miss Thraxton and escorted Sara to his waiting phaeton. His hand closed about her arm as he assisted her into the seat, and a startling jolt of heat flashed through him. Damn, but he was hot for this woman. He had to take a slow breath before he climbed into the seat beside her.

Nick took the reins from his groom and glanced down at his companion, who sat straight in her seat, her feet planted side by side, her hands neatly clasped in her lap. Nick thought that perhaps women on their way to the guillotine had worn just such an expression—a mixture of tension and resignation, as if she'd agreed to some dire, horrible duty and just wanted it to be over.

With a startled gasp, Sara slid across the seat until her thigh rested solidly against his. Scrambling madly, she scooted away, but not before Nick had felt the shape of her thigh against his. Stifling a smile, he took the next corner even more sharply, but this time Lady Carrington was prepared. She gripped the edge of the seat tightly, her face frozen into a grimace at the effort.

Nick chuckled to himself and won a sharp glare for his efforts. "There are seven corners on the way to the park. I counted."

She was silent for a long while. Nick took two more corners, letting the phaeton sway only the tiniest bit, just enough to remind her of what he could do, if he was of a mind.

Finally, she drew a slow breath between her teeth, and said, "What a lovely phaeton." She showed her teeth in what he suspected was supposed to resemble a smile.

"That was very well done," he said approvingly. "Have you ever considered a career onstage? I don't think Keane could have managed quite so well." He feathered his way through the next corner, careful not to make so much as a fold of her gown tremble. She noticed the difference, for she frowned up at him.

Nick was assailed with the sudden desire to kiss her frown away. "Sara, I know you did not come for a ride merely to admire my phaeton. What exactly do you want?"

"I wish to ask you about the comte."

Nick raised his brows. "Henri? What of him?"

"Is he a true comte?"

"In France, there are no false comtes." Since the revolution there were a surprising number of never-before-heard-of ducs, comtes, and other quasi-noblemen that had miraculously appeared overnight. If nothing else, the revolution had managed to thicken the blood of the aristocracy with good, healthy common stock.

Sara shook her head. "That isn't an answer. I want to know if his title and position are legitimate."

"Why?"

"Because my aunt—" Sara glanced up at him, then away, her lashes shadowing her eyes. "I was just wondering."

So the indomitable Henri was making progress with his duchess, was he? Nick considered what he actually knew about his friend and realized that it wasn't much. "I don't know Henri's history."

She tilted her head to one side, the wide ribbons of her bonnet framing her face. "But . . . he travels with you. He is even staying at Hibberton Hall."

"Yes, but that doesn't mean that we've discussed his title." Of course, Nick had his suspicions. But it would be rude to ask and, frankly, he didn't really care. Titles were nothing. They came to one only because of the unfortunate circumstances of one's birth.

Lady Carrington appeared less than enamored with his lack of interest in the comte's credentials. "What *do* you and the comte discuss?"

"Horses. Cards." He slid a glance at his companion. "Women."

She colored adorably, scooting away, though the narrow seat did not give her much reprieve. "Where in France is the comte from?"

Nick considered this for a moment. "Paris, I would imagine."

"Imagine? Don't you *know*?"

"The subject has never come up."

"I cannot believe this! You would let a complete stranger live with you, travel to England with you, all without even asking him the most basic questions? How long have you known the comte?"

"Three years."

Her mouth dropped open and she seemed unable to say a word. Nick wondered what she would do if he kissed her, then and there, slipping his tongue between her lips and tasting her deeply, completely. The thought made him harden immediately and it wasn't until he'd turned the last two corners to the park that his ardor cooled. He found a wide path in the park and let the horses fall into a slower pace before turning his attention back to Sara. "For a certain price, I might be willing to discover all you wish to know about the comte."

She stiffened. "I will not pay you to spy for me."

"I wasn't going to spy. I was going to ask him."

"Won't he think it strange, after you've known him for so long?" Sara's brow creased, then she suddenly brightened. "What if you got him drunk? I daresay he would tell you everything then."

Nick could have told her that getting Henri drunk was nearly impossible. Instead, he nodded thoughtfully. "It's possible, I suppose."

"Then you'll do it?"

"For a price."

She bit her lip and looked away. Nick noted the edge of her even, white teeth as they worried her plump lower lip.

She looked back at him, her lashes so long they tangled in the corners. "What is your price?"

"A dance."

Her face fell, though she quickly recovered.

"I'm surprised you didn't demand more," she said coolly. "Like a kiss."

"When you kiss me, it will be because you want to and not because I tricked you into it."

She sniffed. "That is the only way you'll get another kiss from me."

Nick leaned over and whispered in her ear, "Forget the comte. There are other ways I can help you, Sara."

She regarded him suspiciously. "How?"

"I've been thinking of your plan to find a husband. Without funds . . ." He shrugged.

Her color rose. "I've plenty to offer without a large dowry."

"If you had time, I'm sure you could bring any man you chose to heel. But as you pointed out to me in the garden, time is the one thing you don't have."

"What do you suggest?"

"If you wish to catch a man, you must learn to appeal to him on all levels. I can teach you all you need to know."

"I'm sure you can. Fortunately, I am not so desperate as that. Not yet, anyway."

He regarded her narrowly. "You have already found another victim."

"I prefer the term 'prospect,' " she said haughtily.

Damn it, how was he going to seduce her if she

was chasing men so determinedly? Nick set his jaw. "Who is it?"

"Sir Bawton," Sara said, trying not to look directly into the earl's eyes. The darkest of blue, they appeared almost black and as fathomless as the night. She had to bite back a sigh.

"Sir Bawton. Where do I know that name? Is he—Oh, yes." A slow smile touched his mouth. "Just when do you plan on making your proposition?"

Sara didn't like the look on the earl's face. It reminded her far too much of Anthony's expression when she'd told him about Anna's supposed fascination for Bawton. "I will be seeing him tomorrow," she said suspiciously. "Why?"

"I just wondered when the, er, festivities were scheduled."

Sara had to bite back a scowl. "I think it is time I returned home. My brother is due shortly, and it wouldn't do for him to see me out with you."

"Of course." He turned the horses toward the gate without demur.

That irritated Sara all the more. How could the man go from relentless pursuit to silent mockery in the next instant? And he'd been far too quick to agree to take her home.

The rest of the ride was silent. He pulled the phaeton up to the front steps and climbed down, reaching up to assist her.

Sara put her hand in his, determined to show him that she was completely unaffected by him. She was doing an excellent job of looking bored when the earl slipped a hard arm about her waist and hauled her against him. Standing against the carriage, they were sheltered from prying eyes, his body pressed to hers in a most intimate fashion. With his hips against hers, Sara could feel his manhood straining against the fabric of his breeches. Her breath trembled to a halt, and she looked up at him, instantly lost in the depth of his gaze.

With a sharp sigh, he set her on her feet and stepped away. Sara was glad to know he was as affected as she; his breath was harsh as he adjusted his cravat.

"Think about what I said, Sara. I can teach you many, many things." He took her hand and brushed his lips across her knuckles.

It was just a polite gesture, but there was something so sensual about the way he looked at her through his lashes, something hotly possessive in the way he traced his lips across the back of her hand. It made her think of silk sheets and glistening bare skin, of entwined passion and mind-numbing pleasure.

But it was not to be. She'd been at the mercy of one rake and she'd be damned if she fell under the spell of another. Already she was too fraught with desire for the earl, too eager and too fascinated.

Forcing her traitorous body to obey, she stepped away from Bridgeton. "Thank you for your offer, but I'm certain it will not be necessary." She managed a brilliant smile. "Thank you for the lovely drive in the park. Perhaps we can do it again someday."

With that, she turned and walked into the house, wishing she felt as nonchalant as she had sounded.

Nick watched her until the door closed behind her. He ached for her. It was a new and unpleasant experience, to yearn for a woman in such a way. But perhaps it would make the final moment of surrender all the sweeter.

Holding that thought firmly in place, he turned back to his phaeton and came to an abrupt halt.

"I suppose I should ask your name before I kill you," Sara's brother said, his smile far from pleasant.

Nick knew very little about the Earl of Greyley, only that the man was massive in size and overly assiduous in protecting his sister.

"That would be the polite thing to do," Nick agreed, wondering how much the man had actually seen. If he'd seen Nick holding Sara, they would not be talking now. "It would also be polite to explain exactly *why* you intend to kill me."

"I know who you are, Bridgeton. Leave my sister alone."

"I merely took her for a drive," he said in a bored tone. "My groom was present the whole time."

The earl cast a glance at Nick's groom, who stood staring stoically ahead. "Your groom can go to hell. He's in your employ. That makes him an untrustworthy chaperone."

"It is conventional to—"

"I don't give a damn about convention," Greyley snapped. "The next time you see my sister, do yourself a favor and stay away. She is not the type of woman to associate with a man like you. Surely you have realized that by now."

Nick did realize it, and he knew it was madness

to pursue her. But she was just too damned tempting. He managed a shrug. "I don't answer to you, Greyley. Not now. Not ever."

"Don't press me, Bridgeton," the earl growled.

"And don't press *me*, Greyley. You have as much to lose as I. More, in fact."

For one glorious instant, Nick thought he would have the fight he was yearning for. It would cool his ardor and allow him to vent some of the heat that boiled through his veins. But the sound of an approaching carriage made them both look up to see Lady Langtry's landau.

Cursing, Greyley turned back to him. "Don't let me find you sniffing around my sister again." With that, he went into the house.

Of all the events held each year at the imposing estates outside of Bath, the Fairfax spectacle was considered the grandest of them all. Invitations for the indoor picnic, followed by a stroll through the lit gardens to view breathtaking fireworks, were highly prized and freely given. It was said that old man Fairfax had made his fortune in trade and was therefore more open-minded about mixing his company.

Nick had planned on approaching Lord Fairfax directly to secure an invitation, but it turned out there was no need. He received the coveted card in the first round issued, which filled him with satisfaction.

That night, attired in a black coat and a blue waistcoat, his cravat a wondrously tied French concoction adorned with a flashing sapphire, Nick arrived at the Fairfax estate just in time to see the first colored explosion dance across the sky. Bright red ashes drifted to the ground as a collective gasp rose from the crowd, followed by an appreciative sprinkling of applause. Though the evening was cold, a series of large fires and the continuous flow of Lord Fairfax's special rum punch warmed the guests.

Nick had more exciting games in mind this evening. He strolled across the lawn, his hands loosely clasped behind him, searching for a small, heart-shaped face and a cloud of black hair.

After thirty minutes, he stopped. Where in the hell was she? As if answering his thoughts, Sara's brother came into view. But the Earl of Greyley was not enjoying the spectacle, either; like Nick, he was walking through the crowds, scanning every face.

Nick stood for a moment. Greyley was now coming closer, barely waiting until he was in front of Nick before saying through his teeth, "Where's Sara?"

"I am not her keeper, Greyley." He paused, then added silkily, "However much I might wish otherwise."

The earl's nostrils flared. "I will find her, and when I do, she had best not be with you." With that, he turned on his heel and stalked away.

Nick watched him go. Sara's brother might think Nick was the only wolf hot on his sister's trail, but he knew otherwise. He strode back toward the house, noticing Miss Thraxton, who was apparently caught in conversation with Edmund Valmont.

Anna's gaze kept slipping toward the low shrubbery that marked off a small maze. Nick cursed silently as he crossed to the curved shrubbery that marked the entryway to the maze. With his superior height he could see over the top edge of the brush, but the warm glow of the Japanese lanterns obscured his vision, casting shadows in some places instead of lighting them. Up above, the moon played hide-and-seek behind pale wisps of clouds. With the flashes of color from the fireworks and the gently bobbing lanterns, the maze was the perfect place for a clandestine meeting.

Nick walked quickly through the maze, stopping to listen every now and then. Finally, the low murmur of voices sounded just ahead. Nick stopped and tilted his head, trying to decide if one of the voices belonged to Sara, when a sudden shriek rent the air.

Nick's jaw tightened. Good God, had he been mistaken about the man's character? Of all the men in Bath, Sara should be safe with Sir Bawton. Nick ran down the pathway toward the sound, arriving at the center of the maze just in time to hear a loud splash.

Sara turned a white face to his. She stood on the edge of a small fishpond, trying desperately to pull something from the depths. "Oh, thank God!" she cried. "Help me get him out before he drowns!"

Nick was beside her in an instant, strangely gratified by her reaction. "What's happened?"

"It is Sir Bawton. He fell into the water, and I cannot get him out."

Nick looked down into the pond. A delicate-looking fop reclined amongst the reeds, his body half-submerged in the green, slimy depths, his face nearly covered by a lily pad. To all intents and purposes, he looked dead. Had Sara not caught the fool's arm, he could have indeed drowned.

"Bloody hell," Nick said as he unceremoniously grabbed the man by his wide lapels and lifted him to a sitting position, disturbing a huge frog that hopped out of the way. "What did you hit him with?"

"Don't be idiotic," she snapped. "The fool fainted."

Nick paused in hoisting Bawton out of the water. Even in the glow of the moon, he could tell that Sara's cheeks were brightly colored. "Fainted?"

"Yes. When I tried to kiss him."

Nick's lips twitched. He hauled Sir Bawton's limp form onto the ground, trailing water across the stones as he went. Then Nick straightened and looked at Sara. "You had better tell me everything."

"I tried to kiss him and he reeled backward, stumbled against the wall, and fell. I think he hit his head when he landed, for he hasn't moved since."

"I see," Nick managed in a fairly normal voice.

Sara sent him a fulminating glare. "If you continue to grin at me in that odious fashion, I shall hit *you*. With a rock, if I can find one."

"I won't even smile," he promised, managing to control the impulse by noticing how fetching his companion appeared this evening. Attired in a gown of white silk that attempted to hide her abundant charms behind a high neckline and a loosely fitted skirt, and with a blue pelisse buttoned securely about her throat, she looked far too respectable to be caught in the garden with a man like him. "May I ask you why you attempted to kiss poor Sir Bawton?"

"Because he would not kiss me," she replied stiffly.

Nick looked down to where Sir Bawton's heavy lace ruffles lay in sodden piles about his hands and throat. "I don't suppose he would."

"It wasn't my fault; I did everything just right."

"Just what is 'everything'?"

She sighed loudly, then counted off on her fingers. "I smiled too much, leaned too close, and—" She bit her lip, her glance slipping away.

He raised his brows. "And?"

"Oh, very well. I even brushed my breasts against his sleeve. And all he did was back away and start stammering."

Nick had an immediate image of the feel of her breath along *his* cheek, the softness of her breasts as they pressed against *his* arm. He had to fight a sudden urge to loosen his cravat.

Sir Bawton stirred, moaning quietly.

"He must get up." Sara nudged him with the toe of her shoe. "Sir Bawton!" she called. "Pray rise. It is getting late." Nothing happened, and she made a noise of disgust. "What will I do now?"

Nick shrugged. "Start screaming. Your brother is bound to come running, then you can tell him that Sir Bawton waylaid you in the garden and tried to have his evil way with you. You would be ruined and on your way to the altar, just as you wish."

Sara plopped her hands on her hips, her reticule swinging from one wrist, and glared up at Nick. "It is one thing to embrace a man in a garden and quite another to have him almost kill himself in an attempt to get away. I won't have it said that I am desperate."

Sir Francis moaned louder and covered his eyes with one hand. "What happened?" he mumbled in a thin, lispy voice. "Was I attacked?"

Nick rubbed a hand over his mouth in an attempt to hide his grin. "You fell in the fishpond. Just rest a moment, and you'll feel better."

Sara blew out her breath in a disgusted sigh. "Who knew he was such a ninny?"

"I daresay that was part of his charm," Nick murmured. She turned a dark glance on him, and he raised his hands. "You were the one looking for a complaisant husband."

"I still am," she said, lifting her chin. "But Anthony has scared off every man worth speaking to. Sir Bawton was the only hope I had left."

Nick looked down at the dandy, whose color was returning to normal. Other than a huge knot on his forehead, the man did not seem the worse for his misadventure. A firework burst almost directly above them, the bright yellow light sparking off Sir Bawton's silver-laced waistcoat, which was an extravagant creation of rose, mauve, and silver. His shoulders were puffed out with buckram wadding, his coat was adorned with a series of preposterous buttons, and his stockings sported ridiculous red tassels.

Nick said, "I'm sure Sir Bawton is quite aware of your brother, though not in the manner you would imagine."

Her brows drew together. "What do you mean?"

"Perhaps we should continue this conversation on our way back. Bawton can find his way home on his own." Nick leaned over the dandy and said loudly, "Pardon me, Bawton. Do you wish me to send someone for you?"

"No, no," Sir Bawton muttered. He rolled to his side, then staggered to his feet, where he stood swaying. "Gad, was I set upon by footpads?"

Nick raised his brows. "Don't you remember what happened?"

The foppish lord began to shake his head, then moaned and pressed his fingers against his temples. "I don't remember anything."

"Well then, you slipped on the path, hit your head on the wall of the pond, and then fell into the water. Lady Carrington found you and called for help."

"Thank God she came along when she did." Bawton looked down at his clothes and shuddered. "Lud help me! I can't let anyone see me like this. I shall leave from the garden."

"Excellent. I will have your carriage brought around to meet you there."

Thanking Nick profusely, Sir Bawton staggered off, his hand on his head.

Nick watched the man until he was out of sight before he turned back to Sara. "Tell me, sweet. Have you ever seen Sir Bawton in the company of a woman?"

"Of course I have. He dances with nearly everyone. Anna says he is the most graceful man she knows."

"Exactly my point."

A frown puckered Sara's brow. "What do you mean?"

"Has he ever courted anyone?"

"No. Aunt Delphi says he is a confirmed bachelor. He is a little silly and too aware of his own looks to pay attention to anyone else, but I vow, I never thought he would scream in such a way and then faint."

Nick took her hand in his, curving his fingers about her wrist. "Sara, Sir Bawton is not . . . er, how shall I put this? He is not fond of women."

She stilled, looking up at Nick with a wide, unblinking gaze. "He's not?"

"No. In fact, he prefers the company of men. Very pretty men, in fact."

Overhead, a loud round of bright green sparkles exploded into the night. Sara yanked her hand free from Nick's. "You are teasing me."

"I would never tease about something as serious as a man who has forgotten that he is a man."

Sara stared at Nick. He wasn't smiling, not even a little. In fact, there was only a rueful certainty to his expression. Dear God, he was telling the truth. Never had Sara felt like such a fool. She pressed her fingers to her temples. "That's why he . . . and then I . . . oh, dear!"

Nick shrugged. "A simple mistake, and fortunately Sir Bawton cannot even remember what occurred."

She closed her eyes. "I am so embarrassed."

"Don't be. Return to the lawn and find Miss Thraxton. Your brother is looking for you and is likely to show at any moment."

"And you?"

Nick's lips twisted in a bitter smile. "I'm sure your brother has already discovered that I'm missing as well. I'll follow the hapless Sir Bawton and leave through the garden."

Gratitude overwhelmed her and she took a step forward. "Nick, I—"

He placed the tips of his fingers over her lips. In the distance, she could hear the murmur of voices on the path. "You had better go," he said in a low voice.

But she didn't want to go. She wanted to stay where she was, a fingertip away from Nick. The warmth of his fingers against her lips sent flashes of excitement through her body, to her breasts, and much lower.

Sara closed her eyes and leaned forward, capturing his wrist to place a single kiss in his palm. The gesture was meant to be one of gratitude for his help, but the second her lips touched his skin, it became something else.

The silence lengthened, then turned heavy with desire. Overhead, a cascade of light danced across the velvet sky, dusting the silence with a faint crackle.

The voices on the pathway sounded again, this time closer. Nick dropped his hand and stepped back. The look he gave her was so intense that she blinked. "You owe me, Sara Lawrence, and I will not forget it." With a swift bow, he turned and disappeared down the path.

Her heart pounding an irregular beat, she watched him go. It was a damned shame the Earl of Bridgeton was not interested in marriage.

Sara slowly walked out of the maze, away from the sound of the voices. Her plan was quickly unraveling. Potential husbands were not as easy to find as she'd thought they would be, especially with Anthony now doing his damnedest to keep the field as barren as possible.

Sara wrapped her arms about her as she stepped out onto the hill, the cool evening breeze toying with the edge of her skirt. Despite her determination to stay away from Bridgeton, he had proven himself invaluable again. And now she did indeed owe him.

Perhaps Bridgeton was still her answer—surely he knew some men who would fit her purposes. The idea made her smile. It would serve the earl right if she used him to glean the name of a potential husband or two. The only thing that gave her pause was what he'd ask for compensation for such a favor. Hm . . . what if he wanted her to—

"Sara!"

She looked up to see Anthony bearing down on her, frustration and anger in his face.

Whatever the cost, Sara needed Bridgeton's help—and the sooner, the better.

Chapter 10

The morning after the Fairfax spectacle, Anna arrived at Aunt Delphi's town house as Sara had instructed. Dressed in her best walking dress of white muslin adorned with a new lace collar, Anna was as fashionable as her limited wardrobe allowed. She didn't possess the resources Sara did, and at times she was slightly self-conscious about her appearance.

Not that Anna begrudged her friend the wealth she'd been born to. Grandfather had taught her the pitfalls of wealth, and she was truly glad she was not so burdened. Most of the time, anyway. She fingered the edge of her cuff, pleased to note that her tiny, even stitches were so perfect as to be almost invisible.

Bowing, the butler showed Anna into the front parlor. "Her Grace and Lady Carrington will be down shortly." With a final dignified bow, he closed the door, leaving Anna blissfully alone in the small morning room.

"Thank you," Anna said to the air, relaxing as the sound of the servant's even trod faded down the hallway. She wandered aimlessly about the room, enjoying the faint smell of beeswax and the way the bright sunshine filtered into the room to warm away the morning chill. As the minutes grew, Anna, having run an admiring finger over all of the furniture, picked up a novel that had been left out. Sitting in the large chair by the window, she was soon lost in a wonderful world where a much-put-upon heroine fought her evil uncle for control of her fortune.

The sound of the front door slamming echoed through the narrow hall and made her look up with a start. She slapped the book shut and replaced it on the table just as the door opened and Sara's brother walked in. Impeccably dressed in a morning coat of olive green and a waistcoat of deep brown, Anthony Elliot was a sight to behold. His golden brown hair fell over his forehead, warming his eyes to chocolate. Anna had always had a weakness for chocolate.

He halted on seeing her. There was an instant of hesitation, and he turned as if to leave. But just as his hand closed back around the doorknob, he halted, then turned to regard her with a considering gaze. "I beg your pardon, Miss Thraxton. I didn't realize you were here." His eyes narrowed thoughtfully. "But since you are . . ." He closed the door and advanced into the room with that indolent grace that was all his.

Whether it was due to her awareness of his title and position, or because of his large size, or the lazy, quizzical way he watched her, Anthony Elliot had the ability to make Anna feel like an awkward sixteen-year-old, all elbows and too-large feet. Until she'd met Sara's arrogant brother, it was a feeling she'd thought she'd outgrown.

Annoyed with herself, Anna stood, suddenly unsure of where to put her hands. She dipped a quick curtsy, then made an abrupt gesture toward the settee. "My lord."

The devil! Was that my voice? The undignified squeak infuriated her, and she tilted her chin, ready to meet his mockery. Instead he dropped his hat and gloves on a table by the door, then lazily crossed the room and waited until she returned to her chair. Then he folded his long length onto the settee, carefully moving a small table out of the way where it brushed his knee.

He looked ridiculous, like an adult propped in a child's chair. Being of above average height herself, Anna could sympathize. It was awkward always being too tall, though she doubted it was as much of an inconvenience to a man.

Anthony stretched his long legs before him and fixed her with a relentless gaze. "I hope you do not have too arduous a day planned. It looks as if it might rain."

"Sara and I are accompanying Her Grace to search for a new bonnet."

"How absorbing," he drawled, clearly indicating otherwise. "Miss Thraxton, I hope you will forgive me for intruding on you thus, but I have some concerns about my sister, and I feel you are the one who can answer them."

Anna glanced nervously toward the door. "I'm not sure I know what—"

"You are in my sister's confidence, are you not?" he asked, his voice soft.

"Of course." Though she couldn't quite tell why, she thought she detected a threatening note in his voice. She wished Sara would hurry.

"Miss Thraxton, I'm sure you are aware that my sister is not happy here in Bath."

"She has mentioned as much to me."

"I knew she would," he returned dryly. "While I am more than content to play nursemaid, it would be easier for us all if you would serve as her good friend in the upcoming months and keep me apprised of her actions."

Anna stiffened. "Lord Greyley, Sara is like a sister to me, and I do not feel comfortable speaking about her while she is not present. And I certainly would never *spy* on her."

A flicker of annoyance crossed Anthony's face, quickly hidden. He leaned forward, and Anna noted that his eyes were actually the color of cognac, flecked with slivers of green and gold. "Miss Thraxton, I know something is already afoot. I am determined to discover what it is."

"Then ask Sara. Even if I knew what you were talking about, I would never reveal myself to you."

Anthony's eyes narrowed. "Listen here. If I discover that my sister is up to something reprehensible and you had prior knowledge of it and did nothing to stop her, I will personally see to it that you pay for your part in her schemes."

Insolent ass. "Lord Greyley, anything that your sister says to me in confidence will remain that way, with or without your approval. So do your worst—I really don't care."

His eyes took on an almost feral gleam. "My dear Anna," he said, his voice caressing her name as if he alone possessed it. "I would advise you to be cautious where you throw challenges. Someone may just accept one of them."

"My dearest Lord Greyley," she replied immediately, mocking his tone so well that his eyes narrowed, "I would advise you to be more cautious in how you speak to a lady. I find your manner so offensive and arrogant that I am quite willing to do whatever I can to thwart you." Anna met his gaze calmly, though her heart pounded against the base of her throat. She hadn't been her grandfather's assistant for the past seven years for nothing; she knew oppression tactics when she saw them.

Anthony's jaw tightened, and he had just leaned forward to speak, when the door was thrown open and Sara walked energetically into the room dressed in a becoming pink-striped gown with a matching spenser. Anna smiled at the way Sara's presence brightened the room.

"There you are," Sara said, pulling on her gloves. "Aunt Delphi is getting in the carriage, and—" She stopped. "Anthony, what are you doing here?"

Sending a quelling glance at Anna, he stood. Every movement he made was unhurried and purposeful, and Anna had to control the urge to shiver. "I was just speaking with Miss Thraxton."

"Oh?" Sara said, obviously suspicious. She glanced from him to Anna and back again. "Were you, indeed? And was your conversation productive?"

He picked up his hat and gloves, turning a hard stare toward Anna. "No. Not this time."

Anna returned his gaze steadily. It was better all around if he knew where they stood. Which was on very rocky ground indeed. "Good day, Lord Greyley."

A flash of something lit his eyes to gold, and then his habitual half-asleep expression returned. Anna watched him leave with a sense of relief. He was a formidable man, one who would remember every slight and injury, no matter how accidental or valid they might be.

Sara whirled on Anna. "He wanted to know what I was doing, didn't he?"

"Yes, though I didn't tell him a thing."

"I could tell that, since he looked like a thundercloud." She linked her arm with Anna's. "Come. Aunt Delphi's already in the carriage."

It didn't take Anna long to realize that there was far more to the shopping expedition than she'd realized. Sara was alternately in far too high of spirits, chattering nonstop and making them all laugh, then becoming silent, examining each carriage that went by as if looking for a specific face.

The dowager duchess had a multitude of errands to run. As she entered the lending library to exchange her books, Sara and Anna wandered down the street, peering into store windows. Several stores away, they stood looking at a display of enameled boxes.

Sara gripped Anna's arm. "Drop your reticule."

Anna looked up from a particularly charming box trimmed in delicate scrollwork. "Drop my what?"

"Don't ask questions!" Sara whispered urgently, turning back toward the window. "Just drop it."

Mumbling to herself, Anna unlooped her reticule and dropped it on the pavement. A tall shadow crossed her, causing her to shiver.

"Pardon me, but I believe this is yours."

Anna recognized the low, seductive voice of the Earl of Bridgeton and suddenly understood her friend's odd behavior. "Why, thank you. I didn't even realize it was missing." She nudged her friend. "Look, Sara, it is the Earl of Bridgeton."

Eyes wide with feigned surprise, Sara turned toward the earl. "What a pleasant surprise!"

The earl's mouth curved into a heart-thumping grin, the sun burnishing his dark gold hair. From the width of his shoulders to the fine line of his muscular legs, everything about him bespoke male power. Anna sent a glance at Sara from under her lashes and noticed that she hadn't missed a single aspect of the earl's appearance.

Sara dipped a curtsy. "My lord, and how are you this morning?"

"Quite well, Lady Carrington. And you?"

"I'm fine, thank you."

"And how is Miss Thraxton?" He bowed, slanting Anna a cool, knowing kind of smile. "You really should be more cautious with your valuables."

"It was an accident," Sara said. "I've dropped my reticule dozens of times."

"Come, Lady Carrington," he protested gently. "Enough of this pretense. You asked me to meet you here, and here I am. What service may I perform for you?"

Cheeks bright, Sara cast a guilty glance at Anna. "Lord Bridgeton, I don't know what you are talking about. I never asked you to meet me here."

"But I have the note right here, in my waistcoat." He proceeded to reach into his pocket, but Sara's muffled curse stopped him, his eyes bright with amusement. "What's that? Did you say something, my love?"

"Yes, I did," Sara answered promptly, eyeing the earl with a strange mixture of exasperation and humor. "And I have not given you permission to call me 'my love.' "

Anna lifted her brows at that. In the year since Julius's death, Sara had shown no interest in any of the men of her acquaintance. In fact, she hadn't shown much interest in anything other than raising as many eyebrows as she could.

Sara had changed drastically while she was married to Julius. It had taken Anna months to piece together what had happened, most of it from cryptic comments in Sara's letters. Much of what she knew came from what her friend did *not* say. Anna rather thought that Julius's concept of love had been very different from Sara's and she had suffered horribly as a consequence, turning her back on the fiery, exuberant way she'd approached life.

Now, watching her friend glare at the Earl of Bridgeton, her mouth pressed into a mutinous line, Anna experienced the first stirring of hope. Perhaps it was time Sara reclaimed her own life. But was the earl worthy of Sara's regard?

Nick caught sight of Miss Thraxton's speculative look. Smothering a sense of irritation, he looked down the street, his gaze narrowing as he heard a familiar voice. "Ah, Valmont! Just the man I was looking for."

Edmund Valmont looked up from where he was assisting his great-aunt out of the library. His arms piled with books, a cashmere shawl, a fan, and a small pillow, he blinked uncertainly at Nick. "Looking for me? Haven't offended you, have I? Because if I have, then I didn't mean it. Least, I don't think I did. I once thought about calling you out, but that was years ago. Of course—"

"Edmund," Nick broke in. "I was just asking Miss Thraxton and Lady Carrington to stroll with me through the park, and we would like to request your company."

Her back ramrod straight, Sara said, "I don't recall any such conversation."

Nick lifted a brow. "Yes, but we've already established you have a faulty memory. After all, you did not remember this." He touched the pocket that contained her note. "And you wrote it only this morning."

Sara's smile tightened, and she spoke through clenched teeth. "Perhaps we can find a place to have a more *private* communication."

"Exactly my point," he murmured, then turned to Lady Birlington, who was just following Edmund out of the lending library. "Would you be so kind as to give your nephew leave to escort one of these young ladies through the park?"

Lady Birlington came alive at the mention of young ladies. She looked down her nose at first Sara and then Anna, brightening as she did so. "Why, it is Delphinea's niece and her friend, Thraxton's granddaughter. Good hips, the both of 'em. Of course Edmund may go."

Edmund's mouth opened and closed, then opened again. "But Aunt Maddie! I don't think you want me to be gone for—"

"Nonsense. You'll never find a wife if you stay tied to my side." Her carriage pulled up to the curb, and her rather elderly footman slowly climbed down and went to open the door. "Just put those things in the carriage for me and go for a walk."

"But Aunt Maddie, I—"

Sara's aunt bustled out of the lending library next, two books clasped in her hands. She came to a halt when she saw the small group.

Lady Birlington waved her cane. "There you are,

Delphinea. We have just been arranging a small party for the young people. Why don't you come and travel in my carriage while the children walk to the end of the park?"

"Children?" Lady Langtry looked at Nick, her face coloring vividly. "I don't think that would be a very good—"

"Poppy seeds," Lady Birlington said. She turned to her carriage and allowed her footman to assist her inside. After disposing herself on the plush velvet squabs, she gestured to Delphi. "Come on. We haven't got all day."

"Yes, but I have errands to run and—"

"I have some errands myself. We'll do them together. Come along, now. Let the young people have their fun."

Frowning, Delphi allowed the footman to assist her inside the carriage. "I'm not sure it's proper to leave them alone with—"

"They won't be alone; they'll be all together. No harm in that. Not unless Bridgeton decides to do away with Edmund." Her blue eyes narrowed, and she leaned out the window to look thoughtfully at Nick.

He bowed. "I shall attempt to restrain myself."

"Thank you. Though the urge is understandable, it would be quite rude in front of the ladies."

Edmund tugged on his cravat. "Aunt Maddie, I really think I should—"

"You'll escort Miss Thraxton. I think Lady Carrington would be best left to Lord Bridgeton; she'll know what to do if he gets out of hand. Just to be certain, we'll send my footman to walk with you." Lady Birlington leaned out of the carriage. "Mathers!"

The elderly man stood at attention, his eyes watery and unfocused. "Yes, my lady?"

"The young people are going for a walk. Stay with them." She settled back into the seat with a satisfied sigh. "There. That should take care of the proprieties."

Within moments, the carriage was inching its way down the street and the small group was on their way to the park, hindered only by the slow pace of the footman.

Nick wondered if it had been Lady Birlington's intention all along to saddle them with as slow a creature as she could find, thereby prolonging their walk. She wasn't known as Mad Maddie for nothing. Her elderly frame held an iron-hard spirit and a mind that was sharper than most realized.

They reached the edge of the park and started down one of the shaded paths. It was quite cool, the pale sunlight dappling the pathway before them.

Anna and Edmund trailed behind, the footman following. Nick sent a side glance down at his companion, who was staring straight ahead, unappreciative of the beauty around her. "Well, my love? You wished to see me?"

"Not here," she said with some asperity, glancing over her shoulder. "I asked to speak with you in private."

"If we were alone, we would be doing far more than just talking." Just walking beside her, not even touching, was a heady experience. Had they been alone . . . his breeches tightened, and he cursed his lack of concentration.

Sara sighed. "I wanted to ask you about Sir Bawton. Is he . . . I wanted to make sure he was well."

"He's fine. A little dizzy, but not enough that anyone will notice. He never made much sense to begin with."

"You saw him today, then?"

Nick nodded. "He had the devil of a bruise on his forehead, but other than that, he was fine."

"Thank goodness. I was concerned that he was more injured than he appeared."

"No," Nick said, taking the moment to appreciate the way she walked, with quick, decisive steps, as if she knew exactly where she was going. He'd never seduced a woman of such character, and it was proving to be vastly amusing.

"I wonder if he's told anyone—" She caught herself and shrugged. "Not that it matters, of course."

"Never fear. I took it upon myself to make sure that Sir Bawton will not utter a word about your little meeting last night. He was very embarrassed when he saw me. In fact, he crossed to the other side of the street as if afraid I might recognize him."

Her brow wrinkled. "Perhaps I *should* wish him to start a rumor. God knows, it can only help my cause."

Just as it would weaken Nick's. If Lady Carrington were successful in publicly ruining herself, he would have to give up his hopes of making her his mistress.

He glanced down at Sara's profile, admiring her thick, black hair and the sweep of her absurdly long lashes. He wanted to trace the pure line of her straight little nose and the stubborn tilt of her chin with his mouth, ending with the taste of her on his lips. "Sara, why did you send for me?"

Faint color rose beneath the paleness of her skin. "I wish to ask a favor."

"What?"

Gratitude warmed Sara's heart. She'd lain awake most of the night pondering her options. As day broke, she'd bounded out of bed and dashed off the note to Nick, sending it before she could change her mind. "As you are aware, I haven't had much luck in locating a suitable man to wed."

"So I've noticed." Though there was a decided smile in his eyes, he didn't appear to be mocking her.

"It has dawned on me that I may need some assistance."

"Ah. You wish me to teach you the arts of seduction so that you can capture your quarry more quickly?"

"No, I just need assistance in locating the proper candidate. I'm perfectly capable of handling the rest."

"Are you, indeed?"

She knew he was referring to her abortive attempts with Hewlette and Bawton. "If I had been more careful in my selection, I would already be married and free to go my own way."

"I see. So my only duty is to point out likely candidates for a seduction?" Glancing around, Nick realized that Edmund and Anna had fallen so far behind that they were nowhere to be seen. He immediately took Sara's arm and left the path through a break in the shrubbery.

Some distance away, he found a low bench beside a large, knobby tree, its branches spreading far over the thick grass. He led her to the alcove and watched as she stood near the edge of the bench as if ready to flee at a moment's notice. "I think I'm beginning to understand."

She sent him a sharp glance. "Do you?"

"Since you are asking for my assistance in locating a suitable husband, I can only suppose you wish me to find someone who possesses a complete lack of morality."

An expression of disbelief crossed her face. "No. I was simply looking for someone more . . . malleable."

"Malleable?"

"Yes. Someone who will not interfere with my life."

He laughed—she was a delight. He placed his foot on the bench, then leaned forward to trace his thumb across her bottom lip. The touch was as velvety soft as it was forbidden. "To begin with, you should avoid men like me."

Sara's entire body flushed, and she was hard-pressed not to turn her face toward his touch. She held her breath until he dropped his hand from her cheek.

"It's possible, but it will take time. And what about Greyley? He will get in the way."

"I'll find a way past Anthony." Perhaps with some help from Anna, who seemed able to capture Anthony's unalleviated attention without even trying.

Nick smiled. "I have no doubt you will rid yourself of your brother once you put your mind to it. But that's just the beginning." He crossed his arms over his broad chest and watched her like a wolf stalking its prey. "You must realize the dangers. To make your proposition, you will need to be alone with this man. There is a possibility that he might get carried away."

"Then I shall scream."

"And if no one hears you? Or worse yet—" He stepped closer. "What if this paragon won't let you scream?"

"Then he wouldn't be a paragon, would he?"

"No man is a saint, Sara."

Sara wasn't sure she'd like a saint. "How could he stop me?"

Nick kissed her. One moment he was standing beside her, and the next he was holding her against him, his mouth covering hers, his hands roaming at will.

Her first impulse was to fight him, but his kiss stole every thought from her head. Nick's passion wrapped fiercely about her, drowning her in a wave of sensuality so overwhelming it frightened her.

Suddenly he released her and she staggered backward, her knees hitting the edge of the bench. She sat down so hard her teeth rattled. Her mind whirled at the feelings that raced through her, that his touch evoked. *Good God, no wonder the man has women lying in wait for him.*

Nick stared down at her with eyes so dark they were almost black.

Sara pressed her trembling fingers to her lips. "You didn't need to do that."

"You've been begging to be kissed since our first meeting."

"Not by you," she replied, stung at the faint sneer she thought she detected in his voice.

"No," he agreed with a faint smile. "Not by me."

Slowly Sara's heartbeat calmed, her face cooled, and her hands stopped shaking. But her thoughts were still distracted by his kiss. He was right; she had no idea how to deal with an onslaught like that. "Will you show me how to deal with kisses?"

Nick's gaze fixed on her mouth. After a prolonged silence, he said, "It would take practice."

"Practice?"

"Oh, yes. Plenty of practice. A few hours, perhaps."

Something inside her melted. "Hours?"

"To build your resistance." Amusement softened his expression. "If you'd been kissed properly before now, my sweet, you wouldn't have responded so eagerly. It's rather like wine: If you drink a little each night, it doesn't affect you as strongly when you imbibe more."

She didn't believe him for a second, but the thought of hours of drugging kisses sounded too delightfully sinful to refuse. "How do I know this isn't a trick?"

"You are wise to question me. Men don't always tell the truth." He glinted down at her. "Let that be lesson one."

"I already knew that," she sniffed. "Shall we rejoin the others?"

Nick grinned. His little widow was not only exciting, she was no one's fool. He supposed he should feel guilty, but he didn't. He felt more alive than he had in months. If it took pretending to be her friend to gain her as his mistress, then so be it. "Very well. Together, we will reach your goal."

"Thank you." She hesitated, then said, "But what will you want in return?"

"One kiss—one that has nothing to do with our lessons. Whenever and wherever I choose."

"That's all? You'd go to such trouble just for a kiss?"

She was so delightfully innocent. Nick tipped her face to his. "That and your word that you will keep our agreement secret. You may wish to ruin yourself, but I do not."

"Fair enough."

"Very good." The faint murmur of voices reached them. "Ah, Miss Thraxton and the estimable Edmund. Shall we return to the path and wait for them?"

Sara nodded.

Anna and Edmund soon arrived, exclaiming over how they'd been searching for the missing couple. Panting, the footman lurched up the path in their wake. Nick turned their questions aside with a casual confidence that left Edmund gaping and Anna watching him with a suspicious stare.

As Nick walked beside Sara to the waiting carriage, his thoughts were engaged with their agreement. He'd been wanting a way to reach her, and now he had it—and the fact that she'd sought him out made it all the more delicious. Smiling, Nick handed her into the carriage.

He would enjoy teaching his charge very, very much.

Chapter 11

⟨~∽◯◯∽~⟩

Like a butterfly emerging from a cocoon, Hib-berton Hall shook off the must and mold that had held it prisoner for so many years. The east hall was finally finished, the roof repaired, the fireplaces reinforced, and the odors of paint and wax mingled in the large, empty bedchambers. New rugs had been ordered and would soon arrive. The furnishings deemed salvageable would soon be returned to their places. Mr. Pratt was making a list of items that needed to be purchased.

The great hall was almost completed, as well. The walls had been replastered and painted, the floors sanded and refinished, the paneling cleaned and shined. All that was left was the replacement of the oak paneling in the foyer.

Last would come the renovation of the west hall. Because of the extensive roof damage, that would take months, even with the army of skilled craftsmen.

The late-afternoon sun was resting in the tops of the trees when Nick returned from town, his mind lingering on his walk with Sara. He left his phaeton with the groom and entered Hibberton. A footman took his hat and gloves and withdrew with a quiet murmur. Nick paused and looked around the great hall. Beautifully refurbished, the floors gleaming, the furnishings sumptuous—he should have felt the stirring of triumph, but found simply a sense of belonging. Of coming home.

He'd never recognized that low hum of dissatisfaction that had always pervaded his actions and thoughts for what it was—the desire to have a home of his own. Nick walked slowly through the hall, his footsteps ringing in the silence. He supposed he shouldn't have been surprised; the nomadic existence he'd led with his mother, following her as she went from protector to protector, had never given him the luxury of belonging anywhere.

Nick walked to the front window of the library to look out at the leaf-scattered lawn. Thank God he no longer had a heart to break—Violette's death had effectively ended that possibility. He would never allow himself to suffer from the surfeit of emotion that had crippled his mother's life.

He trusted in something far stronger than love's illusions: pure, unadulterated lust. Which was exactly what bound him to Sara. He rubbed a hand across his mouth as if he could still feel the pressure of her lips on his. There was passion in her, and a warmth of spirit that made being with her a delight.

Nick looked around the library and for an instant, he imagined her coming into the room in that impetuous way she had, a smile on her lips, her eyes sparkling. Suddenly the room warmed and brightened, the weight of the silence disappearing.

As he turned from the window, a sudden flicker of light flashed in the corner of his eye, then vanished. Nick clenched his eyes closed, pressing a hand over them. *Bloody hell, not again.* As he stood, the tightness behind his eyes increased; a slow, tormenting pressure built against his temple. Why did this have to happen now, of all times? He was to meet Sara tomorrow.

Still, the pain increased. Unable to stand it any longer, he left the library and made his way to the huge master chamber. Someone had opened the curtains and blinding light streamed in through the windows. Cursing, he closed the curtains and fell onto the bed, praying the pain would cease.

Aunt Delphi floated into the room, coming to an abrupt halt when she saw Sara standing by the window. "Oh! I didn't see you—Why, Sara! Are you crying?" She set a bandbox on a table and came forward, her face folded in worry.

"Heavens, no, Aunt Delphi." But she felt like it. Anthony had received word this morning that Marcus was on his way to Bath. Her time was drawing short, and she had not seen Nick in over four days.

Where was he? He'd promised to assist her and then disappeared. Well, she knew the dashing Earl of Bridgeton was no saint. Whatever kept him from meeting his promise to her was undoubtedly reprehensible, and she wished nothing to do with it.

Sara caught Delphi's curious gaze and forced a smile. "Did you hear that Marcus is coming for a visit?"

"Anthony seems relieved."

"I'm sure he is." He'd been furious when he'd discovered Lady Birlington's matchmaking had led to a walk in the park with a man he castigated as a bounder, a rakehell, and worse. He'd vowed that it would take an army to watch her, then he'd clearly called in the troops. Sighing a little, Sara turned toward her aunt, catching sight of the bandbox. "Have you been shopping?"

A look of inexpressible mischief crossed Delphi's face. "Yes, all morning. And I bought a hat!"

Sara blinked, as much at her aunt's enthusiasm as at the unfamiliar expression on her face. Aunt Delphi *never* looked mischievous. "May I see it?"

Delphi glanced at the door. "I suppose so . . . just wait." She scurried across the room and closed the door, then brought the box to where Sara stood. "I've been wanting this since I first saw it, but I was afraid it was far too unconventional." She opened the box and pulled out an extraordinary confection of ribbons and bows and feathers.

More feathers than any hat had a right to. And the colors . . . "My, that's quite—Have you tried it on?"

"Not yet," Delphi said, her eyes bright with excitement. Her hands fluttered over the hat, as if unsure what to stroke first—a red-velvet ribbon, a lavender bow, or one of the *many* huge orange feathers. "Do you think I should?"

It was so uncharacteristic of her aunt that Sara smiled. Perhaps Delphi was just trying to amuse herself since the comte's disappearance. He was rarely about now, and Sara could only hope that Nick had warned the man off, although it seemed too chivalrous a gesture for the decadent earl. She pulled the hat from the box. "Of course you must try it on. Here, I'll help."

Within moments, Aunt Delphi stood in front of the small mirror above the mantle, the preposterous hat on her head. She looked anxiously at Sara. "What do you think? Is it too shocking? I don't want anyone to think I'm fast."

Sara gave Delphi a considering look. "No. I don't think it's too shocking." In fact, the bonnet framed the older woman's face in a most attractive way, the profusion of color highlighting the color in Delphi's face. "In fact, it looks wonderful."

Delphi gave a sudden laugh, looking years younger. "Do you think so? I had hoped . . . that is, I was thinking that perhaps I should also purchase a new gown." Her hand smoothed over her sensible gray walking dress.

"Definitely," Sara said. "If you'd like, I'll go with you."

"I wish we could leave this instant, but I promised Lady Birlington I would attend her this morning, and she would be disappointed if I did not come."

"Tomorrow, then. I've nothing planned." *Thanks to that wastrel Nicholas Montrose*, she thought sourly, as her aunt almost skipped from the room.

There was something strange going on with Delphi. But since she seemed to have gotten over her infatuation, Sara could only be thankful. Perhaps her aunt was just beginning to realize her possibilities, taking control of her own life for the first time in years.

It was a pity Sara couldn't do the same. Frowning, she wondered yet again what had happened to Nick. She was tired of waiting, of wondering where he was and when he'd contact her. Her gaze drifted toward the secretary and rested on the inkpot. Within moments, Sara's quill scratched across a missive addressed to the less-than-honorable Earl of Bridgeton.

"Hopkins will tell," Anna said in a low voice.

Sara glanced at the coachman's narrow back where he sat perched in front of the landau, his gnarled hands clenched about the reins. "Let him. I'm not doing anything improper." *Not yet, anyway.*

"Sara, you invited a man—a dissolute rake—to secretly meet you in the park. You have to admit that's a bit reprehensible."

"Nonsense," Sara said heartily. "All I'm going to do is speak with him for a moment. Surely there's no harm in that." *If he even comes.*

At her directions, Hopkins pulled the landau to a

stop in front of a small clearing. Sara nervously rubbed her gloved hands on her knees and wondered if she should dismount. She didn't want to appear too eager, but by the same token, she and Nick had a bargain, and she was determined he was going to live up to it.

The sound of a lone horse cantering closer made her heart leap into her throat. Nick's tall form came into view, and it was difficult for her not to stare. No man rode a horse so well, nor looked so dashing while doing it.

When he got closer she noticed that he appeared pale, his eyes heavily set, his mouth deeply lined. Her mouth tightened at the sight—she'd seen just such signs on Julius after a night of debauchery. She didn't know why it mattered, but it hurt that he would come to see her after a night of carousing.

Worse was the fact that his wan appearance only increased his handsomeness, the pallor complementing his blond good looks. It was infuriating, to say the least.

He approached the landau and pulled up, tipping his hat as he did so.

She jutted out her chin. "What did you do last night? You look horrible."

"Sara!" Anna said, her face as pink as the rosettes on the collar of her pelisse.

But Nick appeared amused. His gaze flickered over her, a wry smile touching his lips. "I've been ill."

"Perhaps you should leave the wine to those who are more used to it."

"Oh, I'm used to it, sweet. Never doubt that. Now, do you wish to sit there and berate me, or would you like to take a walk? We have unfinished business, you and I."

Sara winced as Hopkins gasped in surprise. "Couldn't you be a little more circumspect?" she asked under her breath.

"No," he said in an equally low voice. "Not for what you have in mind."

"And just what *do* I have in mind?"

He grinned, and her heart flipped over. "Lessons," he said, the word a caress.

It was a wonder she didn't poof into a cloud of ash. He dismounted and looped his reins over the back of the landau, then returned to her side and opened the small door, holding out his hand to assist her.

Sara hesitated, glancing uncertainly at Anna.

"Afraid?" he asked softly.

She was climbing out of the seat before the word faded into silence. By God, she'd not let him cow *her*. He reached for her as she hesitated on the last step of the carriage and she recklessly released her hold, hoping to reach the ground before he could touch her. She was successful only in losing her balance. As she spun around she came into contact with the warm wall of Nick's chest, and his hands, the ones she'd so assiduously avoided, clasped about her waist.

With his fingers burning through her clothing, a wild tingling raced through her. She was agonizingly aware of his chest against her back, of his thighs against her bottom.

He set her away from him. "My, how graceful."

She shot him a baleful glare. Anna remained in her seat, staring rigidly ahead; Hopkins merely gaped.

Sara cleared her throat. "I am going to speak with Lord Bridgeton in private. We will be sitting on that bench, in plain view. Hopkins, you stay with Miss Thraxton."

The groom closed his mouth, a stubborn light in his eye. "I should go with you, my lady."

"And leave Miss Thraxton unattended? I think not. We'll be back before you know it."

Nick took Sara's arm and led her to the bench. It was well shaded, though directly in sight of the landau.

Sara took a seat and looked up at Nick. "I am sorry to disturb you, but—"

"I have discovered the man for your schemes."

She swallowed. "Already?"

"When one knows what one is looking for, it is not so difficult."

"Who is he?"

"All in good time, my dear. First, there is the little matter of a lesson." His gaze locked on her mouth. "You cannot run with the wolves without knowing how to fight like one."

"I took care of Lord Hewlette."

"But not before he'd gotten far closer to you than you wished." The sudden grimness in his voice made Sara pause.

"Very well. But you mustn't forget that Hopkins is watching us this very moment."

"Then we will have to leave. Give him a moment to doze." Nick sent her a sardonic glance. "I'm surprised you didn't invite your aunt and your brother along, too."

"Well, I like that! It isn't my reputation I was worried about—it was yours. You are the one who wanted to remain scandal-free, not me."

That must have startled him, for he looked down at her for a long time. "Thank you."

His voice was low and sweet, and it unexpectedly made Sara want to weep. She cleared her throat. "It was no bother." She looked back at him, curiously examining his expression. "What makes you so different from every other man I've ever met?"

He didn't ask her what she meant. It was one of the things she liked about him. He shrugged. "Life has never favored me."

"Ah, your mother."

He sent her a sharp glance. "What do you know about my mother?"

"Only what Lady Birlington told me, and it was amazingly little."

"If she told you anything, it was too much." He glanced at Hopkins and smiled. "Look. He is already beginning to nod off."

"It won't take long at all. Sometimes he falls asleep while he's at the reins." She glanced back at Nick. "How old were you when your mother died?"

His face closed. "Thirteen."

"How horrible for you."

"Was it?" he asked without a bit of emotion in his voice. "In a way, it was a relief."

Sara could only guess at the pain that simple statement hid. She looked at the earl's cool demeanor and realized how successfully he managed to keep all conversation away from himself. "Do you want to talk about it?"

His expression slipped, and she glimpsed a flicker of pain so raw that her own heart ached. Then he reached down and drew her to her feet. "We have better things to do than talk." So saying, he led her down the path, well out of sight of the carriage, to a halt by a wide grassy spot. "Are you ready, sweet?"

A slow, slumberous smile softened the lines around his mouth. He took her hand and turned it palm up. With an expert flick of his thumb, he unfastened one of the tiny mother-of-pearl buttons. Her glove parted to reveal the tender skin of her inner wrist. Her skin tingled as if he'd stroked it.

"Wh-what are you going to do?" Heavens, was that her voice sounding so breathy and unsure?

He lightly skimmed his fingers over the exposed skin, and Sara drew in a sharp breath. Thousands of chills danced up her arm and settled in the most unexpected places.

Nick flicked open another button, and another, then gently drew the glove from her hand. "The mistake most women make when dealing with a man is in believing that all pleasure comes from the sexual act itself. It is far, far more than that. The beginning, the expectation, can be almost as sweet as the act itself."

"Can it?" She cursed her voice for quavering in such a hideously weak fashion.

"It takes a certain amount of knowledge to tempt a man without getting . . ." his gaze dropped to her lips ". . . bitten."

The fingers of her free hand found the loop to her reticule and she clutched it to her. "I'm not afraid of getting bitten."

"You should be."

"The only time a woman is in any danger with a rake is if she loses her heart." She met his gaze evenly. "I have too much control to allow such a thing to occur."

His sudden smile made him all too appealing. "Do you, indeed?"

Sara boldly placed her hand on his chest, her fingers curving slightly so that they pressed into his skin. "I thought we were coming here to practice kissing."

His gaze narrowed into a frown. "You don't know what game you are playing."

"Don't I?" She was glad to see the tension along his jaw. She slowly slid her hand up his chest.

His hand covered hers, halting it. "You are an intoxicating woman, Sara. I don't think you know how much so."

Agonizingly aware of the warmth of his hand over hers, Sara wished her heart wouldn't gallop in such a reckless way, that her head didn't feel so light.

Nick removed her hand from his chest. "You certainly seem to understand the basic principle behind a seduction."

"Have you forgotten that I've been married before? I also have five brothers, and none of them is saintly."

"No, but they are honorable, and in a man that is often the same thing." The glint in Nick's eyes made her shift uncomfortably. "I don't blame your brother for keeping such close watch on you. You are dangerous."

"But you haven't paid him the least heed." She looked at him consideringly. "Why aren't you afraid of Anthony? Everyone else is."

"Perhaps I've decided the reward far outweighs the danger."

The seductive timbre of his voice made her shiver. She hated it when he did that—made her feel as if she were special. She had the lowering conviction that he did the same to all women, that it was as natural to him as breathing.

"I was afraid you'd refuse to come today," she blurted.

He slanted a gaze at her that left her unaccountably hot. "And miss this?"

Sara swallowed. "You said you had a potential husband for me. Who is it?"

"All in good time, love." He loosened the ribbons of her bonnet. "Will you be at the theatre on Wednesday?"

"Of course. The new play opens. But who is—"

Nick lifted the bonnet from her head. "I will meet you there and point him out to you. Then . . ." He tossed the bonnet to the ground. "As you say, you can deal with that part."

"Of course," she said with false bravado, looking at the discarded bonnet with some alarm.

"Excellent," he said, taking her arm and guiding her into a secluded alcove. "I won't worry, then. In the meantime, aren't we supposed to be practicing something?"

The amusement in his eyes made her grin in return, and she suddenly felt as light as a feather, almost giddy with humor. The sun shone, they were alone in an idyllic setting, and Nick's arms were slipping about her waist.

Then his mouth covered hers. He kissed her as if he would devour her, and she matched his ardor with her own. When he finally broke the kiss Sara's heart was thudding dangerously, and she belatedly realized she was grasping his lapels.

When she had caught her breath, she asked, "Lesson two?"

He looked down at her, a strange glint in his eyes. "Lesson two: never underestimate the power of a simple kiss."

"Is that why you asked for a kiss as payment?"

His mouth curved into a smile that made her heart thud an extra beat. "Of course."

She watched him warily. "It isn't very chivalrous of you to ask for payment."

"If I were chivalrous, I wouldn't be helping you ruin your life."

A sudden wave of uncertainty made Sara change the subject. "What other lessons must I learn?"

He took her hand and placed it on his arm, his

fingers trailing a heated path across her knuckles. "Number three: If you want to show a man you are interested in him, then touch him."

"Touch?" Her voice was so husky that it was almost a whisper. She cleared her throat. "In what way?"

His mouth quirked into a self-satisfied smile. "Directly."

Her gaze drifted downward to his perfectly fitted breeches. The expensive cloth clearly outlined his male member—long and thick and taut with desire. And the man was *smiling* at her, as if he found his arousal amusing. Or was it anticipation of her reaction?

Without taking time to consider her actions, she reached out and placed her hand on the line of his turgid member, her fingers closing over him and squeezing ever so slightly.

Nick's smile froze in place. Slowly, his thick lashes dropped over his eyes, and, for an instant, he stood, not moving.

"Well?" she said silkily. "Did I do it right?"

"Not quite. My breeches are still buttoned."

She snatched her hand away, her cheeks hot. The man was completely without honor.

His mouth twitched into a painful smile. "Actually, that wasn't quite what I meant by 'touch.' "

Embarrassment heated her face. "No?"

"No. I meant something a little more . . . subtle. Like the brush of a finger along a man's arm, the feel of your cheek against his as you dance. Men find that intoxicating—though *not* as intoxicating as what you did to me."

"I think we've had enough lessons for today," she said stiffly, turning away.

He caught her hand and pulled her back around to face him. "You are a surprising woman, Sara Lawrence."

The low timbre of his voice softened her embarrassment, and she looked at him expectantly.

"What would you do if a rake whispered that your eyes shimmer like a pool of water, that your skin is as soft as silk, that your voice is like the brush of velvet over bared skin?"

"I'd laugh." Unless it was Nick who spoke such ridiculous platitudes. Especially if he were attempting to seduce her.

"Tsk, tsk, Sara. Such a heartless response would discourage your opponent and make him slink off into the shrubbery and leave you to your own devices. That is not what you want, sweet. You want him bold, passionate, crazed with lust."

That was true, especially the crazed with lust part. "I will need to encourage him. Which you have already shown me how to do."

He smiled, slow and sure, his eyes warm. "So assume I am a man you have just lured into the garden. Why don't you practice your wiles on me?"

Sara bit her lip. If she were ever truly alone with Nick, there would be no stopping.

He leaned closer so that his voice brushed over her like the touch of wind on damp skin. "Come to

Hibberton Hall this evening, Sara. I'll send a carriage. We can practice in earnest there."

Before today, she would have agreed. But now she knew all too well the danger of being alone with him. "What would that accomplish?"

"There are things you should know if you are going to attempt to seduce a man, Sara."

"I just want him to agree to marry me, nothing more."

He waved an impatient hand. "If you want a man to come to that point so quickly, you are going to have to seduce him. It's the only way."

As much as she hated to admit it, he was right. "Still . . . I think you are just trying to get me alone to kiss me again."

"If I wanted to kiss you, you would not be talking right now."

"What if I didn't want to be kissed?" she asked, intrigued.

His eyes darkened and Sara's breath caught in her throat. They were completely secluded, the landau too far away for Hopkins or Anna to hear her cries. Her heart pounding, she took a step away from Nick, the rough bark of a tree pressing into her back.

Nick placed his hand by her shoulder and leaned closer. "Lesson four: Never challenge a man unless you are prepared to deal with the consequences."

A shimmer of hot lust fluttered in her stomach and she was agonizingly aware of his mouth, just a scant inch from hers. She looked at the sensuous line of his lips and found that she couldn't swallow.

"You aren't kissing me," she whispered, trying to make her mind work when all it wanted to do was explode in the white heat of his embrace.

He straightened, a faint smile on his lips. "I don't need to. See? You know far less about men than you think, my love."

"I know enough to know they cannot be trusted," she blazed up at him. "*Ever.*"

"True. So what will you do once you are married?"

"Whatever I want."

"And what if what you want is . . . me?"

Her mouth went dry. "You?"

He lifted a finger to trace the edge of her mouth to her chin, the touch leaving a trail of heat. "You want me, Sara."

"How do you know?"

"Because you disarmed yourself." At her look of confusion, he pointed to her feet. "You dropped your reticule."

As if asleep, she looked down at where her reticule rested by her foot, right beside her forgotten bonnet. Damn it, it was unfair. He had but to bring his lips near hers and she lost her mind.

A tiny prickle of heat stirred in her stomach. Nick's subtle cologne was a deadly mixture of sandalwood and raw heat. "I drop my reticule all of the time. It is something of a bad habit for me."

"And this is something of a bad habit for *me*." Nick placed his other hand on the tree by Sara's other shoulder, trapping her in the makeshift prison of his arms.

He smiled softly, and Sara could not look away

from his mouth. "Poor Sara. To be so much among men and still not understand the most basic tenet. It is the pursuit, not the capture, that thrills most men." His gaze slid over her face, touching on her brows, her cheeks, then coming back to rest on her mouth. "A kiss is just the beginning of the war, the first skirmish. As such, it is vastly important."

"If I wanted to get free, I could kick you," she said, although her bones were turning to the consistency of warm butter.

"Could you?" He leaned forward and trailed his lips across her forehead, stopping at her temple, where his warm breath stirred the tendrils of her hair. Sara closed her eyes against the onslaught of raw sensuality that melted the last of her resistance. For an instant, she wanted him so fiercely she was hard-pressed not to lean into his arms and toss her inhibitions to the wind.

"Sara," he murmured against her cheek, "your objective is to tempt the man you decide to marry until he is crazed with lust. Until he decides he must have you at all costs—even marriage. A simple kiss will not be enough."

"No?"

Nick had to stifle a grin at the look of pure astonishment on her face. "Of course not. He must be so crazed for you that he will brave those angry brothers of yours and commit himself to the wedding vows before **he** knows what he's done."

She frowned. "What are you suggesting?"

"In addition to a kiss, you want to look a little . . . disheveled."

"Disheveled?" Her voice rose an octave. "How?"

His brows rose devilishly. "You might want to muss your gown a bit." His fingers dropped to her neck. Her skin warmed his fingertips and heat stirred in his loins. Keeping his face bland, he trailed his hand across her shoulder and pushed down the shoulder of her gown. Her skin gleamed white and perfect, the delicate hollows at the base of her throat pooling with seductive shadows.

She stared up at him, her breath coming swiftly, her chest rising and falling rapidly.

"Do you—" She broke off to swallow. "Do you think this would cause him to want me more?"

"Oh, yes," he said, aware of the tightness of his breeches.

She wet her lips, her pink tongue tracing a quick line across her mouth before disappearing. "Then I shall have to try it."

"Then I think," he said, one finger following the delicate slope of her neck where it met her shoulder, "it would be even better if you were to do this." He removed a pin from her hair and a thick, dusky curl fell across her luminescent skin. He removed another pin and another, until a cloud of rich waves fell about her, caressing the curve of her bared shoulder. Nick took a slow breath, inhaling the scent of lavender.

She raised her eyes to his. "Do I . . . do I look seductive?"

"God, yes," he whispered as he stared down into her eyes, mesmerized by the pale blue, so startling between her black lashes. Pounding lust roared in his ears—and before he knew what he was doing, he kissed her. Burningly.

He had to have her. To taste her. To make her his. He wanted her thoughts to be of him and no one else.

At first, she stiffened beneath his onslaught. He yanked her against him, his hand kneading her tender flesh through her dress. Instead of pulling away, as he half expected, she clutched his shoulders and was soon returning his kiss with the same passion. The kiss shifted, expanded into something else. Something more. Nick stilled in shock, and Sara leaned into him, moaning into his mouth, her hands entangled in the folds of his coat.

Passion crashed through him, tightening his groin painfully with deep-seated need. He'd wanted her since he'd first seen her, and now she was his for the taking.

But not entirely. He wanted her in his bed, willing and pliant beneath him. He wanted her spirit and fire tangled in his sheets, the heavenly scent of lavender on his pillows. Every sinew of his being yearned for her, and it was with the greatest difficulty that he broke the embrace and released her, his breathing loud in the silence. She staggered backward toward the tree, her hair a cloud of black about her flushed face, her lips swollen and red from his kiss.

For a long moment neither spoke, they just stood and stared as their breathing slowly subsided to normal. Nick rubbed a hand across his neck. "Sara, we must—"

"Hopkins will be frantic and so will Anna." She shoved herself away from the tree and adjusted her gown, her face red. She put a trembling hand to her hair. "My pins."

He retrieved three from the ground and held them out. She snatched them as if afraid she'd burn her fingers on his skin. Considering the smoldering embers of desire that scorched him still, she was wise to fear it.

Sara attempted to put her hair back in some sort of order, her hands trembling. After a moment, she muttered a curse and then pulled her bonnet back over her hair. "Thank you very much for your lessons. I've learned quite a lot."

So had he. Far more than he'd anticipated. "I hope you don't think my actions were too forceful."

Her gaze flew to his. "You had a very valid point. I—I never knew that some men could make a woman forget her objectives." She took a breath, calming herself. "I shall have to prevent that from occurring. But now, I must return to Anna. I look forward to seeing you at the theatre on Wednesday."

She left, the scent of lavender trailing in her wake. Nick stared down at her reticule at his feet. The next time he kissed Lady Carrington, it would be as he carried her to his bed. Smiling to himself, he made his way back to his horse.

Chapter 12

Hibberton Hall rang with the sound of an off-key baritone, the French ditty echoing down the stairs and into the foyer. Nick paused in handing Wiggs his hat and gloves.

After a thoughtful moment, the elderly butler said, "I believe the comte is very talented. For a Frenchman, that is."

The voice increased, careering even more wildly off-key.

Nick grimaced. "I would grant him 'loud,' but I draw the line at 'talented.' "

The butler's blue eyes twinkled. "Yes, my lord." He took the earl's coat and made as if to turn away.

"Wiggs," Nick said, "I believe I owe you ten guineas."

The ancient butler drew himself up. "Yes, my lord. The staff worked hard to complete your task. It was quite gratifying to see them work together in such a way."

"I will have Pratt bring the money to you today. I hope the staff has resolved their difference of opinion over the water stain in the sitting room?"

Wiggs sighed. "I fear we are never to resolve that issue, my lord. Now that the room has been redone, the stain is no longer evident. However, I venture to think that the ten guineas will go a long way to keeping them more focused on their tasks."

"Thank you, Wiggs. Please convey my compliments to the staff."

The elderly butler bowed, then hobbled away.

It was gratifying how the efficiency of the servants had increased right along with the improvements on the Hall. Like Wiggs, they walked taller, held themselves with pride, and were quicker and more efficient in completing their tasks. As more and more of the house opened, Nick had asked Mr. Pratt to hire more maids and some new footmen. The infusion of new faces delighted the old staff, who suddenly had a whole squadron of underlings to order about.

Nick continued to the library, where he sank into a chair behind the large desk. The memory of the kiss burned brightly. He'd never met anyone quite like Sara Lawrence. Her emotions were never far from the surface; she was a woman who would care deeply when she chose to.

The thought disturbed him more than he wanted to admit.

The door to the library opened. "Ah, there you are." Henri sailed into the room and threw himself into a chair opposite the desk. "It is a beautiful day!"

"Isn't it?" Nick agreed. The sun was shining, his servant woes seemed to have resolved themselves, and the woman who was going to be his mistress had sought him out. All in all, it was a damned good day to be master of Hibberton Hall.

Henri sent him a considering glance. "You seem to be feeling much better this morning."

Nick shrugged. He did not like to talk about his illness, especially not now, when the day gleamed golden and his heart was unexpectedly light. There would be time later, when the illness caught him in its final grip and he was unable to fight the pain without the assistance of the little brown bottles that had lured his mother to her death. But this was not a day for thinking of such things.

The comte sighed happily. "It is unseasonably warm today, isn't it? But then, you know that—you were abroad early this morning, *mon ami*. Where did you go?"

"The park."

"But you detest the park. You said it was too small and too crowded and too—"

"I was wrong." Nick pulled a stack of papers to him that Mr. Pratt had requested he sign. "I am beginning to like the park very well. In fact, it is becoming one of my favorite places."

"Oh ho!" Henri said, his gaze bright, his nose almost quivering with interest. "There is a woman, no?"

Nick ignored him.

"There must be. What else could make you light up in such a way?" The comte stood and then came to perch on the edge of the desk. "Are you going to tell all? Or will I have to chatter it out of you?"

Nick leaned back in his chair. "I have no desire to discuss my personal life with a fribble like you."

"Ah! You are being chivalrous, no?" A frown settled on Henri's brow. "This could be serious. Are you certain you have not found the future Lady Bridgeton?"

Nick's humor fled. "Marriage is not for me, Henri. You know that."

"Then why the secrecy?"

"It prevents people like you from nosing about in my business."

"Bah! It would be sad if you were so unimportant that no one took notice of your business. Being anonymous is a painful state of affairs, and I would not wish it on my worst enemy."

"Trust me, Henri. I would enjoy anonymity."

Henri's brow creased. "Perhaps you would. I do not understand it, but then, that is the charm of our friendship." He stood and smoothed his jacket. "I have come to ask a favor of you. Do you remember the little gatekeeper's cottage we stayed in when we first arrived?"

"Of course. What of it?"

"Well, there is a woman whom I wish to . . ." The comte paused delicately. "She is very shy, this lady. And I have been wooing her oh, so carefully. Like a little mouse, she comes to nibble. But alas, I cannot get her to take a big bite."

Nick raised his brows. "That sounds painful."

"Oh, not this kind of nibbling. The only pain I will feel is that of unbearable pleasure." Henri sighed deeply, a dreamy expression on his face. "Thus I need a place that is private, a place where I can tempt her to partake of me."

For one instant, Nick wondered if perhaps the comte was indeed still wooing Sara's aunt, but he quickly discarded the thought. It had been over a week since he'd seen them even speak to one another in public. "Use the cottage. Ask Wiggs to send some of the servants over there to organize it as you wish. But I warn you, it will take some weeks to make it truly habitable."

"That is fine. This lady cannot be hurried." The comte flashed a smile. "She hesitates, yet I know she is tempted. It is only a matter of time."

Nick had to smile at Henri's certainty. "Good luck."

"Perhaps I will ride there now and see what needs to be done. Until luncheon, *mon ami*." Whistling a jaunty tune, Henri strode from the room.

Nick watched him go, aware of a faint sense of envy. He'd never met a person so capable of living in the present. Henri was never bothered with the future, never worried what might happen tomorrow. There was a charm in such uncertainty—in not knowing one's fate. But Nick knew his fate too well, and while it had ceased to terrify him, he could not shake the weight of it.

Nick pushed himself away from the desk and strode from the room. He was dwelling far too much on his illness, and he knew from experience that such behavior only worsened it. What he needed was a distraction.

Perhaps he would join the comte in examining the cottage. He had several days before he would see Sara again, and he couldn't spend all of the time wondering what her reaction would be to the man he'd chosen as her future husband.

Normally he preferred to dally with married women, as they did not demand more from the relationship than he was prepared to give. But now he didn't want to waste any of his limited time on the ridiculous intrigue of such an affair. For though Sara believed marrying would leave her free to wander, Nick knew differently. A man would be a fool to give an ounce of freedom to a wife as lovely as Sara, especially one who issued challenges with her every breath.

But Nick was no fool. He'd have her to mistress before the end of the week. And he'd be damned if he'd let another man touch her—until he was finished with her.

Smiling to himself, he called for his horse and went to change.

Sara almost dropped her glass of punch. *"Him?"*

Nick hid a grin. She was just as outraged as he'd wished her to be, her eyes wide with shock, her chin firming mutinously. "I think Lord Keltenton is perfect."

Her mouth dropped open. Lord Keltenton was known as a lecherous, depraved, ill-mannered rogue with an unfortunate habit of belching in public. But as Nick had pointed out, the man was more than willing to slip away for a few illicit moments—at least, he had been before age and senility had caught up with him.

Now Keltenton was reduced to stealing pinches from unsuspecting ladies who ventured too near the punch table, where he lay in wait.

"He will suit your purpose well," Nick said.

"He's ancient! He wouldn't last a week."

"That's a possible benefit, I suppose."

"Why? As soon as he died, my brothers would be right back where they are now, trying to get me married!"

Nick looked thoughtfully at Keltenton, whose hunched back was silhouetted against the sweeping red-velvet hangings that decorated the theatre walls. "At least you'll have won a reprieve. They cannot marry you off until at least a year of mourning has passed."

She rewarded him with a flat, incredulous stare.

Nick tsked. "What happened to your sense of adventure? Your *joie de vivre*?"

"Just the thought of embracing . . . *that*"—she gestured toward Lord Keltenton—"has cured every inclination I had for adventure."

"He isn't that bad," Nick said, moving to stand by Sara. To his amusement, the dissolute old man leaned unsteadily against the refreshment table, his beady eyes assessing every pretty face in sight. Once in a while he would leer openly, his hands clenching in a clawlike manner, as if he was imagining himself groping the tender flesh that passed nearby.

"He reminds me of my maternal grandfather," Nick said.

"Oh? The hunched back?"

"No, his coat. My grandfather was buried in one exactly like that. Very fashionable, he was. Of course, that was twenty years ago."

She turned to glare up at him. "And you want me to marry *that*."

"Why not?"

Sara stood staring at him with a wide, uncertain gaze. "You must be joking."

"Not at all; he's the only man who will do. I have investigated every potential spouse in Bath, and there was a flaw with every one, but him." Some were too ambitious, some too jealous, and one was too handsome by far.

"What makes him so"—she shuddered—"perfect?"

That was simple: Lord Keltenton was the only rakehell in Bath incapable of the physical act of love. Nick had paid a pretty penny to the man's valet to verify the rumors. Still, the lovely Sara didn't need to know such trifling facts. "He's wealthy, so he won't care if you've a fortune or not."

"Yes, but—"

"And he's lived a totally debauched life, so he won't be averse to giving you the freedom you desire once you are wed. All you'll have to do is prop him against the refreshment table at a few social events each month, and he will be completely happy."

Sara toyed with one of her sapphire bracelets. She'd never imagined that Nick would pick the most disgusting, depraved example of shriveled humanity available in Bath. It was true Lord Keltenton seemed to meet her requirements, but still . . . She glanced at him and barely contained another shudder. Yet perhaps Nick was right. After all, her selections hadn't worked at all.

She turned her gaze to her hands, which gleamed beneath a profusion of rings. She had on every piece of the Lawrence sapphires—the necklace, earrings, brooch, bracelets, and even the tiara, and three rings glittered on her fingers. Gifts from Julius, one for each year of their marriage.

When she'd discovered the true details of his death, she'd considered throwing them out. But the more she looked at them, the more important they seemed. After all, she'd earned them. And now they served as her armor for the upcoming battle.

She'd been mad to ask Nick for assistance. "I don't know if I can go through with this."

For some reason that seemed to please Nick, for his smile warmed until it was a caress. Sara flushed, then said stiffly, "This is not a matter for levity. Anthony has grown remarkably suspicious, and my brother Marcus is due tomorrow." Had Aunt Delphi not developed a headache and asked Anthony to escort her home, Sara wasn't sure she'd have man-

aged even this small amount of time to speak with
Nick.

"Sara, you had best hurry if you want to make
your proposition before Anthony returns."

Sara cast a grimace at Keltenton. It was something of a shock to look from Nick's golden handsomeness to the older man's hunched figure. Deep
sags marred the man's eyes, and loose skin hung
about his neck—which, along with his bald pate,
made him look remarkably like a turkey. He looked
more like two hundred rather than a mere sixty-two.

Nick sighed. "Perhaps you are right. I shall have
to find another candidate for you." He pursed his
lips thoughtfully. "It may take a few days, but I'm
sure—"

"A few days! I don't *have* a few—" Sara took a
deep breath, though her chest ached with the effort.
"I suppose it will be Lord Keltenton, or no one." She
bit her lip. "You . . . do you think I should ask him
here? Or should I lure him into an antechamber?"

Her ice-blue gown a perfect foil for her eyes, her
black hair pinned up with a few intriguing tendrils
curling over her ears, Nick thought she should lure
him into an antechamber. "There are a number of
private rooms, many of them heavily curtained to
afford privacy."

She straightened her shoulders. "Very well. I will
try to convince him to accompany me to one of
those."

"He's a rake, Sara. You won't have to do anything
but look at him and smile. Then, allow him to lead
you away."

Her hand clutched at his sleeve. "Where will you be?"

"Close by if you need anything. Just call."

"Thank you." She released his sleeve, a frown appearing. "If this works, you will want your payment."

"Of course," he said smoothly. "One kiss, when and where I demand it."

"Very well. I will do it." Bravely pasting a smile on her face, she marched toward Lord Keltenton.

Keltenton flipped open the curtain that covered the alcove and gave Sara a leering stare. "After you, my dear."

Sara glanced down the deserted hallway, wondering where Nick was. Gathering her courage, she managed an uncertain smile and slipped behind the curtain.

The alcove was remarkably spacious, larger than most sitting rooms. Used as a private reception room, it was luxuriously decorated in lush red. A small settee rested in the center of the room, piled high with cushions.

Sara smoothed her hands over the skirt of her gown, letting the pale blue satin slide beneath her fingertips. The gown was heavy, the bottom banded with yellow-satin roses. A wide flow of lace formed the collar and decorated the matching gloves. Expertly cut, the neckline was designed to draw attention, while the flow of the skirt emphasized the curve of her hips.

Lord Keltenton pulled the curtain closed, then walked toward her, his gaze devouring her from head to foot. To Sara's chagrin, she discovered that he smelled of musty linen and licorice.

She turned away. "My, this is certainly a lovely chamber."

"Not as lovely as you," Lord Keltenton replied, his voice cracking with age. He watched her with an unholy gleam in his eyes that made her back up warily.

"I'm surprised you know about this room."

"I come to the theatre quite often." He picked up a cushion from the settee and plumped it suggestively. "I like soft things. Soft, young things."

Oh, dear. Sara tightened her grip on her reticule.

Lord Keltenton advanced toward her, and she caught a glimpse of his patently false teeth where his wrinkled lips stretched in a leering smile. The thought of facing such a man over the breakfast table made her stomach heave.

For some reason Nick's steely hard gaze slipped into her mind, and Sara knew she could not continue with her plan. She turned toward the doorway, but Lord Keltenton, apparently energized by his unexpected luck, had imposed himself between her and the door, his hands outspread as if he meant to grapple her to the ground.

"I'll have you to bed, my pretty." He leered. "Such a tasty morsel."

Sara stared at him in amazement. With an ungraceful leap, she skittered around the couch, snatching up a pillow on her way.

Delight dawned in the aging roué's eyes. "Oh, so you want to play games, do you? I *like* games."

Sara held the pillow before her like a shield. "Don't come any closer!"

He cackled and rubbed his hands together. "That's right! You be the terrified virgin, and I'll be the ravager!" He took another step closer, then stopped. His eyes widened and he looked down at his breeches in amazement.

Sara followed his gaze. There, faintly evident against the loose cut of his breeches, was the outline of a tiny erection.

"By Gad, that's famous!" he exclaimed. His eyes gleamed with new determination. "Hold on, my sweet! Old Harold has a little present for you."

Sara lobbed the pillow with all her might and it hit him square in the chest. Without waiting to see the outcome, she gathered her skirt in one hand and leapt over the back of the couch, landing neatly on her feet. "Nick!" she called, glancing toward the door expectantly.

But Nick didn't appear. Instead, Lord Keltenton rounded the edge of the settee. Somehow he'd managed to undo the buttons on his breeches and they now sagged about his narrow hips, his drawers plainly visible, a tiny telltale bump at his crotch.

Dear God, help me now. Sara darted past the settee and around a small table, grabbing a heavy metal statuette as she went.

Lord Keltenton scuttled after her, dancing sideways like a crab. "Hee, hee! Such a lively one!"

Sara turned and cocked the statue in a throwing

stance. "Don't make me use this, Lord Keltenton. I don't wish to hurt you."

He grinned yellowly. "Perhaps I like being hurt. Especially by young ladies with pretty bosoms like yours." He brightened. "I say, would you like to beat me with a riding crop?"

The idea actually had some appeal. "Lord Keltenton, you seem to have made a mistake, as have I. I thought I could do this, but I can't. I just can't."

Her desperation must have reached him, for he stopped in his tracks, his face softening. "Having doubts, are you? Well, never let it be said that old Harold took an unwilling girl to bed."

Sara sagged with relief. "Thank you so much. I thought—"

He lunged for her, cackling wildly. "Tricked you, my pretty!"

Cursing madly, Sara dropped the statue and ran for the door. Lord Keltenton stumbled over the statue and fell heavily, his hands grabbing the bottom of her skirt.

His full weight yanked her to a halt and she stood, straining forward with all her might.

No sound came from behind her. Not a single sigh or pant. The suspense was agonizing. "Lord Keltenton?"

Nothing. Sara turned. He lay on the floor, his pants about his thighs, his fingers gripping the bottom of her skirt. His eyes were wide-open, his tongue hanging from his mouth.

Damn it, must every man she tried to seduce drop into an unconscious stupor? She pulled on her skirt, but nothing happened. Lord Keltenton's fingers remained clenched on her hem as if he were hanging on to her for dear life.

Sara frowned. "Lord Keltenton, release my skirt!"

He didn't answer. He didn't move. In fact, he didn't even blink.

Sara bent closer. The old man's eyes stared in an eerie, unseeing fashion. "Lord Keltenton?" she said louder, her voice shrill in the silence.

She poked at one of his hands with the tip of her slipper, and the truth slipped slowly into her mind. "Oh, fudge," she breathed as panic filled her chest. "I've killed him."

The curtain was suddenly shoved aside and Nick appeared. Tall, broad-shouldered, his hair gleaming in the intimate lamplight, he looked like a knight from a picture book.

He took two swift steps into the room, his gaze dropping to the floor. He froze. "My God, what's happened now?"

Sara couldn't speak. She could only point.

Nick cursed, then crossed to where Lord Keltenton lay. "Bloody hell! Three in a row? I begin to fear for my own life."

"I didn't do anything! He was chasing me and he fell."

Nick stooped to look at Lord Keltenton, who lay on his side, his chest moving slowly. "He's not dead."

"Thank God," Sara said with relief.

Nick's gaze went lower and then stopped. "Good God, he's . . ." He glanced up at Sara. Her blue eyes were wide, her hair tumbled about her face. She looked young and innocent and altogether too enticing. Nick felt the beginning of a smile. "Congratulations, my dear. You have the ability to raise the dead."

She frowned. "What do you mean?"

"Lord Keltenton is aroused. According to his valet, he has not been able to perform such a feat in over ten years." Nick stood, brushing his knees.

"When did you speak with his valet?" Sara asked in confusion.

"Last week. I wanted to ascertain that the rumors were true."

Her face cleared and the slightest hint of a smile appeared on her face. "That's why you said he was a perfect candidate."

Nick nodded shortly. "It appears he's had a fit of some sort, but he's still breathing, and his color is returning. I need to—"

The curtain was thrust aside and the Earl of Greyley burst into the room. His steely gaze found first Sara and then Nick. "What the hell is going on here?"

"Damn," Sara muttered, tugging on her skirts.

Damn, indeed. Nick had sincerely hoped they would be spared her brother's presence until after this little incident was settled. He knelt and pried one of Keltenton's hands from Sara's hem. "Lord Keltenton has had an accident."

Greyley came to stare at the fallen lord, his face grim, white lines about his mouth. "Is he dead?"

"I thought he was," Sara said helpfully.

He shot her a hard glance. "Why is his hand clenched about your skirts?"

Nick loosened the other hand. "Lord Keltenton had an attack and your sister kindly tried to assist him. I'm afraid he grabbed her skirts as he fell."

The earl glowered, his eyes dark with suspicion. "His trousers are loosened."

Before Anthony could say anything else, Nick said, "Assist me in getting him to the settee, Greyley. We can discuss this later."

After a tense moment, he nodded. The two men quickly lifted Lord Keltenton to the settee and dropped him rather roughly on the cushions, then yanked his breeches back into place.

Nick stood looking down at the man. "I suppose one of us should seek some help."

The earl nodded grimly, but made no move to leave.

Nick showed his teeth. "Or perhaps he will recover on his own."

Anthony returned the false smile. "One can only hope."

"Oh, for heavens sake! I'll go!" Sara sent them both a black glare, then marched to the curtain. She flipped the heavy velvet back and disappeared into the corridor beyond.

Greyley closed the space that separated him from Nick. "I know you are somehow to blame for this, Bridgeton. Sara has already been hurt once; I will not have her hurt again."

"She is a grown woman. She can make her own decisions."

"Not with you around, she can't. I know too much about you. So you will stay away from my sister."

Had he any sense, Nick would have agreed and gone his own way. But having this lumbering ox of a man try to tell Nick what he could and could not do infuriated him. He met Greyley's gaze head-on. "You do not dictate to either me or Sara."

The earl's mouth thinned. "Damn you, Bridgeton. I will see to it that you are never welcome in Bath again."

Nick was risking everything with his stubbornness, but for some reason, the idea of resuming his place in society paled when compared to the thought of having Sara in his bed. Nick gave him a faint smile. "We shall see, won't we, Greyley?"

The curtain was shoved open again.

"*Voyons!* What has happened?" Henri entered the room, followed by Sara's aunt and several other people. "Has there been an accident?"

"Not yet," Anthony muttered. "But soon."

Sara's aunt bustled to the settee. "Oh, dear! It's Lord Keltenton!"

A plump lady in lavender satin shook her head, her improbably yellow curls bouncing with the movement. "Given to fits, he is. Best loosen his neckcloth."

This service performed, a somber gentleman was sent to fetch a doctor. More people entered the room, and Nick gladly stepped aside, the whole scene adding to his irritation.

His plan had gone disastrously awry. He'd subjected Sara to the advances of a man he'd thought incapable of such, and put his relationship with her in full view of her brother.

"Perhaps we should pour water on him," Henri said over the din.

His suggestion was met with a welter of approval, and two women were sent to request some water.

Sara stood to one side, her hands nervously clasped in front of her.

Nick watched her, his heart tight at the sight of her distress.

"Bridgeton, this is all your fault."

Nick sighed. "You are beginning to repeat yourself, Greyley. I find it boring."

"That does it." Anthony's face darkened, his mouth white with anger. "I have had enough of you. Name your second."

"No."

"*Name your second.*" Anthony's voice rang over the confusion, bringing instant silence.

Sara took a half step forward, then stopped, alarm darkening her eyes.

Nick turned to Anthony. "I will not fight you. There is no cause for a duel."

"Afraid to die, Bridgeton? I promise I'll make it quick."

Damn the arrogant bastard. "Henri?"

"*Mon Dieu!* Not again." He looked at Sara's aunt and said, "We go, he fights, he kills, we eat breakfast . . . it is always the same."

"Not this time," Anthony said grimly. "Tomorrow, the only place Bridgeton will eat breakfast will be in hell." He glanced around the room, his gaze indifferent. "I need a second as well."

Over by the curtain, Viscount Hewlette said boldly, "I would be glad to be of service to you, my lord." He leveled a malicious glance at Nick.

Anthony nodded. "Very well. Hewlette is my second."

Sara took another step forward but Greyley caught her arm. "Wait!" she said, trying to free herself. "This is not necessary. Please, Anthony, don't do—"

"Pistols at dawn?" Nick cut in.

Greyley nodded abruptly, then stalked out, dragging a protesting Sara with him.

Chapter 13

Much later that night, Nick sat in the library at Hibberton Hall, his feet stretched toward the fireplace as he watched the flicking light from the embers dance across his boots. The corners of the room were clothed in darkness; only the dying fire and one solitary lamp spilled a faint golden glow across the patterned rug.

He was a fool. He'd come to England to reestablish himself, and what did he do but allow his contretemps with a lady of quality to become public fodder. Nick shook his head in disgust. Somewhere along the way, he'd lost what little sense he'd once had for a pair of wide blue eyes.

Not that his interest in Sara had dimmed. On the contrary, he was more eager to have her than ever, now that she'd cost him so much trouble. Nick leaned his head back against the high back of his chair and watched the dying embers struggle for life.

Julius Lawrence had been a fool. To have had access to the bed of such a tender, succulent woman like Sara, yet leave her virtually unawakened, was a blatant sin. Every instinct Nick possessed rebelled at such waste.

He reached for the flagon of brandy on the table at his elbow, and splashed some into a glass. That was the problem with Englishmen: They didn't understand the intrinsic beauty of being the one to awaken a woman, to pleasure her until she cried your name and became part of your soul for a fleeting moment.

Nick absently swirled the liquid in his glass and blessed his French ancestors. Such knowledge was power, and it made the act of making love all the more poignant.

The mantel clock chimed the hour: It was midnight, the witching hour. A prudent man would want to be alert and ready for the duel at dawn, and go to bed. Nick poured more brandy into his glass and toasted the ticking clock. He didn't want to be careful. He just wanted to enjoy the moment, to savor the pleasures left to him until Sara's ox of a brother ended his life on the dueling field.

The thought made him stir restlessly, and he rose to stand by the open terrace window, letting the cool breeze brush across him. He never thought about the possible outcome of a duel. Always before, he'd been defending his honor or the honor of his mother's memory. But for some reason, tomorrow's duel was different. For once, he had no desire to win. Greyley had been right to challenge him; he deserved much worse for placing Sara in harm's way.

He imagined her face if he happened to kill her brother. She'd never forgive anyone who harmed so much as a hair on his head, no matter how much the lummox deserved it. Nick sighed. He shouldn't care, but he'd decided Sara was to be his mistress—so it bothered him to see his hopes blow away like chaff in the wind. Of course, he couldn't very well let Sara's brawny oaf of a brother just shoot him in cold blood, either. Damn it, he'd never lost a duel.

He rubbed his forehead wearily. Either way, he was damned. "What the hell does she expect me to do?" he asked aloud. Worst of all, it had been years since he'd let desire interfere with his life—but then, he'd never had to work so long or hard to woo a woman into his bed.

His mouth twisted into a bitter smile. It was a sad truth that while he'd inherited his mother's tendency toward wildness and her damnable headaches, he'd also inherited his father's weakness for a beautiful face. There was no good blood in his veins. Not a single drop.

Nick took a sip of the brandy, warming it on his tongue, savoring the heavy, mellow taste. What was it about Sara that tantalized him so? Her face wasn't as breathtakingly beautiful as some of the women he'd been with. Perhaps it was her exuberance for life, her determination to win no matter the cost. He'd never met a woman more determined to make her own way in the world, circumstances be damned. She approached every second as if it were an adventure, her heart wide-open, her emotions on display to the world.

Nick marveled at Sara's capacity to make even the most mundane activities or conversations quiver with meaning and emotion. He looked into his glass, and a smile turned up the corners of his mouth. God knew she never left him bored. Perhaps that was the reason he could not let her go.

But no, it was more than that. It was her intelligence, coupled with the hint of naïveté. He was fascinated to think he might be able to touch that innocence and make it his. Yet every time he got near her, that same innocence made him pause. He'd had ample opportunities to seduce her; why had he stopped each time?

Was it chivalry, or his desire to regain his respectability? He shook his head and looked at the half-empty glass in his hand. What a damnable tangle.

Part of Nick welcomed the duel, welcomed it with a hot yearning that was almost frightening. Perhaps this was the way to end it—to just let the bullet take him.

He closed his eyes. No more pain, no more nights wondering if he would make it until morning. Nothing but blessed emptiness.

But the thought didn't bring the relief he thought it would. It was ignoble to just give up. He was not his mother, too weak to fight the demons. His pride forbade him from taking such an expedient route. His hand tightened about the glass. Whatever the outcome, he would welcome it.

The door opened. "My lord," Wiggs said, his voice thick with disapproval.

Nick turned from the window. "Yes?"

"A young lady has come to call." Wiggs's mouth was pressed in a stern line. "She gave her name as Lady Carrington. Shall I tell her you are not available?"

So she has come to plea for her brother's life, has she? "Give me a moment, then show her in."

"Yes, my lord. Shall I request Mrs. Kibble to attend you, to serve as chaperone while—"

"No, thank you, Wiggs." Nick wanted complete privacy. "Let Lady Carrington wait for at least ten minutes before you allow her in." That would give her time to worry a bit.

After a pause, Wiggs replied, "Very good, sir." He bowed and left, moving even more slowly than usual.

Nick smiled at the closed door. The thought of Sara kicking her heels in his foyer, waiting impatiently to see him, was very pleasant indeed. He finished off the remaining brandy, his mind humming ever so slightly. The room had a slightly skewed look to it, as if he were in a long, narrow hallway.

He glanced down at his shirt, smoothing it with one hand. It was still tucked in, his cravat still knotted about his throat, though he'd shed his coat and waistcoat hours ago. He thought briefly of replacing them, then discarded the idea. Sara had invaded his territory—let her find him in all his glory. He undid his cravat and tossed it over a chair, and loosened the neck of his shirt. Grinning, he dropped into a chair, stretched his legs before him, and waited.

Several minutes passed before the door opened again. "Lady Carrington," Wiggs intoned, sounding like a death knell.

Nick noted that she hadn't shed her pelisse; it was still tightly buttoned about her neck in a definite "keep the rake at bay" manner. He couldn't decide whether he was amused or annoyed.

She hesitated on the threshold, her gaze widening when she saw his attire, then she curtsied abruptly. "Lord Bridgeton."

Nick smiled, but made no move to rise. "Lady Carrington. What an unexpected pleasure." He glanced toward his silent butler. "That will be all, Wiggs."

The butler sniffed. "Yes, my lord. If you require anything else, you have but to ring."

"Thank you," Nick said with finality.

With a morose nod, Wiggs shuffled out of the room and closed the door behind him.

Nick turned his gaze to Sara. She stood rooted in the middle of the room, her hands tightly clasped in front of her, her feet slightly apart as if she was prepared for battle.

"To what do I owe this pleasure?" he said, with a slight sneer.

"You know why I have come."

For some reason, that quiet admission irritated him. "Does your brother know you are here?"

She shook her head. "He thinks I am in bed, asleep."

"Your brother is a fool." Nick waved a hand at the seat opposite his. "You might as well sit."

The chairs were grouped around the terrace windows, which he had opened to let in a bit of fresh air. A faint breeze stirred the curtains ever so slightly, washing the heat of the fire from the corners of the room.

After a slight hesitation, she nodded. "Thank you." She took the chair opposite him and perched on the edge.

"Why don't you take off your pelisse? It is quite warm." Using his groin as a gauge, it was more than warm. It was hot, and she was still draped head to toe in yards of material.

Her hands almost reached for the top button, but then she stopped and shot him an uncertain look, her gaze resting on his empty glass. "I'm not sure I should."

He rose and went to the fire, stirring it to new life. "I rarely ravish my guests. In fact, it is usually the other way around."

"I will try to restrain myself," she said in a dry tone as she unbuttoned her pelisse and pulled it off, defiantly tossing it on the chair opposite hers.

"I'm sure you will," he murmured.

She still wore the gown she'd worn at the theatre, the ice-blue silk outlining her curves, the color brilliant against her skin. "So, Sara," he said, lingering over her name, drawing it through his teeth to taste it thoroughly. "Would you like a drink? Sherry, perhaps?"

"No, thank you. I came to speak with you about the duel."

He walked toward the desk. "You'll have a drink first." He pushed aside the carafe of sherry and poured brandy into a glass, then handed it to her. "This will soften that frown of yours."

When she took the glass, he could see how her fingers shook. Nick watched her take a sip and grimace at the strong taste. It was unmannerly of him to offer her such strong spirits, but for some reason he wanted to push her, to taunt her, to torment her as he was tormented.

Frowning at the thought, he went to the terrace door and leaned against it, letting the cold glass dissipate some of the brandy fumes from his mind. "So, love, what brings you? Are you one of those morbid curiosity seekers who crane their lovely necks for a last glimpse of the dying?"

"Nick, please."

"You heard your brother—according to him, I haven't a chance. I will be a dead man on the morrow."

"That's why I've come." She swallowed convulsively. "I heard you're quite good at dueling."

"I've never lost."

She leaned forward, her eyes glistening with tears. "Nick . . . please, Anthony may be pigheaded, but he's my brother."

The soft voice sent a solid thrum of sexual excitement through him. It wasn't fair that he should meet this tender flower just as he was on the verge of death. It was the ultimate irony, and Nick did not find it in the least amusing. "What do you want, Sara?"

"Stop the duel. Please."

He reached out for the curtain tassel and threaded it through his hands. "I can't."

"There must be a way." She licked her dry lips, the innocent gesture sending a flood of awareness straight to his groin.

Good God, she was the most unassumingly sensual woman he'd ever known and he was burning to taste her. "You are asking me to do something that is quite out of my power. Your brother challenged me, not the other way around. If this duel is to be stopped, he has to be the one to do so."

"I've already asked him," she said despondently, staring into her glass.

"He doesn't take his honor lightly."

"Neither do you."

He smiled without humor. "I have no honor. Which is why I have allowed you to join me here, in my house, alone. And why I placed you at such risk with Lord Keltenton in the first place."

Her brow creased. "You have honor."

"No. I have pride, which is a vastly different thing." He could tell she was going to disagree. "Sara, you know nothing about me. I've done things that—" He stared at the tassel dangling from his fingers. "You don't know me at all."

Sara bit her lip, her fingers curling into her palm

so tightly that her nails cut the skin. Nick was different this evening. Intense, quiet. And lonely, somehow. Perhaps it was the strain of the duel.

She'd never seen him without his usual polished veneer. He'd shed his jacket and waistcoat and his shirt was open at the neck to reveal his strong throat. His eyes had a bright, hard quality to them, the result of the brandy, no doubt. But it was more than that: It was the way he watched her, his expression intent as if he were trying to memorize her every feature. "Nick, what do you want?"

"What?"

She ran a finger over the edge of her brandy glass. "What is the one thing you yearn for above all?"

"Freedom."

"From what?"

He didn't answer for a long while, but stood staring out the window. Finally, he sighed. "From pain. I have hurt for so long . . ."

"Are you injured? Or ill?"

"I have headaches. It's an inherited tendency. My mother—"

"Mother? I thought it was your father who suffered from headaches."

"No. Where did you get that idea?"

"Lady Birlington. She knows everything about everybody."

"What else did she say?"

"Nothing; that was all."

His face shuttered. "She told you that I would end up the same way as my mother, didn't she?"

After a moment, Sara nodded.

Nick's jaw tensed, and he looked back out the window.

What could she say now, how could she bridge the gulf that seemed to be growing between them as the silence stretched? But no stroke of brilliance came to her. Unable to bear the silence, she had just convinced herself to leave when he began to speak.

"My mother's name was Violette." Low and intense, his voice was filled with pain.

"That . . . that is a lovely name."

"She was a lovely woman. Quite beautiful, in fact. She was the only daughter of a French aristocrat, and she was a woman of extreme passions. When she was happy, you could not ask for a more exciting companion. But when she was sad . . ." His face darkened. "For her, love was a temporary state. And since she was as selfish as she was beautiful, she floated from man to man, on a never-ending search for something she couldn't have."

"What about you?"

"I was part of the baggage. Where she went, I went. Sometimes I was wanted. Other times—" He shrugged.

Her heart ached. "Where was your father?"

"He was a brief passage in Violette's life, the marriage over before it had truly begun. I have no memory of him, but I do have a letter from my grandfather announcing his death."

"Then your grandfather cared about you."

"Why would he? He left me his title and a house, but nothing else. I don't suppose I blame him, really. By the time we met, I was already beyond saving."

He'd been so alone, his entire life. She could imagine him as a child, watching his mother, yearning for affection, but never receiving it. In that instant, Sara decided she hated the beautiful Violette. No decent woman would ever abandon her child in such a way.

Something fell on the back of Sara's hand, and she looked down at it. A single drop of water glistened on her skin. Yet another drop fell beside the first, and she realized that she was crying. Crying for the love Nick had never known. Crying for the fact that he might never know it now.

She thought of his life, of his behavior, and she realized that he kept a barrier about his heart—one so tall and so thick that no one would ever be able to climb over it. He had closed himself off, and even Henri, his closest friend, did not know him. She cleared her throat. "I heard a rumor about you."

"Which one?"

"That you wanted your cousin's fortune and that you abducted his wife to get it."

Nick turned to look out the window, his face hidden in darkness as he gently swung the tassel to and fro. The silence grew.

"It's true, isn't it?"

He turned back to her, his face devoid of expression. "Every word."

"Did you love her?" Sara clenched her jaw as she waited for him to answer. She didn't know why the question was so important, but it was.

"Love is an illusion, Sara. There is no such thing."

"Not everyone is like your mother, Nick."

"Thank God for that."

Sara swallowed, but a lump of emotion remained in her throat. Somehow, she had to make things right for this man, to show him that not all women were like his mother, that all of life wasn't as devoid of hope and cheer as his childhood. She stood. "I suppose there is nothing I can do to talk you out of the duel."

"No."

"Then I suppose the time has come for me to pay my debt."

He stilled, his gaze locked on her. "What debt?"

"The kiss."

"I would hardly call Lord Keltenton a success."

"No, but our agreement ended when you found him for me. The rest was up to me. Remember?"

His gaze locked with hers. "Do you know what you are saying?"

Her voice deserted her, and all she could do was nod. She wanted the kiss and more. She wanted him to hold her, to touch her, to ease the pain she felt for him. For one brief hour, she wanted to forget about the duel and her need to marry and every other thing that loomed over them.

"I want more than a kiss," she heard herself say. She held her breath, unable to look at him, unable to face his rejection.

There was a quiet step on the carpet, and then he was beside her. His fingers closed over her chin and he lifted her face, his expression harsh. "What do you want from me?"

The tears spilled free, falling silently down her cheeks. "I am not a lady, Nick. I never have been."

He gently ran the back of his hand over her cheek, his expression softening. "That's no sin, Sara. In many ways, it's a blessing."

"Not always." She turned her face into his hand and closed her eyes at the warmth of his touch. "I long for this," she whispered. "Surely that will see me in hell."

His hands slid to her arms. "You are wrong, Sara; you are indeed a lady. But alas, I am no gentleman." He pulled her against him, his voice lowering to an intoxicating whisper. "A gentleman would have sent you home in a carriage, safe and warm. He wouldn't be standing close enough to you to see your heart beat in the delicate line of your throat."

"No?" she managed to whisper.

"And a gentleman certainly would never have discovered that you smell like fresh summer linen, the scent as sensual as the delicious curve of your lower lip." He trailed his finger over her mouth. "No, Sara. I am not a gentleman, and I am damned glad of it."

Her fingers twined in the folds of his linen shirt. "Nick, I want to be with you."

He held her to him tightly. He was so wonderful, so masculine, and she longed for him in a way she'd never known. He pushed aside the wide collar of her gown and dropped a kiss on her shoulder, his voice low, caressing. "I have dreamed of this. Dreamed it so often, it is almost a memory." He followed the contours of her shoulders with his mouth, placing light, sensual kisses on her throat, her neck, beneath her ear.

Sara closed her eyes and let the passion engulf her. She yearned for him so much, needed him so badly, that she pressed her thighs together to still the ache that was growing with each touch, each caress.

"I've wanted you since the moment I first saw you." He rubbed his arousal against her hips, his actions bold and daring as the man himself.

Slowly, surely, she lifted her fingers and placed them on his bottom lip. He was magnificent standing in the firelight, telling her he wanted her. She could barely think, her mind galloping with a thousand thoughts as he lowered his mouth to her cheek and traced a line to her ear. A deep tremor shook her. He was a man of such contradictions, both harsh and gentle at the same time.

"I want you, Sara," he whispered, the words tingling through her.

Simple words, yet they sent a longing through her that made her breasts ache as if he'd touched her. Kissed her. Loved her.

Slowly, fearful of even breathing, she sank onto the edge of the settee and looked up at him. He answered her immediately, his body lowering over hers until they pressed together intimately.

His hands slipped beneath her skirt, sliding up to her thigh. He cupped her intimately, boldly, daring her to stop him. She gasped, a violent tremble racing through her, but she did nothing to halt him. Instead, she clung to him, her cheek pressed against his shirt, enveloped by his masculine scent. Their relationship might not be based on love, but it was based on a mutual need—on the desire for forgetfulness, for the release from pain, even for the space of an hour.

Nick's mouth covered hers as he undid the lacing of her gown. Cool air touched her skin as he pushed her chemise aside and exposed her breasts. Sara felt uncovered, vulnerable. She was doing this to help Nick, she told herself, even as she knew it was a lie. She wanted him for herself, for her salvation, her pleasure, and for no other reason.

He stared down at her bared breasts. She forced herself to sit still, her nipples tightening at his silent regard.

His broad shoulders were outlined by the reddish gleam of the fire, his hair lit to burnished gold. She knew what his expression would be—fierce and protective, the way he looked every time they had kissed. This time it would be all for her.

He bent and closed his mouth over one of her nipples, his tongue teasing it mercilessly. Sara gasped and arched against him, closing her eyes at the torrent of pleasure. Within moments, their clothes lay in the floor about them.

It had been too long. Much too long. And this

was different. Nick didn't take—he gave. And he gave with a single-minded determination to make her long for him even more. She writhed with need, with desire.

"Sara," he whispered, the name a plea.

She opened to him, and they came together in a fierce, desperate motion that sent a wave of fire through Sara until she could no longer think. All she knew was the passion and the pleasure and the fact that Nick was here, with her, and that for the moment, he was all hers.

Sara savored the feel of him, losing herself in the exquisite torture of his touch. He was everything she'd dreamed, and more. And she was lost, just as she'd been lost the first moment she'd seen him in the Kirkwoods' ballroom.

Their passion mounted and grew, each movement an agony and an ecstasy. Nick murmured her name over and over as the heat built within. Just as Sara thought she could stand no more, release flooded through her, washing through her veins and sending her senses reeling. Nick followed a moment later, collapsing on top of her, his breath harsh in her ear.

Neither spoke, their panting breaths the only sound in the room. Then from outside, a commotion sounded in the outer foyer. Nick raised his head, meeting Sara's gaze. Over Wiggs's protests came the sound of another voice, masculine and raised in anger.

"Heaven help us," Sara said. "It's Anthony."

Nick and Sara moved as one, grabbing clothes and yanking them on as fast as they could, but they were still not quick enough. Nick had only one arm in his shirt and Sara was still trying to reach behind her to pull the laces on her dress closed when the door flew open and not one, but two hulking figures stalked in.

Sara's face paled, but she kept her chin high. "Nick, I believe you know my brother, Anthony. With him is my brother Marcus St. John, the Marquis of Treymount."

Chapter 14

Wiggs appeared behind them, his thin face tight with frustration. "My lord, I could not keep them out. I—"

"That's quite all right," Nick said, dropping his cravat back onto a side table. "You did what you could."

The butler's startled gaze drifted from his disheveled master to Sara, who was attempting to right her twisted dress. Red-faced, he all but bolted out the door.

Nick raked a hand through his hair. He had the strangest sense that this moment was not real. But it was. He was standing barefoot on the thick, library carpet, dressed in nothing but his breeches and a hastily donned shirt. Sara had finally managed to refasten her gown, though it was horribly crushed. And looming behind the settee, breathing fire and brimstone, stood Sara's brothers. God, what a coil.

"To hell with the duel," Anthony snarled. "I'm going to kill you here and now."

He started forward, but the marquis grabbed his arm. "Leave them be." He spoke quietly, but every word was clear and deadly, his gaze never leaving Nick.

Marcus St. John had his sister's eyes and the same black hair, but there the similarities ended. Where Sara was small-boned and delicate, Treymount was as tall as Anthony, if not quite as broad. Nick nodded coolly. "I wondered when I'd have the felicity of meeting you."

The marquess neither smiled nor offered a greeting. "I think it would be best if Sara left."

"I'm sure you do," she replied tartly, dropping back onto the settee. She turned to glare over her shoulder at her brothers. "If we are going to have a conversation, then I suggest you all take a seat."

"Perhaps you would care for some brandy?" Nick asked, stepping into the role of host purely to irritate his company.

Anthony's face darkened. "It's probably too coarse."

"Have some brandy, Anthony," Treymount said. "Bridgeton just returned from France, and I daresay his stock is superior to ours."

"I don't care. I won't stand here and—"

"Then leave. Your temper has caused enough problems as it is."

Anthony hesitated, his hands clenching and un-clenching. Finally, he managed to say in a surly voice, "Very well. One glass won't hurt."

Nick noted how pale Sara's face was. Frowning, he poured three glasses and handed them out. Sara took hers with a grateful smile.

"It isn't proper for a woman to drink brandy," Anthony said.

Sara resolutely tilted the glass, taking a huge gulp. She immediately went into a paroxysm of coughing.

Nick shot a hard stare at her brother. "Don't pun-ish her for my sins, Greyley. You and I will be set-tling this at dawn."

"No," the marquis said, savoring the brandy. "I'm afraid that won't be possible."

"Why not?" Anthony demanded.

"Lord Bridgeton is about to become a member of our family. It would be improper of you to shoot him before the ceremony."

"What?" Anthony roared. "Marcus, you cannot mean to tell me that you expect this—this—"

"Braggart," Nick supplied helpfully.

"Bastard," Anthony returned without pause.

Sara set her glass down with a thump and stood, her chin tilted to a pugnacious angle. "I am not get-ting married, and neither is Bridgeton."

"You have no choice," Treymount replied evenly.

"Oh? What are you going to do? Tie me to the altar and place a knife at my throat?"

"If I have to."

"I *still* wouldn't marry him." She turned to Nick.

"Thank you for your hospitality. Feel free to toss these two fools out any time you wish." So saying, she swooped up her pelisse and jammed her arms into it, then stomped to the door. She yanked it open, slamming it behind her with so much force that a picture dropped from the wall and thunked to the floor.

A long silence followed her departure.

"I don't believe I've ever seen her that angry," Anthony said.

"Except the time Chase threw her in the pond on her sixteenth birthday," Treymount replied. "She had just fixed her hair in some sort of curled ... thing." He glanced at Anthony. "You had better see her home. I will take care of things here."

Anthony shot a dark glance at Nick. "Be forewarned, Bridgeton. I'll be watching you."

"How tedious for you," Nick murmured.

Treymount's lips twitched, but Anthony merely stalked out of the room, much in the same manner as his sister.

The marquis leaned back in his chair and stretched his long legs before him. "I fear that Sara has a very romantic idea of you."

Nick turned away. Disappointment was inevitable. Sara didn't understand the circumstances of his birth, of his hereditary weakness. How could she? "She is an innocent, Treymount."

"Yes, and you are the only man she's shown a genuine interest in since Carrington's death. Whether you like it or not, you will marry her. And then ..."

"Then?"

"You will make her happy."

That was the one thing he could not do. How could he, a man plagued with headaches that would one day draw him into a haze of opium addiction? "What if I refuse to marry your sister, Treymount? What then?"

"Anthony will have the chance to fight his duel."

"And Sara?"

The marquess looked down at his boots. "She can go abroad. No one will know of her errors in Italy. She can start anew there, and—"

"You would banish your own sister?" All the years he'd spent, wandering the Continent, waiting for his chance to return home, flooded him. "You cannot care for her if you would do such a thing."

"And what of you? You attempted to seduce her. You took advantage of her desire to taste life and sullied her name with yours. Now you wish to walk away and leave her to bear the consequences." Treymount's dark brows snapped together. "Tell me, Bridgeton. Which of us has her interests more at heart?"

Nick could not argue. He clenched and unclenched his hands, his mind racing over the possibilities. No matter what the outcome of this conversation, Nick was doomed. He'd been a fool to think he could reestablish himself. But the thought of Sara bearing the ignominy of banishment was more than he could stand. It would kill her in a way that had not killed him. He was used to deprivation, used to the hardness of life, but she was young and tender, still filled with hope. He could not let it happen. And looking into Treymount's cold, icy gaze, he knew with a sudden wave of certainty that the marquis would deal as harshly with Sara as he deemed necessary.

Had Treymount attempted to fight him, Nick would have fought with his last breath. Had Treymount threatened to ruin him, Nick would have laughed. But the fact that the marquis had coldly placed his own sister on the altar as a sacrifice to the gods of propriety, made Nick furious.

There was little he could do. "Sara doesn't like being ordered about."

"Then you'll have to convince her that a wedding is in her best interest," Treymount said, his gaze fixed on Nick.

"I will convince her to marry me. Shall we discuss settlements?"

Treymount's gaze narrowed. But after a moment, he said, "Ten thousand pounds and not a penny more."

"Twenty thousand, and I want it set up in her name alone," Nick said. "Two accounts; one for investing. My solicitor will see to it that it is properly handled."

"And the other account?"

Nick managed a cold smile. "Pin money." When he inevitably followed in his mother's path, he would not leave his wife without recourse. Sara wanted her freedom, and he would see to it that she received it.

Treymount took a thoughtful sip of his brandy. "That is very generous."

"I can afford to be. After all, it isn't my money."

The marquis sighed. "Bridgeton, I'm afraid I don't understand. Just what did you hope to gain by dallying with my sister? From what I've heard, she is not your usual fare."

The question caught Nick by surprise, and it was several minutes before he answered. "I have no apologies for what I've done." Regrets were another matter altogether. Lately, it seemed he could not awaken without wishing he had the opportunity to change some aspect of his life. "I would like to marry her as quickly as possible."

"You will leave the arrangements to me."

A slow burn heated his eyes, as if one of his headaches ached to be released. "I have already said I would marry your sister, Treymount. But I will do so in my own time and fashion."

The marquis smiled, and for the first time, Nick was allowed to glimpse the fury behind the icy blue eyes. "You will marry her when and where *I* say. You have lost your rights in this game." He placed his empty glass on a table and stood. "I'll send you a note. In the meantime, stay away from her."

With that, he strode from the room, leaving Nick staring at the closed door.

Damn the St. Johns to hell. What made an entire family so arrogant, so certain, so incredibly over-bearing? For the first time, Nick had a glimmering of why Sara had been so willing to marry just to escape the clutches of her brothers. He'd been with them for under a half hour, and already they were attempting to run his life.

But Nick was made of sterner stuff. He would marry Sara Lawrence, but because *he* wanted to, and in order to free her from her noxious siblings. But that was where it would end. He'd made love to Sara tonight as if it were his last night on earth. He'd lost himself in her without regard for anything—including whether or not she became pregnant.

The thought clutched his heart with icy fingers. He could only pray he hadn't pushed his luck too far already. Once they were married, he'd put an end to their physical relationship—there would be no children from this union. Violette's illness would die with him.

Lost in his thoughts, he sat in the library until the slow fingers of dawn climbed over the garden and warmed the cold room. Then, stiff from sitting, he rose and left, calling for his bath as he went.

Chapter 15

Marcus St. John, the indomitable Marquis of Treymount, was being scolded. Normally, it wasn't something he greeted with much enthusiasm. But Sara, when angered, reached a level of eloquence that bordered on genius. Since he'd been sitting at his desk when she'd stormed into his study and begun her prolonged diatribe, he'd even managed to write down some of her best phrases. They might be of use when composing his next speech for the House of Lords.

"Are you listening to me?" she demanded, coming to a halt in front of him, her fists planted on her hips, her face flushed.

He looked down to where he'd just written

"flamboyant, persnickety nodcock." "I'm not missing a word."

"Good, for I'll say it only once more: I won't marry Nicholas Montrose. Not now. Not tomorrow. Not ever." She whirled and began stomping back and forth in front of his desk. "You have humiliated me! How could you demand such a thing from him? God, what a schemer he must think me!"

"Who cares what he thinks?"

"I do! He was helping me with—" She clamped her mouth closed and flushed a deep red. "It doesn't matter."

Oh, but it did. Marcus had a very good idea of what his imprudent sister had been up to, and it did not please him at all. On another piece of foolscap he reread the names, "Hewlette, Bawton, Keltenton." Written below that in a bold sweep, was the name "Nicholas Montrose, Earl of Bridgeton." He'd pieced together what he could from Aunt Delphi and Anthony, as well as a few tidbits he'd garnered from the groom who'd escorted Sara on many of her outings. All told, the picture had been very disturbing indeed.

"Sara, what is done, is done. You put yourself in this position, and you will have to pay the consequences." He leaned back in his chair. "You wished to marry a man of your own choosing, and so you shall."

A startled expression lit her eyes. "Who told you I had decided to—" She bit her lip.

Marcus stifled a smile. He so loved surprising people, and within the last twenty-four hours, he had

managed to surprise two. His interview with the earl
was one of his most successful endeavors of all time.
In less than a half hour, he'd managed to sway
Bridgeton, a confirmed bachelor by all accounts, into
agreeing to marry Sara. It was not a match Marcus
would have welcomed three months ago. But considering the damage his sister had done to her name
owing to Lord Keltenton's unfortunate illness and
Anthony's precipitous challenge, it was a marvel
he'd managed to get Sara a husband at all. It was
even more fortuitous that he'd managed to find one
with surprising strength of character, and for whom
she had some fondness. Perhaps more than fondness.

Anthony shifted in his chair by the fire as Sara
began to catalog his part in "her persecution." It
would do his brother some good to be made uncomfortable. As far as Marcus could tell, Anthony
had allowed his emotions to overwhelm his good
judgment, culminating in calling Bridgeton out and
putting Sara's name on the tongue of every gossip
in town. To Anthony, there was no worse candidate
for Sara's husband. But Anthony was wrong.

Marcus replaced the pen in the inkpot, remembering Bridgeton's reaction to his threat to banish
Sara. Though he would never do such a thing, the
earl hadn't known that, and the threat had worked
just as he'd planned.

Feeling quite satisfied, Marcus rose and went to
look out the window at the busy street below. "Sara,
resign yourself. You will marry Bridgeton, and that
is the end of it."

Aunt Delphi looked up from where she had been

pretending to embroider by the fire. "The earl is a very handsome man, but I cannot imagine he would make a good companion."

Still fuming, Sara stopped by Aunt Delphi's chair. "It doesn't matter what type of a companion he would be. He doesn't wish to marry me, and I don't wish to marry him."

"He's the devil's own spawn," Anthony said. "It goes without saying that he'll be difficult to live with."

Sara continued to pace the floor, her skirts swishing over the Persian carpet. She'd awakened this morning to the shocking news that Nick had agreed to marry her. It was the last thing she'd expected, for if anyone could hold out against her brothers, it would be he.

Her heart ached to imagine what Nick must think of her. She wouldn't be surprised if he was even now cursing her name. Shoulders sagging, she pressed a hand to her temple. "Nick will not dance tamely to your bidding, Marcus, no matter what you say."

"He'll do as he's promised," Marcus said.

The words made Sara grind her teeth. "Why would he bother? He has no more wish to wed than I."

"How do you know?" Anthony asked. "Did you ask him?"

Her face heated, and Anthony covered his eyes. "Pray do not say another word. I don't wish to know."

"Bridgeton had a choice, Sara," Marcus said. "And he chose marriage."

"Get married or die. I vow, how *did* he make up his mind so quickly?"

"I wanted to shoot him," Anthony offered. "But Marcus would not allow it."

"You are both insufferable!"

"Sara, it is already set," Marcus said. "In two weeks' time, the Earl of Bridgeton will marry you. It is his duty. He may not have the moral quality I would wish, but he is at least a gentleman."

"He's a bastard," Anthony growled.

"That, too," Marcus agreed.

"You don't know anything about him," Sara said, crossing her arms beneath her breasts. It was just like them to judge Nick solely by the face he showed to society.

"I know several things about your infamous earl," Marcus said. "I made inquiries the first moment your path crossed his, the night of the Jeffries ball."

"How did you know about—" Sara turned to look at Aunt Delphi, who was suddenly engrossed in picking a knot from her embroidery. "I should have known."

Delphi had the grace to look shamefaced. "I was only trying to protect you. I could see at once that you were far more interested in that man than was good for you. And I dared not speak out, for you have a deplorable tendency to do the opposite of everything I say."

"I'm sorry you feel I am so unreasonable," Sara said stiffly.

"Aunt Delphi did not mean to hurt your feel-

ings, but you know it's true," Marcus replied.
"You are headstrong and willful, and completely
unmanageable."

"Yes, a perfect St. John by any measure," Sara retorted. How Nick must rue the day he'd met her. An
unexpected lump of sadness clogged her throat.

Marcus turned from the window to sit on the
edge of his desk. "Don't worry, Sara. Bridgeton will
make an honest woman of you. His pride will not
allow him to do else."

"I don't want to be an honest woman. I tried it
once, and the price was far to high."

"She has a point, Marcus."

Anthony raised his head. "Aunt Delphi!"

Delphi's hands fluttered. "What? It's true, you
know. And I always thought—but that doesn't—
Sara knows what I mean."

"Delphinea, don't let Anthony rattle you," Marcus said, sending a black look at his brother.

Anthony showed no remorse. "I'll wager ten
pounds Bridgeton doesn't even show up for the
ceremony."

"Done," Marcus said promptly. "Bridgeton is not
like Julius. A man's reputation and his quality are
often a different thing." He met Sara's gaze and
smiled. "You, of all people, should be aware of
that."

It was true. Julius had been society's darling, the
most pleasant, likable man on Earth, yet a total
wastrel, a compulsive gambler, an unfaithful husband.

But what of Nick? Was it possible that he, too,

was the opposite of his reputation? That beneath his caustic exterior lay tenderness and the ability for true emotion? The idea haunted her. Sara waved a hand. "It doesn't matter. I just want everyone to let me be."

"You are acting irresponsibly."

"And enjoying every minute of it." She dropped into a chair and stretched her legs before her, ignoring Aunt Delphi's disapproving murmur. "Why must we follow the dictates of society every second, even when we're alone? Life is too short to waste on propriety."

Anthony made a disgusted sound. "I can't believe you are talking about propriety."

That fired her. She jutted out her chin, and said, "Bridgeton wasn't anywhere he wasn't invited. I happen to find him attractive." And sensual. And tantalizingly forbidden. And, oh God, as delectable as apple tarts covered with rich, heavy cream. "Unfortunately, he isn't the kind of man one would marry."

"Then what kind of man is he?"

"One made for sin."

Anthony reddened. "I don't want to hear any more of that, if you please. For your sake, I hope that you are wrong and there is more to him than you think."

Sara hugged herself, suddenly cold. "He won't come," she said dully. "You will schedule the ceremony, and he won't show up."

Aunt Delphi reached over to pat her hand. "I'm sure he'll come, though he's bound to be nervous. Marriage does that to men."

"Nicholas Montrose hasn't a weak nerve in his entire body. He's as calculating as a snake and the most licentious man I've ever met."

"Oh, dear," Aunt Delphi said faintly, blinking rapidly. "Then I suppose it's a good thing that your brothers are here to see to it that he does his duty."

Sara covered her eyes with one hand. That was exactly the problem. She didn't want to be anyone's "duty" ever again. But now, it appeared she'd have no choice.

Time crawled to a stop as the day progressed. Sara thought about going to Hibberton Hall, but every time she went to the door, she wondered what she would say and how Nick would react. Each time, she ended up back in the sitting room, her stomach almost sick with apprehension.

Marcus and Anthony left after dinner, and Sara heard them returning to their bedchambers shortly after she'd retired. Alone in her room, Sara leaned her heated face against the cool windowpane. Damn Marcus. She could only pray that Nick didn't think she had anything to do with this. The deep burn of humiliation made her move impatiently from the window. She would go see Nick tomorrow and assure him that all they had to do was stand firm in their denials, and Marcus would let them be.

In a way, she was surprised Nick had not come to visit her already. "The jackanapes," she muttered. It was the least he could do. She plopped down at the vanity and stared at her reflection, pulling the pins from her hair and tossing them onto the cluttered surface. "He didn't come because he didn't wish to. I will be as welcome in Hibberton Hall as the plague." She could almost imagine him recoiling in disgust when next he saw her, his fine mouth curved in a sneer.

The image was so vivid that her throat tightened. She'd managed to hold her tears at bay this long by steadfastly keeping in motion. But in the quiet of the night, the reality was almost too much to bear.

A soft knock startled her. It was well past midnight, and she'd thought everyone was abed. Opening the door, Sara discovered Aunt Delphi clothed in a heavily ruffled robe, a tray in her hands.

She offered a hesitant smile. "I hope I'm not bothering you, but I brought you some tea."

"I don't really want—"

"It will make you feel better."

Sara couldn't refuse such a hopeful look. She stood back and allowed her aunt into her room. "I was just getting ready for bed."

Aunt Delphi swept past, the edges of her robe opening to reveal a lacy gown beneath. Sara lifted her brows at the sight of such a racy garment, but she refrained from comment. In the past month, Aunt Delphi had shown remarkable signs of improvement, and Sara was not about to discourage her now.

Sara took the cup her aunt held out to her, and sat down.

"There," Aunt Delphi said, settling back in her chair and beaming. "This is much better, isn't it? I vow but it has been an eventful few days."

When her aunt then sat fiddling with her teacup,

Sara's curiosity increased. "Is something wrong, Aunt Delphi?"

"Well, I . . . that is—I just wanted you to know that despite what you think, despite what your brothers think, I'm very proud of you."

Sara blinked. "Proud?"

A smile touched Delphi's mouth. "You remind me so much of your mother; she always went after what she wanted in life. I never did anything adventurous except . . ." She looked down at her cup, a wistful expression on her face.

"Except what?"

"When I was sixteen, there was a young man—a boy, really. We were young and impressionable, and neither of us had a feather to fly with, but oh, how we did dream."

"What happened?"

Her smile turned sad. "He wanted me to run away with him, but my mother was very ill, you know. So I stayed in Herefordshire. His father sent him on a tour of the Continent. When I saw him next, he was married to a young lady who possessed a much greater fortune than I."

Aunt Delphi ran a finger around the rim of her teacup, her gaze faraway. "I think he was happy. He seemed to be, at any rate."

"Oh, Aunt!" Sara said impulsively. She put her cup aside to grasp her aunt's hand. "I'm so sorry."

Delphi laughed so genuinely that Sara blinked. "Nonsense; I'm sure it was for the best. I would not have traded those last few months with my mother for the world."

"I daresay it was difficult at the time."

"Of course. But later, Langtry asked my father for my hand in marriage. He was wealthy, titled, and his family had always been particularly close to mine."

"Did you love him?"

Aunt Delphi set her cup on the saucer, the gentle clink loud in the silence. "I came to respect him greatly. He was a very deserving man."

"But did you love him?"

"Eventually. Sometimes one doesn't get everything one wants in life. Sometimes you just have to make do."

Sara stood, her arms crossed as if to ward off a chill. "I don't want to make do!"

"No one does, but—" Aunt Delphi tilted her head to one side. "Did you hear that?"

"Hear what?"

"I daresay it was the wind, for there's a storm brewing. Marcus said it was starting to rain when he returned." She gathered the tray and rose. "Sara, whatever happens, commit yourself with all your heart and never look back."

"To Bridgeton?"

"To whoever will make you happy." With one last smile, she left.

Sara remained in the center of the room, listening absently to the far off rattle of china as Aunt Delphi carried the tray downstairs. For a wild moment, she wondered what it would be like to spend the rest of her days with Nick. She closed her eyes and imagined wakening to finding him asleep at her side.

The thought simmered contentedly, and for the first time in two days, the tension left her shoulders.

But then she remembered Nick's look of fury the night he'd discovered her with Hewlette and had accused her of laying a trap. Sara shivered. For all of his passion, for all of the pleasure she knew instinctively to find in Nick's arms, he would *never* forgive her for this forced marriage.

There was no help for it. In the morning, she'd go to Hibberton Hall and free him from the horrible bargain her brothers had made. Finally content that she'd found the best course of action, Sara readied for bed. She'd just put her arms into her night rail and tugged it over her head when a loud click and the brush of cold air made her whirl toward the window.

She was immediately crushed against a powerful chest. She fought wildly, swinging her fist with all her might, a thrill of satisfaction breaking through her panic as her knuckles connected with solid flesh. Her assailant cursed, then picked her up and tossed her on the bed, pinning her to the mattress with his body.

"Damn it, Sara! Be quiet," Nick's voice sounded in her ears.

Sara instantly stilled, peering at him through the curls tangled across her face.

He released one of her hands and brushed the hair from her eyes. Though his touch was gentle, his face was grim. "I'm sorry to frighten you, but we've no time."

Her heart skipped a beat. "Time for what?"

"For our wedding, dearest Sara." He said the words without a trace of tenderness.

"But we don't need to do that. I was going to slip out tomorrow and tell you that it is all a mistake. Marcus can't truly force us to do anything."

Nick rolled off her and went to her wardrobe, reaching in and grabbing the first gown he found. "Get dressed."

"Nick, I—"

He tossed the gown at her. "When I get married, it will be at a time and place of my choosing. And I choose now."

"*What?*"

"You heard me. We are getting married this very night, and to hell with your brother."

"But I don't want to marry you!"

His eyes blazed hot blue and then suddenly, he wasn't standing in front of her but lying on top of her once again, his body pressing hers intimately into the mattress. She struggled to free herself, but he caught her hands and held them over her head. "Let me explain something, Sara. We have been embroiled in a scandal. In order to avert disaster, we must wed. Those are the rules. You don't have to like them, but by God, you will follow them."

"Don't be ridiculous."

"I'm not. Now are you coming willingly, or do I wrap you in a blanket and throw you over my shoulder?"

For some reason, the idea held immense appeal. Still, she worried he would fall trying to navigate the ladder. "I could scream."

He grinned, the sight sending her heart into a spin. He rolled off her and leaned back against the headboard, his arms crossed behind his head. "Then scream. I'm sure your brothers would be all too happy to discover me in your room."

He was right. And knowing her brothers, they would be all too glad to get their fists on Nick. Furthermore, they would see Nick's presence as yet another reason why they should marry.

She pushed herself upright and noted the way his gaze flickered across her breasts. She glanced down and realized the thin muslin of her night rail hid very little. Blushing profusely, she crossed her arms over her breasts. "Damn it, I don't want you in here. In fact, I don't want you at all."

"Too bad, sweetheart. Neither of us has a choice." He lifted a brow. "So, what's it going to be? Are you coming willingly, or do I abduct you?"

She sat staring at him as if she'd never seen him before. Nick smiled. If he couldn't appeal to her emotions, then he'd appeal to her sense of adventure. "Perhaps you're afraid."

She glanced at the window for a long moment, a sudden gleam in her eye. "What did you use to reach the window? A rope ladder?"

"No, a rather mundane, wooden one."

Sara scrambled from the bed, pushed the window farther open, and looked out, forgetting to cover herself. "Wherever did you find the ladder?"

Nick dragged his eyes from the graceful line of her legs revealed through her thin night rail. "I borrowed it from the carpenters at Hibberton Hall."

"And you brought it all the way here?"

"In a cart. It's only three miles." Nick crossed to the window and leaned against the curtain, admiring the tumble of her hair. "Of course, I had to tell the carpenter an outlandish tale."

"What did you say?"

"That I intended to abscond with a beautiful maiden."

Her lips twitched, and Nick relaxed. He should have realized that she would be as upset as he had been by her brothers' high-handed behavior. "Come with me, Sara. We shall have a grand adventure."

"I thought you didn't wish to marry."

"I didn't. But what propriety demands . . ." He shrugged, then slipped his hand into his pocket and pulled out a folded piece of paper. Sara took it and opened it, tilting it so the candlelight fell on the writing.

Her lips moved as she read the words. "It's a special license." She lifted her eyes to his. "You really do mean to marry me."

He took the paper and replaced it in his pocket, then bent and placed his lips to her ear. "Have you ever climbed out of your window in the dead of night?"

She sucked in her breath in excitement. "It *is* an adventure, isn't it?"

The sight of her smile made his chest ache, and he knew that this moment would be with him when he finally died, no matter how mad he became.

"I've never climbed out of a window before. Or eloped," she said.

"Neither have I. I must warn you, though—your brothers will be furious."

She let out her breath in a satisfied puff. "I'll do it." Then she added, "But first, we have to reach an agreement."

"Oh?"

"There are things we must discuss. I have certain requirements of a marriage."

It was a damnable shame he would never meet the late Viscount Carrington, for he would have taken a great deal of delight in beating the hell out of the man. Stifling his impatience, Nick sat on the edge of the bed and waited.

She crossed her arms, blocking the enticing outline of her breasts from his view. "You know what type of husband I was looking for."

"I'm not that kind. I won't share what's mine." She opened her mouth to speak, but he held up his hand. "Before you begin making a lot of rules which neither of us will be able to abide, let's just agree to take our relationship one day at a time."

"I want honesty. If at any time you plan on . . . leaving me, I want to be told."

"That seems fine."

She met his gaze steadily, a hint of mistrust in their depths. "And what of our future?"

"I have a house, I possess a fortune, and I promise to leave it all to you when I die." He stood. "Do you need to know anything else?"

Disappointment lingered in her gaze, but she shook her head. "No. I suppose not."

Nick reached out and pulled her to him, then

lowered his mouth to within an inch of hers. "There are other compensations for our marriage." He nipped at her lower lip, then moved his mouth to her temple. "Lovely, erotic compensations."

Within the circle of his arms, she shivered, and he became aware of her nipples pressing against the white linen of her nightgown. Moving slowly, careful not to startle her, he gently cupped one of her breasts, his palm kneading the tempting mound.

"Stop," she said, her voice trembling with desire. "I'll go with you."

Nick captured her hand and placed a kiss on the palm. "Excellent. Then don your clothing and let's be off."

She dressed quickly while Nick pretended not to watch. It was difficult, the way his body ached for her. The thought that she would soon be his was almost too tempting to contain.

"Nick, how am I to climb down a ladder in a dress?"

"Hmm. I hadn't thought of that. Fortunately, there is another way out."

She blinked her confusion. "What—"

He opened the door to the hallway and bowed. "After you, madam."

"Nick," she whispered, trying to push the door closed again, "you can't go through the house! If my brothers see you, they will kill you!"

"Their own future brother-in-law? Surely they wouldn't be so crass."

"Shhh! Nick, I—"

He stopped her protests by swinging her up into

his arms. "I'm through arguing. We are leaving through the front door, and that is final."

She frowned, but looped her arms about his neck. "At least try and be—"

He kicked the door back, the heavy wood slamming into the paneling and echoing throughout the house.

"—quiet," Sara finished. She closed her eyes for a pained moment and then sighed. "You are determined to start a fight, aren't you?"

"Not if it means I'd have to set you down."

"Anthony will not be happy."

"Anthony can go to h—"

"Bridgeton, what in the hell are you doing?" Anthony demanded. He stood blocking the hallway, wearing nothing but a pair of breeches.

Nick nodded pleasantly. "Greyley. And how are you this evening? Or should I say morning?"

"Put her down."

"No. She's mine." A devilish smile touched his mouth. "Treymount gave her to me." Nick walked forward, but Anthony did not budge.

Sara peeped at them as they stared at one another, two gladiators prepared to battle to the death. Only she was between them, and had nary a weapon on her. She cleared her throat. "Perhaps we should sit down and discuss this calmly."

"I have a better idea," Anthony said. "Bridgeton will set you down, then he and I will settle this between us."

"Winner takes all?" Nick asked softly.

"Of course," Anthony bit back.

"Bridgeton." Marcus's voice came from behind them. "State your intentions."

For a moment, Sara wondered if Nick would answer. But after a long silence, he shrugged. "I have a special license. I'm taking Sara with me, and I'm marrying her, to keep her from being banished or foisted off on the first stodgy old man who comes along. She deserves more, Treymount. Far more than either of you is willing to allow her."

Marcus flickered a glance at Sara, then said, "Anthony, let them go."

Anthony's huge hands fisted, but he nodded. "So long as he plans to marry her tonight."

"As soon as we arrive at Hibberton. The vicar is waiting even now."

Marcus waited until Anthony had moved aside. "I'll be out to see Sara tomorrow, Bridgeton. I will want to speak with the vicar when I come."

"Of course." Nick tightened his hold on Sara and continued to walk down the hall, down the stairs, and out the front door.

Sara shivered in the night air. Nick pulled a large blanket from beneath the seat of the carriage and tucked it about her, then sat beside her. The carriage jolted forward, and they were on their way.

Sara pulled the blanket closer about her shoulders. This was madness, to abscond in the night like two lovers when they scarcely knew one another. She suddenly wondered if he liked plum pudding. Did he have a favorite color? What did she really know of the man?

Panic swept through her. *Bloody hell, I'm marrying a complete stranger.*

Well, that wasn't strictly true. She knew the little he'd told her about his mother. And she already knew she was attracted to him—that was something, at least. He was also a hardened rake, and if anyone understood rakes, it was she.

The carriage finally rolled to a stop. Nick hopped down, then lifted a hand to assist her from the carriage.

Sara scrambled down, her foot tangling in the blanket and sending her tumbling right into Nick's arms.

He swept her up once again and turned toward the house. "I know you wish for pretty words, but I've never been good at those. I fear you'll have to take me"—his gaze dropped to her mouth—"as I am."

"Damn," she muttered.

A devilish light lit his eyes. Sighing, Sara looped her arms about his neck and let him carry her. It was rather pleasant to be held so. He walked right past the startled butler and went up the stairs into the front hall.

"M-my lord," the ancient retainer sputtered. "My lord, where are you . . . who is . . . should I have Mrs. Kibble prepare a chamber for the lady?"

Nick stopped at the door to the library and glanced at the harassed butler. "This, Wiggs, is the future Lady Bridgeton, whom I am to marry in less than ten minutes."

The butler's mouth opened and closed. "Here, my lord?"

"The vicar is on his way."

"My lord, it is nearly one in the morning!"

"I am well aware of the time. Notify me when the vicar arrives."

Blinking rapidly, Wiggs bowed. "Yes, my lord." He barely waited for Nick to turn before he scuttled down a side hall, ready to repeat the tale for the entire household.

Nick carried her to the settee and placed her on it. "You look lovely in pink, my dear."

"I prefer red. Bright red."

A deep chuckle rumbled in his chest, the sound teasing past her ears to settle in her bones. "So do I."

There was a soft knock at the door, and Wiggs appeared. "The vicar has arrived, my lord."

"Show him to the blue salon."

Her stomach clenched, Sara moved to stand before the mirror that hung over the mantle. She ran her fingers through her tangled curls.

"Leave it. It looks fine." His voice was so close behind her that she started, tensing when he slipped an arm about her waist to pull her against him. He lowered his face and pressed it against her hair. "You smell like lavender," he murmured, then pressed his lips to her temple.

He took a last, deep breath before releasing her. "Come. It's time." He took her hand and led her from the room.

As they walked down the hallway, she glanced furtively at him. Gone was the sparkle in his eye, the teasing note in his voice. He was silent, his expression serious. A heavy weight pressed against Sara's chest. What had she gotten herself into?

The vicar met them in the study, his kindly face dispelling some of Sara's fears. He spoke quietly with Nick, and then turned and opened his book to begin the ceremony.

Before he'd spoken more than two words, a commotion was raised in the foyer. Amazingly, Sara heard Aunt Delphi's soft voice pitched for combat.

"Damn it," Nick said, taking a quick step toward the door.

Sara forestalled him with a single touch. "It's just Aunt Delphi."

As if in answer, the door flew open and Delphi stood in the opening, Nick's decrepit butler hovering behind her. Her back as inflexible as a steel pole, Aunt Delphi sniffed. "I came to witness the wedding, but this creature would not allow me to pass."

Wiggs sent a helpless glance at Nick. "I tried to tell her that you were not home, my lord, but she would not believe me."

Nick came to stand beside Sara. "Wiggs, bring us some tea. I'm sure Her Grace is chilled."

Though obviously loath to retreat from the battlefield, Wiggs complied. Aunt Delphi watched him go with a martial gleam in her eye. "Thank you, Bridgeton."

Nick bowed. "Of course, Your Grace. I'm delighted you came to witness the ceremony."

"I wouldn't miss it for the world."

Sara supposed she shouldn't be surprised. She

glanced around the entry, but saw no one else. "And Marcus and Anthony?"

Delphi's face pinched with disapproval. "They were halfway through their second bottle of port when I last saw them. I daresay they won't be coming."

Sara was glad of that much, at least. To her relief, the ceremony was quick. When the time came to place the ring on her finger, Sara was surprised when Nick pulled a small circle of gold from his pocket. Moments later, the ceremony was over.

Sara stood in the center of the room as Nick escorted the vicar to his waiting carriage. She was married. Thoughts of her other wedding intruded, and she couldn't help contrasting the two. Her wedding to Julius had been a display of wealth, an exhibit of perfection. Every detail had been meticulously planned, with nothing left to chance. Her dress alone had cost a fortune, the church filled with flowers, a wide assortment of friends and family gathered to witness what should have been her finest hour.

Ha—*that* hadn't come until almost three years later, when she decided she wouldn't mourn the husband who had long before left her.

Sara gazed at the band on her finger. The warm light of the fire touched the gold and made the delicate design stand out in relief. Tiny flowers had been etched into the surface, a single vine twining about the whole. It was beautiful, elegant, and simple, and she somehow knew that Nick had selected it himself.

"Sara?" Aunt Delphi hesitated. "If you need me to stay—"

"I'm afraid that will not be possible," Nick said, coming into the room. "The house is still being repaired, and no extra rooms are ready for inhabiting. Lady Langtry, thank you for attending."

Delphi flushed. "Yes, I suppose I should go."

Unrepentant, Nick escorted Delphi to her carriage. Sara watched them go, suddenly feeling alone. She felt like a stranger here at Hibberton Hall, but she was now the mistress and responsible for all aspects of the house. The thought slowly settled into her mind, and she sank to the edge of the settee, looking about her with startled wonder.

How could she be mistress of a residence like this? Oh, she'd run an establishment before, but she and Julius had confined their housekeeping to a narrow town house in London. This was something altogether different. A slow, uncertain pressure began to press on Sara's shoulders.

After several moments the door opened, and Wiggs came into the room. He stopped on seeing Sara. "My lady! I thought you were with Lady Langtry."

Sara stood, nervously smoothing her gown. "No. I was just sitting here and . . ." What? Feeling sorry for herself? Heavens, but she was being ridiculous. She was a St. John, born and bred, and it was time she began to act like it. "I would like to retire now. Could you lead the way to the master chamber?"

The butler hesitated. "Yes, my lady. However, I believe—"

"Excellent," Sara said briskly. She went to the door and waited for the butler to open it.

He followed at once and led her up the grand staircase in silence, then escorted her down a bewildering set of halls. Wiggs finally stopped at the very end of a long and drafty corridor before a set of wide oak doors. He opened them and stepped aside.

Sara walked into the room, refusing to even look around until she was alone and more in control. "This will be fine. My clothes will be arriving tomorrow, and I will need the services of a maid."

"Yes, my lady. I will inform Mrs. Kibble in the morning."

"Thank you, Wiggs," she said, turning away.

"As you wish, my lady. If you require anything else, please do not hesitate to ring." So saying, he bowed and left, shutting the doors behind him.

As soon as the door closed, Sara whirled to look around the room. Though spacious and opulently furnished, it was also stark. The heavy red curtains that draped the windows and the bed were without decoration, and even the walls were unadorned. Yet everything was neatly in its place—a wardrobe filled one wall, several chairs were meticulously grouped about a crackling fire, and a robe was neatly folded on a small stool by the bed.

She walked toward the huge bed, admiring the heavy piece of furniture. It was large enough to comfortably sleep five or six people. She placed a hand on the mattress, and the memory of Nick's warm body atop hers flittered through her mind and lingered. She smiled and trailed her fingers along the heavy red cover. Perhaps there *were* compensations for being married that she hadn't yet considered.

Sara glanced at the closed door, then climbed onto the edge of the bed, wondering what Nick looked like in the mornings—his hair mussed, his eyes heavy with sleep. Her breasts tingled at the thought—she knew exactly what he would look like.

Still, despite the fact that she found him irresistibly attractive, she must remember that this was not the marriage she'd hoped for. Nick was not a man who would sit tamely by while she went her way. Worse still, had it not been for his pride and his desire to be respectably established, he'd have refused to wed her, no matter what threats her brothers employed. It was a very lowering thought.

The door opened, and Nick entered. He came to a halt when he saw her sitting on the bed. "Sara. I thought Wiggs had taken you to your room."

"I thought this was—" Her cheeks heated. Of course there was a separate chamber for her; she'd been foolish to think otherwise.

Nick closed the door and crossed to stir the fire. "I'm afraid I'm using the connecting rooms as storage." He replaced the poker. "Shall I show you to your room now? You must be tired."

Sara nodded, feeling betrayed in a way. She'd assumed that she and Nick would enjoy an even greater physical intimacy than they'd already shared. She followed him toward the door, but then stopped. "Wait, Nick. I don't understand why is there . . . am I . . ." She gestured, unable to frame the question.

"Sara, I have no wish for children." His expression was dark, almost bitter.

"But last night—"

"I should never have allowed last night to happen. We'll blame it on the brandy and the fact that I was certain I was shortly going to my death."

"But do you ever want children?"

"No."

Sara bit her lip. "I see. Then we will not be sharing a bed or . . ." Disappointment colored her voice.

He smiled then, his gaze warming as he reached out and stroked a finger down her cheek. "There are ways to give each other release without actually making love." His hand dropped from her and he stepped away. "But tonight, you are no doubt tired and—"

She wrapped her arms about his neck and pulled his mouth hard to hers. He responded immediately, his mouth hot and possessive. Sara melted against him, all her pent-up emotions swirling to the fore. She clutched Nick's lapels and held him closer, but even that was not enough. She wanted him closer, to assuage the uncertainty that threatened to overwhelm her.

He moaned, sweeping her up and carrying her to the bed, his hands moving everywhere—across her breasts, down her sides, sliding a pathway from her breast to her hip and back again. He laid her on the bed without breaking the kiss, and with his mouth still hot over hers, he wrapped a hand about her ankle and slowly slid it up her leg.

His fingers drew a heated line past the inside of her knee, leaving a trail of delicate fire all the way up until he could cup her womanhood. She shifted to give him better access, and he gently stroked her.

Nick's excitement grew as he watched Sara's face. She glowed with passion, her eyes closing as he teased her to the brink of madness. God, but she was beautiful. Beautiful, and all his. The thought was unexpectedly erotic, and he grew even harder.

Her back arched, Sara pressed against his hand, moaning deeply. Nick was aroused beyond belief. He longed to thrust himself into her, to feel her hot sheath clutch about his straining erection. He stroked her more deeply, urging her on.

She gasped with need; her hands clutched his shoulders as she suddenly tightened her thighs about his hand. "Nick, *please*."

"No," he said, his breath as ragged as hers. He parted her thighs and cupped her once again, moving his fingers quicker and quicker.

Watching Sara made his blood simmer and boil. His brow grew damp as he felt her sudden ripple of pleasure, and she finally climaxed against his fingers.

His breath harsh in his throat, Nick sank his face into her hair and held her close, fighting to keep his tenuous control.

After a moment, Sara moved uncertainly, but Nick held her tightly. "Don't move," he murmured, fighting for the air to speak. "Not yet."

For several long moments they lay still, legs entwined, arms about each other. Finally Nick took one, last shuddering breath before he pulled back to look into Sara's eyes. He could see the lingering remnants of their passion, the hunger that had made her grasp his shoulders so tightly.

Nick gently cupped Sara's face and looked into her eyes. "See, love? Though we can't enjoy each other as we did last night, we can still give each other pleasure."

A tremulous smile touched her lips. "But what about you?"

He took her hand and placed a kiss on the palm. "We will talk about that another time. Right now, you are tired." He released her hand and tugged her skirts back down. "Come, let me show you to your chambers. Your aunt brought a portmanteau with some of your clothing, to last until we send for the rest of your things."

Careful not to meet her gaze, Nick saw Sara to her chamber. He'd selected one that was a safe distance down the hall. Though the chamber adjoining his was meant to serve as the private sanctuary of the mistress of the house, he didn't trust himself to have so much heady temptation within such close reach.

It was better for them both if they had to traverse a goodly length of chilled corridor before coming to each other's rooms. The coldness of the hallway would surely deter the passion that too easily flared between them.

Wiggs had already been to Sara's chamber, so the

fire was blazing, the bed made and turned down, the portmanteau unpacked. Mrs. Kibble sat dozing by the fire, jerking to awareness as soon as Nick opened the door. With a sense of relief, Nick said good night and returned to the privacy of his own chamber.

There, he stood staring down into the fire, wondering at the fates that had caused his marriage to a woman like Sara. He would not allow himself to become a slave to the desire he felt for her, nor would he allow her access to his heart. After all, there was no future for them.

His relationship to Sara would be confined to the here and now, to the safety of the present. That decided, he put another log on the fire and got ready for bed.

Chapter 16

Morning sunlight streaked across the empty hallways of the Duchess of Langtry's town house. Silent as a dust mote, Delphi pulled the hood of her cloak over her head and slipped noiselessly outside. The door latch made no sound, and even the birds seemed to have forgotten to sing.

The sun did little more than brighten the cold day, but Delphi didn't notice. Heart pounding, she walked away from the house and hurried to the corner. Once there, she hugged herself to stave off the cold and waited. Beneath her cloak, she wore a scandalously cut red gown that shimmered like the light of a thousand fires. Delphi shivered at her own temerity, but never had she felt so alive.

From a distance came the clop-clop of an approaching vehicle. A heavily curtained carriage pulled up, the door swinging open before it came to a complete stop.

Her whole body tingled with anticipation. Glancing over her shoulder, Delphi climbed into the carriage. It was off again before the door had time to close, and soon she was surrounded in semidarkness.

Large, powerful hands grasped her arms, and she was lifted and then deposited on a warm, masculine lap as if she weighed no more than a feather. "Ah, my little Delphinea," murmured a husky, lightly accented voice.

Delphi lifted her face to the comte and accepted his kiss. His mouth teased and tested her, making her mad with a nameless desire. It was always like this—the passion, the furor.

Thump.

Delphi lifted her head. "What was that?"

"Ignore it, *ma petite,*" Henri murmured, his hands caressing her beneath her cloak. Each brush of his fingers was delicious torture. Henri placed his lips to her ear. "You are a seductress and I cannot stay away."

Thump. Thump.

Delphi pulled the hood of her cloak tighter over her head to block out the troublesome sound, but still it came.

Thump. Thump. Thump.

"My lady?" came a soft, feminine voice.

Delphi moaned.

"Ah, *ma chère,*" Henri said, his voice fading. "I must leave."

"But I don't want you to," Delphi cried.

"But I must," he said, tipping up her chin and smiling into her eyes. "Never fear, though; I will wait for you. Always."

He bent to kiss her good-bye and in that moment, Delphi awakened.

She was not in a carriage with Henri, dressed in a scandalous red gown and wrapped in a fur-lined cloak. Instead, she lay in her own bed, her sheets pulled over her head, her maid knocking at the door.

Delphi rolled to her back and pulled the sheets off her head, the dream so vivid that she could almost feel the pressure of Henri's mouth on hers. Every night, she dreamed the same thing—of the comte holding her, touching her, making mad love to her. But it was all such a futile effort. At one time he had shown a great interest in her, and she'd thought— no, she'd *hoped*—that it might become more. But his insistence that they meet clandestinely had sent her into such a quiver of uncertainty that she'd cut the connection. He'd been disbelieving at first, and then hurt, culminating in a huge row in which he had said all sorts of hurtful things, calling her "weak-willed" and "afraid to live."

The words rang hollowly in her mind as she watched her maid enter with the breakfast tray. It had been almost a week since Henri had last spoken to her, though he let her know with his every look that he thought her foolish to have refused him.

Delphi closed her eyes and wished with all her heart that she had the courage to take him up on his offer, even though the practical part of her rejected the idea—she knew the man wasn't even a real comte. Nor was he wealthy, as he liked to imply. He was a scoundrel, and any relationship they might have would only lead to heartache.

The maid stoked the fire and arranged the tray on the table beside it, then left. Delphi waited until the door closed before she gathered her pillow and let the tears fall.

Sara's second week at Hibberton Hall passed much like her first. From morning until night, she sorted out a variety of household problems that spanned the state of the linens to the placement of the new desk in the morning room. Sara was glad for the nonstop barrage of work, for it kept her from thinking about Nick—a topic that was beginning to consume her every waking moment.

Though she would never have credited it, he continually managed to pleasure her in new ways, still keeping away from true consummation. And true to his word, he had shown her ways to pleasure him, as well. She'd reveled in them all. Yet the more they refrained from the actual act, the more she desired it. It was as if he withheld a part of himself from her, something more precious than the physical aspects.

Sara had the feeling that their marriage was a dream, an illusion that would only last until Nick tired of her. And the day would come; she knew it. It was there in his eyes, in the way he spoke to her, as if, in some indefinable way, he was reminding her that he would not always be with her. She stored the unsettling comments away and refused to think of them.

Instead, she concentrated on Hibberton Hall. Every inch of the house fascinated her, from the ornate plasterwork on the ceiling of the library to the newly tended pathways in the garden.

Sara sighed and leaned against the stone wall that surrounded the small pond, pulling the collar of her pelisse to her chin. Unsettled and alone, she felt her spirits sinking lower every day.

"Dreaming of where you are going to put the fountain?" Nick stood several paces away, immaculate in a deep blue riding jacket, his hands shoved into the pockets.

An immediate wave of desire rippled across her, a desire that was growing stronger every day; that he was so close and yet untouchable made her yearn for him the more. She had to look away from him just to get her mouth to form an answer. "I was trying to decide if we should use the pink stone or the yellow for the pathways."

He came to stand beside her, dropping a kiss on her cheek, his voice shivery-hard against her ear. "Ah, the difficulties of gardening. I'm glad it is you, and not I, who has to struggle with such items." He let his hands wander up her waist, past her ribs and on to cup her breasts, his hands warm and demanding.

Sara arched into his palms and closed her eyes, desire sparkling along her spine. She shivered and pulled away, turning to face him. "Where have you been today?" She noticed a hint of pallor beneath his tan, and frowned.

He looped an arm about her shoulders and pulled her against him, resting his chin on the top of her head. "I've been with the workmen in the west wing, doing what we can to salvage some of the original paneling."

"How engrossing."

A chuckle sounded deep in his chest. "Trying to lure me from my work, are you? I hope you are as lusty this evening as you are today, madam."

Sara wondered if she'd imagined that look of strained illness, but before she could answer, Henri came charging across the lawn.

"There you are! Wiggs has just announced luncheon. I came to see if Lady Bridgeton would like a real man to escort her indoors and not a lovesick boy."

Sara managed a smile as she took the comte's arm. She'd developed a new appreciation for Henri, and rather wished Aunt Delphi and the comte had been able to resolve their differences. Perhaps marriage to Nick had softened her, but she'd begun to believe that Henri was capable of sincere feelings. Certainly, his concern for Nick was proof of that.

They went in for lunch, Henri talking animatedly. Nick said little, unusually quiet. Sara noticed that he did not eat, but merely shifted the food on his plate. At the end of the meal, he asked Wiggs for some brandy.

The butler frowned in disapproval. "My lord, perhaps you should forgo the brandy."

Nick turned slowly. "I beg your pardon?" His voice was low, soft, yet Sara felt a tremor of unease.

His expression strained, the butler collected the decanter and set it on the table. "Forgive my intrusion, my lord."

Nick said nothing. His mouth white, he poured himself a deep drink. Sara frowned. Several times in the past week, she'd heard the servants making a variety of comments that bordered on the parental, all of which Nick met with barely concealed impatience.

She glanced at her husband from beneath her lashes. "Your servants are very fond of you."

"They are fools."

"At least they are not rude," she returned.

"*Excellente*, Madame Bridgeton," the comte said approvingly. "Teach him some manners. He needs them very badly."

Nick glared at Henri, but the Frenchman had already turned his attention back to his plate.

Sara leaned forward. "Nick, why didn't Wiggs want you to have brandy?"

"Because he mistakenly thinks it causes my headaches."

"Perhaps he is right." At Nick's scowl, she added, "Surely there is a way to cure them. Aunt Delphi has a headache every time it rains, and she takes laudanum to—"

"No laudanum."

"But if it can help your headaches—"

"No," he snapped.

Sara flushed at the harsh tone of his voice, and even Henri put down his fork and stared at them with a frown.

Sara cleared her throat. "If you won't take laudanum, then your headaches must not be bad at all."

"Precisely, madam. They are nothing." He turned away to talk to Henri about a new banister the workmen had just installed.

Hmmm. There was far more here than she'd realized. Something secretive. Sara waited until the meal had ended and Henri was on his way out for his daily ride before broaching the subject again. "If you don't take laudanum, what do you take?"

A frown marred his brow. "Leave it, Sara. I've told you it was nothing."

"I know you did, but if the servants think—"

"I don't care what the servants think and neither should you. They know nothing about it." He turned and strode toward the terrace doors.

Sara hurried to catch up with him. She grabbed his arm and halted him, pulling him around to face her. "Being your wife gives me the right to interfere in every aspect of your life."

"Nonsense."

She crossed her arms and stared at him.

Nick sighed and raked a hand through his hair, wincing at how bright the sun had suddenly become. Though his headaches had greatly decreased when he'd first arrived in England, the last two weeks had seen a gradual increase. Every day a new sign seemed to indicate that his agony was far from over. Nick closed his eyes and rubbed the bridge of his nose.

"Well?" Sara asked impatiently.

"I begin to perceive that I was a bit naive in believing that our union would be simple."

She met his gaze steadily. "If you won't take laudanum, maybe you'd be willing to try an herbal tisane. Aunt Delphi has found chamomile very beneficial."

Nick had to bite his tongue not to snap at her. His head had ached since morning, a dull throbbing pain that warned him of the severe days he had ahead. Damn it, he'd not wanted Sara to know the true extent of his illness. He remembered the terror with which he'd witnessed his mother's agony, and he was resolved that Sara would never look at him with the same heartsick pity.

He glanced down at Sara and said slowly, "It's possible a tisane may help."

She tilted her head to one side, her dusky curls swinging over one shoulder. "What we need is an herb garden. Perhaps I can plant one come spring." She stepped onto the lawn. "I saw a book in the library on that very subject. Would you mind if I planted one here, between the roses and the shrubbery?"

"I'll send the gardener to you."

"That will be lovely." She smiled at him. "You realize what this means, don't you?"

He raised his brows, trying hard not to let any of his pain show in his eyes. "What?"

"That I will expect you to drink my herbal teas every time I make one. Perhaps I will find the one that will cure you!"

"Perhaps," he said, hope lifting his spirits. If she

could find a cure, they could embark on a normal relationship . . . He shook his head. No. How many
times had he seen his mother attempt to find some
way other than laudanum numb her pain and how
many times had she failed?

His throat tightened. He would never allow Sara
to see him fall to such depths. He'd end his life before he'd let that happen—and happen, it would.
The thought pained him worse than his head. Even
in this short time, Sara had brought him so much
pleasure. She deserved better than to be saddled
with a man destined to descend into the pits of hell.

Perhaps Pratt could help him determine a way to
protect Sara when his ultimate end came. She already had the accounts established for her by Marcus, but Nick wanted her to have more. When the
time came that he knew he could no longer endure
the pain, he would ensure that Hibberton Hall and
all his funds would be hers. In addition, he would
safely invest a healthy sum for her future.

She would be truly independent, with a house
that was worthy of her spirit and beauty, perfectly
maintained by a staff that was trained and ready to
serve her.

He tried to imagine Sara living at Hibberton Hall
after his demise, but he couldn't. All he could see
was the picture she made now, dressed in a
sprigged muslin gown, the sun shining through the
window, warming her hair and touching the tip of
her nose.

For the first time in his life, he realized all that he
was going to miss. The unfairness of it made the

blood pound behind his temples. Small white circles skittered at the edge of his vision, and he closed his eyes against the growing pain.

"Nick?"

He could hear Sara's voice as if she were at the end of a long tunnel, the soft tones echoing. He forced his eyes open and made his mouth curve into a grimace. "I just realized I was to meet Henri in the stables to see his new mount."

She smiled, her teeth glimmering whitely between her rose-petal lips. It was always this way right before he suffered an attack. Colors and sounds stretched, capturing other senses with them until they drove him mad.

The tang of metal in his mouth made him realize how little time he had. "I will be back in an hour." Without giving her time to protest, he left, forcing himself to keep his shoulders straight. As soon as he was out of sight, he let the pain go and almost staggered at the impact.

A steady arm gripped him. "*Mon ami*, you would not listen to Wiggs, would you? You have nearly left it too long." Henri kept him from sliding to the floor. "Come, I shall call Sara and—"

"*No.*"

The comte frowned. "But—"

"I don't want her to know how bad they are. Not yet." *Not ever.*

"*Mon ami*, if you do not tell Sara about your illness, what will she think when she sees you?"

He hadn't thought that far ahead; the senseless, stupid part of him had held out false hope that this episode might be brief. "I will go away. Maybe the cottage. The worst attacks only last a day or two before they pass; I will just tell Sara I have to go away on business."

"I am not one to give advice, but I think you are in error. Sara is a strong woman. Why not just tell her—"

"I won't have her frightened."

Henri's brow creased in confusion. "What's there to be frightened of?"

Nick turned away. Even Henri did not understand. Nick never wanted Sara to see him so desperate, so wracked with pain and terror that he didn't know where or who he was. Like his mother had been, the night she died, so crazed that she hadn't known her own son.

It took all of Nick's strength and Henri's assistance, but he made it to the gatekeeper's cottage. There he collapsed into bed and let the pain take its course.

Chapter 17

❦❦

"**M**y lady, you asked for me?" Wiggs said, standing uneasily inside the morning room.

Sara had been nervously pacing the carpet, wondering where her elusive husband had disappeared. "Yes, Wiggs. Just where is the earl?"

Wiggs hesitated, his watery blue gaze slipping past her to the front door. "Where is who, madam?"

Sara plopped her fists on her hips. "His Lordship. The tall, handsome blond man who owns this house."

Wiggs shifted uncomfortably. "I'm sure I don't know. His Lordship was here yesterday."

"I realize that. I ate luncheon with him, remember? But today he is nowhere to be found."

"I believe he left you a message, my lady."

"Saying that he would be back this morning." She gestured to the late-afternoon sun that was swiftly sinking. "Does it look like morning to you?"

Wiggs's gaze drifted to the window over her shoulder, his expression carefully blank. "No, my lady."

It was obvious Wiggs was not going to give an inch. But she'd been on tenterhooks all morning, her imagination running wild. "Surely you know something!"

Wiggs stared stoically ahead, like a prisoner facing a firing squad. "His Lordship rarely takes me into his confidence."

"He may not have told you precisely *where* he was going, but you at least know when he left." Sara took a step closer to the butler. "You did see him, didn't you?"

His gaze grew wild, but he didn't move. "I-uhm, I believe I might have."

"And when was that? Midnight? One o'clock? Two?"

"Your Ladyship, I'm not sure I should—"

"Let me make this easy for you. If you don't tell me when you saw his Lordship last, I shall lie on the floor and have a fit."

He blinked. "A . . . fit, my lady?"

"A complete, unstoppable fit of hysterics. Mrs. Kibble has already twice suggested that I should lie down, in case I was feeling dizzy."

The butler's thin mouth twitched in a smile that was quickly suppressed. He looked at her for a long moment, then said carefully, "My lady, I assure you I would tell you if I were able. But I cannot."

Sara's jaw tightened. So Nick had forbidden his servants to betray his whereabouts, had he? She could only think of one reason he would go to such lengths. The black ooze of betrayal made her stomach sicken.

Damn his soul, she was *not* about to be made a fool again. But first she had to find the bastard. Taking her emotions firmly in control, Sara sat down in a chair and removed her slippers.

Wiggs's eyes widened. "My lady! What are you doing?"

Sara dropped her shoes onto the carpet beside her. "I am preparing to go into hysterics. I cannot abide women who drum the heels of their slippers while screaming. The one sound drowns out the other, so it is a completely wasted effort."

"My lady, surely it is not necessary—"

"Will you tell me where His Lordship is?"

"No. I cannot."

She sat on the floor and neatly arranged her skirts about her legs. "You'll forgive me if I seem unpracticed in this. I haven't been treated as a child in years, and it is difficult to remember all the nuances of such a performance."

Wiggs wrung his hands. "My lady, I cannot tell you where . . . he expressly forbade me . . ." The butler's voice was growing progressively weaker, his Adam's apple bobbing in an alarming fashion. "My lady, please reconsider—"

"As soon as you tell me when you last saw His Lordship."

The determination in her eyes made him sigh, and his shoulders sagged in defeat. "Very well, my lady. Please do get up from the floor."

Sara accepted his hand as she climbed to her feet. "Excellent, Wiggs. It was going to be very difficult to revive me."

A reluctant smile touched his weathered lips. "Thank you for not forcing me to such lengths, my lady."

Sara grinned, pushing her feet back into her slippers. "So, Wiggs. I understand you cannot tell me exactly where His Lordship went. You are honorbound to do as the earl requests, and if he expressly told you not to tell me about certain aspects of last night, then you cannot do so. However, it will not hurt you to impart what information he *didn't* order you not to pass on."

Wiggs looked impressed. "That is quite true, madam."

"Then let us begin. Where is His Lordship?"

Wiggs looked at the ceiling.

"I see. Well, then, at what time did you last see His Lordship?"

"Shortly after lunch, madam."

"Where did he go?"

Again the butler stared at the ornate ceiling.

Sara sighed, her brow furrowed in thought. "I assume he was ready to leave when you saw him?"

The butler nodded.

"Hm. Did he receive a billet of some type, a message that sent him out?"

"No, madam."

Sara frowned. "Did he seem distressed?"

Wiggs leaned forward eagerly. "If I may venture to mention it, my lady, His Lordship did not look well. In fact, someone had to help him to his carriage."

He'd been ill and he hadn't told her. Suddenly, the conversation they'd had yesterday took on a more ominous meaning. "Who helped him into the carriage?"

The butler's rheumy gaze lifted toward the ceiling once again.

"Ah," Sara said. "The comte."

Wiggs bowed. "Very good, madam."

"And is the good Henri here now?"

"He returned just this morning. I believe he is in the breakfast room."

Gratitude warmed her heart, and Sara placed her hand on the butler's thin arm. "Thank you, Wiggs. If the earl is ill, I need to know about it. Some men let their pride do their thinking, and it can be very damaging."

He smiled in such a fatherly way that Sara was tempted to rest her head on his shoulder.

She found Henri facing a plate of ham and eggs, his usually cheerful mien gone. As soon as he saw Sara, he flashed a brilliant smile and stood. "Ah, *chère*! There you are!"

"Here I am indeed." She crossed the room and took the chair by his side, turning it to face him. "Henri, I am not a woman given to dissembling."

Henri's smile froze as he resumed his seat, eyeing her warily. "No?"

"No. I'm much more likely to demand an explanation forthwith."

Henri sighed. "I warned him how it would be, but he would not listen."

"He is ill, isn't he?"

"The headaches, they plague him. He did not wish to frighten you."

Frighten her? "How bad are they?"

"There are days when he does not leave his bed." Henri began to say something else, but stopped and shrugged. "It is a family illness. You should ask him."

"I will if I can find him. Where is he?"

"The gatekeeper's cottage."

"Is he alone?"

"No. There is a manservant who will stay with him, should he need anything. I, too, planned on returning after—"

"After you had convinced me that he had left on a matter of business."

The door opened, and Sara was surprised when Aunt Delphi traipsed in. The older woman halted when she saw the comte, bright pink touching her cheeks. Sara absently noted the blush as a thought occurred to her. "Aunt Delphi, do you have the recipe for that tisane you made when your head pained you so last year?"

Delphi blinked. "I think I remember it. Why? Do you have the headache, dear?"

"No, no. It's not for me." Sara jumped up and

grabbed Delphi's hand, pulling her from the room. "Henri, I will be back shortly."

"Very well, *ma chère*," he called, waving her away, though his gaze was fixed on Delphi's retreating figure. "I will escort you to the cottage when you are ready."

Sara bustled Delphi into the library and set the elderly lady to the task of writing her tisane recipe while Sara quickly packed. She returned to the library just as Delphi was folding the recipe into a neat square.

Sara grabbed the paper and handed it to Wiggs. "Have Mrs. Kibble find these ingredients and bring them to the gatekeeper's cottage."

"Yes, madam," he said, beaming with importance. He immediately hobbled off.

Henri entered the room. "Are we ready to go, then?"

"Almost. Aunt Delphi gave me the recipe for her tisane."

"He won't take it. He does not like medicine, you know."

Sara straightened her shoulders. Nick would drink it if she had to pour it down his throat.

"Sara, what of our shopping?" Delphi asked, pulling her gloves back on.

"Shopping?" Sara turned a confused gaze on her aunt.

"We were going to look for a hat to go with my new pelisse of Brussels green. You sent me a note just yesterday saying that you would be here and had nothing to do, and—"

"Oh, yes. I had forgotten." She couldn't go anywhere now; Nick needed her. "I'm afraid something has come up this morning, and I cannot come with you."

"But I—"

"Fortunately," Sara interjected smoothly, "the comte has agreed to escort you to town."

"Mon Dieu!" the comte burst out, though he quelled his outburst when Sara turned a minatory stare on him. "I—"

"Would be pleased to escort Her Grace," Sara finished inexorably. "Don't worry about Nick. I'll tend to him myself."

Sara didn't wait to see them off. Her portmanteau neatly strapped on the back of the curricle, a basket of food at her feet, she was soon on her way to find her foolish husband.

Chapter 18

❦

Sara found the cottage curtains drawn, the door tightly closed and locked. She knocked repeatedly, pounding until her fists felt bruised. Finally, just as she was considering climbing in a window, the door opened. Sara recognized the servant as one of the new footmen. He bowed low, an unmistakable flash of relief in his eyes as he informed her that His Lordship was in his chamber.

Ordering the man to see to her portmanteau and the basket, she dashed up the stairs. Once she stood outside the door, she faltered, suddenly unsure. What if Nick refused to see her? She almost knocked, then thought better of it. Thankfully, the knob turned easily in her hand.

The room was dark, the curtains drawn, and the

air heavy with the scent of the beeswax candles that guttered on a low table. Sara could just make out Nick's dark form across the room in a chair. Girding herself, she walked closer and could see his head resting on the high chair back, his eyes closed, his hair in disarray. There was a tenseness to his face, a sign of the pain that raged through his head and the fight he made to maintain his pride.

Sara quietly stood at the edge of the rug. His pride would hate her being here, but hers wouldn't let her retreat.

He opened his eyes and turned his face toward her; her hands fisted at her sides when she saw the torment in his gaze.

"What do you want?" His voice sounded as if the pain had scraped the edges of it raw.

She took a step toward him. "I came to help. Can I get you—"

"No. Just leave me alone." Eyes closed, he turned his face away. The faint light touched the length of his lashes and played along the hard line of his mouth.

Sara longed to reach out and trail her fingers through his hair, to touch the bold lines of his mouth, to brush her lips across his unshaven cheek. But she dared not; he would welcome no hint of affection from her now.

Nick stirred restlessly, his brow furrowed. His face was pale beneath his tan, his hands tightening about the arms of the chair until the knuckles shone. The demons were in full force.

Sara took a step closer. "Nick," she said softly, "you must get into bed."

His eyes opened to a slit, the hard blue gleam startling between the thick lashes. "I told you to leave."

"No, you *ordered* me to leave. I don't take orders well."

His mouth curved into a sneer. "Which is why I was left with no choice but to wed you."

Although she should have expected such a reaction, the words stung. She cleared her throat. "You should be in bed."

"I don't want to be in bed. I want to be left alone." He raised his head, his mouth white. "This is my fight, Sara, my problem. Not yours." She didn't answer and he sighed. "It is already easing, or I wouldn't be in this chair. I just need another day, and then I shall return home."

"Surely there is medicine—"

"No!" He winced at his own raised voice, dropping his head back against the chair once again. "Damn it, Sara, I don't want anything or anyone. I just want to be left alone."

Sara's frustration began to simmer. Here she was, trying to help the man, and all he did was order her about. "You, sir, are an ungrateful devil and a coward."

He turned slowly to face her, his hair a warm gold in the dim light. "What did you say?"

"I said you were an ungrateful devil."

"And?" he prompted softly, his eyes unnaturally bright.

Pushing Nick when he was ill was pure madness, but his refusal to accept her assistance angered her—as if she were too unimportant to be bothered with. She'd had enough of that with Julius, and she wouldn't allow it to happen again. She lifted her chin. "I said you were a coward."

He was out of his chair and facing her in the beat of a heart. His eyes blazed down at her. "Say it again," he said softly, the threat heavy.

She squared her jaw. "You are afraid of this illness. I can see it in your eyes. I just don't know why."

He grabbed her by the arm and stalked toward the bed, yanking her along behind him.

"What are you doing?" she demanded, her heart pounding furiously.

His grip tightened and he increased his pace. Fear chaining her feet, she stumbled on the edge of the rug. Nick gave a muffled curse, then picked her up and tossed her onto the mattress.

Sara scrambled madly for the edge of the bed, but he was too quick. The weight of his body forced the air from her lungs and she lay caught, his large, warm body pinning her into the softness.

His mouth touched her temple, his breath hot on her skin. "You wanted me in bed, and by God, that's where you'll have me."

"Get off me," she responded through clenched teeth. "This is ridiculous. All I did was request that you get in bed because you are ill."

"Ah, to be blessed with such a caring and tender wife." His voice brushed her ear, hard and unforgiving. "It isn't a very natural role for you, Sara. Find another."

His sneer fired her anger to new heights. "Damn you, Nick! I'd appreciate it if you would move so that I can breathe."

His weight shifted slightly to one side, but his body still pinned her down. "There. Are you better now, dearest wife?"

Sara hated the way he said the words, as if they tasted foul. "What do you want?"

He lifted a strand of her hair and rubbed it against his cheek. "If I must go to bed, then it will be with my lusty wife. I'm glad you didn't arrive last night, when I would have been unable to oblige your demands."

Sara sighed and ceased struggling. "Nick, I was just trying to alleviate your headache."

"How? By giving me an ache somewhere else?" He moved against her suggestively, and she could feel his arousal against her hip. Her body warmed instantly.

His gaze darkened. "If you must doctor me, then tend me where you can do the best good." A sensual smile flickered in his eyes, and he whispered huskily, "I should not be doing this, but I no longer care. Besides, who am I to refuse such a compelling woman?"

"What you need is good food and rest. You've been working much too hard on the Hall."

His smile curved slowly. "If you want me to stay in bed, Sara, then you will have to entertain me."

She looked at the tempting line of his mouth, at the masculine strength of his throat, and she burned for him. Heavens, but he was enticing, and he was finally saying all the things she'd wanted him to say for the past week. But he was ill, she reluctantly reminded herself. "If you must be entertained, then I'll find some cards for you to while away the time."

"I'd rather while away my time with you, madam. And on you." He nuzzled her neck and murmured, "And in you."

Surely this couldn't be good for him. Though she knew she should refuse him, her ability to do so was melting with each word.

He cupped one breast through her dress, sending hot shivers to her stomach. "Ah, Sara. You smell heavenly; all fresh and spicy, like a walk through a summer garden after a rain." His lips touched her throat, and tremors raced through her.

His other hand slowly pulled up her skirt. The fine material slid along her leg, inching past her calf, where he finally slipped his hand beneath. His fingers were unnaturally hot as they skimmed her leg, her thigh. He found her most secret place, his long fingers opening the folds and touching her in a way that made her arch against him.

She was on fire. She yearned for him, ached for him deep within. He kissed her cheek with the softest of touches, his mouth leaving a damp trail as he traced a line to her ear. His breath fluttered against her earlobe and sent a deluge of delicious shivers through her. He was slow, deliberate, his intent all too clear—he meant to make her crazy with desire, and then he'd take her, slake his pain in the ecstasy of their lovemaking.

And why not? Why not use this method that

gave them both such pleasure? If it gave him respite for an hour or two, it was the least she could do.

He unlaced her gown, and before she knew it, he had her bare before him. She touched his face, gently smoothing away the lines about his mouth, then she tugged at his shirt. Without a word, he stripped. Sara ran her hands over his hot skin, kissing his throat, his chin.

His hand cupped her breast again. "Look at me, Sara."

She opened her eyes. He was so incredibly beautiful, his golden skin damp with perspiration, his blue eyes vivid. Holding her gaze, he dropped his mouth to her breast and laved the peak, his hands now stroking higher, up her thigh, returning to the taut core of her womanhood.

She gasped, her head thrown back. Nick soaked in the sight of Sara's face as she gave herself to the passion. Her face flushed, her eyes glistened, her face softened with wonder.

He covered her mouth with his and kissed her softly, deeply, mingling his soul with hers. Thank God she hadn't come until this morning, after the unholy terror of the night had passed. But this . . . this was madness. Yet he was beyond caring, beyond anything other than the feel of this moment, this second. He lifted himself and poised above her, his hands tangled in her midnight black hair. "Love me, Sara. Let me come in."

Her thighs widened and she held him close. Nick lowered himself into her slowly, so slowly that she moaned her impatience. He held still, savoring his entry, reveling in the heat and tightness. Suddenly, he could take it no more and he pushed deep within, cupping her closer to him, losing himself inside her silken softness. Her eyes widened and she gasped, her body clenching about him. He ground his teeth against the waves of pleasure she gave him, losing himself in the onslaught of sensation. The silky tug yanked him over the edge, and he climaxed deep inside her.

For a long moment he lay there, absorbing her softness, her warmth. Then realization of what he'd done crept into his awareness. *Dear God, no.* What the hell had he been thinking? Cursing his own weakness, he forced himself upright, swinging his legs over the edge of the bed. He dropped his head into his hands. "*Damn.*"

Sara lifted herself onto her elbow, and her voice instantly filled with concern. "Oh, no. Did it make your headache worse?"

He glanced back at her, then could not look away. Her hair was tangled about her shoulders in a midnight cloud, her face flushed. A soft light shone in her pale blue eyes, her face alight with worry.

Surely one mistake would not be a disaster. After all, she'd been married to Julius for three years and had not gotten pregnant. Relief washed over him at the thought, and he managed to shake his head. "Actually, my headache is almost gone." And it was true—the pain was still there, but distant now, a mere memory of what it had been.

"Almost?" She frowned and he could tell her

mind was working furiously. "Nick, perhaps physical exertion is good for you."

It was possible, he supposed; he'd never really tried it. As he wondered if perhaps she was right, her hand slipped into his lap and found his manhood. It leapt to life at her touch, growing harder as her fingers tightened about him. "Nick," she said softly. "If our first try didn't rid you of all your pain, then perhaps once more would completely cure you."

She stroked him and Nick had to bite his lip to keep from moaning aloud. She was erotic and yet innocent, the combination as intoxicating as brandy. And he was addicted—he craved her, desired her, wanted her with every breath he took.

Yet the thought of her face when she realized he was too weak to fight the pain by himself, of what she'd think of him when he finally had to turn to laudanum for relief, made him cringe inwardly. He could bear a lot of things, even the loss of Hibberton Hall and his own pride. He could accept the loss of everything but her.

He took Sara's hand from his groin and placed it above her head. Then he captured her other hand and held it there as well. She immediately rubbed her hips against his, her nakedness brushing over his manhood in a way that made him grit his teeth. "Sara, stop. We can't do this."

She looked at him and smiled, thrusting her hips toward him again. "Why not?"

"Because I said so." He placed a quick kiss on her forehead, released her, and rolled out of bed. He must be crazed to have taken this as far as he had. He yanked on his trousers, pulled his shirt over his head, and grabbed his boots, feeling guilty.

"Nick." Sara's voice was low and husky, the voice of a woman who wanted to be touched. "Please come back to bed."

He kept his back to her and fastened his breeches. He didn't trust himself to even look at her. "Not now." He heard a rustle from the bed as if she had moved to the edge.

"Nick, I—"

"Get dressed, Sara." He dropped a quick kiss on her hair, then left, closing the door behind him.

Out in the hallway he paused, his hand still on the doorknob, his heart aching worse than his head ever had. He rested his forehead against the smooth wooden door and closed his eyes. God help him, he was becoming too attached to Sara, his happiness too involved in hers. It would be better for them both if they maintained their distance, coming together for mutual pleasure and no more.

He should not have allowed her to muddle his thinking, but he'd been powerless to resist her. And once he'd had her in his bed, he'd been unable to let her go. He craved her fiercely; his every waking thought was tangled up with images of her. Was it simply because of her proximity day in and day out? Or was it more?

Though he'd thought it would have the opposite effect, the fact that she now belonged to him made her all the more entrancing. He'd never thought of marriage as an erotic experience, but it was, intensely so—Sara's every move, the timbre of her voice, the fresh scent of her skin, the thick tangle of her hair—they belonged to him and no one else. To his shock, he was discovering he was a possessive man.

He closed his eyes as a massive rope of tightness banded about his throat and threatened to stop his breathing. His headache had melted during their lovemaking, but now it returned, pounding through his brain. He had to resist her. And if he could not, then he would leave her.

For Nicholas Montrose, there was no middle road. There never had been.

Chapter 19

$\sim\!\!\infty\!\!\sim$

A week later, Anthony Elliot, the Earl of Greyley, climbed out of his carriage and turned toward the house he'd rented for his stay in Bath. It was well built and free from the frills found in most Bath architecture, so he was considering purchasing it, if the owner could be convinced. After all, Sara was established here now, and it would be convenient to have a permanent residence nearby.

He walked up the steps to the front door. It had been three weeks since Sara had married. Marcus and he had taken turns going to visit her, reporting back on what they found. Yesterday it had been his turn, and the visit had unsettled him.

Sara had been pale and restless, her thoughts far away. But it had been her expression when

Bridgeton walked into the room that had caused Anthony to wince. Whether she knew it or not, Sara was in love. Worse, it was obvious from the longing glance she turned toward her husband that she didn't believe that love reciprocated.

Anthony balled his hand into a fist. What had Marcus been thinking in arranging the marriage? Hell, what had *he* been thinking? He should have put his foot down and prevented the whole damnable match.

The door opened as he reached the landing, and he passed his coat and hat to the waiting butler, then turned to the study.

"My lord," the butler said. "Lady Bridgeton arrived a half hour ago."

Sara? A sense of foreboding engulfed him as he crossed the foyer and entered the sitting room. Sara stood before the fire, her arms wrapped around her as if she was trying to ward off a chill. Her mind was obviously far away for she hadn't heard him enter, but continued to stare with unseeing eyes at the flickering fire.

Anthony noted the delicate shadows beneath her eyes. What had Bridgeton done to his sister? He took a step forward. "Sara?"

She started. "Oh, I didn't see you! How long have you been there?"

"I just came in." He regarded her closely. "I take it this isn't a social call."

She managed a wan smile. "I need your advice, Anthony."

For God's sake, his advice would be to walk

away from the bastard and never look back. Still . . . Anthony looked into his sister's eyes and saw tears welling. "Of course," he said hastily. "Come and sit down." He waited until she took a chair and then he sank into the one opposite. "Sara, what has happened?"

She took a shuddering breath. "This is so awkward. But I must talk to someone and . . . Anthony, I need to ask you something very—"

"Perhaps you should speak to Aunt Delphi?" Anthony said, alarmed.

"I thought of her, but she's been acting so unusual lately."

Anthony had noticed that himself. Bloody hell, he was surrounded with teary-eyed females, and there wasn't a drop of decent brandy in the house. "Aunt Delphi is probably just missing you."

"I think it is more than that," Sara said with a watery smile. "But I cannot ask her to help me with my problems when she obviously has her own. I also thought about asking Anna for advice, but—"

"No," he said vehemently. "That blasted woman doesn't know a damn thing about men." Not that she'd admit such a thing; women like Anna Thraxton never admitted they weren't an expert on any topic.

"Her experience is rather limited in this area, so I—" Sara bit her lip. "I thought perhaps you could assist me."

Anthony braced himself. "What is the problem? I assume we are talking about Bridgeton."

"Yes, and I would appreciate it if you would put

your dislike of him aside." She suddenly stood and paced a short distance away, then returned, her movements jerky and unsettled. "Anthony, I need to understand how men think."

Well, that didn't seem too difficult. "Oh?"

"Nick . . . wants me."

"Wants—" Surely she didn't mean—

"I can tell that he does. He touches me all the time and—"

"Good God," he muttered.

Sara looked at him. "What?"

"Nothing," he said hastily. "Go on."

She eyed him uncertainly. "Very well. Nick wants me, but he's decided not to . . . to . . ." She floundered to a halt and the tears that threatened in her eyes became reality. One, single drop slipped down her cheek.

Bloody hell. Anthony raked a hand through his hair. "Do you mean to tell me that Bridgeton is not . . . er, fulfilling his husbandly duties?"

She nodded miserably. "Oh, Anthony, what am I to do?"

He closed his eyes. *God above*. He was a decent man, one who took his responsibilities seriously. He was a good friend, an excellent landlord, and he never cheated at cards, unless it was with one of his own brothers. What had he done to deserve this?

"I knew I shouldn't have asked you," Sara said, her voice quavering. She pulled a handkerchief from her reticule and mopped her eyes. "Never mind; I'm sorry I bothered you—"

"Damn it, Sara, you haven't bothered me at all,"

Anthony snapped. "Sit back down while I think this through." If he didn't help her, she'd go to that Thraxton woman, and heaven knew what harebrained advice she might give.

Sara's eyes brightened. "You're thinking?"

"Don't look so surprised." She had the grace to smile a little, and he relaxed. "Now sit." He pointed to the chair she'd abandoned. She obediently came and perched on the edge, her gaze glued to his face.

Anthony seriously wished he'd had a drink. Hell, two would be better. "You'll have to give me more details. Has Bridgeton ever . . ." He gestured vaguely, not quite believing he was having this conversation.

She turned a bright pink, a dreamy expression softening her eyes. "Oh, yes."

Damn Nicholas Montrose to hell. There was so much in that "oh, yes" that Anthony did not want to think about. "But now he refuses. Does he say why?"

"He says he doesn't want children, but I know there are ways . . ." She looked down at her hands, tightly clenched about her reticule. "When we first married, he . . . but now he won't even—" She bit her lip. "Anthony, what would you do if your wife wouldn't . . . you know . . . ?"

"I'd seduce her." And he'd be successful, too, for if there was one thing Anthony understood, it was how to arouse a woman.

"I never thought of that," Sara said, her voice almost wondering. "I could seduce him." Her gaze was soft, and there was a faint bloom of color in her cheeks.

Oh, Lord. She stood and gave Anthony a brilliant smile. "If I seduce him, then he will see that we can still be close without risking anything."

What the hell have I done? "Yes, well, there's no need to be hasty, Sara. You might want to wait a while before you—"

"Anthony, thank you so much. I knew you were the one I should talk to." She pulled her gloves from her pocket and briskly tugged them on.

He nodded dumbly and stood. "Yes, but—"

She reached up and patted his cheek. "I wish I had time to stay and talk, but I have so much to do before this evening." With a blinding smile, she turned and whisked out of the room, leaving Anthony staring after her.

As soon as she'd realized the extent of Nick's illness, Sara had changed one of the old pantries at Hibberton Hall into a stillroom and began experimenting with herbs. Between Mrs. Kibble's considerable knowledge and the thick tome she'd discovered in the library, she was confident she'd discover a cure. If only she could convince Nick of that.

Now, armed with Anthony's advice, she spent part of the afternoon running errands and returned home flushed but triumphant. She took special care in dressing, wearing a deep blue gown from which she removed the lace collar. Once devoid of that, the neckline plunged to a fascinating depth. Sara looked down and then tugged it even lower as she set about readying the stillroom.

Somewhat secluded at the end of the east wing, with a small window that opened onto the courtyard, the room had the added bonus of staying warm even on cold days. Everything readied, she sent a message to her husband and waited.

He'd not risen this morning as usual. Another of his headaches had claimed him, for he'd disappeared yesterday after lunch, and she'd not seen him since.

Her heart ached to think of him suffering alone, but his room would be locked tight, with only Wiggs given entry—and then, only to bring more brandy. Brandy was *not* the way to cure a headache, and the sooner she convinced her stubborn husband of that, the quicker he would heal.

But first she had to convince him to let her into his life. Sara set a small cup of honey on the low table, then loosened her hair, removing all but a few of the pins. Then she tugged at the low neckline of her gown until it was slightly askew. That done, she checked her reflection in the lid of a pot and was pleased to see that she looked disheveled, like a woman who had just experienced the ultimate passion. Oh yes, Nick had taught her well.

The thought of what she was about to do made her skin tingle in anticipation. With a determined effort, she banished those thoughts, picked up a pestle, and began to make powder of St. John's wort for the new tisane.

She had worked less than a minute when a deep,

husky voice came from the doorway. " 'And all that's best of dark and bright, meet in her aspect and her eyes.' "

A flood of heat washed across her, so strong that her knees trembled. Gripping the mortar tightly, she put a smile on her face and turned. Unshaven, Nick leaned against the doorjamb, his hands in the pockets of his breeches, his shirt undone. His intense gaze followed her every move. At the sight of him, so close, and so . . . vulnerable somehow, her yearning flared to life. It was all she could do not to reach for him.

"It's good to see you up and about," Sara managed with false cheerfulness.

"Liar. I look like hell, and you know it."

"I am fixing another tisane for your headache."

Something flickered in his eyes, then faded. "Is that why you sent for me? I was afraid something had occurred with the workmen."

"No, I just want you to try this. Mrs. Kibble claims it can cure everything from pains to rashes."

His gaze raked across her, lingering on her low neckline. "Can it cure the longing to sin?" His mouth hardened when she blushed. "I'm no saint, Sara. Sinning is one of the few things I do well."

No, he wasn't a saint. He was delectable. Irresistible. Everything Sara had ever wanted. A pang settled in the pit of her stomach, heating her from the inside out and making her hot and restless.

Nick moved from the doorway and stalked closer. She shivered in anticipation. He was so beautiful, and he was all hers.

He stopped before her, his warm, masculine presence completely surrounding her. "Just being with you makes me a better person."

His voice dropped, and she could feel the brush of his breath against her ear. "I would like to sink into your goodness, surround myself with your sweetness. But I can't. Do you understand that, Sara?"

His gaze rested appreciatively on the low-cut gown, on the way her hair was tumbling about her shoulders. She could almost feel the heat rising from him in thick, languorous waves. "Losing yourself inside me will make all of your aches go away," she said.

He froze, then turned on his heel as if to leave, but Sara was quicker. She dropped the mortar and pestle and reached for him, locking her arms about his chest.

"Sara, don't—"

"Your head is not the only place that aches." She rested her hand on the bulge that evinced his desire. "Why don't we work on this one, first?"

He tried to pull away, but she held him tighter. "Remember lesson one, Nick? You cannot run with the wolves without knowing how to fight like one."

His eyes closed as if he were in pain.

Sara rose on her tiptoes and ran the tip of her tongue along his lower lip.

His brow creased, but still he didn't move. He stood, hands fisted at his sides, an expression of longing on his face.

He wasn't going to push her away! Sara took one of his hands and unfisted it, then placed it on her breast. "Touch me, Nick," she whispered against his cheek, trembling with desire.

He opened his eyes and groaned. Then, as if unable to stop, his hands gently stroked her, pulling her nipples to taut readiness. She swelled at his touch, her flesh fuller, riper.

The air about them thickened, growing heavy with their need. Sara reached behind her and found the small cup of honey. "Lesson two," she whispered, dipping her finger into the honey. "Never underestimate the power of a kiss."

She placed her finger on his bottom lip. Nick's body tightened and he wondered if he was dreaming. Perhaps he was still lying in bed, his brandy-soaked mind creating the ultimate fantasy. The honey beaded on his lower lip and Sara slowly pulled his mouth to hers. As she kissed him, her hands tugged at his shirt and she pulled it free, then dropped it to the floor. Her hands roamed everywhere, caressing, touching, stroking.

Just as he thought he could take no more, she pulled back and met his gaze, her eyes dark with desire. "Three: If you want a man to know you are interested in him," she whispered, "then touch him."

Her hand closed over his erection. It was exquisite. Pleasure and pain mingled and became one. Nick knew he could not let Sara's seduction continue, but he was powerless to resist her. Powerless to do anything but stand still and let her do what she would.

She dipped her finger into the honey once more

and touched his chest. The drop quivered a moment, then trickled down his chest and to his stomach.

Her finger traced the line left by the honey, her eyes slumberous and mysterious. "I wonder if you are as sweet as the nectar." She pressed her mouth to his bare skin, her tongue flickering across the base of his throat, branding him.

He ground his teeth to maintain control. She had learned seduction all too well, and with each delectable lesson, he was condemned to a hell of his own making.

Sara followed the errant trickle of honey, stopping to press her hot mouth to each of his nipples. Nick's hand sank into her hair, the silken tangles catching his fingers. "God," he whispered hoarsely, watching as she knelt to kiss the final trail to his stomach, "you are so beautiful."

She smiled up at him, then reached into her pocket and pulled something out.

As lost as he was, Nick managed to gasp out, "What's that?"

"Lesson four," she said, peeping up at him through her lashes. "Never challenge a man unless you are prepared." She opened her hand.

Nick immediately recognized what it was. It was a French sheath, used to prevent pregnancy. "Where did you get that?"

"Anna's grandfather. He believes that these should be given freely by the crown in order to control the population." She grinned. "He even sent one to the King by post."

Nick tried to concentrate on her words, but his

mind was too preoccupied with her fingers as they undid his breeches. This was madness. Utter madness. His hand clamped about her wrist and she looked up at him, a plea in her gaze.

He looked at the sheath she held. Normally he didn't trust them, but his body was pushed beyond endurance. He wanted Sara so badly he shook. He released her hand. "We can try it."

As if afraid he'd change his mind she swiftly tugged down his breeches. Nick helped her, yanking them off and kicking them toward the door. She then placed the sheath over his turgid manhood.

Nick pushed down the sleeve of her gown, exposing the delicate lace of her chemise. She reached up to unlace it, but he stopped her. "Keep it on."

"But I thought—"

"Don't think. Feel." He cupped her breast through the fine material, his thumb finding the crest and teasing it to a peak. Then he dropped his mouth to her nipple, the wet cotton clinging, rubbing, erotic.

Sara arched in surprise as sheer pleasure raced through her.

He lifted his head. "You are too succulent a dish to leave untasted." He placed his hands on her waist and lifted her to the edge of the table. Then he took her hands and placed them on her breasts, his gaze dark with passion. "Touch them, Sara. Touch them for me."

She hesitantly held her hands to her breasts and he sucked in his breath, watching her every move. Somehow the seduction had changed, and now he was in charge. He dipped his fingers into the honey, then pushed her skirts aside and knelt before her.

"So beautiful," he murmured. He threaded his honey-coated fingers through her nether curls, his thumb sinking deeply into her.

A moan escaped her and he could feel the waves of sensation ripple through her. She wriggled on the table, trying to get closer. His head dipped, and he sucked every drop of honey from her.

Sara moaned his name, her hands clenched in his hair. Nick replaced his mouth with his fingers, so he could watch her face. His thumb circled her, tormenting her. She moaned again and all thoughts of pain, of anything, were washed away. The scent of her beckoned to him stronger and stronger, and he finally pressed his sheath-enclosed manhood against her.

Sara locked her legs about him and pulled him deep inside, drawing him home until they were merged, melded completely. He sank his hands into her hair as he began to move, slowly at first, and then with increasing speed. She could feel his tension building, could feel his need rise. At the last moment he pulled back, but Sara clenched her legs all the tighter, jealous of that part of himself that he wanted to withhold. She wanted him there, deep inside as he crested the peak of his own desire. She wanted to feel him swell and explode in wonder.

"Sara, no!" he gasped. "The sheath—"

She moved against him, pulling him deeper.

Waves of desire caught them both and Sara crested on their passion, tightening her hold when

Nick cried out her name and then collapsed against her.

Sara wrapped herself around him, holding him to her, wishing this moment could last forever. After a long moment, he pushed away and untied the sheath. She watched him through her lashes, aching for him to wrap his arms about her and to hold her.

"Sara," Nick said, his voice strained.

"Yes?"

"You said you got this from Anna's grandfather. How long has he had it?"

"I don't know. It's the one he shows when he gives lectures. He gave it to me because it was time he bought a new one—"

Nick's face darkened. "Damn it, Sara, do you want to have children?"

"Actually, yes. I think it would be lovely to have a child." Heavens. Where had that come from? But even as she wondered, she knew. It was having a home of her own, and feeling that she belonged here, with Nick.

Nick cursed and whirled away, snatching up his breeches and yanking them on. "Damn you, Sara. Don't *ever* do that again."

His anger was as shocking as a plunge into icy cold water. Sara slid from the edge of the table and pushed her skirts down. "Nick, I didn't mean to—"

He caught her face between his hands, his touch less than gentle. "I am my mother's son, Sara. I would *never* curse a child of mine with this illness."

Her gaze met his steadily. "That is not for us to decide." Unafraid, she wrapped her hands about his wrists and held him there. "There has to be a way to stop the pain, Nick. I believe I can find a way to help you, but you have to give me some time."

"I don't have time."

"Nick," she whispered, her voice a plea. "I won't stop until I find it. Even if it takes forever."

He realized that she was telling the truth—she was committed to helping him. Just as he had been committed to helping his mother. He closed his eyes. He loved Sara too much to let her throw the rest of her life away on him.

In that moment, he knew he was truly cursed—that his life until now, with all its tragedy and emptiness, had been but a rehearsal for this terrible moment. He could not keep away from her, nor did he have the heart to leave.

This couldn't go on. He had to find a way to get Sara out of his life before it was too late.

Trembling from head to foot, Nick pulled his wrists free of her grasp and left, closing the door softly behind him.

Chapter 20

Wiggs took a deep breath, then knocked on the door. At the muffled greeting, he entered. "Pardon me for disturbing you, my lord."

Henri blinked. In the three months he had resided at Hibberton Hall, this was the first time Wiggs had ever come to his chamber. Henri pulled the tie on his red-velvet robe tighter. "You are not disturbing me at all. Is something wrong?"

A look of relief crossed the butler's face. "Yes, my lord. It's His Lordship. He has locked himself in his library and has not come out since yesterday. It is most unlike him."

"Voyons!" Henri exclaimed. "I will go immediately."

"I shall send Roberts to assist you in dressing, my lord."

"There is no need. I have on a robe—and a damned expensive one, too." Henri slipped a cravat pin in his pocket and walked past the outraged Wiggs. He went directly to the library and knocked on the door. As he'd expected, there was no answer.

He slipped the pin from his pocket and bent to the lock. Less than a minute later, the door opened with a click.

"Ah, there you are, *mon ami*," he said as he walked into the darkened room. He pulled the door closed and locked it behind him. "Is there any brandy left?"

Nick sat at the desk, his feet upon it, his face drawn and haggard. Surprisingly, he didn't look drunk at all.

A stirring of concern made Henri frown. "*Mon ami?* Are you ill?"

"What do you want?"

"I awoke this morning and became very thirsty. So, I came here. I see you have brandy."

"The door was locked."

Henri held up the cravat pin.

A reluctant smile touched Nick's mouth. "The world is not safe with you wandering through it."

"True." Henri dropped the pin back into his pocket and came to sit on the edge of the desk, facing Nick. "So what are you doing here, sitting behind a locked door?"

Nick shrugged, but offered no answer.

Henri wondered at the stark despair he saw in his friend's eyes. "Nicholas, you must talk to me. Maybe I can help."

Nick rubbed a hand over his face. "There is nothing you can do. The headaches are worsening, Henri. I don't want Sara to see me when I—" He clamped his mouth shut.

Pride, Henri knew, was not the noblest of emotions. But it was one he was very familiar with. "You must leave her."

"I can't." It was a cry of pain.

Henri was not surprised. "Then what will you do?"

Nick's jaw hardened. "If I cannot leave her, then I must make her leave me. I must make her so despise me that she will stay away from me."

"How will you do that? She is crazy in love with you."

Nick sent a dark glance at the comte. "You are a fool, Henri."

"Not where women are concerned," Henri said. Except, of course, for Delphi. He had wooed her, oh so carefully, and at first, she had warmed to him. But then he had become too eager. Too precipitate. He'd asked her to join him for a romantic tryst, and that had ended their budding romance.

He'd thought she was ready; all of the signs had pointed to it. And he was, after all, something of an expert in reading those signs. But she'd recoiled from his invitation with horror, cutting the connection and refusing to even speak with him.

Henri had been hurt. It wasn't as if he'd had the

audacity to ask her to marry him; that would have been an insult of the highest order. Still, he could not mistake the look of utter hurt that had filled her eyes at that instant, and the thought had made him most uncomfortable.

The more he thought about it, however, the more disgruntled he became. Finally, armed in building indignation, Henri had set out to punish Delphi. He flirted shamelessly in front of her and dallied with whoever was available.

But the foolish woman didn't even know the proper way to respond to such treatment. Instead of flouting him and flirting heedlessly herself, she merely watched him with large, sad eyes. Eyes that caused Henri additional hours of unhappiness.

Voyons, it was enough to drive a man insane. And now this. Henri cast a surreptitious glance at his friend. There was something almost despairing about the way Nick sat so still, his face devoid of all emotion. Henri had seen similar expressions on the face of some of his countrymen when they'd lost everything they possessed in the war.

Henri sighed and stood. "I think you are making a mistake, *mon ami*. Sara is your wife, and it is her duty to stand by your side, whatever occurs."

"You say that as if you envy it."

"Perhaps I do. But it is your decision, and you must do what you think is right. If you need my help, Nicholas, you have but to ask."

Nick watched as the comte left the room, closing the door behind him. For a long moment he simply sat still, wondering if he had the strength to do what needed to be done. But he had no choice. Sara had proven that when she'd seduced him so thoroughly in the stillroom. He was powerless against her—too besotted to walk away.

So he had to make Sara leave.

He knew her well. Better, perhaps, than she knew herself. Julius had betrayed her, leaving her hurt and alone. Because of that, she would never again allow herself to be so used.

He looked down at the desk where a missive lay on the top of the blotter. It was addressed to Lucilla Kettering, the nefarious Lady Knowles. For all her faults, Lucilla would serve his purpose perfectly. By this time tomorrow, Sara would hate him as much as she hated Julius.

Why did the thought fill him with grief, instead of relief?

". . . and then the elephant stepped on Lady Birlington's hat and—"

"Elephant?" Sara blinked.

A lopsided grin graced Anna's wide mouth. "I wanted to see if you were listening."

Sara hadn't been, of course. Her mind was too occupied with her errant husband. Since last week's interlude in the stillroom, he had assiduously avoided her company. She met Anna's curious gaze and managed a wan smile. "I was listening."

"No, you weren't. I also had a baboon riding in a carriage, a dog kissing Lady Elderton, and a blue fish at the Fretwood ball, and you didn't catch a one."

"I'm sorry. I've just been preoccupied."

Anna placed her hand on Sara's. "What happened?"

Sara picked up a blue tasseled pillow and held it against her stomach. Damn her impulsive tongue. Why had she blurted to Nick that foolish thing about having a child? But she knew why she'd said it . . . "I believe I have made a mistake." And she was baffled as to how to fix it.

Until that moment, having a child hadn't really occurred to her. But somehow the combination of Nick's sultry presence and the remnants of their passionate encounter added to her realization that she was really and truly happy, and had made her reach out for just a little bit more. If only she'd known that that little bit would drive Nick away.

Perhaps if she told him that she'd been teasing, that she didn't really want a child at all . . . but she *did* want children. Not right now, of course, but soon . . . Nine months seemed about right. Sara held the little pillow more tightly. Perhaps he just needed a little time to adjust.

The door opened, and Nick strolled in. Sara's heart leapt at the sight of him. He looked wildly handsome in his riding clothes. He hesitated when he saw Anna, but then smiled and came forward, bowing gracefully. "Miss Thraxton. How delightful to see you."

Anna returned his greeting and he turned to his wife. "Sara, I came to tell you that I will be leaving this afternoon."

She dug her fingers into the pillow even as she said in a voice of great unconcern, "Oh? When will you be back?"

Nick adjusted his cuff, careful not to meet her gaze. "A week. Maybe more."

He was lying. She knew it as clearly as if he'd told her so, himself. "Where are you going?" She hated the words as soon as they left her mouth.

His gaze hardened. "That, my dear, is none of your business."

Anna gave a shocked gasp, but Sara's training as Julius Lawrence's perfect wife stood her in good stead. She was able to hold Nick's gaze, though her eyes burned and her throat ached.

Nick put on his hat. "If you need anything, Wiggs will know how to get in touch with me." With another quick bow to Anna, he left.

This time not only was her pride being shredded, but her heart, as well. Sara closed her eyes, listening to the sound of his booted feet as he crossed the foyer and went out. Moments later he cantered by, riding as if the hounds of hell were at his heels.

Then she let the tears fall. Anna put her arm about her shoulders and murmured words of consolation, but none helped. For the first time since Julius's death, Sara cried—and it was for another man.

After Anna had gone and Sara had had time to compose herself, she found Wiggs. "Where is he?"

"My lord is at the gatekeeper's cottage. He said he was going to work on some estate business."

Sara blinked, surprised Wiggs had answered her so readily and that Nick was so close. "Have the landau brought up."

The butler bowed and left. Sara remained in the

foyer, pacing impatiently. This was *not* the way one ran a marriage. Problems should be discussed, debated, even yelled about. But apparently things had been different in the Montrose family than in the St. John family, and Nick did not feel comfortable expressing himself. Not beyond lust, at least.

The landau was finally ready and Sara stepped outside. Just as she reached the carriage, a clatter arose in the yard. She turned and found the Comte du Lac astride his bay.

"Ah, the lovely countess. Have you seen Nick? I must ask him—"

"Nick is not here."

Henri paused, his bright gaze quickly assessing her. "What has happened, *chère*? You appear disturbed."

"I am going to visit my husband and have a word with him."

"You are in a passion, no? I will ride with you. A woman in a passion should never travel alone."

She climbed into the landau with more energy than grace. "Thank you for your concern, but it is unnecessary." She nodded to the groom, and they were off. They had almost reached the cottage before Sara realized that Henri had followed her. When they arrived, he hopped off his horse and came to assist her alight.

The cottage was awash with light and color, the windows thrown open. Sara frowned to hear voices and laughter spilling from the upstairs window.

Henri glanced uneasily at the cottage. "Perhaps we should not be here. Why don't we—"

Sara pushed past him and entered. Somehow, she climbed the narrow stairs and walked straight into the main bedchamber.

Nick stood in the center of the room, his shirt off, his breeches undone, his hair tousled. Standing beside him, her hands intimately splayed over his chest, was Lucilla Kettering, her sumptuous body clothed in a diaphanous gown that showed every curve.

Lucilla saw Sara first, and a crafty catlike smile curved her mouth. "Why, darling. We have a visitor." She leaned her head against Nick's shoulder and purred up at him, "I do hope this doesn't mean you can't stay to play."

"I can stay as long as I wish." It was Nick's voice, yet it wasn't. Nick's voice had never been so cold, so hard. He flickered an impersonal gaze Sara's way, and asked, "What do you want?"

She wanted for this moment to never be. She wanted to disappear in a puff of smoke and wake up in a dream where Nick loved her. Loved her as much as she loved him.

"I came to talk to you," Sara said, amazed to discover that her voice worked. "Nick, don't do this."

Lucilla gave a throaty chuckle, her eyes filled with false pity. "I don't know how to tell you this, but he already has." She trailed her hand down Nick's chest to where his breeches hung open. "Several times, in fact."

Nick caught Lucilla's hand before it went any farther, though his gaze never left Sara. "Leave, Sara. Now."

Sara's mouth filled with an acrid taste, and her heart clenched in pain. Yet something seemed off about the scene. There was no intimacy between the two who stood before her. Nick seemed unyielding and stern, and Lucilla's voice held a tinge of desperation. She didn't sound anything like a woman who had just won the man of her dreams.

And despite Lucilla's claims, the covers on the bed behind them were still tightly drawn, the pillows unmussed. Like Lucilla's gown, everything in the room was perfect. Too perfect.

"Sara," Nick said, wondering why she was still standing there, an arrested look on her face. "Sara, please go." His chest ached and a dull pressure thudded behind his eyes. No matter what hell he descended into, he would never forget the expression on Sara's face when she walked through the door and saw him with Lucilla.

Sara raised her eyes to his, and in that instant, he knew that she'd seen through his deception.

"If you wanted me to leave, all you had to do was say so." She flicked a glance at Lucilla. "As for you, you can have him." She turned on her heel and walked from the room.

Nick stared at the empty doorway, his heart thudding slow and sick against his throat. Desolation held him in its icy grip and he felt nothing but the echo of a deep, soulless emptiness that was so overwhelming he almost staggered.

Just as he'd intended, she was gone. And he would never see her again.

Henri's startled face appeared in the doorway.

When he caught sight of Lucilla, his face hardened. He whipped his gaze to Nick. "*Mon Dieu*, what have you done?"

"Where is she?"

"She jumped into her carriage and fled as if running for her life."

"Go after her. She shouldn't be alone." For an instant, Nick feared that Henri would argue with him, but after one more glance, the older man left.

Frozen, Nick stood staring at the open door. His life was over. Nothing mattered now. He would see to the restoration of Hibberton Hall and leave it to Sara along with his fortune. At least she would have something from him. Some small gesture that might let her know what she meant to him.

A slender female hand came to rest on his shoulder. "Nick," Lucilla said, her voice brushing against his neck. "That was rather enjoyable, wasn't it? Just like when we were in Paris."

Nick turned away. "You can go now, Lucilla. I will send a draft to your house that more than covers your gaming debts. You should be able to live quite comfortably for a while without being forced to sell yourself yet again."

"But Nick," she said, placing her hand on his. "Now that Sara's gone—"

"I can go straight to hell, where I belong. And you, my dear, can leave." He strode toward the door. "Don't worry about locking up. By tomorrow, this place will be burnt to the ground."

Lucilla blinked and glanced around at the fine furnishings. "All of it?"

"Yes," he said, his heart as bleak as his soul. "I never want to see this place again." With that, he turned and left.

Several days later, Anthony arrived on his aunt's doorstep. Damn the Elliot family and their constant squabbling. He'd been called back to London to sort out a dispute, and it had taken Delphi's missive almost a week to find him. He followed the servant to where his aunt sat waiting.

"Thank God you have come," she said, starting up from her chair.

"Where is she?" Anthony asked.

"In her room. I vow, Anthony, I'm at my wits' end."

"Bloody hell," he muttered. "Have you talked to her?"

"I've tried, but she won't say a word. I had a tray taken to her room, but she won't eat, either." Delphi took a shaky breath. "I heard what happened from a very reliable source."

"Who?"

"That's none of your business," Delphi snapped, then colored. "Sara caught Bridgeton with another woman. It must have been difficult for her, after Julius."

It would have been more than difficult, especially if she'd attempted to seduce him. *Thanks to my misbegotten advice.* Anthony rubbed a hand over his face. "Maybe she'll talk to me."

Delphi looked unconvinced. "I hope so. I'm worried about her."

Moments later, Anthony knocked hesitantly on Sara's door. When there was no answer, he opened it. "Sara?"

He expected to see her collapsed on her bed, tears streaming from her face. Instead she was pacing, her hands fisted to her side, her face pale and tense. He closed the door behind him, then crossed to lean against the bedpost.

She slanted a furious glance his way. "If you've come to talk, you are wasting your time."

Anthony shrugged. "I've never been one for conversation. I'm just here to keep you company."

She crossed her arms and increased her pace. "Nicholas Montrose is a bastard."

"I know."

"And a . . . an ass."

Anthony nodded, noting how her eyes blazed. His heart ached for her. "Shall I kill him for you?"

"No," she snapped. "Death is too good for a man like him. Let him be alone, if that's what he wants. I want nothing more to do with him."

"Are you certain?"

"I'm positive." She took two more steps then came to an abrupt halt, her face crumpling.

Anthony closed the space between them, catching her to his chest as sobs wracked her body.

After an interminable time, she hiccuped to a stop. "Oh, Anthony," she whispered. "He didn't love me. Not even a little. I thought he might come to, but—" Pain convulsed through her and she gripped Anthony's jacket and pressed her face against him.

Anthony rubbed his cheek against her hair. "Ah, sweetheart. Just forget this part of your life. Let it go."

"I can't."

"It will be hard, but you can do it, Sara. I know you can. One day, you'll look back on this and—"

"No, I won't." There was quiet surety in her voice.

He pushed her hair away from her face. "Why not? You started over after Julius died. This will be the same."

"It will *never* be the same. Never." She raised her pain-filled eyes to his. "I'm pregnant, Anthony. I'm going to have Nick's child, and he hates the very sight of me." With that, she dropped her head against his chest and broke into fresh sobs.

It was a pity the Earl of Bridgeton was not present at this exact moment, because Anthony would have killed him with his bare hands—as slowly and as painfully as he could. As it was, he was forced to stay with his sister and hold her until her tears finally dried.

Uncertain what to do then, Anthony ordered her to bed. To his surprise, she went, falling quickly asleep as if exhausted. He stood for a long while looking down at her, noting the bluish circles beneath her eyes, the sad turn of her lips even in her sleep. It was painful, he knew. But perhaps it was for the best.

Anthony bent over and kissed his sister's cheek, then turned and quietly left the room.

Chapter 21

A week passed before Sara declared herself ready to leave the house. After careful consideration, Delphi chose the Boswells' dinner party. It was to be a very small, select sort of party with only ten couples present. After dinner, a musical performance by Lady Boswell was to serve as the evening's entertainment. All in all, Delphi thought it was the perfect event for Sara to make her reappearance.

Lady Boswell, a large, imposing woman who wore a turban, fixed her cheerful gaze on Sara. "Lady Bridgeton, what a pleasure to make your acquaintance. May I say that you are even prettier than was reported?"

Sara managed a smile. "Thank you. Aunt Delphi has told me so much about you, as well. I hear we are in for a rare treat this evening."

"Well, never let it be said that I don't know how to entertain, be it a countess or a princess. Speaking of which, we have some relatives of yours coming this evening. I doubt you've met them yet, for they've been in the country for a while and everyone knows that—" A stir at the door made her look up. "Ah, there they are now. If you'll pardon me, I must greet them." She turned to meet two new visitors.

Sara watched as Lady Boswell greeted a tall, slender woman dressed in the height of fashion and wearing a pair of spectacles. But it was the man beside her that caught Sara's attention. She could only see him from behind. Tall and well formed, with hair as black as night, he reminded her of someone.

Sara was just about to ask Delphi for his name when he turned her way. Her heart contracted painfully. With the exception of his dark coloring, the man looked exactly like Nick.

Lady Boswell brought the newcomers over and introduced them. Sara knew immediately that this was Nick's cousin. She glanced curiously at the viscountess and encountered such a frank look from the woman's amazing green eyes, that she colored and dropped her gaze. Uncomfortable, she mumbled her greeting and made her escape as soon as possible.

The rest of the evening was agony. Sara could not look away from Lord Hunterston. After dinner, she thankfully escaped to the music room and took a seat in the farthest corner, hoping she could escape the poignant reminder of her husband.

Lord Boswell, a bluff, pleasant man with a loud

laugh, escorted his wife to the pianoforte and made ready for the evening's entertainment. Sara saw to her dismay that Viscount Hunterston was sitting near the front of the room with Aunt Delphi, directly in her line of sight. Almost moaning, Sara closed her eyes.

"Alec looks amazingly like your husband," said a voice to her side.

Sara jerked her gaze around and found herself looking into the deep green eyes of the viscountess. "Yes," Sara heard herself say. "Yes, he does."

"Quite disturbing, in a way. But then, one doesn't think of 'Bridgeton' and 'comfort' in the same sentence."

The viscountess's voice held a touch of an accent, but Sara couldn't place it. "I'm sorry if I've been staring."

"Oh, Alec is used to it. No one can see the two of them without commenting on the similarities. It is even more pronounced when they are together." She looked at Sara and offered a frank smile. "Devilishly handsome, aren't they?"

Sara found herself returning the smile. "Far more than is good for them."

"Exactly what I've been telling Hunterston for years now. Since we are family, I wish you would call me Julia. I still don't care much for titles and all that. I'm an American, you know."

"Only if you'll call me Sara."

"What a pretty name! I must say, you caught us by surprise. We've been in the country and didn't realize Bridgeton had returned. Or married, for that matter."

"It wasn't really his decision," Sara said, then colored when Julia raised her brows.

"Don't look like that," Julia said. "It wasn't Alec's decision, either. But it was good for him, nonetheless. Where is Bridgeton?" She turned her sharp gaze around the room as if she expected Nick to step out from behind the curtains. "I can't see him just leaving you to wander about without him."

Sara's expression must have given her away, for Julia immediately patted her hand and turned the topic. When the viscountess revealed she had just three months ago given birth to her second child, Sara's curiosity was caught and she found herself asking an unusual number of questions. Catching a speculative gleam in the viscountess's eye, Sara feared that she had revealed far more than she meant to.

The musical performance finally started. Julia remained with Sara throughout, including the pause for refreshments, and told her a great deal about the entire Hunterston household. The party broke up as soon as the entertainment ended.

As Julia and her husband returned home in their carriage, she said, "That was a lovely evening."

"The soup was cold, the meat overcooked, and the pianoforte out of tune."

"Besides *that*, it was pleasant."

"Hmm," he said in a noncommittal voice.

Her gaze narrowed. "In fact, I thought the company made the gathering especially interesting." When her husband didn't respond, she said pointedly, "Didn't you?"

Alec pulled his hat over his eyes, then crossed his arms as if preparing to nap.

Julia moved to his side of the carriage. "I spoke at length with Lady Bridgeton."

Her husband pushed his hat back and sighed. "Lady Langtry seemed to think there is a rift between them. A permanent one, to judge by the way she mentioned it."

"We can't let that happen. Sara is despondent. And with a baby on the way . . ." She bit her lip, her eyes filling with tears.

"Julia, you cannot expect me to get involved in Nick's business."

"He's your cousin, Alec. The only family you have."

"Do you remember what he tried to do to you?"

"Do you remember how your grandfather treated him?" she countered. "What his mother was? How you believed him a thief and worse? You were wrong then, and you are wrong now."

"He's not worth the effort."

"Sara thinks he is."

Alec made an impatient noise. "Julia, I am not going to visit Nick and that is that. Besides, we're leaving in the morning."

"Then go and see him now." She leaned against him, looping her arms about his neck. "Alec, please. If you won't do it for Nick, then do it for the baby. Find out what is wrong and see if you can set it straight."

He could never refuse Julia when she pleaded for one of her lost causes. Sighing heavily, he took her hand and placed a kiss on it. "Very well."

Still, he couldn't help but wish to hell that Nick had stayed in France.

"I'm sorry, but His Lordship is not at home," the elderly retainer announced.

Alec shoved his hat and gloves into the man's hands. "He will be home for me."

"But sir—"

"I am His Lordship's cousin, and he will be most distressed if you do not give me entrance." To Alec's surprise, the butler regarded him suspiciously.

Alec sighed. "Look at my face. See the resemblance?"

The butler peered at him, squinting in a horrendous fashion. "My eyes aren't as good as they used to be, but I don't think—"

"Damn it." He stepped past the butler and cupped his hands to his mouth. "*NICK!*"

"My lord, please!" the butler said.

Alec had just cupped his hands to his mouth again when he heard a door to his right open.

"What—" Nick stood in the doorway, his shirt undone, his face shadowed and lined with fatigue. "Hunterston. What the hell do you want?"

"Julia sent me."

Nick turned, slamming the door closed behind him.

Alec winked at the butler, then followed Nick into the room.

"Bloody hell," Nick muttered as he dropped into a chair. "What have I done to deserve this?"

Alec noticed that a half-empty bottle of brandy sat on the table at Nick's elbow, but no glass was in sight. "I met your wife last night."

An arrested expression crossed Nick's face.

"She looked fine—or as fine as can be expected. Do you mind if I sit?"

"As if you'd remain standing if I said no."

Alec grinned. "True." He picked up a glass lying on its side on the desk, then sat in a chair across from Nick.

After a noticeable pause, Nick handed him the bottle. "Where did you see Sara?"

"At a dinner party. Julia was quite taken with her." Alec poured himself a healthy measure of brandy and passed the bottle back to Nick. He wasn't interested in drinking at this hour, but the more he put in his glass, the less would be in Nick's bottle. "Of course, Julia is taken with every creature in need."

"Sara's not a charity case," Nick said harshly. "I saw to that. And she'll have this house, too, once—" He broke off, his mouth clamped shut.

Alec raised his brows. "Once what?"

Nick didn't answer. Instead, he stared down at the bottle in his hand. "From the first moment I saw her, I wanted her. But not as a wife. As a mistress."

"Then why'd you marry her?"

"A rare moment of altruism. That, and she has a brother the size of a mountain. Several, in fact."

"I can't imagine either of those things affecting you."

Nick shrugged. "However it was, I married her and then . . ." He lifted the bottle in a silent salute, then took a long drink. "And then I found I'd made an even greater mistake."

Alec knew this story all too well. "Something changed."

Nick's mouth curved into a sneer. "Don't look so pleased with yourself, Hunterston. I'm not completely besotted. Just somewhat."

"I see." Julia had been right. Alec marveled at his wife's ability to ascertain people's needs with the barest of conversations. "Julia thinks Sara cares for you, Bridgeton."

"She . . . No, it doesn't matter. I can't have her."

"Don't be an idiot. She's your wife."

"She's everything. But if she stayed with me, I would just hurt her." Nick's mouth twisted into a bitter smile. "So here I am, alone in my grand house, waiting for the end, while the only woman I'll ever love is only three miles from my bed."

This was a different Nick indeed, Alex realized with surprise. When Nick had first come to live at their grandfather's, they'd been close, almost like brothers. Unfortunately, that had all changed when their grandfather had accused Nick of theft and Alec had blindly believed the old man. It hadn't been true, and that one moment of doubt had killed the warmth between them. "What happened between you and Sara?"

"Why do you care?"

"I don't. But if I go home to Julia without a complete explanation, my life will be hell."

"I'm already there." Nick sighed and leaned his head against the back of his chair. "I sent her away."

"Why?"

"Because I don't want her to see me become my mother."

Alec frowned at the bleakness in Nick's voice.

"Your mother was addicted to laudanum. How could you possibly become like her?"

"She suffered from headaches—just as I do. The laudanum came later, to kill the pain."

"Are the headaches that bad?"

"God, yes—and getting worse. I can fight it now, but the day will come when I cannot. Alec, I can't let Sara see me like that."

"I see. And what will you do about your child?"

At first, Nick thought he'd heard incorrectly. But Alec's steady gaze told him otherwise. "*God, no.*" He bolted from his chair. "She can't be! I sent her away as soon as I realized—" He sank back into his chair and dropped his head in his hands.

Alec swore. "You didn't know."

Nick stared with unseeing eyes at the floor, the room shimmering out of focus. All week he'd dreamed about Sara, yearned for her with a burning that never lessened. He feared it was only a matter of time before he weakened and went after her, and he prayed she'd hate him enough to resist him. "How far along is she?"

"I don't know. Julia just said . . . Maybe she's wrong, Nick. Julia sometimes assumes things and it's possible—"

"No. She wouldn't make a mistake like that. Bloody hell." Nick pressed his hands over his eyes. "But I don't want her to see me when—"

"Damn it, Nick, don't you understand what marriage is all about? You made the vows. You promised to be with each other forever. No matter what happens to you, no matter what happens to her, you are *together*. It's not fair for you to shut her out just because you fear something is going wrong."

"You don't understand—"

"Like hell I don't. Every man fears dying, Nick. But you don't know when, and you don't know how. You could get thrown from your horse tomorrow and break your neck." Alec shrugged. "And Sara might fall down the stairs and—"

"No!" Nick surged from his chair, the image of Sara's broken body flashing before his eyes. "Damn you, Alec. Get the hell out of here!"

His jaw taut with anger, Alec rose. He went to the door and then paused, his hand on the knob. "Think about it, Nick. You can live your life wishing for what you don't have, or you can accept the many gifts you already possess. The decision is yours."

Nick closed his eyes as Alec's steps retreated down the hallway. His mind raced, flickering through a thousand possibilities.

Perhaps Sara had been right about his headaches. Perhaps there *was* a cure, or at least a way to lessen the pain. He was afraid to hope, but for Sara, he would at least try. He owed it to her and their unborn child. *His child.*

Every fear he'd ever had congealed in his breast, pressing against his heart, suffocating him. "Oh, God, no." The words slipped from his stiff lips, an agony and a cry.

Nick looked at the bottle of brandy still clamped in his hand. With a feeling of disgust, he threw it as hard as he could. The bottle crashed against a wall and broke into a thousand pieces.

Chapter 22

The sitting room of Lady Langtry's town house was an especially pleasant room. Facing the front of the house, it caught the warm morning sun. Sitting in her favorite chair, Delphi looked up from her embroidery and watched Sara and Anna contemplate a particularly absurd fashion plate. All told, she thought Sara was coming around rather nicely. Although there was a sad turn to her lips and her eyes held a rather tragic expression, her color was returning, and her appetite was healthy. Which was a good thing, considering she was to have a child.

The thought of a baby made Delphi unaccountably sad. She'd always wanted children, but fate hadn't given her the chance. She looked down at the perfect row of stitches she'd just sewn. Maybe it hadn't been fate. Maybe it had been she, herself.

The thought caught her. Had she unwittingly put her own life on hold all those years? But why? Why had she spent her adult life tending her relatives' children, serving as nursemaid for her own aunts and uncles, and even serving as chaperone for the younger ones? She cast a furtive glance at Sara. Not that she begrudged her family whatever assistance she could offer, but still . . . she wasn't sure she knew what life really was. She'd gone from dutiful daughter to dutiful wife to dutiful widow in a matter of months.

Perhaps Henri had been right. Perhaps she was afraid. And now . . . when she looked ahead, all she saw was more of the same. Years and years of living for other people. A lump in her throat, Delphi blinked away her tears.

Anthony entered the sitting room, pausing briefly when he saw Anna sitting with Sara. Delphi thought they made a lovely picture together, Sara's dark coloring a striking contrast with Anna's vibrant red. Apparently Anthony didn't agree though, for his face darkened and he looked away, coming to Delphi and placing a kiss on her cheek. "How are you today, Aunt?"

She managed a smile. "Very well, thank you."

"I think Sara should go to London," Anna said. "She has no reason to stay in Bath. Besides, London has the best doctors, and she will be far more comfortable there, among her friends."

Anthony's mouth stretched into a semblance of a

smile. "Perhaps *you* should go. I'm sure we'll all miss your company, Miss Thraxton."

"Oh, I plan on going to London." She smiled sweetly. "I shall make it a point to visit *all* of you."

His smile knocked askance, Anthony opened his mouth to reply when a soft knock sounded at the door. The butler appeared, holding a silver salver bearing a single calling card. He crossed the floor and held the salver out to the duchess. "Your Grace, the Earl of Bridgeton has come to call."

Delphi took the card, sending an uncertain glance at Sara.

"I will not see him," she said, a stricken look in her eyes.

"And so you shan't," Delphi said soothingly. She tossed the card back on the salver. "Please tell the earl that we are not in."

He gave an impassive nod, then left. As soon as the door closed, Anthony said, "You can't keep him away forever, Sara. He's your husband."

"Nonsense," Anna said with a sniff. "He may be her husband, but he has wronged her, and she shouldn't be made to suffer his presence."

"Perhaps what he has to say is important," Anthony said. He shot a harsh look at Anna. "*Very* important."

Sara continued to look at the fashion plates, but the color in her cheeks told Delphi she was listening intently to every word.

"Oh, dear," Delphi said, "perhaps it wouldn't hurt just to see him—"

Anna made an impatient sound. "Lord Bridgeton doesn't deserve such courtesy!"

"Pardon me," Anthony said, "but I don't believe this conversation has anything to do with you, Miss Thraxton. Kindly keep your opinions to yourself."

"It is a pity you don't follow your own advice, Lord Greyley," Anna shot back.

A brief scuffle sounded out in the hall. Anthony turned toward the door as it opened and in walked Nick.

He immediately looked toward Sara, whose gaze was now rigidly fastened on a fashion plate. Anna, likewise, appeared engrossed.

Anthony nodded. "Bridgeton."

Nick returned the greeting, then looked back at Sara. "I hope I'm not intruding, but I must speak to my wife."

Delphi bit her lip. There was something intense, almost frightening in the way Bridgeton was staring at Sara.

It was all so confusing. On the one hand, it would be best for the child if Sara and Bridgeton could work out their differences. On the other hand, it would be best for Sara not to have to deal with such an undiscerning man.

Of course, there really wasn't such a thing as a *discerning* man. Just look at the comte.

As if in answer to her thoughts, another soft knock sounded at the door. The butler reappeared with yet another card. "Your Grace, the Comte du Lac."

Delphi blinked. Henri? Here? Her thoughts in

disarray, she stared at the card with unseeing eyes. Taking her silence as agreement, the butler bowed and left. A scant moment later, the door reopened and Henri appeared.

He came straight to her side and took her hand. "Your Grace." He bowed, his lips brushing her knuckles.

Heat suffused Delphi's face, and she wondered suddenly if fate had given her another chance. She hoped she had the strength to accept it. She managed to smile, tightening her fingers over his.

Henri's gaze widened, a flush touching his cheeks.

"Henri!" Bridgeton's low growl came from behind him. "What are you doing here?"

Henri reluctantly released Delphi's hand. "I was walking past the house when I saw the young ladies seated here, and they made such a charming tableau that I had to come in."

"This is the second floor, Henri," Nick said dryly. "You must have had a very long neck to win such a sight, fetching though it is."

Delphi watched with interest. It was difficult to imagine two more different men. The one was so suave and warm, the other cold and controlled. Today, though, the earl lacked his normal air of command. Dark circles surrounded his eyes, making him appear more intent, more dangerous; his hair was mussed and his cravat hastily knotted. A faint sheen of golden stubble even covered his cheeks. He looked disheveled and, if possible, more handsome than ever.

She slipped a glance toward Sara, but her stubborn niece was glaring down at the fashion plates as if they had offended her. Things did not bode well for the earl. Oh, dear; it was such a difficult predicament.

At a loss, Delphi caught Henri's gaze. He nodded toward the door.

Delphi's hand tightened on her embroidery frame. Here was her chance. Her one and, perhaps, *only* chance. Collecting her shaky resolve, she stood. "Well, it is certainly warm in this room. If you don't mind, I believe I will retire to the breakfast room. It is much cooler there."

Sara promptly stood as well. "I shall accompany you—"

"Actually," Henri interrupted, "I must take my leave, so I will be happy to escort your aunt on my way out."

Delphi almost shivered at the excitement that trembled through her limbs. "That would be very nice, indeed. If you will excuse us?" Without waiting to see anyone's reaction, she hurriedly left.

Anthony immediately stood. "Miss Thraxton, would you like to look out at the garden? There are some particularly lovely flowers I would like to show you."

Anna opened her mouth to argue, but Anthony grabbed her arm and unceremoniously pulled her to the window at the far end of the room.

Sara turned for the door, but Nick stepped forward and cut off her one avenue of escape. She glared at him, then decided not to give him the satisfaction of rattling her. This day was bound to happen, if not here, then in public. It was better to get it over with now. Chin in the air, she resumed her seat and opened her book to a random page, resolutely staring at the blurred picture.

Nick took a chair across from her, leaning forward so that his knees almost touched hers. "Sara, I've been a fool."

He certainly wasn't going to get an argument from her on that score. She kept her gaze fastened on her book.

He placed his hand on her knee. "I've rued my actions every minute I'm awake, every second I'm asleep. Sara, I was stupid to use Lucilla to trick you. I just . . . I wanted to frighten you away."

She jerked her gaze from the book. "Why?"

"Because I didn't want you to see me like—" He briefly closed his eyes. "Sara, the headaches—they are just the beginning. Eventually I will not be able to fight the pain, and I will be forced to turn to laudanum, like my mother.

"You've never seen what laudanum can do to a person. At first she only took it to ease the pain. Later, she *had* to have it. Then there came a time when she ran out. We had no funds, no money at all. The pain was horrendous."

Sara's hands gripped the book harder. "You are not your mother."

"No, I'm far, far weaker than she. When she realized there would be no more laudanum, she put a gun in my hand and begged me, on her knees, to end her torment. So I—" He closed his eyes, his face a mask of torment. "I went out and I did what I had to, to procure more. I got her laudanum that day and the next and every day that she asked me to. And the things I did to pay for it—" He looked away.

Tears welled in Sara's eyes, and her heart went out to the boy Nick had been, the man he'd been forced to become—all because of one woman's addiction to poison. "But perhaps there's another way to combat your headaches, Nick."

"It is the only thing that ever helped her," he said grimly. "And it is what killed her."

Sara set her book aside. "Nick, how did Violette die?"

"She threw herself from the roof of our chateau when I was thirteen."

Sara gasped.

"Her body fell past my window, and I saw her for an instant—" His voice broke, and he swallowed. "She didn't even leave a note. Nothing."

Sara sat in stunned silence.

"And that is why I didn't want to have children. I didn't want my child to be cursed the way my mother and I were." He looked up at her, his eyes almost black. "Sara, I know about the baby."

She froze. How had he found out?

"I want you back, Sara."

"Because of the child?" Her heart contracted.

"*No.* I wanted you back before I discovered about the child." He reached for her hand, but she yanked it away, aware that his touch could undo the tenuous control she had.

"Sara, I made a terrible mistake. Please forgive me." Nick held his breath and waited.

She shook her head. "I'm truly sorry for your pain and fears, Nick. But that doesn't change the fact that when you faced a problem, you didn't turn to me. You shut me out, banished me from you and the home we were making. I can't live that way. I want to be part of a family. And that means facing problems together."

"I'll try to—"

"You made decisions that affected both of our lives without ever consulting me. And you have treated me so cavalierly that I may never be able to forgive you. Good God, why didn't you just tell me you thought you might become addicted to laudanum? Am I so insignificant that I did not even deserve that?"

"Sara, I wanted to tell you, but I couldn't bear the thought of you turning away from me."

She raised tear-filled eyes to his. "Is that how little you think of me?" she whispered.

Oh, God, he was driving her farther and farther away. He desperately wished she'd let him touch her, show her how he felt. But this, trying to express himself while she sat there with hurt and accusation in her eyes—the words froze and tangled. "Sara, you don't understand—"

"But I do. You would risk everything on the basis of what *might* happen. Yes, you have headaches, though Lady Birlington seems to think it was your father who suffered from headaches and not your mother."

Nick froze at a sudden thought. Was it possible? If his mother's only flaw had been laudanum addiction, then he would gladly bear the pain of the headaches. Sudden hope rose in his heart, though he dared not trust it yet.

"Sara, I pray to God that what Lady Birlington said is true, especially now that you are carrying my child. But you have to understand that I did what I thought was best for us both."

"By faking an assignation with Lady Knowles? Brilliant, Bridgeton." She stood. "Perhaps the next time you decide to rid yourself of a wife, you will have the courage to do it without so much dissembling. Good-bye."

She stood, and the movement wafted the faint scent of lavender to him. He closed his eyes, struggling to find the words he needed. None came.

The sound of the door softly closing ripped through him like the thunder of a cannon. She had left him. And she would never return.

His heart was beyond pain, his mind numb with the realization that he had finally found love, and he'd killed it. Destroyed it with his senseless fears and his inability to open his heart to the very woman who owned it.

"Bridgeton?" Greyley murmured from behind him. "She just needs some time."

Unable to bear the man's pity, Nick nodded shortly. Without a word, he turned and left.

Somehow, he made it back to his carriage. He climbed in and mutely sat there.

"Are we returning home, my lord?"

Home? There was no home without Sara. There wasn't anything without Sara. Nick closed his eyes. "To Hibberton Hall."

The footman closed the door and soon the coach was rumbling out of Bath. Nick stared with unseeing eyes at the green rolling hills. Outside all was light and beauty, but in his heart was the empty desolation of aloneness, of being without Sara.

Heat prickled against his eyes, and he touched his hand to his face, then stared uncomprehendingly at the wetness from his cheek. He loved her. And she could not stand the sight of him.

His fingers curled into a tight ball. Whether she wanted it or not, Sara was part of his life as he was part of hers. He'd fought for too many years, against too many demons, to sit tamely by for the most important battle of his life.

A slow calm began to build around his bruised heart. He had won past her defenses once, and he would do so again. Staring blindly out the window of the carriage, he began to plan his attack.

"Ah, this must be the breakfast room," Henri said. He patted Delphi's hand where it lay on his arm. "I suppose I should be going . . ." He waited expectantly.

Her fingers tightened on his sleeve and he thought he saw hesitation in her eyes.

But after a moment, she smiled uncertainly and then stepped away. "Of course you must go."

Disappointment raked through him. He'd been foolish to even come here, but he hadn't been able to stop thinking of the delectable Delphi. This morning he'd found himself outside her house, standing on the stoop. It was a strange thing, this compulsion he had to see her, but he would not renew his offer. If she wanted him, she would have to make the first overture.

He managed a polite smile. "Good morning, then, Your Grace."

Just as he turned away, she said in a breathless voice, "Perhaps you would like to wait for Bridgeton?"

Henri looked at her. She appeared flushed and uneasy, but because she wanted him to stay or because she didn't wish to await the outcome of the interview between Nick and Sara alone, he could not say. Still . . . he shrugged. "But of course."

She immediately turned and led the way into the breakfast room.

He followed her, noting the luxurious appointments of the room. A large but delicate rosewood table filled the center of the room, while a scattering of side tables and buffets filled the walls.

Delphi gestured to the few dishes remaining on the table. "Lord Greyley must have just finished his breakfast. I will call the servants to clean this up."

"They will come in their own time." Henri feared his nervous companion might flee if she opened the door again. "Just leave it."

"Very well." She took one of the chairs and faced him with a tremulous smile. "Pray have a seat, my lord."

He obediently took the one across from hers in an effort not to startle her, and waited.

"It is . . . quite cold this week, is it not?"

"Oh, very," he agreed pleasantly.

She swallowed, her fingers nervously folding and unfolding a pleat in her skirt. "A pity it might rain."

"Indeed."

She dropped her gaze and stared at the carpet.

Silence filled the room and Henri became aware of how loudly the clock ticked on the sideboard. After a long moment, he noticed the *Morning Post* sitting by the forgotten dishes. He gestured toward the paper. "If you don't mind?"

Coloring, she shook her head and Henri thankfully retreated behind the paper.

Delphi stared at the back of the *Morning Post*. It was a hopeless passion, and she knew it. He was a counterfeit count, completely penniless, and far too handsome.

But some small spark of her soul yearned for a change, screamed that it was time she found some happiness before it was too late. If she wanted life, then she was going to have to force herself to embrace it.

Delphi looked at the newspaper wall, and whispered, *"Let not love drop from thy lips."*

The *Morning Post* remained firmly in place.

Delphi closed her eyes. What was she doing? He would just laugh at her, tell her she'd had her opportunity and had frittered it away. She opened her eyes. But what if he didn't? What if he swept her into his arms and made mad, passionate love to her? After a long moment, she said in a slightly louder voice, "*Hear me, oh love. Teach mine heart to despair not.*"

The *Morning Post* trembled slightly, and Henri murmured something vague.

Delphi stiffened. Here she was, baring her soul and Henri didn't even have the politeness to respond. She stood.

Henri looked around the edge of the paper. "Is something wrong?"

Delphi looked into his bright blue eyes and froze. After a moment, she shook her head dumbly. He gave her a quick, impersonal smile, then disappeared behind the paper once more.

She closed her eyes. *Oh, God, give me strength.* A faint trembling shook Delphi's knees, excitement warming her from the toes, up her calves, to her thighs. She gasped and pressed her hands together and clasped them to her breast. "*Oh lustful knave, tease me unto death, I care not.*"

Henri's astonished gaze appeared over the top edge of the paper. "Pardon?"

Delphi wondered how his voice would sound when raised in passion. Her heart hammering an erratic rhythm, she leaned forward against the breakfast table. She felt powerful, alive, and amazingly fierce. "*From thy honeyed mouth, sweetness drips.*"

Slowly, ever so slowly, Henri dropped the *Morning Post* to the ground. "Delphi, what—"

She flattened her hands on the table and leaned even closer to Henri—her love, her life. "*Betwixt us lies a river of passion. Come drown with me, beloved! Be one with me."*

He stood, his face bright with hope. "Delphi . . . do you know what you are saying?"

How could he look at her and not know? Delphi swept the remaining china aside with a magnificent sweep of her arm. *"Come, my love! Let us lie among the gentle breezes and part the waves with our passion."* Without a thought, she lay on the table, rolled to her side, and held her arms out toward him.

Silence filled the room, broken only by her own fast breathing. The table was cool and hard beneath her, and one of her shoulders seemed to have landed on a plate. But Delphi ignored it all. She held out her arms and waited.

Henri cleared his throat. "I . . . ah, Delphi?"

His tentative voice sent her confidence crashing to the ground. What was she doing? *Oh, God, I am such a fool. He doesn't want me, and here I lie . . .* She'd allowed her passion to overcome her judgment, and she had just made the biggest mistake of her life. Face burning, Delphi pushed herself from the table and stood. "Oh, dear," she said, her face so hot she wondered that it didn't burst into flames.

She couldn't bear to look at Henri, couldn't bear to see his embarrassment. Her whole body seemed to shrink in humiliation and a tear gathered in her eye, quickly followed by another.

"Ah, my sweet Delphinea," Henri said. "You have butter."

She had . . . what? She looked at him.

He gestured to her shoulder. "You've butter on your dress."

She glanced down where a smear of butter marred the white muslin. Suddenly the tears could not be contained. She'd made the most wretched fool of herself, and Henri would never want to speak with her again. She turned and ran for the door.

"*No.*"

She froze in place, her hand on the knob.

"You love me." He said it in a voice of wonder, as if he couldn't believe his fortune.

Breathless hope held her in its grip. "Yes," she managed to whisper.

"My sweet, shy Delphi," he said, his voice closer. His fingers slipped along the edge of her collar. "You have utterly ruined your dress. I'm afraid it must come off."

She turned slowly to face him. "You want me to take off my dress," she repeated stupidly.

"More than anything in the world." He pulled a jeweled pin from her hair and tossed it aside.

Her hair falling about her face, Delphi now swiftly tugged at her laces. With the comte's help, her dress was soon removed. He kissed each bit of her skin as it was exposed, making her a mass of tingles.

Before Delphi knew what had happened, he carried her to the table and set her on the edge. She wrapped her arms and legs about him and kissed him deeply. It was as if a well of passion had suddenly burst forth, and Delphi could not contain it.

He moaned against her mouth, then placed his foot on a chair and joined her on the table, struggling to undo his breeches as he did so.

Crack. Henri froze. *Crack. Crack*. The table shook and then, with a final creak, collapsed onto the floor. Spoons and forks clattered, dishes bounced into the air, and chairs went toppling.

The door to the breakfast room flew open and Anthony stood in the doorway, Anna peering over his shoulder. Shock and disbelief warred on their faces. From where she lay amid the china and splintered wood, Delphi buried her face in Henri's neck and burst into laughter.

Chapter 23

I t began with a letter. Addressed to Lady Bridgeton in a strong, simple script, it arrived shortly before breakfast the next morning.

Sara's heart pounded on seeing the footman's livery, recognizing him as one of Wiggs's underlings. For one mad moment, she stared at the missive, the vellum crisp beneath her fingers, and wondered if she should open it. But her good sense returned. There was nothing more to say. Nick had lied to her and left her alone, just like Julius.

She was weary and stretched, too tired to deal with such painful emotions. It was strange, but she could not remember ever feeling this way about Julius. But then that was because she didn't love him like—

She caught the thought before she could finish it. Love was the last thing she should feel for Nicholas Montrose. She handed the letter back to the footman and ordered him to return it to Hibberton Hall, unanswered and unopened.

Nick arrived shortly afterward. Sara had been on her way to her room when she heard his voice in the front hall. Reacting instinctively, she'd crouched on the landing, peeking over the banister. His face set in determined lines and looking devastatingly handsome, he listened impatiently to the butler's explanation that no one was home before saying in a loud voice, "Inform Lady Bridgeton that I will return." With that, he'd replaced his hat and left.

Sara had closed her eyes and inhaled to see if the scent of his cologne lingered in the foyer. If she sat still enough, she thought she could detect just a trace. Finally, she'd shaken herself off and retired to her room.

An hour later, she heard a solid knock on the front door. She tiptoed down the hallway and peeked down the stairs. The footman from Hibberton Hall had returned, this time with an armful of flowers. The arrangement was so large that it barely fit through the door, the exotic scent filling the entire house. Sara stared at the flowers, aware of a strange well of disappointment. She waited until the footman had left before she raced down the steps, gathered the flowers from the astounded butler, marched into the street, and threw the entire arrangement in front of the carriage. The shocked footman watched as the wind had lifted the flowers and scattered them far and wide, a white note fluttering free and tumbling down the street. Dusting her hands, Sara returned to the house, slamming the door behind her.

But the image of that note stayed with her, and she began to envision what words it had held. Was it a letter of abject apology? An impassioned plea for forgiveness? Sara couldn't see Nick writing such things, but still . . . she almost wished she'd read it.

To ease her mind, she went in search of Aunt Delphi. She found her aunt sitting in the breakfast room, tracing her hands over the rosewood table. Sara frowned. "Is it still broken?"

Just yesterday, the table had inexplicably collapsed, shattering some of their good china. Sara had been in her room, having fled there after Nick had left, and she hadn't seen the wreckage, though Anna later assured her it had been spectacular.

"The table is just fine," Delphi said in a repressive voice. "You can't even tell it's been fixed."

"I wish hearts were as easily repaired."

Delphi patted her hand. "Give yourself some time, dear. You'll feel better soon. I'm sure of it."

Sara wasn't so sure but she kept silent, merely suggesting they keep busy by visiting the lending library. Once there, deciding to stay away from anything having to do with love or romance, Sara selected two very worthy tomes on horticulture. It wasn't until later, as they rode in the carriage back to Delphi's house, and she caught herself studying the medicinal properties of various herbs, that Sara realized she was still thinking about Nick.

Disgusted with herself, she tucked the books

away and decided not to read them. She entered the foyer still feeling out of sorts, and discovered a small box on the table in the front hall. She knew immediately that it had come from Nick, and had the footman who delivered it still been there, she would have sent it home without further ado. But he'd already left, probably rejoicing that he'd managed to deliver at least one item successfully.

Frowning, Sara left the box on the table in the hall for return on the next day, glancing at it whenever she happened to see it. When Anna arrived that evening she exclaimed over the gift, wondering aloud at the possible contents and finally carrying it into the sitting room, where it sat in solitary splendor on a side table. As the evening progressed, it seemed to Sara that the box was as alone as she. She found herself moving it to one side while looking for Aunt Delphi's missing thread, tapping a finger on its smooth side while listening to Anthony and Anna bicker, or just holding it in her hand and staring at it.

Finally, while turning the pages of her book, Sara accidentally knocked it to the floor.

Anna looked up from her book by the reformer, Mary Wollstonecraft. She gazed at the fallen box with a considering frown, finally saying, "I suppose you will have to pick it up."

Sara thought she detected just a hint of sarcasm in Anna's voice, but she wasn't certain. "Perhaps I should just leave it."

Anna raised her brows, but made no comment. Moments dangled by during which Sara tried valiantly not to look at the box.

"Perhaps," Anna said into the silence, "*I* should pick it up. Just in case it falls open."

"That would be best," Sara agreed, her heart racing a little at the thought.

Anna wasted no time in scooping up the box and, just as she predicted, the top fell off. She stood gazing into the box, a dazed expression on her face.

"What is it?" Sara demanded impatiently.

Eyes wide, Anna held the box toward Sara. There, reclining on a bed of red velvet, sat a large square-cut ruby ring with an intricately carved gold band. The gem winked up at her, blinding in its brilliance. Set with diamonds, it made the Lawrence sapphires pale in comparison.

"Fudge," Sara said. "I have to give that back."

"Nonsense. It's the least that bounder can do for you—plaster you with jewelry and beg for forgiveness. I like that in a man." Anna shot a hard look at Anthony, who was too immersed in the newspaper to notice.

Sara took the box from Anna and replaced the lid, setting it back on the table. "You know why I have to give it back." She resolutely returned to her book. What was Nick thinking, to send her such a thing? What was he trying to prove?

"There is a note with it," Anna said. "Perhaps you could just return the note and keep the ring."

"No," Sara said firmly. "It all goes back—the note *and* the ring."

"That's not a very practical way of doing things." Sighing heavily, Anna returned to her book, though her gaze drifted to the box as frequently as Sara's.

Later, after Anna left, Sara found herself looking at the ring again—just to admire it. She even took it upstairs so that she could try it on away from Anthony's prying eyes. It was a perfect fit. The ruby looked especially lovely on her hand, the deep red mesmerizing against her white skin. It was a truly lovely gift, and one that showed how well Nick knew her taste.

That night, she slept with the ring tucked beneath her pillow. The next morning, collecting every bit of her determination, Sara put the ring back in the box and ordered that it be returned to Hibberton Hall. She stood in the window of the sitting room and watched the footman carry it away, feeling a strange urge to cry.

So it went for two more days. Nick visited often and always the butler turned him away. And when Nick wasn't present, a steady flow of gifts and flowers flooded the house. It was, Sara decided as she stared down at a gorgeous ruby necklace, enough to drive a woman mad. Yet somehow, it still wasn't enough.

Delphi bustled into the room, a shawl of Indian silk fluttering about her. "I will never speak to Lady Merton again."

Sara replaced the necklace in the box. "Lady Merton? But you've known her forever."

"Apparently Ophelia has forgotten that fact." Delphi settled onto the edge of the settee, her lip quivering. "She had the audacity to try and hint me away from Henri."

"Why would she do that?"

"She says that he is no more a comte than I. In fact, she is telling everyone that he is an imposter and that he has made a fool of me."

Sara looked down at the ruby necklace and shut the box with a sigh. "Does it matter what she thinks?"

Delphi toyed with the fringe on her shawl, her face folded with worry. "I daresay he has no income whatsoever."

"Most likely."

Delphi's lip quivered again. "And no prospects, either."

"Probably not."

"And he's a full eight months younger than I." There was a hint of a wail to her voice.

"No one would ever credit it. You don't look a day over forty."

Delphi brightened. "Do you think so?" At Sara's nod, Delphi sighed. "I don't know why I let that man affect me so."

"Sometimes we don't have a choice in who affects us," Sara said softly. "It just happens." And sometimes there was no way to stop it from happening, even when you knew it would lead to heartache.

Delphi took her niece's hand and gave it a gentle squeeze. "No, we don't. But life comes to visit but once, and only a fool would have the door locked and bolted. I fear I have kept the doors to my heart locked for so long that they have rusted closed."

"Aunt Delphi, you are being too harsh on yourself."

"No, I'm not. I instinctively retreat from that

which has the power to hurt." She stared down at the floor for a moment with a frown. "And it hurts to be in love. Doesn't it?"

Yes, it did. But not always. Sara could remember a time when just the feel of Nick's warm hand on hers made her heart leap with joy. Damn it, why did life have to be so complicated? She stirred restlessly, suddenly assailed with the desire to escape her cares. "Do you know what we need?"

Delphi shook her head.

"A complete change of scenery. Why don't we go on a tour of the North Country, just you and I? We'll have a delightful time."

"I don't know. I promised your cousin Althea that I'd come and stay with her while—"

"Althea has two sisters who are perfectly capable of assisting her. We can leave next week. It would do us both good to get away from Bath." Maybe the time away would clear her head.

"I suppose you are right," Delphi said thoughtfully. "And if we stay gone long enough, certain people just might miss us."

That was a thought. Sara's heart suddenly lightened. At least she would be doing *something*. "We'll pack this very evening and leave in the morning."

"Yes, dear." Delphi stood and began digging in her reticule. "That reminds me, Anthony caught me in the hallway and he wished me to give you—ah, here it is!" She pulled out a small square of white paper and placed it in Sara's hand.

"What is it?"

"He didn't say. I wonder if I should pack my new

pelisse?" Giving Sara a quick smile, Delphi floated off, her mind already busily engaged in their new plans.

Sara looked at the folded vellum and recognized Nick's writing. Her first impulse was to toss the note into the fire, but Delphi's words stayed with her. What was she afraid of? It was just a letter, and she didn't have to finish reading it if she didn't like what it said.

Setting her shoulders, she opened the missive. She didn't know what she expected—poetry or an eloquent plea of forgiveness, perhaps. But only five words adorned the thick vellum.

"I will always love you."

And she would always love him. Tears clogged Sara's throat, and the great ache of loneliness broke free. He'd made a mistake so great that it had ripped the delicate fabric of their relationship, leaving her unsure if she could ever find it in her to forgive him. And had he been truly involved with Lucilla, there would be no possibilities, no forgiveness. Sara would never again be a betrayed wife.

But neither would she accept being treated as less than an equal partner. Delphi was right—doors could be closed so long that they rusted shut. Like the doors to Nick's heart. And maybe the doors to her own, as well.

Sara placed a hand over her stomach, where the small life grew. It was time she moved on with her life, whether she was ready or not. The only question that remained was, would she move toward Nick, or away?

Chapter 24

Nick tossed the reins of his horse to the waiting groom and walked up the front stoop of Hibberton Hall. He was riding at least an hour a day now and was already beginning to feel the benefits. His head was clearer, the pressure behind his eyes less. All he needed was to heal his heart and he would, for the first time in his life, be whole.

But his courtship wasn't progressing at all. The traditional methods had gotten him nowhere. Perhaps it was time for a more untraditional wooing . . . but what?

Wiggs was waiting for him in the foyer. "My lord, the Earl of Greyley has arrived. I escorted him to the library."

Nick didn't wait to hand his gloves and hat to the

butler, but spun on his heel and went straight to the library.

Anthony was standing at the window, arms crossed, one shoulder against the frame. "There you are," he said without rancor. "I delivered your note."

Nick was instantly on his guard. "I was surprised you offered to do it."

Anthony shrugged. "You looked so forlorn, standing in the street."

"I am not beaten yet, Greyley."

"No, I don't think you are. You have lasted longer than I would have. She's not been very accommodating."

"But then that has always been part of Sara's unique charm," Nick replied with a tight smile. To what do I owe this honor?"

"She's leaving."

"When?" Nick bit out.

"Tomorrow."

"Dear God." Nick raked a hand through his hair.

"I tried to talk her out of it, but she's determined."

Nick looked at Anthony with sudden suspicion. "Why are you helping me?"

"I don't know what's going on between you and Sara, but I know the child needs a father." He shot a hard glance at Nick. "Are you willing to assume that responsibility?"

"I will, whether Sara wants it or not."

"That's all I need to know." Anthony pushed himself from the window and strolled to the door.

"Will she be home this evening?"

"I'll make sure of it." Anthony met Nick's gaze. "Don't muck this up, Bridgeton."

"Thank you, Greyley. I owe you." And it was a debt he would gladly repay the day Sara was his once again.

Well after midnight, Nick lifted the ladder from the back of the old wagon and hefted it to his shoulders, staggering a little under the weight. "Damn it," he muttered. "I need a carpenter's assistant."

He managed to get the ladder around the side of Lady Langtry's town house and laid it beside the rosebush. Then he tipped his head back and stared up at the window far over his head. In the entire house, it was the only one where a light burned. Sighing, he grabbed the ladder and hefted it upright. It began to tilt precariously to one side, and he hastily righted it, stepping backward into a thick puddle of mud. "Bloody hell," he swore, resting the ladder on the side of the house, right by Sara's window. The next time he attempted this, he was going to bring one of the stable hands with him. He glanced at his muddy boots and grimaced, then tried to scrape the mud on the gravel path.

"*Mon Dieu!* What are you doing here?"

Nick whirled around. Henri stood facing him, his silver hair bright in the moonlight.

"That, Henri, is none of your business."

"Ah, but it is my business." The comte came to stand beside the ladder, looping an arm through a rung. "Did you know Delphi and Sara were leaving?"

"I'd heard," Nick said shortly. He placed his foot on the bottom rung of the ladder and looked pointedly at the comte's arm. "Do you mind?"

Henri obediently stepped back. "Pray continue. You can thank me later."

"For what?"

Henri tucked his thumbs in his waistcoat and rocked back on his heels, the very picture of a self-satisfied male. "It has taken, oh, such an effort, but I have convinced my little Delphi not to go away. And if Delphi does not go, then Sara does not go."

"That was very good of you."

"Ah, it was nothing." Henri glanced up the ladder to Sara's window. "Perhaps I will wait for you in the carriage."

Nick nodded and began to climb. He'd nearly reached the top of the ladder when Henri's voice drifted up to him.

"One more thing, *mon ami.* The terrace doors are never locked. You might want to try that way next time."

Nick turned to glare down at him, but Henri was already wandering down the path, humming the refrain of a waltz.

Damn Henri. Nick climbed the last two rungs and reached Sara's window.

Inside her room, Sara was unsuccessfully trying to read about the proper planting for St. John's wort, but her mind kept drifting to the herb garden she'd planned at Hibberton Hall. It would have been lovely. Furthermore, it would have kept her stillroom stocked for Nick's tisanes. She wondered if his headaches had worsened, and if he was eating well. The idea that he might be suffering at this very moment, all alone at Hibberton Hall, made her throat tighten painfully.

"He deserves to suffer," she said aloud, blinking away the moisture that had gathered in her eyes. Still . . . it didn't seem fair that *she* should suffer as well. Every moment without Nick was an agony.

She loved him so much. Too much to let him ruin their marriage with his fears. Still, he hadn't had the opportunities she'd had to witness a truly loving relationship. Considering his dread that he might end up like his mother, she shouldn't have been surprised that he'd attempted to push her away in such a horrible manner.

Yet the question remained: Could he learn to treat her as a respected partner in this marriage? After her experience with Julius, Sara could accept no less. A wave of restlessness swept through her, and it was with a very heavy heart that she readied for bed, looking forlornly at the trunks that lay open in the center of the room, packed and almost ready for her journey on the morrow.

Just as she slid under the covers, a scratching sound came from her window. Sara slid to the edge of her bed, her gaze on the curtain.

There was a creak as the casement was opened. The curtains trembled, then were tossed aside as a man's figure was silhouetted against the night sky.

He was here! Sara scrambled to find her robe, stubbing her toe on her trunk in the process. Cursing wildly, she hopped to where her robe lay across a chair and yanked it on.

Nick closed the window and entered, looking far more dashing and handsome than any late-night visitor should.

"Wh-what do you want?" Sara asked, tying the sash about her waist in a double knot.

A smile flickered in his eyes. "I want you."

Her heart beat faster, but she sternly quelled it. "You had me once, and you sent me away."

"I was wrong."

They stood staring at one another, neither moving. Sara wanted nothing more than to walk into the circle of his arms, but for the sake of their child, she couldn't. Not yet.

There was so much more she needed to hear him say, but he just stood looking at her, his face dark with some emotion. Finally, just as she decided to break the silence, he said, "I'm leaving Hibberton Hall."

That startled her. "But . . . you love that place."

"No—I love you. Without you, Hibberton Hall is an empty shell."

"Where will you go?"

"That depends on you."

She frowned, shoring up her defenses. "What do you mean?"

"Sara, I'm not good at saying what I feel. I never have been." He reached into his pocket, withdrew a sheaf of papers, and held them out.

She took them hesitantly. "What is this?"

"The deed for Hibberton Hall. I've decided to sell it."

"How could you?" she asked, her heart squeezing painfully. He was leaving Hibberton—leaving her. His fingers tightened over the papers. "I can't believe you'd just let it go."

His gaze narrowed. "Why do you care?"

"I'm very fond of the Hall. I thought you were, too."

"I am," he said simply. "But I want you and our child to have a roof over your heads, a place of your own. Hibberton Hall is yours."

She looked at the packet. "You said you were *selling* it."

"I'm a rake, Sara. There is always a price."

A fluttering hope warmed her heart. "What's your price?"

"One kiss." His voice hung in the air between them, husky and seductive.

Could he mean . . . ? Sara shook her head. "I'll not be made a fool of," she warned.

"I'm perfectly serious. All I ask is one kiss, and the house is yours—every board and brick. I had Pratt draw up the papers this evening. It's why I came so late—I've been waiting for him to finish with the blasted document for three hours."

He looked so annoyed that a giggle almost slipped out. Sara quickly turned away, aware of a lightening in her heart. Would she deny him even this? Could she? The thought of a kiss was too tempting. Her loneliness swelled to an ache, and she turned back. "Only one."

Just one, tiny kiss. What harm can it do?

She closed her eyes and waited to be swept into a passionate embrace. Instead, Nick slowly placed his lips to hers, the gesture hesitant, almost reverent.

And she realized it wasn't just a kiss, but also a promise. A promise of change, so tender, so overwhelming, that she leaned into the embrace, tears springing behind her lids, her own heart leaping in answer.

Nick murmured, "I love you, Sara. I always will. And I will never again close you out of my heart." He gazed into her eyes, then turned back to the window.

She watched him push back the curtain and swing one leg over the casement. Then he turned to look at her, his heart in his eyes. "Good-bye, Sara."

She managed to swallow. "I'm leaving in the morning. I hope . . . I hope you'll at least write to me. I'm not sure where we'll be staying, but—"

"Wherever you go, I will find you. I promise." He turned and stepped onto the ladder.

There was a note of finality to the sound. Suddenly, Sara was moving toward him. "Nick?"

He looked back.

Sara crossed the room to stand in front of him. "I want another kiss."

His breath passed sharply through his lips. "Of course."

Just as he leaned toward her, she placed her hands on his chest. "But first, there are a few things we must settle."

His gaze burned into hers. "Name them."

A feeling of power tingled through Sara. "I am not a child. In the future, whenever you have a problem, you must promise to bring it to me. I daresay I could handle your illness much better than you have."

A faint smile touched his lips. "More than likely."

"Second, you will promise to love me and only me, for the rest of your life."

"I do."

"And if you ever again dare presume to decide what I want and don't want, I will leave you and I will not come back, whether I love you or not. Do you understand?"

He sat very still, his eyes a brilliant blue. "You love me?"

"Of course I love you! Why else would I care if you were with Lucilla—whom I will never forgive for her part in your little deception. I may have to be severe in my dealings with her."

He swung his leg back over the casement. "I almost pity her."

"Don't waste your time." A thought suddenly dawned. "Oh! And one more thing . . . the ruby ring? Do you still have it?"

A slow smile crossed his face and he nodded. "I have the whole set, my love."

Smiling, she twined her arms about his neck and drew him to her. "I believe it's time I gave up the Lawrence sapphires for the Bridgeton rubies."

He placed his hands on her waist. "Whatever you want, Sara. Just stay with me and love me. I wish I could promise you that our life will be easy, but I can't."

"No one can promise that. And so long as you don't mind if I continue to try and find a cure for your headaches, I think we will be fine." Sara met his gaze steadily. "May I come home?"

His eyes darkened, and he pulled her against him. "Every night before I go to bed, I stop by your stillroom and imagine you there." His voice grew husky. "Do you remember the last time, Sara?"

She could feel him, hard and ready, straining against his breeches. God, how she had missed his touch, the ardor they shared. She ached for him even within the clasp of his arms. "I have to warn you, Nick. Some of the remedies may not taste as good as my last one." She traced a finger down his chest, lingering at his nipple. To her satisfaction, he caught his breath as it puckered. "And some may require direct application to your naked skin."

He caught her hand and pressed a kiss to it. "Perhaps we should invest in more beehives, my love."

"Oh, yes," she said breathlessly as her handsome husband placed delicate kisses on each of her fingers. "I have the feeling we're going to need lots and lots of honey."

At Avon Books, we know your passion for romance—once you finish one of our novels, you find yourself wanting more.

May we tempt you with . . .

- **Excerpts** from our upcoming releases.

- Entertaining **extras**, including authors' personal photo albums and book lists.

- Behind-the-scenes **scoop** on your favorite characters and series.

- **Sweepstakes** for the chance to win free books, romantic getaways, and other fun prizes.

- Writing **tips** from our authors and editors.

- **Blog** with our authors and find out why they love to write romance.

- **Exclusive content** that's not contained within the pages of our novels.

Join us at
www.avonbooks.com

AVON *An Imprint of* HarperCollins*Publishers*
www.avonromance.com